BROTHERS
OF CAIN

Berkley Prime Crime Books by Miriam Grace Monfredo

SENECA FALLS INHERITANCE
NORTH STAR CONSPIRACY
BLACKWATER SPIRITS
THROUGH A GOLD EAGLE
THE STALKING-HORSE
MUST THE MAIDEN DIE
SISTERS OF CAIN
BROTHERS OF CAIN

CRIME THROUGH TIME
CRIME THROUGH TIME II
(edited by Miriam Grace Monfredo and Sharan Newman)

BROTHERS OF CAIN

Miriam Grace Monfredo

BERKLEY PRIME CRIME, NEW YORK

BROTHERS OF CAIN

A Berkley Prime Crime Book
Published by The Berkley Publishing Group,
a division of Penguin Putnam Inc.,
375 Hudson Street, New York, New York 10014.

Visit our website at
www.penguinputnam.com

First edition: September 2001

Library of Congress Cataloging-in-Publication Data

Monfredo, Miriam Grace.
     Brothers of Cain / Miriam Grace Monfredo—1st ed.
     p. cm.
     ISBN 0-425-18189-8 (alk. paper)
     1. United States—History—Civil War, 1861–1865—Fiction.
I. Title.

PS3563.O5234 B7 2001
813'.54—dc21

                                                    2001037518

Printed in the United States of America

10   9   8   7   6   5   4   3   2   1

For my brothers,
Mark and Kevin and Craig,
and for the sisters they have given me,
Lisa and Candace and Sandra.

ACKNOWLEDGMENTS

—ɯ—

My sincere gratitude to the following:

Eivind Boe, my skilled and painstaking copyeditor, who has taught me more than I ever learned in school.

Joel Emerson, reenactor, for information on uniforms.

David Feinberg, reference librarian at the Library of Virginia in Richmond, who found the Spotswood Hotel site and its neighbors.

Rachel Monfredo Gee, for a remarkable memory and, together with husband David, for a prospective new reader.

Woody Harper, treasurer and assistant general manager of Richmond's Hollywood Cemetery, for his ready assistance.

Bob Marcotte, for the willingness to share his prodigious knowledge of just about everything.

David Minor, of Eagles Byte research, who was always there when most needed.

Gerry Reilly, director of West Virginia Independence Hall, who generously educated me about his state and the Wheeling Custom House, where so much history was made.

And, as ever, Frank Monfredo.

AUTHOR'S NOTE

—ɯ—

Brothers of Cain, like the preceding *Sisters of Cain,* is based on an actual episode of the American Civil War— the 1862 Virginia Peninsula Campaign. Union general George B. McClellan's plan to capture the Confederate capital of Richmond became the single largest campaign of the war. Intelligence information, or the lack of it, figured significantly in its outcome.

The major characters in *Brothers of Cain* are fictitious, but historical figures frequently appear. Some information on those who are less well known is given in the Historical Notes section at the end of the novel. Although *Brothers of Cain* is a work of fiction, recognized historical facts have not knowingly been altered.

Visit Miriam Grace Monfredo's website at
www.miriamgracemonfredo.com

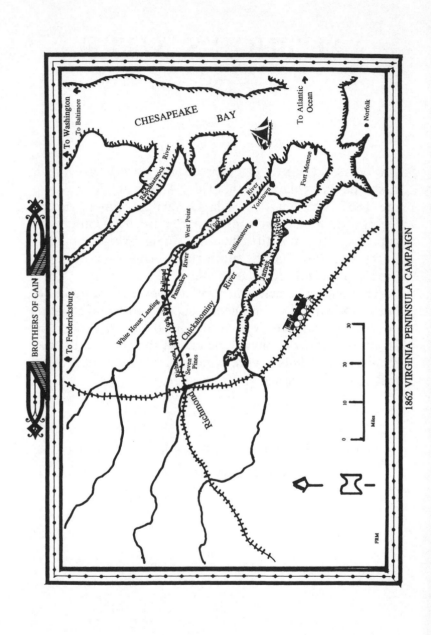

BROTHERS OF CAIN

CHESAPEAKE BAY

To Washington
To Baltimore

To Atlantic Ocean

Norfolk

Rappahannock River

Fort Monroe

To Fredericksburg

West Point

York River

Yorktown

Williamsburg

James River

White House Landing

Pamunkey River

Railroad

Richmond and York River R.R.

Chickahominy River

Seven Pines

Richmond

Miles
0   10   20   30

1862 VIRGINIA PENINSULA CAMPAIGN

FRM

Were half the power that fills the world with terror,
Were half the wealth bestowed on camps and
courts,
Given to redeem the human mind from error,
There were no need of arsenals or forts;

The warrior's name would be a name abhorréd!
And every nation that should lift again
Its hand against a brother, on its forehead
Would wear for evermore the curse of Cain!

—Henry Wadsworth Longfellow,
"The Arsenal at Springfield"

1

Sleep, the brother of death.

—Hesiod, c. 800 B.C.

MAY 1862
Williamsburg, Virginia

"You won't be leavin' me?" the boy asked.

"I won't leave," said the young man sitting slouched against the trunk of an oak. "Just have to shift myself some." He stretched out his long legs to ease the cricks, but did it slowly, so as not to jar the boy slumped against him.

"You won't go . . . an' leave me here alone?" the boy asked again with more urgency, pressing his forehead into the man's shoulder.

"I won't go," Seth told him once more. Several times in the past hour he had tried to change his cramped position without disturbing the wounded boy, but even the slightest movement brought him awake, and each time he had that same question.

"Can you . . . take me home?" the boy said, his breath rasping. "I want my . . . my pa. Tell him I didn't . . . run . . ."

Choking drowned the next words strung between his gasps, and bloody phlegm ran down his chin. His voice sounded more feeble every time he spoke.

"I'll take you at sunrise," Seth lied. "Can't see where to go right now."

That much of it rang true. Only an alien land lay ahead, and it was dotted with Rebel campfires. Even the air held a foreign smell, a thick metallic smell of smoke and blood and rain. Always rain. Sometimes it would stop for a spell, but after a time it would start again, dropping from low dark clouds that hung over woods and farmland like a leaden shroud.

When the rain last began, thinning the battle smoke that lingered above a once-greening field, Seth had found himself lying in a muddy ditch with no clear memory of how he had come to be there. He could remember only a burst of gunfire and the sensation of falling. When he had dragged himself from the ditch, he saw sprawled across the rutted field the silent gray bodies of Rebel troops. They looked rigid, unnatural, as if a regiment of tin toy soldiers had been tossed helter-skelter over a rumpled green counterpane. There were blue-coated dead there, too, but not near as many. And maybe, Seth thought, he had been left for dead himself.

After struggling to his feet, he had come upon the boy, somehow still alive despite his fearsome wound. Seth had known it was dangerous to be there, and more so for him to stay there. He had to find the road leading back to his company's camp, and would stop only long enough to take the boy to the nearest sheltering tree.

Now the rain had stopped again and a milky moon swam between breaking clouds. Water still dripped through the oak leaves, and Seth threw back his head, mouth open, his canteen emptied by the boy's need that had been greater than his own.

"I'm mighty tired, sir," the boy said in no more than

a whisper. "Wish I could . . . could see my pa 'fore I sleep. Could you fetch him?"

"I'll fetch him soon."

The boy began to slip sideways. Seth caught him by sliding his arm around the narrow shoulders wrapped in his own dark blue coat, and looked down at the waxen face. It was very young. The lad could be no older than Seth's brother Harry, maybe ten or eleven, or twelve at the most. He was a drummer boy. When Seth had found him, the drum had been a few feet away, its sheepskin head smashed by some stomping boot, and the sticks still clutched in the boy's hands. The wooden drum had been painted dark green and bore the stenciled black characters 5TH N.C.

"Pa?" the boy murmured against Seth's chest. "Pa, you shur you ain't 'shamed of me?"

"No, not 'shamed," Seth answered. Lord, he was tired, bone-tired. Why was he still here? He could not save the boy, and could likely not even save himself if it came to that.

"I'll be home 'fore long, Pa . . . I reckon."

"I reckon," said Seth, a damp cold seeping through his flannel shirt as night settled. He tried not to fix on the hole in the boy's belly made by the savage tearing of a minié ball. Earlier Seth had drawn off the shredded, butternut-colored musician's tunic and bound it around the boy's mid-section, thinking to give him some comfort and maybe stanch the blood. Not that it was any use. Gut wounds almost always meant death. Even the surgeons turned from them in despair.

"Say somethin', Pa . . . please say somethin'!" came the boy's soft whimper. "It's so dark I cain't see . . . an' I'm 'fraid."

"Nothing to be afraid of here, son," Seth told him, stroking the boy's wet hair, because he could not think what else to do. He wondered why he did not feel more foolish, being as how he had never had a son, but he guessed this lad could be Harry in a few years' time. God, let this war be over by then.

His arm supporting the boy had grown stiff, and his right ankle throbbed something fierce. At first he had thought it was broken, but he could move his toes inside the boot, so it might only be sprained. How it had happened he didn't know, because he could not dredge up the memory.

"I have to shift again," he said, and lowered his arm, holding the boy's shoulder with his other hand.

When Seth went to lean him back against the oak, the boy toppled over like a sack of loose grain. The young man sat there without moving, not wanting to know, but at last he searched for a pulse even though the rattle of the boy's breathing had stopped. So had his heart.

Seth knuckled away a smart of tears before he closed the boy's eyes, aware that every minute he remained there was foolhardy. He rose on his knees to draw his coat free, then straightened the boy to lie flat, crossed the hands and tucked the two drumsticks between nail-bitten fingers. After that he mumbled the Lord's Prayer, the only prayer that came to mind, for whatever good it might do.

"*. . . and forgive us our trespasses as we forgive those who have trespassed against us . . .*"

With legs so numb he could barely feel them, Seth got to his feet and shrugged into his coat, which was damp with rain and the boy's blood. He went to fetch the drum, and while he was placing it beside the small form, he heard behind him a rustle of leaves.

"You come 'round real slow now, Yankee!"

Seth turned to face four soldiers in mud-streaked jackets who were standing some yards beyond. One had a rifle trained on him. They looked to be about his own age, maybe a few years older, and although the moonlight was bright enough, Seth didn't need it to know the color of their uniforms.

"He done dyin' yet?" asked one, gesturing toward the boy.

"He's done," Seth answered, and wondered how long they had been there.

"One of your regiment?" asked another.

"No," said Seth. "One of yours."

He saw the rifle barrel waver, then hold steady. Could be they meant to shoot him instead of take him prisoner, and either way he should put up a fight, but there were too many of them and his ankle would make a mockery of it. He had been three days without sleep, so he was almost too damn tired to care what the Rebels did.

He glanced down at the boy. Sleep, death . . . hardly seemed to matter much which.

One of the soldiers came forward, stooped to look at the boy and glance at the drum. "He's ours, all right. So how come," he asked Seth, "y'all didn't just leave him here?"

"He didn't want to be left."

Slowly, reluctantly, the rifle lowered. "Maybe you just saved me a bullet," said its owner, who looked some older than the others.

They rolled the boy in a blanket, and one of them slung the bundle over his shoulder. The older soldier said to Seth, "Seems like y'all missed the truce time to pick up the dead. Thing is, we lost more'n half the Fifth North Carolina—" he gestured toward the field "—so I s'pect we have to take you prisoner. One way or t'other."

"I expect so."

"Y'all an officer?" asked another, eyeing Seth's shoulder strap.

He hesitated before answering, "Second lieutenant," because it was unfamiliar. His brevet commission had come through two days before.

"Okay, Lieutenant Yankee, it's prison in Richmond, and after that, I bet y'all wish we'd 'a' shot you."

Seth nodded, and after a backward glance at the boy's drum, he limped forward.

His ankle must be swollen, because his boot felt as tight as an iron shackle, and he gritted his teeth as he hobbled over the soggy ground. A strip of woodland lay beyond, stark and still under a wash of moonlight, and his mind gradually began to clear. He kept limping along, while his memory returned what he had lost.

He had been acting as a courier, carrying orders to Brigadier General Hancock from an aged, ranking general who had been miles from here on the Yorktown road and stone-blind to the field of battle.

Seth guessed now that his roan gelding must have been shot from under him. He had been galloping through a woods in the direction of gunfire, and when the trees had thinned he saw ahead a rolling expanse of young green wheat. Lines of Union blue, crouched on a shallow rise of the field, were firing down at exposed, advancing Rebel troops, and men in gray were falling like grain before a sweeping scythe. Their red and blue battle flag, held aloft by a swaying staff, had fluttered like plumage on a snared bird until the staff and its square of bunting went plunging into the howling, churning harvest of men.

Just as Seth had reined in, a burst of cannon fire exploded from the woods and beneath him the horse shuddered. He could remember yanking his boot from a stirrup before the roan fell sideways, and then he had been sinking through clouds of smoke.

That was all his memory gave back. But what had the Rebel earlier said? More than half a Carolina regiment lost?

The soldier with the rifle was telling a younger one, "The man's lame, Billy, so he won't give you trouble. Here, take the gun, and you walk him back through the woods to camp. We got to round up those loose horses, 'cause we head west 'fore sun-up."

Billy took the rifle, and the other men loped off into the trees.

As he walked, Seth could feel the blood start to flow in his stiff legs. Must finally be getting to his brain, too, because it showed him an image of a Rebel camp with the survivors of an ambushed Carolina regiment. Having seen their brothers mown down on that wheat field like green stalks, Seth doubted they would let him leave the camp alive. He couldn't blame them either.

He glanced ahead and guessed he might have maybe one chance. No more than that.

He and Billy moved into the trees. When Seth smelled a trace of wood smoke he began to overdraw his limp, hobbling forward with clumsy steps and hoping the others were beyond earshot. After he had slowed to a near standstill, Billy came up close behind to give him a prod with the rifle barrel. "C'mon Yankee, gotta make camp 'fore mornin'."

Seth shrugged, then stumbled as if tripping over something in his path. Flailing his arms to catch himself, he dropped to his knees, falling hard against the other man.

"Hey, watch it!" yelled Billy, taken off guard and staggering backward. "Jest what the hell'r y'all do—"

Seth lunged for the rifle, and caught the barrel in his hands. He twisted it out of Billy's grip and swung the stock hard against the other's knees. As Billy's legs buckled, Seth heard shouting from beyond the trees at the same time a bullet went whining past him. He hunkered down, raised the rifle to fire, and from the corner of his eye saw only a gray blur before the blow struck him. As he pitched forward, he heard again the whine of a bullet.

His last conscious thoughts were of his brother and of the drummer boy, of sleep and of death.

"Damn fool!" yelled Billy, leaping to his feet and throwing the rock aside to grab the rifle. He took a few steps backward and aimed the gun barrel down at the sprawled figure.

"No!" said a brusque voice.

The barrel was pushed aside by the man who had come pacing through the trees, a lean, crisp-bearded man, his eyes narrowed and keen as those of a fox, with a forage cap pulled low over his forehead.

"No," the man said again.

The one word was all he spoke, but the intent of the command and its authority could not be mistaken.

"Aw, sir, lookit all thet there blood on his coat," Billy complained. "General Hill, sir, this here's one of them Yankee bastards kilt all—"

"It's over, boy! Stand away. You don't shoot a man in cold blood lest there's a damn good reason, and I don't see one here. Now bring him into camp."

2

Men dropped by the thousands, exhausted, sick, and wounded, [and] the Medical Department, unprepared, flung itself upon the Sanitary Commission when it became known that our transports were lying in the river.

—Katharine Prescott Wormeley, May 1862

The York River

On and on toward the ships they came, emerging from the fog like ghosts of ancient warriors bound for the river of no return. Bloodied and haggard, the soldiers made their way down the muddy embankment. Most of them limped or hobbled on crutches made of forked tree branches, and some with limbs missing were brought groaning on stretchers. None of the men appeared whole. If not injured and maimed, they bore the marks of disease.

And these were the victors, Bronwen Llyr thought. And the ones able to make it this far. No one yet knew how many were not able.

The young woman stood in the bow of a moored hospital ship aptly christened the *Aeneid,* forced to watch the ragged march because there was nowhere she could avoid it. Several times she had leaned over the rail, certain she would retch from the smell of blood and rotting flesh. Each time she expected to see the river running red.

From those around her Bronwen gathered that the few

ambulance wagons requisitioned by a distant army quartermaster had become mired in mud, clogging the road from Williamsburg.

"Stuck up to their wheel hubs in the stinkin' muck!" offered one feverish-looking soldier. "And not goin' anywhere soon. 'Fore long they won't need to, 'cause the wounded are dyin' fast as flies in those wagons."

How could any office clerk in Washington City know what type, and how many, vehicles would be needed on a battlefield more than one hundred miles away? thought Bronwen with disgust. Or could even begin to estimate how many men would fall sick? These soldiers had been forced to make it here on their own. What if there were no hospital ships of the Sanitary Commission? And the Sanitary was not even connected to the military, but was instead a civilian volunteer organization.

Blocking the path to the York River wharves were lighter carts with the most dangerously wounded who were judged to have some chance to survive. The carts were jerking through the thick red mud, hauled by mules braying complaint with every step. Again and again foghorns bleated, and steam whistles shrieked from the transport ships, along with the shouts of those loading the soldiers bound for unprepared, makeshift Northern hospitals.

Because of the heavy mist, Bronwen could catch only brief glimpses of her sister, a Sanitary Commission nurse who was tending the sick and wounded.

"You look worn out, Kathryn," Bronwen had said to her a few hours earlier after reaching there by gunboat from Fort Monroe.

"I'm a little tired," her sister had admitted, and with a soft sigh had shaken the hem of her muddied skirt. "But I shouldn't even say that, because it's nothing compared to the exhaustion of these men. Most of them have come miles."

Kathryn was working her way, back and forth, between

the *Aeneid*'s wharf and the York riverbank, her shoulders drooping beneath a shawl, her face so pale and drawn that the past few days seemed to have aged her thirty years. She went from man to man, stopping to give them beef broth ladled from buckets that swung above a shallow fire pit. Now and again she would stop to clean dirt or vomit from a soldier's face, stanch with cotton lint the blood from a wound, and dole out her meager supply of whiskey. Then she would point the men toward the ships and move on to the next ones stumbling down the path.

Their trek to the river had been fairly steady during the two hours since Bronwen had arrived. To watch it was almost beyond bearing. For relief she lifted her gaze to the riverbank farther upstream, lined with weeping-elm and flecked with the pink of magnolias and the white of fringe trees. Spread against a ceiling of swollen clouds were the dark, tilting wings of turkey vultures as they glided in searching flight. They too had been brought here by war.

There had been time to speak only briefly with her sister. "This must be how Hades looks," Bronwen had said, "from the shore of the river Styx."

"I expect so," Kathryn had murmured, using the back of her hand to push a strand of deep-bronze-colored hair from her dirt-smudged forehead. "But it's worse at Williamsburg. The first men to reach us told of wounded still lying in the rain without food or even the most basic care."

"Why don't I see more than a handful of doctors?"

"Most are at the field hospital tents a few miles upriver," Kathryn had told her, "because so many of the injured need immediate surgery. But the doctors there are overwhelmed and they're sending on the men who can walk."

"Walk" was not the word Bronwen would have used to describe what these men, especially the amputees, were compelled to do. "Lurch" or "sway" or "totter" would have been more fitting, but she did not say so. With limited success she was trying to curb her tendency to voice every thought that came to mind.

Then shouts for help with more arriving casualties had sent Kathryn hurrying off again.

Bronwen had trailed reluctantly after her, but felt useless in the face of such need. Nursing was not what she had been trained to do, and never would have chosen to do, so this was a view of the war she had until now been spared. The stoicism of these survivors was dumbfounding, in light of their injuries and the diseases that followed an army like grim reapers. It was all she could do to keep her stomach down while handing out tin mugs of the broth.

At last one of the two big transports, its cargo the most seriously sick and wounded, headed into mid-river and steamed east toward the Chesapeake Bay. The stream of men from the Williamsburg road began to thin. That did not mean there were fewer sick and wounded, Bronwen guessed, but only that there were fewer who could reach the river.

Men were still being carried from the *Aeneid* onto the one remaining transport, and had been for several hours, so Bronwen could not think there would be space for more. Some time ago she had lost sight of Kathryn, and now spotted her at the foot of the hospital ship gangplank. She was gesturing at the transport, although Bronwen, glancing toward it, could not see for what reason, but her sister's distressed expression was enough to make her start toward the ship. After reaching the gangplank, she found it jammed with stretchers and limping men, and when she looked again, Kathryn was gone.

The two young women stood side by side on the upper deck of the hospital ship, their long skirts laden with moisture and sagging onto the wood planking. A short time before, the second transport ship had left. The rain had slackened and shafts of sunlight thrust between clouds, but they brought small comfort to the wounded forced to wait until the ships could unload and return for them.

While the transport headed downriver, Bronwen had waited for her sister on the *Aeneid*'s upper deck. When Kathryn appeared from below, she had pointed at the stern of the ship, asking with a worried frown, "It's left?"

"Yes, finally, but why do you look upset by that?" Still shaken by what she had seen, Bronwen had added, "Given the surroundings, though, I suppose you wouldn't look any other way."

"There's something I need to tell you in private," Kathryn had said, "before I go to anyone else about it. Let's walk forward."

They now stood in the *Aeneid*'s bow.

"There's no one else here, Kathryn, but you seem to have gone mute. Why this secrecy?"

Her sister grasped the upper railing and looked down at the York sliding toward the Chesapeake with only an occasional ripple marring its surface. The yellow flag of the hospital ship hung limp, a splotch of color in the dissolving gray mist.

"I wonder if I've jumped to a wrong conclusion," Kathryn at last answered. "In which case I don't want to disturb the others aboard. Let me think for a minute how to explain it."

"How to explain *what?*" Bronwen prodded, but she knew her sister could rarely be made to speak before she was ready. It was one of many traits they did not share.

Kathryn only gazed at the tranquil river. The *Aeneid*, an excursion ship converted to a floating hospital, was moored some distance above Yorktown. The Union garrison there had been evacuated a week before, when, during the night, the Confederates had stolen away from their entrenched position without a shot fired. General George McClellan, commander of the Northern Army of the Po-

tomac, had declared it "a brilliant success." Since Mc-
Clellan's superior force had been besieging Yorktown for
nearly a month, his pronouncement had left many in
Washington speechless. A week later, they were still groping for words.

In an effort to contain her impatience, Bronwen remarked, "Notice how quiet it's become? You would hardly know what went on here earlier, or that there are still
wounded bunked below."

As if to give this the lie, a sudden anguished cry came
from a lower deck. Another cry, and another and another,
followed like echoes before quiet again descended.

Bronwen, gripping the rail in alarm, glanced at her sister. Kathryn had straightened with every line of her frame
drawn taut. Smudges like coal dust underlined her dark
blue eyes, their whites shot through with the red of fatigue.

When the silence continued, Bronwen ventured, "Does
that happen often?"

"No, it doesn't," Kathryn said quietly. "There are several amputations being performed, and we have very little
ether left. We're expecting a supply boat from Fort Monroe later today, but I suppose the surgery couldn't wait."

She shook herself slightly and smoothed her blue
apron, blotched with stains that might have been dirt or
broth or blood. When she appeared lost in thought, Bronwen's patience reached its limit. She had been granted
leave for only the day and had to return that evening to
Fort Monroe.

"Kathryn, please! What *is* it?"

Her sister gave a start, then glanced around to see if
she could be overheard before saying, "Late yesterday,
when a large group of casualties arrived from Williamsburg, I noticed one man who didn't appear to be injured,
or sick either. He clutched at his chest only when he saw
me watching him, and his grimaces seemed feigned. But

I was busy with others and lost track of him. Then last night I came across him below deck with the worst wounded."

"So he *was* injured?"

Kathryn gazed upward as if trying to clear her mind of everything but recall. "He was sitting on the edge of a bunk, studying something on a piece of paper. When he saw me, he grabbed his chest and doubled over, while he was slipping the paper under a blanket. At the time, I was sure he meant to conceal it."

"You still thought he was faking pain?"

"I don't know. When I asked him how he felt, he just moaned and lay back on the bunk. He refused to let me look at his chest, and when I asked if he wanted to see a doctor, he said he didn't need one. Then he rolled over with his back to me."

"Maybe he'd had enough of battle and didn't want to be sent back to his regiment. I'd be surprised if he were the only one!"

Kathryn shook her head. "I've seen that just a few times, and those men had a desperate look about them. This man didn't. His expression was more . . . determined. But as you saw earlier, our resources are strained, and there's no space for someone who doesn't require im-mediate care."

"You've told no one else?"

"No, I was afraid the man might really have been in pain and was too proud to say so. And I didn't have time to spare, because the needs of others were so urgent. I'm ashamed to say that in all the confusion I forgot about him."

"But why are you so troubled by this now? Someone will spot it sooner or later if the man is malingering. And if he isn't . . . well, is it so important?"

"There's more to it, Bronwen. While that second trans-port was loading, I went below to check the men again, to be sure the worst cases were being taken aboard first.

That same man was standing by his bunk, looking as if he intended to leave. Space on those transports to Washington is scarce—the hospitals at Yorktown and Fort Monroe are both full—so I asked him if a surgeon had approved his passage. He answered, sharply, that he had just been cleared and needed to go directly to the transport ship."

"Did he seem nervous?"

"Not exactly nervous. 'Furtive' is a better word, especially when I asked him to wait while I checked the surgeons' roster. He pulled a paper out of his coat pocket, saying it was his clearance, but when I reached for the paper, he jammed it back into his pocket and brushed past me. He nearly ran down the gangway."

"So he's gone?"

"It seems so. But when he hurried past me, his coat caught on the bunk, and the paper slipped from his pocket. He obviously didn't realize he had lost it, so I picked it up and called after him. He acted as if he didn't hear me. I followed him to the gangplank, and that's when I saw you and tried to point him out. Then I lost sight of him."

Kathryn reached into the pocket of her apron, and withdrawing a crumpled square of paper, she handed it to her sister. "I've already looked at it. What do you think?"

Bronwen smoothed the paper, then stared in confusion at a detailed map of Washington. "Why would a wounded soldier go to any trouble to conceal this? And he must have had it when he was brought aboard, or someone here on the ship gave it to him. Is that likely?"

"I suppose it's possible," Kathryn said. "But why have it at all? He was being transported, so he couldn't have been concerned about losing his way. Unless—"

"Unless, as you guessed, he wasn't wounded. Was faking in order to board that transport as a way north. Now just who, these days, might have trouble freely entering Washington?"

"A Confederate," Kathryn answered. "I thought of that,

but the man wore Union blue and spoke with a northern accent."

"And when I'm in Richmond, I speak with a southern one," Bronwen told her. "It can be learned. The man could easily have come by the uniform—by taking it from a prisoner of war, or a dead Union soldier, or any other number of ways."

Kathryn reached for the map. "Did you notice this pencil mark made on one of the streets? It's faint, but I think there's an X inside a circle."

"I saw it," Bronwen said, peering over her sister's shoulder. "That X seems to be . . . it's marking Old Capitol Prison!" she whispered, an absurd idea springing to mind.

"I was afraid it might be the prison," Kathryn agreed, so readily that Bronwen thought she might be entertaining the same absurdity, although she could hardly believe it of her levelheaded sister.

"If you recall, I've been to Old Capitol," Kathryn went on. "There are more than a hundred prisoners there, and that man could simply want to visit a friend, or even a relative. Nothing more than that."

"Then he went through his charade here without reason," Bronwen objected. "Prisoners are allowed to have visitors."

"But he might not have known that. I can guess what you're imagining, Bronwen, but this could be a coincidence. I realize you don't believe in coinci—"

"A man you didn't believe was wounded is brought aboard this hospital ship," Bronwen interrupted. "He then manages to sneak aboard another Union ship bound for Washington, and he just happens to have in his possession a map marking the location of Old Capitol Prison. A coincidence?"

She paused to study her sister before adding, "You can't have forgotten who is now being held in Old Capitol, Kathryn. Held for trial on charges of treason and murder, as you also can't have forgotten, since you helped to put the woman there."

Kathryn was shaking her head, and Bronwen knew she was trying to convince herself that what they were imagining could not be true. It was too long a leap of reason to make. Still . . .

"Did the man have any identification?" she asked.

"Last night I picked up his coat to look for some, and couldn't find anything. Most soldiers take pains to have names and addresses sewn into their clothing, so their families can be notified if . . . if need arises. But just because this man did not, doesn't mean something sinister."

Bronwen was unconvinced, but said, "All right, since there are some Confederate prisoners of war being held at Old Capitol, that man might only intend to visit a friend, and he fancied intrigue to get himself into Washington. On the other hand, let's speak the unspeakable. The man *could* be a Confederate agent. Who is now on his way to help another Confederate agent escape her rendezvous with a jury and possibly a hangman. Is it simply happenstance that Mrs. Bleuette, code name Bluebell, was arrested only a week ago, giving Richmond just about enough time to learn of it?"

"The thought of that woman gives me a chill," Kathryn said. "What should we do?"

"Describe the man to me."

"He was more or less nondescript."

"That's not much help."

"But he was. He had regular features and no distinguishing characteristics. Average height, average frame, brown hair, and I'm not sure what color eyes. Now that I think about it, he averted his face whenever he spoke."

"Clean-shaven?"

"No, but every soldier in the field for any length of time has some beard." Kathryn paused before saying, "Actually, if he hadn't been irritated, he might have looked quite nice. I think I would recognize him again."

"Let's hope you don't have to."

"But what if we're mistaken and have simply jumped to the worst conclusion? Given our past experience with that woman, it's understandable but not reliable."

"I get paid to jump to worst conclusions," Bronwen said, "and Treasury should at least be alerted to the possibility of her attempt to escape from Old Capitol. Wouldn't be too hard to do, considering the lax security there, especially if Bluebell has an accomplice. I'll wire Rhys Bevan about it from Fort Monroe."

Bevan was her immediate superior in the United States Treasury Department. Its newly formed special intelligence unit, of which she was a member, was the Union's only organized espionage presence there on the Virginia peninsula. However far-fetched the scheme she and Kathryn imagined—and admittedly it *was* far-fetched—Bronwen had to report it.

"Kathryn, when do you expect that next tug from Fort Monroe?"

"Not until late afternoon."

While Bronwen was calculating the time it would take the tug to unload its cargo before returning to the fort—and the military telegraph line to Washington—Kathryn suddenly asked, "Would that woman recognize you?"

"She followed me at a distance in Washington at least once that I was aware of. And she would know you, too, wouldn't she?"

"I was there at the prison to confront her, along with several others, including your Treasury superior."

"Don't worry about it," Bronwen said, "because you'll never see her again. If Bluebell *were* to escape, she would make a beeline for Richmond and Major William Norris. He's head of the Confederate Signal Corps—that's a euphemism for one of their espionage units. I wouldn't be surprised if Norris engineered this, although the woman is treacherously inventive all on her own."

"Bronwen, I hesitated to tell you because I was afraid

you would become entangled with her. Please promise
you won't."

"I can't promise that."

"But why do *you* have to—"

"Because Bluebell can identify me and possibly another Treasury agent as well."

She was trying to remember if the woman Bluebell had
ever seen agent Kerry O'Hara long enough to later recognize him. "It occurs to me," she said, "that identification
may be exactly why Norris wants the woman brought
back to Virginia. If so, his timing would be uncanny, because my next assignment is Richmond."

Since her sister looked so concerned, Bronwen did not
add that Norris's timing might not have been uncanny; he
could have been informed. That would mean, God forbid,
that the Treasury unit might have itself another mole. One
had just been unearthed, but in the past weeks Rhys Bevan
could well have recruited additional members. Or worse
still, there could have been *two* double agents in the unit
when it was originally formed.

An unpleasant sensation skittered down her spine when
she recalled some suspicious incidents involving Agent
O'Hara. Rhys Bevan had insisted her distrust of him was
unfounded, and she hoped he was right, because O'Hara,
too, could be assigned to Richmond.

He might already be there.

It now seemed even more urgent that she get word to
Washington, but there was no transport until the tug arrived. Unless she was prepared to swim down the York,
she would just have to wait.

3

—m—

The atmosphere of Richmond is redolent of to-
bacco; the tints of the pavements are those of
tobacco. One seems to breathe tobacco, to see
tobacco, and to smell tobacco at every turn.

—a Richmond observer, 1860

Richmond, Virginia

Only by some nimble sidestepping did the British intelligence agent Colonel Dorian de Warde manage to avoid an oceanic mud puddle. De Warde was then forced to leap from the cobblestone paving to the Broad Street sidewalk as yet another top-heavy baggage wagon rattled past. This one was piled with expensive luggage that shifted precariously when it jounced around the next corner. Jarred loose by the wagon's careening passage, a steamer trunk tumbled into its wake. When the trunk hit the pavement, it burst open, spilling into the gutter a froth of lace-edged petticoats and a fount of sparkling jewelry.

De Warde, whose elegant appearance called to mind a well-preened falcon, gave the jewels a keen appraising eye. He stepped back into the street, only to be shoved aside by ragged children and shabbily dressed adults who were splashing through the puddle to pounce on the windfall. De Warde paused to reevaluate. The wagon in the meantime had clattered on toward the nearby railroad station.

His innate dignity having won the day, de Warde moved back onto the sidewalk to look after the wagon, observing that the richest rats were always first to leave a sinking ship, whether the ship bore plague or famine or advancing Federal troops. Confederate-held Williamsburg had just fallen and the exodus from Richmond was now reaching fever-pitch. Roads to the train depot were clogged with fleeing citizenry, and even the family of the Confederate president had taken flight. Jefferson Davis himself remained at the helm of his foundering vessel.

De Warde tucked his ebony-shafted walking stick under his arm and set out briskly in the direction of the James River. The Union army was a few days' march from the gates of Richmond, and thus from the Virginia tobacco stored in warehouses along its waterfront. This tobacco had long since been packed into hogsheads, purchased and stamped with the buyer's mark, and now it sat waiting to be shipped. But since many if not most of these buyers were British and French, the Union blockade of Southern ports had made their tobacco as inaccessible as treasure guarded by a fire-breathing dragon. De Warde's personal investment in the treasure was considerable, although less than his queen's; the third French Napoleon's share was larger than both combined, but Louis would not sneeze without first obtaining Britain's blessing, much less go a–dragon baiting.

To make matters more pressing, the compulsion for retribution had reared its ugly head. This compulsion did not afflict only Americans, but they surrendered to it with greater enthusiasm than did their older European cousins, who had learned over time that revenge was frequently more costly than it was worth. De Warde had just come from the Ninth and Broad Street office of the Confederate War Department, where he had met with an officious civil servant named Jones. This toad of a man had informed de Warde that some draconian law required the destruction of *all* stored tobacco lest it fall into enemy hands. Jones had been smugly adamant, and apparently combustibles were even now being brought to the warehouses to facilitate burning the tobacco. Tobacco worth more than sixty million dollars.

Clearly something must be done.

When de Warde approached the row of warehouses strung above the James, he saw a short column of blue-clad men, undoubtedly Union prisoners, being marched through the doors of a three-story brick building half the length of a city block. Over its doors a sign painted in bold black letters read LIBBY AND SON, SHIP CHANDLERS AND GROCERS.

A sudden rumble of wheels made de Warde turn to see a large carriage just drawing to a halt some distance away. From it descended a man whom he recognized with wariness as the French minister Count Mercier. Perhaps Emperor Napoleon III had developed a cold, and this fact had not yet been relayed to de Warde.

"*Bonjour,* monsieur de Warde," Mercier greeted him. "What a charming surprise to see you here."

"A surprise, indeed, sir. I had understood you were in Washington."

"*Oui, mon ami.* And I am there still," responded Mercier, a glint of humor in his cold eyes.

"Just so," said de Warde, amused as always by the French élan when denying reality. "Then I have not been misinformed. But if you are not here, then will you be unable to attend the Confederacy's funeral? A funeral lamentably preceded by an expensive cremation?"

The glint in Mercier's eyes grew brighter, but he did not answer. He gestured instead to another man, who, with his back to them, was just climbing down from the carriage.

Mercier asked de Warde, "Have you met *un Américain*

James Quiller? Monsieur Quiller has just returned from Paris."

De Warde's brows lifted. Now this *was* a surprise. One with perhaps unpleasant implications. Baltimore businessman James Quiller was reported to be a close friend of the United States president Abraham Lincoln. Quiller's business was alleged to be the publishing of railroad and steamship guides, as well as maps of the South, but if this was all the man did, reasoned de Warde, then the sun tomorrow would rise in the west. Quiller had supposedly arrived in Washington from Europe only yesterday. Had his journey here to Richmond been made in the company of the French minister? If so, it could bode ill for British interests in the American fraternal war now raging. To say nothing of millions' worth of British tobacco.

Lincoln was by all unbiased reports an intelligent man and a shrewd politician. Thus he must be aware that his naval blockade, while aimed at preventing European goods from reaching the South, was also preventing the South from shipping to Europe its valuable cotton and its almost as valuable tobacco. He must also be aware that this fact increased the likelihood of Britain and France intervening on behalf of the Southern Confederacy. Count Mercier, given his clandestine trip here from Washington, could be clearing a path on which to bargain with Lincoln.

"Monsieur Quiller," offered Mercier while they waited, "has confided that his stay in Paris was *sympathique.*"

Meaning precisely what? thought de Warde with rising alarm, even as he sent the French count a bland nod. Had Mercier been authorized to agree that his country would refrain from entering the American civil strife, in return for safe passage of French tobacco from the South? If so, where would this leave British interests? And de Warde's own investments? France would not enter the fray without Britain's support, but it could *refuse* to enter and make its refusal profitable. One simply could not trust the French.

De Warde decided an immediate visit to the British

consul here in Richmond should be the next item on his agenda. Followed by a call on Major William Norris, who by this time should have replaced his Confederate mole recently uncovered by a resourceful Federal Treasury agent. That this young agent was beautiful as well as clever made de Warde more kindly disposed toward her than he otherwise might have been—the world being woefully in need of such qualities—but she would bear close watching. Particularly since she had ready access to Lincoln.

Now walking from the carriage toward de Warde and Mercier was a tall, robust-looking man. As he drew nearer, the Englishman's eyes widened, but they had narrowed to conceal his surprise by the time Count Mercier began his introductions.

"A pleasure to make your acquaintance, Colonel de Warde," responded the man, and thrust out his hand with typical American exuberance.

"I assure you, my dear Mr. Quiller, the pleasure is all mine."

As indeed it was. Due to this chance meeting, de Warde had been reminded there was often more than one way to slay a dragon.

Which meant he had just been handed a double-edged sword.

4

—⚭—

*After a battle, when men are brought in so rap-
idly . . . and everyone raving for drink first and
then for nourishment, it requires strong nerves to
be able to attend to them properly.*

—Frederick Olmsted, May 1862

The York River

It was late afternoon before Bronwen saw her sister
again on the *Aeneid*'s upper deck. Kathryn had been min-
istering to a group of soldiers recently brought by
stretcher from the field hospital outside Williamsburg. All
of the men were amputees.

"Are you finished?" Bronwen asked her.

"Nothing here is ever finished," Kathryn answered, either sorrow or fatigue making her voice so low it was
barely audible, and Bronwen had to bend forward to hear
her next words. "Those two transport ships won't be returning for wounded until later this evening, but that supply boat should be here anytime now."

"Good, because I'll leave on it and telegraph Rhys
Bevan from Fort Monroe about your mystery 'patient.'
And let's hope he doesn't arrive in Washington before my
wire does."

The more Bronwen considered the possibility of this
man having been sent by Confederate intelligence, in or-

der to assist an assassin's escape from Old Capitol Prison, the uneasier she grew. She did not tell Kathryn this.

"Is there any chance you won't be going to Richmond?" Kathryn asked, sounding so plaintive that Bronwen hesitated to deprive her of hope.

"I imagine I will be at some point," she hedged.

"But you were nearly killed there!"

"Circumstances are different now," Bronwen said, which was not strictly the truth, but not an outright lie, either. The gravest danger to her in Richmond had come not from Southerners but from those Northerners who had sold themselves to the South. She recalled what Colonel Dorian de Warde, a treacherous if courtly British agent, had said the day Confederates evacuated the Norfolk naval base: *Beware a man who will sell his country for a few pieces of silver.* And de Warde should know. To purchase betrayal he was willing to pay coin of the realm sterling. He had claimed he was there in Virginia to protect his tobacco investments, and Bronwen, aware of de Warde's affection for money, had half-believed him. She believed little else he had said.

Her sister sighed and passed a hand over her forehead as she asked, her voice no more than a whisper, "Why are you doing this?"

"Doing what?"

Kathryn glanced around to see who might be within earshot before she replied, "Intelligence gathering. Espionage. Spying. No matter by what name you call it, Bronwen, it's dangerous beyond measure, and I don't understand why you do it. For what reason?"

The question caught Bronwen off balance, and her recourse, while trying to regain her footing, was to counter, "Why are *you* here, Kathryn?"

"I'm not here to fight in this war. Or to take sides in something so complicated I can't begin to pass judgment on who is right or wrong—nor would I choose to if I *could* sort it out. It makes no difference to me whether

the men who need care are Federals or Confederates, Un-
ionists or Rebels, Northerners or Southerners."

Bronwen could not think of a response. Perhaps there
was none, because what her sister said was unquestionably what she believed. How could she reproach Kathryn
for "giving aid and comfort to the enemy"? Or say that
this was, incidentally, considered to be treason, because
Rebel solders she patched up today could turn round and
kill Union soldiers tomorrow?

Bronwen would also have to admit, now being forced
to consider it, that she had not particularly wanted to think
about why she was involved. At first the novelty and excitement, and the good wages, together with her admiration for Lincoln had been reason enough. But the novelty
was wearing thin, and the excitement was too often coupled with gut-wrenching fear. What had been steadfast
was her trust in Lincoln and what he believed. She had
also seen slavery firsthand. Despite hearing arguments to
the contrary from many decent white Southerners, she remained convinced that if slavery did not exist in America,
and if efforts were not being made to extend it to the
western territories, there would have been no war.

"I have faith in Mr. Lincoln, Kathryn. And no one
should be enslaved!"

She was rather startled by the intensity in her voice.
Obviously so was Kathryn for she said, "If that's your
answer, I didn't realize you felt so strongly about slavery."

"Until recently, neither did I," Bronwen granted, "but
I've never been good at soul-searching. And if you don't
mind, I'd rather not do much more of it."

"Why did things have to come to this terrible pass?
This tragic waste of lives?"

"I agree it's tragic, but I don't know that it's a waste.
And if McClellan's campaign here in Virginia is successful, and there's every reason to think it will be, the tragedy

could end soon. Should be within the next few weeks."

She turned to study her sister. Kathryn had begun to reflect the compassion she had always owned, making hers an uncommon beauty. While she looked fragile, she had always been surprisingly hardy, and hardiness must be a given for the women who joined the Sanitary Commission. Earlier, when she had seen Kathryn helping wounded soldiers, some of them had been nearly twice her size.

As Kathryn tucked stray wisps of hair under the shirred edge of her nurse's snood, she scanned the shoreline. "I can't think what's keeping Natty. I sent him hours ago for dandelion greens to make soup, because that broth isn't enough for some of the men. I expected the boy back long before this."

"If he's survived alone on the streets of Washington, I'll wager he can take care of himself anywhere."

"You don't know him, Bronwen."

"I'm not sure I want to—he sounds like a ruffian. How old is he?"

"He claims he doesn't know, or what his surname is either, both of which could sadly be true. Sometimes he looks seventy and acts as if he is seven, sometimes it's the other way round. And he's not a ruffian," Kathryn added with the hint of a smile, "at least not a confirmed one."

"All right, a promising one."

At a muffled cry from below deck, Kathryn's half-smile vanished. She seemed to feel responsible for every last man on board, Bronwen thought, and while there were other women of the Sanitary Commission here, most were volunteers without her sister's training and hospital experience. The women appeared to be chiefly well-to-do New Englanders who were performing basic housekeeping duties. But even if in the future they attempted to do more, Kathryn had said they would almost surely be rebuffed by the male army surgeon. By nearly *any* male surgeon.

Kathryn suddenly pointed downriver. "Isn't that a tugboat coming, probably from the Bay? It should carry the supplies we need, and if there's mail we might have some word of our brother."

"What did Mama's most recent letter say about him? Other than that he was here on the peninsula," Bronwen asked while she watched the approaching tug.

"Just that he had written home after landing at Fort Monroe, and that his regiment was heading west toward Richmond. Said he had received my last letter, the one where I told him I'd also be down here with the Sanitary Commission ships. He'd just received a promotion, and not to worry because Yorktown had been taken without a battle. For which we can be thankful."

"And there's been nothing from him since then?"

Kathryn shook her head. "In spite of all the men we've treated—and those transferred to the larger ships to be sent on north—those last soldiers said there may *still* be wounded at Williamsburg. I pray that our brother . . . no, it's too terrible to imagine."

"It's too terrible to imagine that the army medical service was so unprepared!" Bronwen responded. "That soldiers were left to die—some simply from thirst and hunger—because there were no means to get them off the battlefield. Thank the Lord your Sanitary Commission is here! Now maybe the army will stop complaining that volunteers are only meddlers."

Kathryn nodded, her expression so grave that Bronwen wondered if her sister would ever laugh again. Would anyone who had been here?

In silence they watched the tugboat steaming closer, and a few minutes later Kathryn said, with obvious relief, "There's Natty! But what on earth is he doing in that tug? Last I saw him, he was running down the wharf."

Without difficulty Bronwen identified the thin, tow-headed boy standing in the prow, his arms waving wildly. A burlap bag that looked to be bursting with greenery was slung over one shoulder, and he was shouting something at the top of his lungs.

"Unassuming little chap, isn't he?" she commented.

After the tug was moored at the wharf, and a few wounded soldiers struggled ashore, the boy nodded vigorously to one of them before dashing toward the hospital ship and clambering up its gangplank.

He thrust the sack of dandelion greens at Kathryn. "Here, Lady, take these stinkin' things. An' I got somethin' to tell you! There's a sol-jur—"

"Natty," Kathryn broke in, "I'd like to introduce you to my sister."

When he spun to face her, Bronwen regarded the boy with skepticism. It was obviously mutual. His speckled hazel eyes held a wariness she had seen in other street youngsters, but despite the ragged helmet of straw-like hair that nearly obscured his face, she could also see something more complicated in his expression. It might be intelligence or bravado or both, but whatever it was, it included an almost feral alertness. Bronwen nodded at him, thinking: *Lock up the valuables and nail down everything else.*

After his swift glance of appraisal Natty turned back to Kathryn. "You shur thet's she's a re-layshun? Don't look nothin' like you, Lady. Them grass-green eyes she got 'minds me of a alley cat. Now lissen up, 'cause I has to tell you somethin'."

"Natty, that was unkind," murmured Kathryn.

"Oh, I don't know," Bronwen said. "I've reminded people of worse things than a cat."

"Yeah, I bet," agreed Natty, and before Kathryn could react, he shouted, "Hey, whadda you know. Down there's the doc!"

He jumped to hang over the rail, swinging his arm

toward the wharf where another tug from farther upriver was just docking.

A number of uniformed men leapt to the wharf and headed for the hospital ship's gangplank. None seemed to be wounded, and Bronwen's gaze was drawn to a dark-haired man with striking looks. She would not have called him conventionally handsome, because his features were too strong, but he had a quality that commanded attention. The aggressive manner in which he came striding toward the ship made her uneasy, until she decided that he looked too clean to be a pirate and too conspicuous to be a spy.

She glanced over the others, looking for the doctor Natty had trumpeted and guessing it might be the surgeon her sister had mentioned briefly in a letter. Since she saw no one who matched Kathryn's one-word description of "dedicated"—which to Bronwen meant dull—she looked to her sister for a sign.

Natty was plucking at Kathryn's sleeve. For some reason she had flushed to the color of an overripe peach, her expression portraying what could only be profound surprise. Following her line of sight, Bronwen glanced down again to see the dark-haired man standing below them, his gaze unmistakably fixed on Kathryn.

When he came up the gangplank, Bronwen realized that her sister's description had not only been lacking but also misleading, since this was evidently the surgeon. And "dull" was not the word that sprang to mind.

Kathryn was standing as if cast in stone. Bronwen wondered why she seemed so stunned to see this man here; he was, after all, a doctor. When he reached the deck, he came to within a few feet of Kathryn, and stopped. Neither said a word, although watching them Bronwen believed she could almost hear the space between them thrumming like a telegraph line. Just how well had they known each other in Washington?

Kathryn, as if suddenly recalling where she was, lowered her eyes and turned to Bronwen to introduce the man.

Dr. Gregg Travis gave Bronwen a nod, but before either of them could speak, Natty elbowed them aside, yelping, "Lady, I been tryin' to tell you somethin'! But if you ain't gonna lissen, I got more things to do than lollygag round here!" He pivoted toward the gangplank, vaulted over the rope, and dashed down the planking with the nimbleness of a monkey.

This succeeded in wrenching Kathryn's attention from the doctor. "Natty, please wait," she called after him, and Bronwen figured the dismay in her sister's voice was exactly the response the little scamp had hoped to achieve. Travis seemed not to heed the boy's antics—possibly, Bronwen thought, because the doctor was studying her as if she were a bug under his microscope.

She had learned, she now realized, more about Travis from her Treasury chief Rhys Bevan than she had from Kathryn, who had neglected to mention his name. Rhys had told her that it finally became necessary to inform Travis of her own activities, because both he and her sister had been involved, unwillingly, in the charges against the Bleuette woman. For that matter, so had Natty. The boy, together with Kathryn and Travis, had gone at Rhys's request to Old Capitol Prison. Natty identified Bluebell as the one who had hired him to follow Kathryn, the consequences of which had been near murderous. It now struck Bronwen with a nasty jolt that the woman could recognize all three of these people. Not that she would ever have the opportunity. Unless she escaped from prison.

With this nightmarish possibility rearing its head, Bronwen peered down to see if the tugboat was being unloaded. It was not.

In the meantime Kathryn had been glancing back and forth between the departing Natty and the wharf. She turned to ask Travis, "Are there more wounded in the tug?"

"No, thank God! And don't worry about the boy—he'll be back all too soon."

Bronwen observed that when he looked at her sister, the deep-set dark eyes clearly saw not much else on the York. Nor did he apparently ever smile, not even when he asked, "Kathryn . . . Miss Llyr . . . how long have you been here?"

So it was "Kathryn," was it? And to think that her sister had not mentioned, had not even hinted at this.

"Several days," Kathryn answered, her own eyes not quite meeting his. "We came up the river the night after the Confederates withdrew from Norfolk, and saw the explosion when their ironclad was destroyed."

"The word is they set the *Merrimack* ablaze themselves," Travis said with contempt and a glance at Bronwen. "It was an unbelievably stupid blunder, unless there's more to it than is generally known."

Did he suppose, Bronwen wondered, that she would announce it if she did know? Which she did. River scouts, among them the disguised Treasury agent Kerry O'Hara, had told the *Merrimack*'s flag officer that the ironclad's draft was too deep to take it more than a few miles up the James River. Either it would run aground, or Union shore batteries would sink or capture it. While the indecisive flag officer pondered what to do, the tide began to ebb. The officer, persuaded he had no choice but to abandon ship, ordered the ironclad burned to keep it from falling into enemy hands. The explosion, when flames hit its powder magazine, could be seen for miles.

"Someone must have made a bad tactical error," Bronwen agreed, since Travis evidently expected her to say something. She doubted if he was taken in by her noncommittal response. The man did not look gullible.

At last crates were being lugged from the tugboat, and several men yelled up at Travis for instructions. After answering that he would be there in a minute, he told Kathryn, "Those medical supplies were needed badly at

Williamsburg. Obviously they didn't arrive in time for too many of the wounded, and the blame rests squarely on the army medical service. There has to be fast action taken to make sure it doesn't happen again. I've come to see your director Olmsted about it. He's here, isn't he?"

Kathryn nodded, and explained to Bronwen, "Dr. Travis is acting as liaison between the medical service and the Sanitary Commission. If you recall, you briefly met Frederick Olmsted earlier today." She turned back to Travis. "Is that where you've been? At Williamsburg?"

"Yes, and when word came of the battle there, I had to leave Washington immediately. There wasn't time to tell . . . anyone."

Kathryn colored again, having apparently recognized herself as "anyone."

Bronwen, aware that she was a fifth wheel here, did not want to intrude further on this tension-fraught reunion, but concern made her say to Travis, "Our brother's New York regiment might have been at Williamsburg. I don't suppose that among the thousands of men there you came across him?"

"No, but the medical service was in such disarray, I wouldn't have known it if I'd tripped over him. Why, is he listed as missing?"

"Not that we know of."

When he turned again to Kathryn his eyes held the same focused attention. "I'll hope to see you again shortly, Miss Llyr."

When he turned and strode down the gangplank, Bronwen watched her sister's gaze follow him to the tug. The man was a compelling figure, and any woman drawn to intense, forceful men would find him attractive. The wonder was that mild-mannered Kathryn did.

"Hey, Lady," a voice behind them chirped. "I figgered to give you 'nother chance, 'cause I still got somethin' to tell you."

It startled Bronwen that Natty had stolen up without

her noticing until she remembered that he was a child of
the streets. When it came to stealth, he could likely put
the entire Treasury unit to shame.

"Natty," Kathryn said, her tone too indulgent to be
heard as scolding, "you can't expect me to drop everything else to pay you heed."

"Yeah, I can. An' if you cain't, I'm leavin' this here
place."

"Where are you going?" Bronwen inquired, not for a
minute believing he intended to carry out his threat.

"To them parts unknown," he said theatrically, thrusting out his arm and sweeping it at the shore.

The rascal could be a worthy successor to the Booth
brothers, but he had certainly managed to capture her sister's attention.

"Why would you do that?" Kathryn asked him, the
alarm in her voice now as unmistakable as Natty could
have wished.

" 'Cause I had somethin' to tell you. But if you don't
care nothin' 'bout a sol-jur who mebbe knows somethin'
'bout yer re-layshun, then—"

"What relation?" interrupted Bronwen, suddenly ques-
tioning if this might be more than just an act to gain
attention. "Who are you talking about?"

Natty pointedly ignored her by telling Kathryn,
"There's a sol-jur what come in thet tug down there, and
he been askin' if'n—" He stopped abruptly, and then said,
"You got 'nother name, right?"

"Another name?"

Bronwen, with growing apprehension, asked, "Do you
mean besides 'Lady?' "

"Nah, thet ain't what I mean."

Determined not to play guessing games, Bronwen said
firmly, "It's Llyr, as I am certain you know! *Llyr.* Now,
what's this about?"

"Okay, okay, don't get huffed! Thet there sol-jur was
askin' if there's somebody here called by thet name."

Bronwen felt her stomach clench, and Kathryn sent her an anxious look as she repeated to Natty, "Llyr? The soldier said *Llyr?*"

"Ketched my 'tention, it did, 'cause I figgered it was the same name as yers."

Bronwen had already started toward the gangplank, Kathryn and the boy following her, when she turned to ask him, "Where did you meet this soldier?"

"Dunno 'zactly. Weren't none o' them dandy-lines 'round here, so's I took . . . I had me a ride in one o' them li'l dinghy boats."

"Right," Bronwen said, by now walking briskly down the wharf and restraining the urge to shake him. "And after you stole this boat, you went where?"

"I told you I dunno *where!* An' I dint steal it! I jest borrowed it."

"Oh, I'll bet!" They had reached the end of the *Aeneid*'s wharf, and she gripped the boy's shoulder, saying, "All right, which soldier is it?"

Natty shoved her hand away and looked around. Finally he shrugged. "Don't see him nowhere."

"Look!" Bronwen told him, herself glancing over the dozen or so men seated in the vicinity of the tug in which Natty had arrived. The boat, being unloaded very slowly, lay moored on the far side of the wharf.

"I *am* lookin'," Natty protested, "an' he ain't here!"

"Excuse me, miss," said one of the men, his arm in a tattered, dirty sling. "Are you looking for Goldman? Private Goldman?"

Bronwen glanced at Natty, who only shrugged again. "I dunno his name," he muttered.

"We aren't sure who we're looking for," Bronwen replied, as Kathryn went forward to check the man's arm.

"Are you a nurse, miss?" the soldier asked her.

"Yes," Kathryn answered, "and I think you should come aboard to have a doctor look at that arm and put on a clean sling."

"Why did you ask if she was a nurse?" Bronwen said to him, not quite convinced that it was merely because he had never seen a female in that role before.

"Goldman was looking for a nurse he heard might be here. Her name's Llyr."

"Why is he looking?"

"He didn't say, just asked us to let him know if we found someone with that name."

"Where is he now?" Bronwen said, beginning to feel even more apprehensive.

"I think maybe he went aboard the hospital ship," volunteered another man. "He was asking for a Miss Llyr who's supposed to be a nurse."

At a fast pace Bronwen started back to the *Aeneid*. She had reached the top of the gangplank when a young man in uniform came toward her across the deck, his head wrapped in a bloodied bandage. She heard behind her the whisper of Kathryn's skirt and saw the man's eyes go to her sister's headdress.

"Miss," he asked Kathryn, "is your name Llyr?"

"Yes," Kathryn said. "And are you Private Goldman?"

He nodded. "I've been looking for you, Miss Llyr. Your brother told me he had a sister with the Sanitary Commission, and that you might be here on the York now."

While Bronwen listened, she told herself this man was merely about to pass on a greeting from their brother. At first a dark premonition made her afraid to ask, but after taking a deep breath she said, "I'm Bronwen Llyr. Do you have word from our brother?"

"Not word exactly. And I'm afraid it's not good news, miss. The Rebels captured him at Williamsburg."

Bronwen, hearing Kathryn's moan, grabbed the rail to steady herself. Desperately hoping against hope, she asked Goldman, "Are you sure it's our brother they've taken? His name is Seth."

"I'm sorry, miss, but yes, it was Seth."

By now she should have been prepared, but his words snatched her breath as if she had taken a blow to her belly.

Kathryn had sunk back against the rail, her face blanched, while Natty began to pull at her sleeve.

"Lady, don't go gettin' skeered. He got *took,* is all. An' with them Rebs shootin' at anythin' thet's twitchin', it's lucky he dint get kilt!"

Bronwen gripped the rail, trying to quiet her heart-thudding fear. "How do you know this, Private?"

"Seth and I are . . . we were in the same regiment. Guess I must have been knocked out during the fighting"—he touched the bandage and winced—"and when I came to my senses I was in a woods. It was pretty dark, but I heard voices and was afraid it might be Rebs, so I crawled behind a tree. It was Rebs all right, and two of them were carrying your brother. Another one was an officer. He said something about 'the prisoner' and about heading west in the morning."

Bronwen swallowed hard. "So Seth was definitely alive?"

Goldman nodded, and seemed embarrassed. "I'm sure I saw his arms move. I guess I should have tried to help him, but I was still groggy and . . . well, there were five of them all told and I was out of ammunition. I'm really sorry," he apologized, swaying on his feet.

Kathryn, her face still pale but holding more composure than Bronwen could summon, said, "Thank you, Private Goldman. It was good of you to find us, and I'm sure there was nothing more you could have done. You need rest, so you should go below. Please ask the doctor down there to look at your head."

She reached out to take his arm, but Natty grabbed it first, saying, "Okay, sol-jur boy, I'll get you off o' this here deck. C'mon 'long."

All Bronwen could do was mumble her thanks as Natty led Goldman to the companionway ladder. She and Kathryn stood there, staring in stunned silence at each other until Natty came dashing back to them. "Thet sol-jur's okay. So whadda you gonna do now?"

A good question, Bronwen decided. She had stood there paralyzed by fear long enough, and possibly she could begin to think straight.

"If they took Seth to Richmond—and chances are they did," she told Kathryn, "he could be held in one of the tobacco warehouses along the James River. Some of them are being used for prisoners of war and—wait! Didn't Mama's last letter say Seth was just promoted?"

After Kathryn nodded, Bronwen said, "When I was in Richmond a few weeks ago, Libby and Son, a ship chandler's warehouse on Canal Street, had just been confiscated to hold captured Union officers. I know exactly where that warehouse is."

She could see that Natty was taking this all in, even though his eyes remained riveted on her sister.

"Then what should we do first?" Kathryn asked. She had straightened her shoulders, her shock clearly retreating before her natural inclination to fix what was broken.

Bronwen looked down at those unloading the tug, and estimated how long it would take them to finish. The result was not encouraging. "We pray," she told Kathryn. "And hope that I can persuade Rhys Bevan and . . . and others in Washington to include Seth in a prisoner exchange."

"I thought those exchanges were only under discussion."

"They are, because the politicians in Richmond and in Washington typically can't agree on the terms. Which means we also need to pray that Major William Norris doesn't somehow learn of Seth's capture. Llyr is not a common name and Norris would almost certainly make the connection with me."

"But Seth's not a spy!" Kathryn protested, and then, too late, covered her mouth with a hand.

They both glanced sideways at Natty, but he was too

clever to have missed the implication and was again eyeing Bronwen warily.

"It doesn't matter what Seth is not," Bronwen stated, disregarding the boy, who was the least of her concern. "If Norris suspects for even a second that our brother might be with Treasury . . ."

She broke off, realizing it would be pointless and cruel to tell her sister that just days before she had seen Timothy Webster, the Pinkerton Agency's best operative, hanged in Richmond. His body had been left for hours to swing from the gallows as a ghastly graphic warning.

When the image of Webster's contorted face rose before her, Bronwen whirled toward the shore and, hiking up her skirt, went down the *Aeneid*'s gangplank at a run. If Dr. Travis cared at all for her sister, he would see that tugboat unloaded fast.

5

What other dungeon is so dark as one's own heart! What jailer so inexorable as one's self!

—Nathaniel Hawthorne

Washington City

Mist rising from the Potomac River meant the glow of gas lamps on First Street scarcely reached the small second-story room, but the woman poised at the edge of an iron-framed bed did not need light. It would not mask the stench of rotting, urine-soaked floorboards, or mute the *click-click* of rats running over the bare wood. Nor could it deaden the guttural breathing of a prison guard sprawled across the stained mattress.

The rats did not very much disturb her. Far more terrifying were the large black spiders infesting the webs that hammocked from corner to corner of the room. The woman grimaced and rubbed her arms with harsh strokes as her flesh crawled. Then came the recurring memory of spiders creeping over the decomposing body of her stepfather, their waving legs extended like long malevolent probes, her mother's coarse, reddened fingers raking them off the corpse and flinging them at her in fistfuls. And the shrieks of "Whore . . . whore . . . whore" echoing over the first hissing flames.

The memory had been made years ago, but it reappeared with such sharpness that it might have been yesterday.

The woman's jaw clenched as she forced the image aside. With a graceful gesture she flung back the nearly waist-length hair that fell like a shawl over her naked shoulders; hair so pure a black that it cast a shimmer of blue. The loose hair irritated her, but her hairpins had been confiscated for fear they would be used for picking locks or as weapons—as if she could not obtain a knife anytime she wanted one. She eyed a basin on top of the commode, then rose to dip a handkerchief into the water and wipe her breasts and thighs to rid herself of the guard's smell.

Feeling something on her bare foot, she reflexively raised it, unable to suppress a hoarse cry when a spider dropped to the floor. Shuddering violently, she glanced at the bed. The guard, snoring noisily enough to cover any sound, did not stir. But he wouldn't, steeped as he was in the whiskey with which she had lured him.

The woman quickly reseated herself at the edge of the bed, pulled on stockings and dress and shoes, and laced the shoes with determinedly steady fingers. When she finished, she stamped her feet to scatter the rats. After glancing again at the guard, she lit a pilfered candle stub in a tin saucer, and as the flame guttered in its melting wax, she inched cautiously off the bed, scanning for spiders that might be skittering across the floor. She spotted one of them, but could not make herself step forward to grind it under her heel, and could not repress another shudder.

Seizing the guard's trousers, which had been thrown over the room's single chair, she unfastened the key ring from his belt. The next part would not be difficult. Security at the prison was so slack that she had often wondered if she might not just walk out through the gate. If she were caught, surveillance on her would tighten, so she had made herself wait. Norris would want her soon.

Standing beside the bed, she prodded the guard with the toe of her shoe until he rolled onto his back. His snores were loud enough to wake the dead—which was fitting, since she had decided that he should join them. While it was not necessary, it would give her some reward for the hours tonight, and the two preceding nights, that she had spent in his hands. Norris would undoubtedly disapprove, but how would he learn of it? In any event, he would not dismiss her. He knew her past and he used that knowledge, needing her for what only she could give him.

Three days ago she had received a note, slipped into the prison yard by one of Washington's many Southern sympathizers: she should prepare herself every night thereafter. Tonight the signal had come. A few hours after midnight, she had seen through the window a series of three tiny flares—matches lit at regular intervals—from across the street.

Now, reaching under the mattress, she withdrew the short-bladed butcher knife obtained from a kitchen worker, the worker who had sold her the whiskey and demanded the same payment as this guard. She leaned over the man to place one hand on his forehead, much as an anxious wife might check a sick husband for fever. So balanced, she deftly slipped the blade between his ribs. His liquid gurgling was silenced by another efficient thrust of the knife. Bending over him again, she satisfied herself that he was no longer breathing and stepped back to clean the blade on his trousers.

After dropping the knife into a pouch hanging from a cord looped over her wrist, she extinguished the candle, then opened the door with a skeleton key on the ring and edged into the darkened hall. The rickety stairs to the ground floor were exactly eleven steps away.

•   •   •

Joshua Jared hoped this woman was worth the time and risk. From the far side of First Street, he gazed up at the dingy, brick Old Capitol, where a few faint lights could be seen through the grimy windows striped with slats of wood. Then, hearing the expected voices, he ducked behind a lamppost before the two sentries who were patrolling the prison's perimeter came into view. Their few words to each other were spoken in obvious boredom. When they strolled past the prison gate, they only glanced at it, and walked on around the far corner. It would be another quarter of an hour before they appeared again.

Jared moved from behind the post and pulled a box of matches from his pocket. He had not lost the box as he had the map. Fortunately, before the loss he had studied the map thoroughly enough—when not under the troubling gaze of the young woman nurse—to find his way here without trouble. The confusion of those unloading wounded men in a downpour of rain had allowed him to slip unnoticed from the moored transport ship. He had then made his way to the warehouses lining a service road that ran from Alexandria harbor.

Before finding a carriage to take him across the Potomac and into Washington City, he had entered the Jubal and Sons warehouse to discard the blue Federal uniform and put on a civilian frock coat and trousers, left for him there with a black, hooded cloak. He had neatly folded his castoff uniform; he would need it again. Lastly, he had made certain there was no revealing bulge from the derringer hidden in the frock coat pocket.

"A derringer won't be of much use," he had said in Richmond. "Why not a revolver?"

"A Confederate revolver cannot be so easily concealed later," he had been informed, "when you will be smuggled aboard a Union navy ship for the return trip to Virginia. In any case, a weapon won't be needed. This will be a simple, straightforward retrieval operation."

"And if something unexpected occurs?" he had pressed.

"It will be dealt with by the one you are retrieving, who is more experienced than yourself."

More experienced did not necessarily promise much, thought Jared now, since this was only his second assignment. At least the rain had stopped, but tendrils of fog still wavered upward from the street's cobblestones. As he struck the first match, he glimpsed a blur of movement on the far side of the prison's iron gate. Leaping back behind the lamppost, he heard the gate rasping as it swung open. A tall woman hurried through it.

After pulling the gate closed, she turned to cross the street. Black hair swirled around her like an exotic fringe, and a damp muslin skirt without petticoats beneath it clung to her thighs, the gaslight outlining their ripeness while she walked toward him through the mist.

He moved from behind the post, holding out the cloak.

"Did you have any difficulty?" he asked as she reached him.

Her face was lowered, and turning to step into the cloak, she answered in a throaty voice, "None at all."

When he drew the cloak around her, she swept the hood up over the dark cloud of hair in a single lithe movement, running her fingers down the hood's edges to gather them under her chin. Jared, finding her gestures curiously erotic, felt himself respond—until she arched her neck to raise her face and he saw her eyes, the empty, cold silver eyes of the dead.

6

---〜〜---

*Washington was a spacious place, its visible
magnitude quite took my breath away. . . . The
White House was lighted up, and carriages were
rolling in and out of the great gate.*

—Louisa May Alcott

Washington City

"*I* need to see Secretary Stanton at the War Department
concerning this," Rhys Bevan had told Bronwen as he
started toward the door of his Treasury Building office.

"But . . . no, wait!" she objected. "I haven't told you
all of it."

"Tell me when I get back. I shouldn't be long."

She now stood alone at the office's open window,
looking over a city strewn with the skeletal frames of
unfinished civic structures, although bristling with elaborate military fortifications and musket-bearing troops.

Suddenly, from the road below her came an upsurge
in what had been for some time a fast-running stream of
loud, fluent curses. If nothing else the language lent color
to the overcast day, coming as it did from burly members
of the army quartermaster corps, who were attempting to
goad into action a six-mule team balked in the middle of
Fifteenth Street. Meanwhile, all traffic had been brought
to a halt. Scores of buggies and carriages stood idle,

backed up for more than half a mile, but the mules refused to budge.

And no fools those mules, concluded Bronwen, because the wheels of the heavily loaded wagon behind them were submerged hub-deep in the bog that was supposed to pass for a thoroughfare. From the window she could see congested roads in every direction. It would certainly be interesting if the Confederate army picked now to attack Washington. With Stonewall Jackson rampaging more or less at will throughout the Shenandoah Valley, and pushing ever nearer to the Potomac, there were those who believed such an attack could be close at hand. But if the Rebels got a good look at the roads here, they might turn around and go home.

The scene below Bronwen was at least a distraction while she waited with growing impatience for Rhys Bevan. What was keeping him? Had he gone to learn the status of the stalled prisoner-exchange talks?

And why had she been recalled to Washington?

She took for granted that her telegraph message about Bluebell's possible escape attempt had caused extra guards to be placed at Old Capitol Prison. If surveillance of Confederate prisoners had tightened accordingly, the woman should remain fast inside its walls.

Late yesterday, when she had reached Fort Monroe to send the wire, a telegram marked URGENT had been awaiting her from Rhys Bevan. It ordered her immediate return to Washington, so she had caught the next transport heading north. After she had arrived here this morning, there was time to tell Rhys only of Seth's capture, the uppermost thing on her mind, before he had dashed off.

In addition to the curses now coming through the window was the rising stench of a befouled river and canal swollen by days of rain. Before Bronwen pulled the window closed, she took a last look down. The mules still held up the traffic, and it was beginning to rain again. The

Potomac shipyards should stop building boats and begin building arks.

The sound of footsteps made her turn toward the door as Rhys Bevan came through it. The usually even-tempered Welshman shoved the door needlessly hard to close it, giving Bronwen advance warning of his mood because his expression did not. Only those familiar with Treasury's chief detective would know that the glint in his cool blue eyes indicated anger. For all the tone of his voice revealed, he might have been commenting on the rain when, rounding his desk, he said, "The Bleuette woman is gone."

"Gone?"

"I've just now learned that she escaped sometime during the night."

"But how could that *happen?*" Bronwen protested, striking the desktop with the flat of her hands. "The wire I sent from Fort Monroe said you could expect her to try something!"

"She did more than try." Rhys seated himself and tossed the several sheets of foolscap he had brought on a stack of other papers. He glanced at the desk clock before adding, "And a guard was murdered in the bargain."

"Which should come as no surprise to anyone. What *happened?* Was everyone here in a stupor?"

"I beg your pardon?"

She swallowed her next remark, telling herself that Rhys, who ordinarily tolerated her surly lapses, was at the moment beyond such indulgence. He was probably almost as furious as she, and it would be wise to watch her step.

"I didn't receive your wire until half an hour ago," he told her, "when I was in the War Department telegraph office. It's unfortunate, but there was an ill-starred assortment of factors at work."

"Such as?"

"David Bates, the telegraph manager, became ill yesterday, and a new man had come on the job. Since your message was in code, which the new operator failed to recognize as Treasury's, he didn't realize it could be urgent. Instead of alerting me, he sent your message on to Secretary Stanton's office. Stanton was home at that hour."

She blurted in exasperation, "Who is some telegraph operator to decide what is urgent and what isn't?"

"He has been so informed."

"Well, that's comforting, now the woman has bolted!"

"Please take a seat, Agent Llyr. I am no happier about this than you, but your stalking back and forth will bruise Treasury's costly carpet and will not put Bluebell back behind bars. I've had extra sentries posted at the bridge to Alexandria, but I suspect she is already long gone."

Bronwen dropped into the chair opposite his desk. "And the man I described? He can't have been stopped either."

"He was not. The sentries have his description, such as it is."

"They're always half-asleep, anyway," she complained. "A third of the Confederate army could waltz across that bridge before they were noticed. And now Bluebell and her accomplice are running around loose. Or more likely, are on their way to Richmond."

"Are you taking the Bleuette woman's escape personally?" Rhys asked, and Bronwen, glancing up in surprise, saw that she was being given close scrutiny.

"You can't have forgotten," she responded, "that both my sister and I were very nearly killed by that woman. So, yes, I *am* taking it personally!"

"Yours is a hazardous occupation."

"Kathryn is a nurse, as you know, and nursing is not usually considered a hazardous occupation."

"We are at war," he said, "where everyone is at some risk—not only you, Agent Llyr."

Bronwen was taken aback by this dismissive remark.

It was not like Rhys, and there must be more to it. Until she knew what, she should tread lightly, especially since he had still not told her why she had been recalled. But first things first. "Did you learn anything about my brother?"

He swiveled in his chair to stare at the reproduction of Stuart's portrait of George Washington that graced the wall beside his desk. Of late Rhys had taken to gazing at this portrait frequently, thought Bronwen with impatience. Doubtless this was because while Washington was in office, he had built a formidable espionage network that had since been allowed to disintegrate. Had it not been, Rhys often said, the intelligence-gathering obstacles that now confronted the North might not seem so insurmountable.

He finally answered, "At the War Department I was told that a list of men missing after the Williamsburg battle had not yet been compiled. So where—" Rhys paused and swiveled back to face her "—did you hear that your brother had been captured? And are you certain it's true?"

"A soldier in Seth's regiment saw Rebel soldiers carrying him," she said, wondering why Rhys questioned it. "I would think they took him to Richmond, so of course I want to know if prisoner exchanges are expected in the near future. Are they?"

"Both sides continue to argue about terms, but I will keep making inquiries. I asked whether you were sure that your brother had been captured because, as you might guess, it could compromise your coming assignment."

"Compromise . . . why?"

Rhys steepled his fingers under a square, clean-shaven chin, and sat regarding her with his usual, self-possessed composure.

She waited, trying not to fidget, but reluctant to say anything for fear of jeopardizing the assignment. If Seth was being held in Richmond, she *had* to go there.

At last Rhys sat forward, saying, "Has it occurred to you what might happen if Confederate intelligence were to learn of your brother's capture? And I agree that he is likely in Richmond."

To hedge or not to hedge. Bronwen pushed the small of her back against the chair, debating with herself, but then gave it up. Rhys was too smart to outwit, and he would be irritated if she tried.

"Well, yes, I've thought about it. Major Norris might make the connection between Seth and me—"

"*Will* make it."

"—and he might presume that Seth is in Treasury's intelligence unit. Which is why it's so urgent for him to be released quickly, before Norris learns of it. How long will it take for both sides to agree on an exchange?"

"You had best not hold your breath waiting for that. Not when there are politics involved."

Before she could form another question, he went on, "Think this through. Let's say Confederate intelligence does learn of your brother. What then?"

Rhys would also be irritated if she played dumb. "Norris might have Seth charged with espionage."

"You were in Richmond when Timothy Webster was convicted of spying," Rhys reminded her, as if she were likely to forget it, "and Webster's case was pleaded by Allan Pinkerton, General Wool, plus any number of others working behind the scenes. He was still hanged."

"But the Confederates had some proof that Webster *was* a spy. Seth is not."

"How do you know?"

Sucking in her breath, Bronwen gaped at him, and it was a moment before she could reply. "You're not saying that my brother—"

"I'm not saying that," he interrupted, "but you can bet the Confederates will, whether Norris has proof of it or not."

Since that was exactly what she most feared, she had no rejoinder.

"There's another prospect," Rhys continued, "one that

is not any more pleasant. Norris could charge your brother despite knowing the charge isn't true, after which a sham trial would be conducted, resulting in a guilty verdict, for the sole purpose of making you surface. But you would not be the only target of this gambit. If you were captured, the entire Treasury unit could be put at risk."

Bronwen burrowed deeper into the chair. Only a fool would dispute what he had said. How did she or anyone know whether under interrogation she could resist naming every last agent in Treasury's espionage unit? Along with everything else she had learned as a Federal agent?

The North already lagged well behind the South in intelligence gathering, since there had been no network in place when the conflict began. The Federal government had been forced to rely on Allan Pinkerton's detective agency, a private firm with next to no experience in the espionage field. Worse yet, although Pinkerton had succeeded in placing four operatives in Richmond, they had all been captured this past February. Webster had been the only one executed, but the others were still imprisoned.

Since then, the need for information had become still more intense. General McClellan's current campaign plan consisted of advancing the Union army westward up the Virginia peninsula, a thick thumb of land lying between the York and the James Rivers. His initial force of 120,000 troops that had landed at Fort Monroe was supposed to be joined by an additional 40,000 men now stationed south of Washington. McClellan's capture of the Confederate capital city of Richmond would end the secession war. At least this had been the conviction that drove the plan's approval by Lincoln and Secretary of War Stanton.

But the North was frantic for information it did not possess regarding Confederate troop strength and movements. Equally if not more crucial was the looming threat of the two strongest European powers, Britain and France, coming to the aid of the Confederacy. So how could Bronwen expect Rhys Bevan to risk what few agents he had to send to Virginia? Who could be caught if she were forced to disclose them?

She could not expect it.

He had been sitting there silently. Although she had felt his gaze on her, she could not meet his eyes when she asked, "Are you saying that I cannot go to Richmond?"

"If I did say that, would it stop you?"

"No."

"I thought not. So there is little to be gained by wasting my breath. However, as you must know—but I am compelled to point out anyway—there is no one who can, or will, bail you out if your boat begins to sink. A trite metaphor, perhaps, but I trust you understand. At the moment, there are also no other Treasury agents in Richmond who could relieve you if need be."

"Then at least I won't have to deal with O'Hara!"

Rhys gave her a cryptic look. "I did not say there would never be another agent."

When she started to protest, he put up a hand to stop her. "We'll return to your brother in a minute," he said, after glancing at his clock, "but if I decide to send you to Richmond on assignment, there are several other issues we need to address. One I've only learned about this morning."

She gave him a swift nod of agreement, relieved beyond measure, because if she were on assignment, she might receive Treasury assistance in freeing Seth. It had also occurred to her that Rhys was not just being magnanimous. He needed agents who were familiar with Richmond. He also would have no choice but to send her there if the president requested it.

Lincoln knew he lacked intelligence information, did not entirely trust his political and military sources, and had gathered unto himself a handful of personal spies.

Bronwen's own history with the president had made her one of them.

"Who in Richmond," Rhys now asked her, "that we need to concern ourselves with, is likely to know you on sight? I'm not overly troubled about it, since what was before the war a city of forty thousand has now grown to three times that size. If you're disguised and are prudent, you should be able to move around without too much danger of recognition."

"I would think only Colonel de Warde could identify me. Of course, there's now every reason to believe that the charming Miss Bluebell is there, too. Or she soon will be."

"She can recognize you, can't she? She followed both of us, but at a distance."

Bronwen nodded. Thinking back over the past weeks, she added dryly, "When Bluebell tried to shoot me in Alexandria, she'd presumably identified me first."

Rhys also appeared to be thinking. "When she made that attempt, your hair was still long and red, correct?"

"Yes. I didn't cut it until I was *ordered* to, if you recall."

Even if her attitude was unreasonable—and she conceded it was—she still resented losing her long, braidable hair, even more than she did dyeing it brown.

He ignored her remark, and reached for the several sheets of foolscap. "There's new information on the Bleuette woman, gathered by the government prosecutors preparing for her trial. I haven't had a chance to do more than glance at it, so bear with me a minute."

Restlessly Bronwen waited while Rhys scanned the sheets. He began to frown as he read, more slowly it seemed, but at last he put the papers down with another glance at the clock. "She has an interesting history, what of it has been traced. Her given name is Simone, surname originally Cartier, born outside of Baltimore in '28. Which means she is now thirty-four."

"Isn't Major Norris also from Baltimore?" she asked. "I wonder how long he and Bluebell have known each other."

"I'll come to that in a minute. Simone Cartier was orphaned, her father having died when she was seven, and her mother and stepfather having both died in a fire when she was twelve. No mention of any siblings. She has no recent criminal record, at least none that's been uncovered in Maryland."

"Recent—so she does have something?"

Rhys nodded. "Years ago, and I'll get to it, but there's been nothing else found."

"Isn't it possible that Bluebell, or Mrs. Bleuette, née Cartier, could have left a trail of dead bodies from here to the Gulf of Mexico—and probably has—but simply wasn't caught? And does she really have a husband whose surname is Bleuette?"

"There's no record of a marriage," Rhys answered. " 'Mrs. Bleuette' may be an assumed name, a play perhaps on Bluebell, with the title 'Mrs.' meant to lend an air of respectability."

"So, other than her being orphaned at a fairly early age, what is there interesting about Bluebell's history?" Bronwen said, her initial curiosity having been dulled by this prosaic account.

"Remember I said she had a criminal record made years ago? At that time she was indicted on two counts of murder."

"Aha!" Bronwen straightened in her chair. "Now *that* sounds more like the Bluebell we know. You said *indicted?* Wasn't she found guilty?"

"The case never went to trial. Shortly after the indictment, and while she was in prison, she suffered a miscarriage. The murder charges were changed to manslaughter."

"I don't understand."

"At first neither did I," Rhys admitted, "until I looked again at the date of the indictment. It was 1840."

Bronwen gazed at the ceiling. "But in 1840, wouldn't she have been only twelve? The same age as when her mother and stepfather died . . . in a fire?"

He nodded.

"She had a miscarriage? When she was *twelve?*"

When Rhys nodded again, Bronwen said, "Well, so who was she charged with murdering?"

"There was apparently evidence that the fire had been deliberately set, and two bodies, those of a man and a woman, were found inside the burned house. An autopsy disclosed that the man had been stabbed, and the woman garroted. They were Simone Cartier's stepfather and her mother."

"Good Lord! But why would she kill—?" Her voice broke off as she suddenly envisioned a reason.

Rhys said smoothly, "I imagine we have thought of the same thing, and while it's exceedingly unpleasant to consider, the evidence seems to make it plausible."

Bronwen listened in shocked silence while Rhys, gesturing at the papers, said, "The twelve-year-old Simone Cartier, after the miscarriage occurred, was visited in prison by a physician and then by a priest. Both men subsequently made pleas to the court on her behalf, the exact nature of which—if they were even taken down—has since been expunged from the record. All we know now is that the charge was changed to manslaughter under the ubiquitous *Extenuating Circumstances.*"

"Which means?"

"That we cannot know with any certainty if she was made pregnant by her stepfather. It may have been by someone else entirely. In any case she served only one year in prison."

"But to kill her mother too? Why?"

"We will probably never know. But there is more to it."

Bronwen, nearly too stunned to absorb what she had already heard, murmured, "What more can there be?"

"The physician and priest I just mentioned were both from the village of Reisterstown, located a short distance northwest of Baltimore. The priest's name is of no consequence, but the physician's last name was Norris."

"*Norris?* But . . . but that couldn't have been William Norris. A few weeks ago, you guessed his age as about forty, so he wouldn't have been old enough in 1840."

"I agree. Norris would have been around eighteen at the time, and probably at Yale, where he earned his law degree."

"The doctor who attended Simone Cartier could have been his father or grandfather, or an uncle," she said.

"I'd wager that was likely, because his father's estate is in Reisterstown. And from there, if at some point William Norris learned of the girl, the imaginable permutations become almost endless. It could go far to explain why Norris, who by all accounts is an intelligent and urbane man, would have reason to be acquainted with someone as ruthless as the Bleuette woman."

Shaken, Bronwen could not remain seated, and climbed out of the chair to her feet. "If she . . . Simone . . . was only twelve at the time of all that, I wonder if she's aware that Norris probably knows her history? Not that I suppose it matters. But now . . . well, what am I to gather from this?"

"That the past is prelude. And that is all, Agent Llyr. We simply know more about her, and it could be useful knowledge somewhere down the road. But while her history may read like a gothic horror tale, it does not alter the fact that she is a dangerous woman."

He looked at his desk clock before rising from his chair. "You were called back to Washington for good reason. I can only hope your brother's situation doesn't interfere with it. No, don't ask—you will learn soon enough, and we need to leave right now. We have an appointment with someone who should not be kept waiting."

7

I must save this government if possible. . . . It may as well be understood, once for all, that I shall not surrender this game leaving any available card unplayed.

—Abraham Lincoln, 1862

Washington City

"Take a chair, Miss Llyr, and we'll talk a spell."

"Yes, sir," Bronwen replied, observing that Mr. Lincoln looked older every time she saw him, the furrows in his face deepening as if cut by a turbulent, fast-flowing river. She seated herself before his desk in the chair he indicated, while Rhys Bevan took up a standing position next to the doorway. But who would dare risk being caught listening at the presidential keyhole?

"Too bad you missed Jim Quiller," Lincoln told her. "He was here day before yesterday. Came back from Paris safe and sound."

"I'm glad to hear it, sir. May I assume that his eyesight is also now sound?"

Lincoln's mouth lifted slightly at the outer corners. "He sounded as if it's fine."

Bronwen could not restrain her own slight smile at the word play. Quiller's "failing eyesight" was a euphemism for what, several months ago, had taken the businessman from Richmond where he had observed someone following him. Before it was known that he had left the country, Lincoln, who had not seen his friend for some time, had requested that she locate Quiller. She subsequently learned the man had sailed for Paris.

"I look forward to meeting Mr. Quiller," she said.

"He allowed as how he wants to thank you himself for clearing up that nuisance," Lincoln told her. "Can't be here, though, because Jimmy left Washington yesterday."

Her hopes lifted at the possibility of an ally, and she asked, "May I inquire if he has gone south again?"

"He has. Said he had another hankering to go on down Richmond way. Understand you have one, too. Is that so?"

Bronwen glanced at Rhys Bevan, who appeared to be especially interested in the books on the shelves above him.

"Yes, sir, I do."

"Better think on that some," Lincoln cautioned, "because we have more trouble brewing down there. Now, we talked of this some weeks ago, Miss Llyr, but it could stand some review. Our British and French cousins are knocking on the South's door like a flock of pesky woodpeckers. Eighteen twelve wasn't all that long ago, though fifty years might appear long to someone your age, when the British tried to push us back into their nest. And here they are, fixing their sights on us again. If they decide to fly straight into our storm . . . well, we just cannot let them do that."

He paused, and Bronwen nodded to let him know she understood the gravity of the European threat.

"I haven't settled yet on what might convince them to point their guns in another direction," Lincoln went on, "but there could be one or two ways to persuade them to hold their fire until I do."

From the corner of her eye, Bronwen saw Rhys Bevan suddenly yank open the office door, look out and around it, then close it again. She inched forward to the edge of her chair. The president might be about to abandon his usual oblique manner of telling her what he wanted in terms enigmatic to anyone who was eavesdropping, and occasionally even to her who was not.

"Our naval blockade of Southern ports is beginning to do its job," Lincoln continued, as if he hadn't noticed Rhys's investigation, "but it's causing some inconvenience to Britain and France. Jimmy Quiller told me the French are upset their Virginia tobacco can't get through it. Tobacco they've paid millions' worth of American dollars to smoke."

"Millions?" Bronwen asked, thinking she couldn't have heard him correctly.

Lincoln nodded. "Seems their tobacco hogsheads are just rolling around down there in some Richmond warehouses, and it's understandable those folks are getting anxious."

"Yes, sir, I can imagine they would be."

"I think it might be a good thing to ease their minds on that score. Mr. Bevan and I have chewed over a few ideas, and he'll tell you about them later. Trouble is, if you want to lend a hand, it's fair to say you could find yourself in a peculiar situation—one that might even strike you as being a breach of your allegiance to the United States."

Bronwen froze in the chair, unable even to turn to Rhys Bevan. *Breach of allegiance?* Wasn't that similar to treason?

"And in that event," Lincoln said without pausing, "I expect you'd like some word, from the best authority in these parts, that you have permission to do what needs to be done."

His gaze was direct while he waited for her response.

Bronwen, thoroughly bewildered, told herself to keep faith, that Lincoln would not request she put her head in a noose, but still answered hesitantly, "If you think so."

"I do. Permission granted."

Lincoln now sat back in his chair, and Bronwen glanced at Rhys, who was again studying the books. She could not imagine what either man expected of her, but apparently she would soon find out. Meanwhile, her brother's straits were her greatest concern. Now if she could just think how to raise this with the president.

Lincoln sat forward again. "Mr. Bevan tells me that you're acquainted with someone in British intelligence."

Bronwen somehow kept from groaning when she said, "Colonel de Warde? Yes, I've had a few encounters with the man."

Then something occurred to her, and she added, "I saw de Warde in Norfolk. He said he was there to protect his *tobacco* interests!"

The president was studying her with an odd expression. If the occasion had not been so somber, she might have seen it as mild amusement.

Startling her with a switch of tracks, Lincoln said, "I hear the Spotswood Hotel is a favorite watering hole in Richmond. If you run into Jimmy there, you tell him I send my regards."

So the hotel was where she should meet Quiller, who had just returned from tobacco-hungry France. "I'll be sure to do that, Mr. President."

"I expect that Jimmy, since he travels in circles that include Union loyalists, just might be able to learn how our young soldiers are being accommodated there in Richmond."

Bronwen jerked upright on the chair, and swung to look at Rhys, who continued to avoid her eyes. She turned back to the president, surprised that Rhys had evidently told him about Seth. And it must have been Rhys when he had left his office earlier, since it was unlikely to have been Secretary of War Stanton, and no one else knew. She sent Rhys a look of apology for having been so surly on his belated return.

She was even more surprised when the president said, "I imagine you are sorely troubled by this matter, Miss Llyr. I regret that it happened."

He pushed away from his desk, his long frame unwinding slowly as he stood and gave Rhys a nod. "We could likely take some coffee, Mr. Bevan."

Rhys was already at the door with his hand on the knob. He yanked it open and disappeared into the anteroom, then returned to shake his head at the president.

Their concern seemed so excessive that Bronwen decided someone must have recently been caught eavesdropping. Washington was riddled with spies, apparently even here in the Executive Mansion.

"Would you ask Sam if he might fetch that coffee?" the president said to Rhys. "And you could mention to him that I'd be obliged if he might allow me some sugar this time."

The first-floor servant Sam was a former slave with a mind of his own, and had Bronwen not been so worried, she might have smiled at the presidential plea.

When Rhys had left, Lincoln walked to gaze through the window at the mansion grounds, which were untended, overgrown, and beginning to resemble a cow pasture. It was said that livestock in fact occasionally rambled in to graze.

Bronwen suspected that the president's request for coffee had been a delaying tactic; that he was now deliberating something that involved her, or else she would have been dismissed. Whatever it was, it seemed unlikely to be Seth. One captured Union soldier could not be expected to occupy much space on his list of concerns.

Rhys returned almost at once to report that the coffee, and perhaps even the sugar, would arrive if and when Sam found time to bring it. Then he again took up his station by the closed door.

"This is a thorny thicket we have here," Lincoln said to her as he reseated himself, and for a second Bronwen thought he was referring to the mansion grounds. "We tried to cut our way through it once before and we failed. When Timothy Webster was captured, there was strong effort made to free him. Did not work. I'm of the opinion that it might have hanged the man faster than if we'd muzzled and leashed our baying hound dogs. Making an almighty commotion just served to persuade Jefferson Davis and his friends that Webster was the fox they thought he was."

He stopped and looked at her with his keen eyes, the question implicit.

"I follow what you're saying, sir. Except that I . . ." She faltered, swallowing hard against the dread of his possible reaction, which could include her dismissal from Treasury if he thought her a loose cannon. But knowing she either had to say it or lie by saying nothing, she drew a deep breath and plunged on.

"I have to tell you, Mr. President, that I am going to do everything I can to free my brother. I was there in Richmond when the Confederates executed Webster, and I doubt they would hesitate to do the same to Seth if they discover he's my brother. I pray they don't, but I can't rely on only prayer!"

Lincoln's expression had altered slightly, and she feared she had made a terrible mistake. He could order her not to leave Washington. He surely had the power to do it.

The fear escalated when his eyes left her and went to Rhys. A long look passed between the two men before Lincoln's gaze returned to her. "Tell me something about this brother of yours."

Bronwen, grasping at hope, tried to think how to make Seth clear to someone who didn't know him.

"He's not just my brother, Mr. Lincoln. He's a . . . well, instead of telling you, I'll give you an instance. Where Seth and I come from in western New York, there can be some fierce winters, when snow falls as high as the . . . the top rail of a fence," she said, reminded of newspaper accounts of Lincoln's own rural, rail-splitting youth.

Encouraged when she saw his mouth twitch slightly, she went on, "When a north wind's blowing, that snow can drift even higher. On the worst, snowiest, coldest mornings, Seth would climb out of bed long before first light, so he could go to our elderly neighbors' houses and dig out a path to the road for them. He got up that early, because then they wouldn't know who did it. So they couldn't try to pay him."

She broke off, swiping at her eyes, furious at the tears welling there. It rarely ever happened, and never before at such a crucial moment. But through the blur, she saw Lincoln nod slowly.

"Sounds to me," he said, "as if the world might be a poorer place without that young man."

"It would. I'm not like Seth—no one is—but I've always wished I could be."

"All the same, you're a resourceful young lady, as I have reason to know, so I expect if anyone can retrieve your brother, it's likely to be you. Now, I am prepared to give help, but it has to be the unseen, quiet kind. And you can understand that."

Bronwen couldn't respond, not overly confident she did understand.

It must have been plain on her face, because the president went on, "Let's say a man's had his favorite racing mare stolen by some horse-thievin' nobody, and the first man, he reckons he'll just steal his horse back. Now if nobody sees or hears him, and he and his horse don't make a great ruckus out of their leaving, then nobody has reason to fret. Can just go right on about the thievin' business as if the horse is right there in the stall and ready to race tomorrow. But all the same, that horse is gone."

Bronwen heard a soft chuckle at the same time she heard a loud knock. She turned to see Rhys Bevan, his

hand on the knob of the opened door. Standing just outside it was an earnest-looking man whom she recognized
as Lincoln's personal secretary.

"Come on in, Mr. Hay," said Lincoln. "Don't tell me
I've managed again to forget about some appointment."

John Hay held up a leather-bound date book, saying,
"It's two representatives of the British crown, sir."

"Been cooling their heels long?"

"If you'll forgive me saying so, sir, it's probably been
long enough."

Bronwen got to her feet, as did the president, who said,
"Mr. Bevan, I need to have a few last words with Miss
Llyr. So I'd be obliged if you two would stay until I see
what the English want this time. Meanwhile, tell her what
we have in mind. Mr. Hay will see you have a place to
do it."

Bronwen took a swallow of the coffee that John Hay had
offered when he turned over his office down the hall from
the president's. The room had no window, and as she had
squeezed past the door and onto a straight chair, she wondered if it had once been a broom closet.

"It's a little cramped," Hay had apologized, "but it's
private."

After he left, Rhys went to sit on the only other chair,
crammed behind Hay's desk. Bronwen did not have to
stretch far to prop her elbows on the desktop, but the
position was uncomfortable enough to make her focus on
what he would say. Her mind wanted to stray to Seth. If
Lincoln could not give her visible assistance, what could
he give?

When she asked Rhys that, he refused to elaborate,
saying only, "In time you'll undoubtedly see what he
meant more clearly. But please take note: only because
the president is persuaded that it's futile to forbid you to
try and free your brother—since you will do it anyway,
and he is not prepared to drag you before a firing squad—

are you being given leave to find a way to rescue him."

"I thought Mr. Lincoln was giving me an assignment involving that costly tobacco."

"And you do recognize, don't you," Rhys immediately countered, "that *it* is the reason you are being sent to Richmond?"

She frowned at a repeat of the obvious. But what she was supposed to do with millions' worth of tobacco hogsheads remained a mystery.

"This assignment is of critical importance," Rhys told her, as if she could not have gathered that from Lincoln's comments. "Clearly the president is prepared to go to almost any lengths to keep Britain and France neutral. If McClellan's present campaign is successful, it may go far to convince the European powers that the South cannot win this war. They assuredly don't want to back an expensive, losing cause. But if, God forbid, McClellan is *not* successful . . ."

He left the rest unspoken, and then added, "Either way, however, the British and French see their investment as threatened. If it appears that McClellan is about to capture Richmond, the Confederates will burn that tobacco, for which the Europeans will hold us responsible. If McClellan does not reach Richmond, and the blockade continues to keep the tobacco beyond their reach, they will also blame us."

"Honestly blame us, or will it only be bluster?"

"It doesn't matter what it is if, in their view, it represents enough of an excuse to involve themselves in this war."

"I guess I see," she said, although flummoxed as usual by the arcane workings of politics.

"We are more concerned about Britain," Rhys explained, "because France would be unlikely to go it alone. But make no mistake, we know both of them are considering it."

"I understand how serious this is," she protested, "but

what is it I'm supposed to do? I know next to nothing about diplomatic intrigue and even less about tobacco. I don't even smoke it."

"This is no time for flippancy!"

Rhys had nearly snapped it out, making Bronwen draw back from the desk. He was probably on edge because he was Welsh-born, making more real to him a vision of the British lion crouching atop the Treasury Building.

As if reading her thoughts, he eyed her narrowly, but went on, "Anything we—meaning the Federal government—attempt must be done behind the scenes. That means as close to invisibly as possible. This is what has been suggested, if you are ready to listen."

Again Bronwen nodded, this time quickly, since her access to Seth would be threatened if she did not agree. While she respected both Lincoln and Rhys, she could see how her brother's peril compelled her collaboration with whatever they had in mind. But she had joined the Treasury intelligence unit of her own free will, and Lincoln was determined to save the Union. She was only one of many who had pledged to help him do it.

"I'm listening, Chief," she said, reaching for one of several small, round black stones clustered near a woman's portrait at the edge of John Hay's crowded desktop. Probably reminders of his Indiana roots in the midst of Washington's mushrooming turmoil. As she turned the stone in her fingers, she looked at Rhys expectantly.

It must have satisfied him, because he said, "All right, listen carefully. The solution to this dilemma may be to play our hand so as to appear that everyone can win it. First, we allow the Confederate government to believe it is granting Britain a favor—and thus increase the chance it will receive European aid—by permitting that tobacco to be moved out of Richmond."

"But even if the Confederacy does permit it, the Union's Atlantic blockade prevents the tobacco from reaching Europe," she inserted with confusion, rolling the stone between her palms.

"So that *everyone* can win," he repeated. "The blockade is immaterial if that tobacco does not go east to the ocean."

Bronwen sat forward. "You mean if it were, for instance, to go north?"

Rhys nodded. "But not too far north. The Confederacy will never allow it to leave Virginia. But if they were promised it would be held somewhere *in* Virginia, they might agree. And here is where the Federal government can do the Europeans a favor—and thus increase the chance they will *not* choose to aid the Confederacy."

"I follow that part, but I'm lost in Virginia."

"What do you know about the western section of it?"

"It refused to secede from the Union with the rest of the state."

"Correct. And just this past month the counties of western Virginia voted to adopt a new state constitution. Now they are working on having admission to the Union approved."

"Who has to approve it?"

"Both houses of the United States Congress. But for the statehood bill to become law, Lincoln must sign it."

"Oh, I see," Bronwen responded, as light began to break.

"West Virginia's bid for statehood has grown directly out of the war, and there are troubled waters to navigate before it's granted," Rhys told her. "Some knotty constitutional issues have been raised, not least of which is its desire to be admitted as a slave state. So while the bill is to be introduced to the Senate in a few weeks, it's a contentious one, and by no means assured of passage."

Bronwen thought she saw what was coming. "So yet *another* favor can be granted! This one to the Federal government by West Virginia if it agrees to store that foreign tobacco—and maybe increase the chance its state-hood bill passes."

"That's the idea. You do understand that the Federal government can't be seen as directly involved in this game of chance, and will simply appear to be looking the other way while it's played out?"

He waited until Bronwen nodded, and then she asked, "But even if Lincoln and the government look the other way, wouldn't the western Virginia warehouses holding the tobacco be under Federal protection?"

"That's right. And now to the game plan. You do re-member, I assume, the Oswego River raid we engineered last year?"

Tossing the stone from hand to hand, Bronwen sent him a disgruntled look, since there was no possible way she could have forgotten it. Treasury had learned that En-glish rifles were being smuggled to the South by way of British-held Canada. The rifles crossed the Atlantic to the St. Lawrence River, were transported from there to King-ston on Lake Ontario, and then sailed across the lake to the port of Oswego, New York. Colonel Dorian de Warde had been implicated, but as usual, his cunning had kept him from being caught in Treasury's net.

And suddenly she saw the reason for Rhys's question.

"If those guns could *enter* the United States from Can-ada through Oswego," she said, "then tobacco could even-tually *exit* the same way from West Virginia. Avoiding the blockade. And Lincoln would agree to look the other way while it quietly travels north to Oswego on Union railroads."

"Very good, Agent Llyr. I congratulate myself on hir-ing clever people," he added.

"So that's what prompted the president's question about de Warde? Chief, are you suggesting I should deal with that . . . that slippery, conniving character?"

"To paraphrase Shakespeare: Misery—in this case pol-itics and war—makes for strange bedfellows." At her reaction to this, Rhys said dryly, "I don't mean that literally."

"I'm delighted to hear it."

"It's a complicated scheme," he admitted needlessly, because Bronwen's head was reeling, "and I've drawn only a possible outline. While I'm not particularly comfortable in giving you this assignment, you do have the dubious distinction of being acquainted with de Warde."

"I should have a raise in pay for that alone!"

Rhys gave her an impatient look. "Again, while I'm not free from worry about this, we know you are capable of improvisation if things go wrong, and your record with Treasury to date says you can likely handle it. Also, your loyalty to Lincoln is unquestioned."

"Meaning what? That I can't be bribed?"

She had said it half-jokingly, and to her surprise, Rhys nodded soberly instead of rebuking her for flippancy. But what, she now wondered uneasily, would she do if it came to choosing between her brother and her country?

"Finally," Rhys said, "if we do nothing about the European tobacco, the potential for disaster is high."

To avoid his gaze, Bronwen's own eyes moved to John Hay's bookcase. She had not told Rhys that on the day Norfolk fell, the way in which she had encountered Colonel de Warde contained a bizarre twist. It could not have been coincidental that he had appeared on the scene just as she disabled a Confederate conspirator intent on sabotaging the Union ironclad *Monitor*. De Warde had then proceeded to kill the man—unnecessarily, as Bronwen saw it. He alleged he had done so to protect her. Since she gave credence to almost nothing de Warde said, she believed it had actually been to prevent the man from naming any others involved in the conspiracy. And she was still nagged by doubt over whether the whole story of the *Monitor* plot had been told.

Did Rhys need to know all this? Probably not. The overriding reason for not telling him was the possibility that he might conclude—mistakenly—that she felt she owed de Warde something. If so, it might jeopardize her assignment in Richmond. She was relieved he had not brought up her brother again, and she wanted it kept that way.

A change of subject might be smart.

She replaced the stone on the desktop, saying, "The president mentioned that he'd talked to Quiller the day before yesterday. Did they discuss any of this?"

"I trust they did not. I urgently requested that if one of my agents was to be involved, the tobacco scheme must remain a completely covert operation. The president readily agreed."

Meaning they both saw it as potentially dangerous, Bronwen thought, and told herself not to think about it again. She should concentrate on the danger to Seth.

"Keep in mind," Rhys cautioned, "that the situation could shift at any minute, calling for a swift reaction, even a withdrawal on our part. You can now see why the president gave you the permission he did. Much of course will depend on McClellan's success in reaching Richmond."

"Your Agent O'Hara questions whether McClellan will reach Richmond in this century," she muttered. "Or hasn't O'Hara informed you of his questionable loyalty?"

"Agent Llyr, we have long since exhausted the subject of O'Hara and your distrust of him. A distrust that is without basis and beginning to verge on the unbalanced."

"Without basis? O'Hara's from Virginia! He attended the U.S. Military Academy with Jeb Stuart, and Lord knows how many others now in Confederate command. He's a walking powder keg!"

"As I have repeatedly told you," Rhys said, "many officers, of both the South and the North, attended West Point. Many of them fought together in the Mexican War, and many of them became friends. And as you well know, O'Hara is from *western* Virginia, the very area we have just discussed in detail. So let us hear no more about him!"

"But—"

"No more, Bronwen!"

When Rhys used her given name, she sank back into the chair, recognizing that he was beyond tolerance. "When do I leave?" she asked contritely.

"I would imagine in the next day or two."

This reminded Bronwen of something she had meant to ask him earlier. "Have you heard anything from Elizabeth Van Lew about Marsh's condition?"

Tristan Marshall was another agent, a young man with whom Bronwen had previously been allied when the Pinkerton Agency had employed her. Over a week ago, Marsh had been shot during a confrontation with a double agent: a man supposedly working for the Federal Treasury while spying for the South. The injured Marsh, disguised as a Southern soldier, had been spirited into the Confederate's new Chimborazo Hospital. Fortunately, it was located a short distance up the road from the mansion of Union loyalist and spy Elizabeth Van Lew.

"I had word of Marsh yesterday by way of a wire from Fort Monroe," Rhys answered. "The information had been relayed east to the fort by way of Van Lew's network of contacts along the James River. The wire said that Marsh still needs a physician's care. I don't know the particulars."

"Which means?"

"If we decide Marsh needs to be removed from Richmond quickly, it must be done with his condition in mind, making it a difficult decision. In any event, it needn't involve you."

Bronwen sat forward. "Who need it involve? Who else would be in Richmond to do it?"

She was afraid she knew the answer. And when he did not immediately reply, she said, "O'Hara! But you earlier said there was no other agent there."

"I merely reserved the information that O'Hara is again at Fort Monroe," he answered smoothly. "It was he who sent the wire, and he who will likely be removing Marsh."

She stopped herself from making another objection to O'Hara, and a good thing she did, because a rap on the office door was followed by it swinging open.

John Hay edged into the small room. "The president is free to see you now," he told them.

"The British are still sorely upset about their tobacco," Lincoln said after they had returned to his office. "Seems their soldiers took a fancy to it during the war in the Crimea, and when they got back home they spread the fancy around."

He turned to Bronwen. "Miss Llyr, now that Mr. Bevan has explained the lay of the land, what do you think?"

"I think I'm ready to go to Richmond."

"I expect we should ask if you would be so ready were your brother not a prisoner there."

While Lincoln did not give it the inflection of a question, Bronwen assumed it was one. "I can't say for certain, sir."

She had to withstand grave scrutiny when he said, "This is a serious matter, and I'm aware it's not a simple task we've set for you. It could be a perilous one, too, and I'm troubled by that. Now, you think on it, and then give me as honest an answer as you can."

Bronwen shot a glance at Rhys, who was staring intently out the window and clearly did not intend to add his voice.

"I'm sorry, Mr. President," she said, "but I'm not much of an abstract thinker. So I can't answer your question because my brother *is* there, and that's as truthful as I can be. But again, sir, I want to go to Richmond."

His scrutiny of her continued, until Lincoln finally said, "Fair enough. There are some things just can't be answered, not by all the abstract thinkers put together, Miss Llyr, or we wouldn't have this war to begin with. And we surely wouldn't be asking young folks like you to fight it for us."

8

—m—

*Citizens were leaving by hundreds in all direc-
tions. . . . Some of the officers of government,
seized with the gunboat panic, decamped with the
flying populace. We have never known such
panic.*

—Sallie Brock Putnam, May 1862

Richmond, Virginia

Gray morning light, when it reached the upper levels of
the vast storerooms in the Libby and Son warehouse,
brought with it little solace. Seth Llyr sat on the damp
floor under a second-story window opening that overlooked Canal Street and the canal. Beyond them was the
James River. None of the warehouse windows held glass
panes, allowing the chill air to sweep in unchecked. Seth
gritted his chattering teeth as he tried once again to pull
on his boot. After a few useless, painful tugs he quit.

His ankle remained swollen, but not as badly as when
it had ballooned during the forced march to Richmond.
Still, its throbbing, together with the stink of overflowing
privies and dank walls swarming with vermin, had kept
him wakeful every night here. So did the groans of sick
and wounded prisoners. Compared to what some of his
fellow officers suffered, the ankle was a mild discomfort.
And then this morning, in the dusky early hours, a herald

of hope had sounded: the distant rumble of artillery from somewhere down the James.

Favoring his ankle, Seth awkwardly got to his feet and stood beside the south windows. Over the dull boom of cannon, he now heard noise from a different direction. He limped across the room, so large that much of it was always dark, maneuvering around men who were still sleeping, or too sick to raise themselves, until he reached the windows overlooking Cary and Twentieth Streets.

He started to lean out of one, when a voice behind him said sharply, "Lieutenant, take care!"

Seth half-turned to nod his thanks for the reminder. Prisoners had been told that anyone seen in front of the windows—and therefore presumed to be plotting escape—would be summarily shot by the sentries posted below. At the moment, there were no sentries in sight.

Outside on the streets a sizable crowd was gathering. Since these were probably the Richmonders who had been unable to flee or had stubbornly refused to flee, the crowd was a motley one, including shopkeepers and prostitutes and uniformed Confederate soldiers. Those faces that Seth could make out held anxiety, and the buzz of their voices was subdued. This might be owing to yesterday's rumor, overheard by officers held on the ground floor and quickly relayed throughout the prison. Since then, too, the guards had been acting edgy.

Five days ago the Confederates had evacuated the Norfolk naval base on the Chesapeake, and Union forces now occupied this strategic position at the mouth of the James River. The rumor had claimed that a squadron of Union navy gunboats and the ironclad *Monitor,* joined by two other newly launched ironclads, was steaming upriver toward Richmond. This could only further threaten a city already endangered by the advance of McClellan's troops up the peninsula. Thus the gunfire heard for the past several hours likely came from the warships. If so, thought

Seth, with a jolt of unqualified joy, he and the others could expect to be freed.

The man who had earlier warned him had come to stand beside the window, commenting crisply, "Apparently the rumor was true, and our navy will arrive here before our infantry does."

"Sounds like it, sir," Seth replied to Major Edmund Randall, who, like many here, had been captured at Williamsburg. "That cannon fire is coming from downriver, so what else could it be but our warships?"

"God, let's hope so!"

"Amen!" said Lieutenant Rafe Andrews, who was approaching them. Another prisoner, close behind Andrews, was a man Seth knew only as Thompson. Since only officers were brought to Libby, Thompson must be one, but Seth had yet to hear the man's rank.

"Hope they're damn quick about getting here," Andrews added, "because Carson over there isn't going to last much longer."

Seth looked at Lieutenant Carson, a member of his own New York regiment, lying on a heap of rags. Unfortunately, Andrews was likely to be right about poor Carson. The day before, a Confederate surgeon had finally amputated the young man's shattered right elbow and forearm, but the surgery had come too late. During the night Carson's moaning had turned to raving, and when Seth grabbed a candle stub to look at him, he found long angry fingers of red streaking up what was left of the arm and extending into his shoulder and neck. Carson had gradually, ominously quieted, the infection clearly taking its toll.

The street below suddenly erupted with wild cheering. Seth, together with Andrews and Randall, lunged for the window, as did Thompson and scores of others rushing forward, all of them ignoring the standing order. A tense hush descended over the room as they strained to hear what was causing the frenzy below. A short time later, thumping noises came from the mouth of a pipe protruding just above the floor. The pipe had been stumbled upon in a corner, and the prisoners, by digging out wood chips with belt buckles and a few undetected penknives, had succeeded in ramming the pipe's length through the ceiling of the first floor.

Thompson dropped to his knees and yanked off a shredded piece of cloth concealing the pipe, then yelled down into it, "What's goes on out there?"

He positioned his ear to it, and shortly after the color drained from his face. Several minutes later, he rocked back on his heels to tell the others, "Navy was comin' up the James all right, but got stopped about seven miles back. Seems the river narrows there below some bluff, where the Rebs have been buildin' a fort with mounted seacoast guns, and they've sunk pilings and hulks of ships in the river to block passage. So with the Rebs' big guns and their sharpshooters rainin' down shells and shot, our Navy's gettin' the hell pounded out of 'em. Even the damn *Monitor*'s retreatin'."

Into the stunned silence that followed, Carson stirred with a barely audible moan. "I . . . I guess they won't be here in time. Somebody . . . please tell my folks."

Rafe Andrews went to stand over him, saying, "Hey, boy, sure you'll make it."

"The hell he will," Thompson growled. "None of us will. We're gonna rot here—"

"That's enough!" Randall snapped. "We'll be exchanged sooner or later."

"Maybe. But too late for Carson there," Thompson argued. "For him and a lotta others."

When Carson moaned again, Seth left the window and went to crouch beside him. The stump of the arm had bloated to twice its normal size. When Seth had felt the young man's flushed forehead the night before, he found Carson burning with fever. Now his face held a waxen pallor, and the pupils of his eyes were enlarged and dark.

And Seth thought, as he often had, of the young drummer boy at Williamsburg.

"Anybody got some water left for Carson?" he asked now.

"Not since last night," answered one of the men. "Maybe we can get a guard to bring some."

"Sure we can," muttered Andrews. "They're down there celebrating the defeat of the Union navy, but I bet if we ask they'll run right up here."

Seth looked at the men's bitter expressions as the cheering below gusted up through the windows. By the sounds of it, all of Richmond knew their city had been saved from seemingly inevitable capture. It would bolster their courage and fortitude, making them more determined than ever to hold fast against the Union because they now believed they could do it.

While hope dwindled in the faces above him, Seth looked at Carson's anguished expression, and the need to ease the man's suffering made him say quietly, "I'll tell your folks, Carson. But we *are* going to leave here. I'm sure we will."

Carson's parched lips quivered. "Can your sister . . . could she get us out? The one you said works . . . works in Washington?"

"Oh, sure enough, boy," scoffed Thompson, who had moved much closer than Seth had realized, along with several of the others.

"What's he talking about?" Major Randall asked Seth.

Seth shook his head, but didn't reply, although Carson was looking at him with desperate hope. They were all Union officers here, all in the same fix, and surely they should be able to trust one another, but Seth suddenly felt uneasy.

He pushed Carson's damp hair off his forehead and said to him, "I'll go find you some water. Be right back."

Seth got to his feet, and limped toward the stairs.

•   •   •

When the guard was told to enter, he opened the door into a clean, well-lit office on the ground floor of the warehouse. In one corner stood a staff holding a bright swirl that was the Confederate flag. At a window stood a tall man in civilian clothes, while another man, beefy and stone-faced and wearing a Confederate uniform, stood with his back to the far wall. This second man motioned to the guard, who stepped back into the hallway. A moment later he pushed a prisoner into the office.

"That's all," said the uniformed man to the guard. "Dismissed."

"Yes, sir, General," the guard said as he backed out of the office.

General John Winder, Richmond provost marshal and prison commandant, seated himself at a desk under a portrait of Jefferson Davis, and gestured to a chair opposite him.

"Take a seat, Yankee," he directed. "Warden tells me y'all might have an interestin' piece of news regardin' one of your cronies upstairs. That true?"

"You said to keep my ears open. If I heard anything out of the way, it could help me. I want out of here. Will this do it?"

Winder glanced at the man in civilian clothes, who, other than swinging from the window to face the room, had not changed his position. He returned Winder's glance with a noncommittal expression.

"Depends," replied Winder to the prisoner, giving him a too-generous smile. "It might, it might not. Let's hear what you've got to say."

9

—⁓—

Northern soldiers! who profess to reverence the memory of George Washington, forbear to desecrate the home of his first married life, the property of his wife, and now owned by her descendants.

—a Granddaughter of Mrs. Washington, May 1862

White House Landing, Virginia

*B*ronwen had caught a tugboat from Fort Monroe to the wharves above Yorktown where Kathryn's hospital ship had been moored. The *Aeneid* was no longer there. Nor were any other ships. From some soldiers in a newly situated field hospital, she learned that the Sanitary Commission vessels were more or less paralleling the overland advance of McClellan's troops. She pulled a map from the pocket of her bibbed overalls, and after a quick glance at it, she realized she did not need it. What she did need was quick cooperation, but a demand would get her nowhere here.

"Captain," she had said to the tugboat's fresh-faced officer, while sweeping off her cap and letting her curls tumble free. "I need your help most desperately, sir. I must go to White House Landing hastily, and I would very much appreciate your taking me."

While the officer had gaped at her transformation, she had handed to him a sheet of velum, accompanied by a lavish smile. The pass had been requested by Lincoln through Treasury Secretary Salmon Chase and issued by General Wool, commanding officer at Fort Monroe. In her exasperation at discovering Kathryn gone, she had nearly forgotten its potential usefulness.

The tugboat captain's eyes had widened satisfactorily as he scanned the signature. "Well now . . . miss, is it? I surely would like to oblige, but I haven't got fuel enough for steam to take you all that way right now. Have to wait until—"

"Could you take me to West Point instead?" she had asked, gazing at him in earnest appeal. "My poor, delicate sister is near there, half-sick with worry that I might be shot by a Rebel."

"Miss, don't you trouble your pretty head about it another minute, 'cause I surely can get you that far."

At West Point the York branched into the Pamunkey River, and there also was the terminus of the Richmond and York River Railroad.

Bronwen knew from experience that this railroad ran west all the way into Richmond, but there was no chance she could safely ride it that far. She had guessed the Sanitary Commission ships might be at White House Landing, a natural harbor on the deep and winding Pamunkey and spanned by a railroad bridge—unless the Confederates had inconsiderately burned it before they retreated.

During a short but tense train ride, she had convinced herself that such must be the case. The Confederate command would never have left intact a bridge that could carry McClellan's army closer to Richmond.

When the train rumbled into the White House depot, she found that she had guessed right about the Sanitary Commission, but not about the railroad bridge. It was, inexplicably, still in one piece. And finally she and Kathryn once again stood on the *Aeneid*'s deck, but this time it was in a rare burst of Virginia sunlight. Over the smell of river and steamships drifted the scent of southern roses blooming incongruously among a burgeoning thicket of army tents.

"It worries me that you are going to Richmond," Kathryn protested.

"I'm not looking forward to it myself," Bronwen confessed, "but Rhys Bevan said the prisoner-exchange bickering could drag on for months. In the meantime, as I said before, Seth might be identified by Confederate intelligence."

"How? No one knows both him *and* you."

"I admit the odds are against it, since he's unlikely to announce who he is to someone like Major Norris. But I don't dare trust those odds, Kathryn—there are almost certainly spies in the prison, same as everywhere else. The sooner Seth is out of Richmond the better."

"You'll be so alone there, though—"

"Not quite," Bronwen broke in, and glanced round before she explained, "The president's friend, businessman James Quiller, is there, and he's acquainted with other Union loyalists in Richmond. He may be able to help. And don't forget our Aunt Glynis's friend, Chantal Dupont. Her Riverain Plantation is along the James, and I've been there before. Since the widow Dupont is a staunch Unionist, I assume I'll be welcome there again."

Kathryn looked unconvinced, and she did not know even the half of it. Bronwen realized there would be no point in trying further reassurances, since she could barely reassure herself. Instead she turned to gaze over the fantastical scene that the formerly tranquil White House Landing had become.

The long, newly constructed pier where the *Aeneid* was moored also accommodated gunboats and cargo transports. Bridging the shallows between the gentle slope of the riverbank and the deeper water were floating docks riding on barges. Beyond them flitted an occasional white-sailed sloop. An extended stretch of the Pamunkey shoreline was hilled with cartons and crates and barrels holding foodstuffs and ammunition for thousands of men, in addition to countless bales of forage for their animals. More supplies and equipment were anticipated from Washington and Baltimore by way of the Chesapeake and the York, and by the eastern section of the York River Railroad, which was now in Union hands. The western section of it, the Richmond and York, was still held by the Confederates.

The headquarters of the Union army's commanding general were supposedly somewhere nearby, but not at the house for which the landing had been named.

"General McClellan has posted guards at the house entrance and forbidden the use of its grounds," Kathryn told her, and indicated a cottage that might at one time have been white but was now painted brown. "It belongs to the son of a high-ranking Confederate officer, General Lee. The general's wife is a descendant of Martha Curtis Washington—Mrs. Lee had a notice to that effect nailed near the cottage entrance."

Kathryn still looked troubled, but apparently recognized that Bronwen wanted to drop the subject of Richmond.

"I assume that if McClellan's here, Allan Pinkerton is too," Bronwen said, "since he fancies himself as the general's intelligence staff. And I do mean *the* staff. Aside from what Thaddeus Lowe's balloon ascents indicate—whenever the weather permits, which is practically never around here—there's no intelligence information making its way to McClellan from anyone other than Pinkerton."

"But so much depends upon this campaign," Kathryn said, her tone incredulous.

"Pinkerton insists that he can learn everything needed from Confederate deserters and prisoners of war. He's so stubborn that he refuses to back away from that position, even after it's been suggested that deserters and prisoners could be planted to provide false information."

Bronwen, after leaving the train, had cautiously made

her way to the pier and crept aboard the *Aeneid,* obeying with resentment the repeatedly voiced order of Rhys Bevan: "Do not get near Allan Pinkerton!"

During the past weeks, Rhys had not been content to just repeat this order with every other breath, but included variations on the theme such as "There is too much at stake here for you to risk refueling the petty feud between you and Pinkerton. I mean it, Agent Llyr. Go around him! Avoid him at all costs. Steer clear of him!"

Et cetera.

Over a year ago, Allan Pinkerton had dismissed her from his detective agency for insubordination. The incident leading to the dismissal had involved the soon-to-be-inaugurated president, and while it had supplied Pinkerton with an opportunity to fire her, he had been unaware until later that Lincoln had witnessed the entire episode. Thus Pinkerton had publicly embarrassed himself, for which he had never forgiven her. Bronwen was not fond of him either.

"I saw Mr. Pinkerton shortly after we arrived here," Kathryn told her. "Given your history with the man, I didn't think it would be wise to make myself known."

"Good thinking! I've been instructed to avoid him like the plague."

"I should hope so."

The blast of a ship's horn made them turn toward a transport ship rounding the bend of the river. At the same time a distant train whistle sounded.

"McClellan's building himself a city here," observed Bronwen. "And it defies reason that General Johnston and his Confederate troops left the bridge and railroad tracks intact when they retreated. They must have been in one all-fired hurry. Maybe Johnston hadn't yet heard of our navy's defeat at Drewry's Bluff, and he had visions of the *Monitor* leveling Richmond. It reminds me of all the equipment left behind when the Confederates abandoned Manassas. When O'Hara and I arrived there—"

She stopped and glanced round again before asking her sister, "You haven't by chance seen *him* here? Would you recognize O'Hara if you did see him?"

"No, I haven't. And yes, while I caught only the one glimpse of him, I'm fairly certain I would know him again. He looked quite good-natured and attractive."

"So does a diamondback rattler before it strikes. I asked because O'Hara's masquerading as a river scout, and you might not recognize him. He's been wearing some getup that makes him look like a cross between Robin Hood and Sam Houston. River scout! I'll be amazed if he hasn't drowned himself in the York."

"Bronwen, that's mean-spirited."

"You wouldn't say that if you knew O'Hara! But speaking of attractive men, where is your Dr. Travis?"

Bronwen had been half teasing, expecting to elicit a blush and a disavowal of "your Dr. Travis." She was surprised at the concerned look she received.

"I don't know where he is," Kathryn replied. "He said he intended to search for more wounded, and then for a field hospital site. I saw him for only a short time back there above Yorktown and haven't seen him since."

"Are you worried that he's lost? If I found my way to you, I'm fairly certain he can. He looked like a man more than capable of taking care of himself."

Kathryn nodded distractedly before a small sloop, tacking toward shore, diverted their attention by coming perilously close to capsizing. When Bronwen glanced beyond the sloop, she spotted the boy Natty crouched on a short dock. Beside him was seated a young girl, who appeared to be about Natty's age, until Bronwen recalled the boy's age was unknown. Both youngsters were holding long sticks to which lines had been tied to dangle in the water.

Pointing to the dock, Bronwen said, "I doubt any self-respecting fish would be swimming through all this boat traffic."

"I'm glad to see Natty doing something that's not illegal," said Kathryn, her slight smile fleeting. "But then, he's not been in any trouble since we heard about Seth. Perhaps his upright behavior stems from fear that he'll be imprisoned, too." She gave Bronwen a quick glance when she added, "He's been asking questions about spies and spying."

"Somehow I don't see that occupation in Natty's immediate future."

"I didn't see it in yours, either," Kathryn responded quietly.

Both youngsters suddenly sprang to their feet, with Natty yelling loudly as he jerked up his pole. The girl jumped back as an elongated, glistening black object as big around as a man's arm appeared wriggling at the end of the line.

"What is *that?*" Kathryn asked.

"I think it's a water snake. They're not as smart as fish. Let's hope the boy's not planning on mounting it as a trophy."

As Natty was unhooking his catch, the girl said a few words, which brought from him a gesture that looked like dismissal. But after a moment's hesitation, he tossed the snake back into the river.

"Atta girl!" Bronwen chuckled.

Natty and the girl began walking along the shore toward the *Aeneid*'s pier, the boy carrying his fishing pole like a shouldered rifle. The girl, after a sideways look at him, did the same with hers.

"Who is she?" Bronwen asked. All she could see was a complexion the color of maple syrup, and dark hair pulled back into a switch that hung down the back of her pink calico dress. The dress looked as if someone taller should be wearing it.

"I don't know," Kathryn answered, "but I expect we're about to find out."

Some yards from the ship, the girl came to an abrupt halt, and even took a few steps backward. Natty could be heard saying, "Whatsa matter? They ain't gonna eat ya!"

The girl shook her head. Saying "C'mon!" Natty grabbed her arm and hauled her forward, while she tried to dig her bare heels into the pier.

"Could be trouble," Bronwen said.

"Why?"

"Because we're not in western New York, and I haven't seen anybody but white people on this ship—or, come to think of it, anywhere else around here."

Her sister looked confused. "What difference does that make?"

Before Bronwen could answer, Natty and his captive came up the gangplank and walked toward them. The boy eyed Bronwen with distrust.

When Kathryn said, "Hello," the girl ducked her head, while below the sagging hem of the pink dress, brown toes curled on the warm deck.

"She don't talk much, Lady," Natty offered.

"They say opposites attract," muttered Bronwen, receiving in return a puzzled scowl.

"What's your name?" Kathryn asked the girl.

"It's Ab-sent," Natty answered. "Weird name, huh?"

"She might talk more, my boy, if you talked less," Bronwen told him. She went down on her haunches and, looking into the girl's velvet brown eyes, asked, "Is that your name? Or is Mr. Know-It-All here making it up?"

Natty began to object, but stopped when the girl, with a shy smile, bobbed her head.

"I thought maybe," Bronwen said. "So tell me what your name really is."

The girl's voice came in a whisper. "It's Absinthe."

"See?" Natty crowed. "I told you!"

"Absinthe?" Bronwen repeated.

The girl said, "Yes, *A-b-s-i-n-t-h-e*. Absinthe. But he is right that it's weird. Mamma might have been makin' a joke when she named me."

Bronwen rocked back on her heels at the matter-of-fact

manner in which this was stated. And the girl's spelling
and grammar were not that of an uneducated slave child.

"What kind of joke?" she asked, throwing her sister a
baffled look. Absinthe was a European liqueur of high
alcoholic content, rumored to cause severe intoxication
often joined by hallucinations. There were some calling
for a ban on its import. Why on earth would someone
name a child for it?

"Mamma said I wouldn't be here if it weren't for absinthe," the girl answered with the same matter-of-
factness.

"I see," said Bronwen, guessing maybe she did. Someone had obviously educated the girl, and since it was
against the law to teach slaves to read and write, her
mother might not have been enslaved. Bronwen felt uncomfortable asking the girl if this were true.

She didn't need to, as Natty said, "She's gotta be a
slave, 'cause she says she got . . . got banded when the
white peoples in thet there ole house up 'n left."

"Do you mean *abandoned?*"

"Thet's what I said. But then she says she runned
away."

"Well, Absinthe, which is it?" Bronwen asked her.

"I s'pect in the hurry of leaving, the white folks forgot
me," the girl answered. "But then I was afraid if they
remembered and came back, they would sell me South.
So I hid. 'Sides, I was scared of all the soldier men coming here."

"Where is your mother?" Kathryn asked her.

"She . . . she passed on."

"I'm so sorry, Absinthe," Kathryn said. "But you can't
stay here by yourself. Not with all these troops."

"I know," said the girl, blinking back tears. "I'll go
somewhere soon."

Bronwen saw several women she recognized as being
with the Sanitary Commission climbing on deck, and she
tried to catch her sister's attention. But Kathryn was look-

ing at the girl with distress, saying, "Where will you go?"

"Why cain't Ab-sent stay here on the boat?" Natty inserted. "She's jest a kid—cain't go wanderin' round by herself."

Bronwen's opinion of Natty went up a notch. And he, an orphan without roots, would be an expert on "wanderin' round" by one's self. This war could result in many abandoned, rootless slave children such as Absinthe.

At the moment, Bronwen just wanted to avoid a possible confrontation with the approaching Sanitary nurses. They were undoubtedly good Christian women, but she had heard too many good Christian abolitionists who, while they spoke with fervor about the evils of slavery, spoke with rather less enthusiasm about the prospect of freed Southern slaves moving north. What if the girl was ordered off the ship?

Kathryn would not accept that quietly. Her position then would be even more awkward than the one in which Natty's unruly presence had already placed her. Bronwen decided, although her fears might be wholly unjust, that it would be better to avoid a potential problem.

Since the women had nearly reached them, she said peremptorily, "Natty, Absinthe, come along with me!" Taking the girl's hand, she drew her toward the *Aeneid*'s gangplank.

"I ain't goin' nowheres!" Natty announced loudly, planting his feet on the deck. "An' I don't see why Absent has got to, neither."

"Bronwen, wait!" Kathryn called after her.

"I'm hunting up something to eat," Bronwen said over her shoulder. "I'll see you before I leave."

With Absinthe in tow, Bronwen rounded the cottage and found, as she had hoped, no guards posted at its rear entrance.

"Is the kitchen in the house or is it separate?" she asked the girl.

"It's back there." Absinthe pointed to a small log structure some sixty feet beyond. The girl's expression was solemn, but she did not look particularly frightened.

"Let's see," Bronwen said, "if some food has been left behind."

"There's bread and honey, and some apples and buttermilk in the cellar," came the soft reply.

"Is that where you've been hiding?"

"Yes, ma'am."

"You don't need to 'ma'am' me. My name's Bronwen, and that will do just fine."

After they reached the kitchen, Absinthe went to fetch the apples and buttermilk. Bronwen sat down at a scarred table to spread honey on thick slabs of bread. Recognizing that she should start for Richmond while there was still daylight, she tried to think what to do with the child. As Kathryn had pointed out, the girl could not stay here alone, with thousands of troops arriving. And she would not have hidden herself if she had wanted to rejoin the people whose house it was.

"Absinthe," she said when the girl reappeared with a brown crock and a lumpy sack, "have you ever been to Richmond?"

"No," Absinthe said solemnly as she poured buttermilk into two mugs, "but almost to there. White folks here went visitin' a big place on the river that was close by the city."

"A big place on the river? Do you mean a plantation? On the James River?"

"Yes, ma'am, Bronwen. And that boy back there was wrong. I'm not a slave, 'cause Mr. Lee, he set my mamma free. She stayed here, and when she passed on, I didn't know anywhere else to go. But today I remembered where my brother is."

"Your brother?"

"My older brother Shandy. He got sold to the folks who live in the place on the river. That's why we went there."

Bronwen gazed at the girl while her mind went back to something her Aunt Glynis had once told her: that a child whose mother had been manumitted was also free. Aunt Glyn had learned that some years ago when, with support from the Underground Railroad in western New York, she had helped a slave girl to escape the long reach of the Fugitive Slave Law. And Aunt Glyn, if she were here, would unquestionably believe Absinthe ought to be helped, too. But what could she herself possibly do for the girl with all that loomed before her in Richmond? Her first concern had to be Seth and Mr. Lincoln's assignment. But this youngster could not just be left to fend for herself.

Maybe Absinthe's brother didn't know about their mother's manumission, since the girl said he had been sold. In which case, he also wouldn't know that he was now free.

"Did the plantation where your brother went have a name?" she asked the girl.

"Yes, it was Ber . . . Berkel . . . Berkeley!"

Bronwen nodded. The immense tobacco and grain plantation, a pre–Revolutionary War landmark, included the good harbor of Harrison's Landing, where the James River widened. Berkeley lay, she recalled, not far from Chantal Dupont's Riverain.

"I would like to go there to see my brother," Absinthe said with a light flaring in her eyes.

"That might not be a good idea just now," Bronwen told her, and had to watch the light all but flicker out. She wondered if the girl knew her father, but perhaps not, since she hadn't mentioned him other than the telling reference to absinthe.

It might be hurtful for her to think about, so Bronwen did not ask, but said, "I need to return to the ship and my sister, but I'll try to think of what you might do. Wait for me here, and I'll be back soon."

Absinthe's lips trembled and Bronwen remembered that she had been abandoned before. She caught the girl's small hand and pressed it firmly in her own, saying again, "I'll come back. Promise."

10

A brother offended is harder to be won than a strong city; and their contentions are like the bars of a castle.

—Book of Proverbs

White House Landing

As Bronwen headed back down the pier to the *Aeneid*, she slowed her pace beside a black gunboat that was docking, having just heard what sounded like a vaguely familiar voice. Not quite believing her ears, she saw a broad-shouldered man in navy uniform descending from the bridge. He was motioning to something or someone as he reached the pier, and it was his gestures and the way he walked that held her attention. When he drew nearer, she confirmed that the naval officer was indeed Lieutenant Commander Alain Farrar.

She had worried about encountering him again. While figuring it would happen sooner or later, she fervently wished it had been later than now. But short of conspicuously bolting back to shore, she would have to face him. There was no time to even rearrange her cap over her forehead.

"Hello, Lieutenant Farrar," she said, deciding to take the initiative.

His initial puzzled expression made it plain that Farrar did not recognize her, even though he had seen her wearing overalls before. When his face suddenly registered astonishment, it was solely astonishment, as far as she could tell.

"Braveheart!" he said with what seemed genuine, if surprised, enthusiasm. "Is it really you?"

"It is."

"You're the last person I expected to see here," said Farrar, as he came up to her. His clean-shaven chin was level with the top of her cap.

"I imagine so," Bronwen replied, waiting for the first verbal blow to fall.

"What brings you to this Union outpost, milady? Still working for Treasury—or can't you say?" he asked, his handsome smile at full force.

Was it *possible* that he didn't know? Bronwen merely nodded, at the same time glancing around to see who else might be interested in his question, and hoping he would not repeat it quite so loudly. How did one hush a lieutenant commander?

He must have seen the glance. "If you're looking for my aide," he said, seemingly oblivious to her discomfort, "I lost him. He was killed during our naval takeover of Norfolk."

He did *not* know. Bronwen's shock must have registered on her face, but Farrar appeared not to notice.

"It was a damn shame!" he went on, "and I can't think why he was even near the area where his body was found. Rebel troops had all reportedly withdrawn by then, so it might have been a Confederate sympathizer who shot him, but we'll never know."

Since he obviously expected a response, Bronwen shook her head, murmuring, "I'm sorry it happened."

From one standpoint she *was* sorry, because she wondered whether she would ever learn the truth behind the aide's death. It had been, she was almost positive, to keep him from talking.

Rhys Bevan had not shown himself to be overly impressed with her suspicion, but for his own reasons wanted the incident kept quiet. It was now clear Farrar knew nothing about her role in it.

Fortunately, someone aboard the gunboat hailed the lieutenant commander, and while he turned to acknowledge it, she gathered her wits. Farrar, giving a light tap to the brim of her cap, started down the pier, saying over his shoulder, "If you're ever again in need of a white knight, Braveheart, I'm your man!"

"I can't stay here on deck long, Bronwen, because we've just had word of sick men arriving here shortly by transport," Kathryn told her. "Can't you at least wait until tomorrow to start out?"

Natty stood nearby at the railing, making no attempt to disguise his eavesdropping.

"I should have been in Richmond before now," Bronwen said, "but I made this detour to see you because I don't know . . . that is, I'm not sure when I'll see you again."

Kathryn's expression made Bronwen add quickly, "Don't worry! I'll be fine—you know nothing ever happens to me."

"Something is *always* happening to you."

"I would have left before now," Bronwen persisted, "except for the girl. Every day that goes by could put Seth more at risk, but I don't know what to do with Absinthe. Taking her to Berkeley Plantation and her brother would be miles out of my way, to say nothing of possibly having to cross Confederate lines to get there. And that's just one among many problems."

"Ab-sent's got a *brother?*" Natty asked. Not waiting for a reply, he said, "So why cain't she go see him?"

"I just *said* why," Bronwen told him, her tone sharper

with impatience than she intended. "Sorry, my boy, but I have things on my mind."

Natty sent her an unforgiving look. "Ab-sent's got to go somewheres, 'cause they don't want her on this here boat."

"Why do you say that?" Kathryn asked him.

" 'Cause I heered some of 'em arguin' 'bout it."

Kathryn began to reply, but suddenly her glance went to something over her sister's shoulder. At the same time Bronwen picked up a faint smell of chocolate. She spun to see an all too familiar figure coming up behind her.

"Begorra, if it isn't Red!" said the laughing voice belonging to the smell. "Fancy meeting you here."

Bronwen, catching her breath, could say only, "O'Hara!"

"The same. I bet you're delirious with joy to see me."

"I can't say that I am. Why are you here?"

"Excuse me, Red, but I believe introductions are in order," O'Hara prompted, his bright turquoise eyes alight with their customary mischief. He swept off his slouch hat to say, "If this beauteous lady here is the one I saw you with some weeks ago, she must be your sister. Kerry O'Hara, Miss Llyr, at your service."

As Kathryn said, "How do you do, Mr. O'Hara," Bronwen noted with annoyance that she was trying not to smile, and was failing miserably. O'Hara had that effect.

He smelled the same and looked the same. Same light blond hair, same short clipped beard following his square jawbone, same jaunty stance, and the same fringe on his buckskin jacket that swung when he reached for Kathryn's hand.

"I asked what you're doing here," Bronwen repeated.

"River scouting," he answered. "Looking over the lay of the water and the land as is my wont."

"And I'm the queen of England," retorted Bronwen, "looking over my lost colonies, and figuring ways to get them back, as is *my* wont."

O'Hara laughed again, and glanced at Natty, who, gawking at O'Hara, seemed for once to be speechless. "And who are you, young chap?"

"Name's Natty," the boy mumbled.

"Natty? Ah, after the fabled frontiersman of the late, lamented James Fenimore Cooper, I presume?"

"Huh? What'd you say?"

"There's no time for this," Bronwen objected. She turned to her sister. "We need to think what to do with the girl."

"What girl?" asked O'Hara.

To Bronwen's irritation, Kathryn proceeded to tell him.

"Well, I'd say the solution is to give her over to McClellan," O'Hara commented. "He's probably always yearned for a handmaiden to kiss his boots."

"O'Hara!" Bronwen snapped, and saw with satisfaction that Kathryn was now regarding him less favorably.

Natty looked downright mad. "You cain't jest give somebody away, and thet there was a rotten thing you said," he accused O'Hara.

"And typical of him," Bronwen agreed. "Natty, where are you going?"

The boy, after an angry look at O'Hara, had turned and was starting down the gangplank. "I'm gonna go see Absent."

"Be back before dark," Kathryn called, and received no response from Natty, who was now running toward the house.

Bronwen was about to pin back O'Hara's ears for his callous remark, but was interrupted by the shrill of a steam whistle as a large transport headed for the pier.

"That will be the men arriving," Kathryn said. "Bronwen, I have to go below. Please tell me you'll stay the night."

"I can't. Before dark I need to catch a train, and I have an idea about the girl, Kathryn, so don't worry about her.

I'll try to be in touch, but don't imagine the worst if you don't hear from me for a while."

Kathryn, obviously trying to suppress tears, nodded and stepped forward to embrace her sister. Then the transport was steaming to the pier, and she hurried toward the *Aeneid's* stern.

Fighting back a spurt of tears herself, Bronwen went quickly down the gangplank, hearing O'Hara's light tread right behind her.

"Hold on, Red," he demanded, as she, ignoring him, briskly walked the length of the pier.

She suddenly had to pull up short. A group of men, all but one in Union blue uniform, came pacing toward the pier from the direction of the army tents. Bronwen identified the straight-shouldered man in the lead as General George McClellan, while glimpsing with dismay the civilian just behind him. It was the brush-bearded detective Allan Pinkerton.

Other than diving into the Pamunkey, there seemed no possible way to avoid him.

If McClellan recognized her as he passed, he gave no sign of it. She tried to edge sideways, but saw that another inch would indeed send her into the river. Not even for Rhys Bevan would she humble herself that much, so she stood her ground. She sensed O'Hara directly at her back. When Pinkerton spotted her, he removed the ever-present cigar from his mouth, giving her a glare that would have stopped a herd of stampeding buffalo dead in their tracks.

"By whose authority are you here?" he demanded. "Unless it's a higher one than McClellan, I swear you'll regret it."

Bronwen very much wanted to ask if he would recognize anyone, even God, as outranking McClellan, but held her tongue and instead pulled General Wool's pass from her overalls pocket. O'Hara remained unusually silent.

Pinkerton scanned the pass, flicking cigar ashes on it,

and handed it back to her. "I see no reason for you to be here at White House Landing. And I question Wool's authority to issue that."

Bronwen disliked him so strongly she did not even try to curb herself. "General Wool issued that pass, Pinkerton, at the request of someone who categorically outranks even McClellan. And if you don't believe me, why don't you wire the White House—the one in Washington."

She instantly regretted saying it. Although she doubted he would do it, she still shouldn't have challenged him. Her mission for the president was covert, and if Pinkerton did make inquiry, Lincoln's secretary would rightly deny any knowledge of her. And Treasury Secretary Chase, who was dubious of her to begin with, could recall her for creating an incident. But she thought she could depend on Pinkerton's overweening pride to cover her lapse. He would fear Lincoln's part in it just might be true.

The detective's ruddy face had flushed to an even deeper shade when he growled, "I don't care by whose authority you're here; unless you leave now, I'll have you placed under arrest and ask questions later. Do you understand?"

Bronwen strained for self-control and, not trusting herself to speak, nodded once. Pinkerton brushed past her and lumbered up the pier without a backward glance.

"You do like living dangerously, my girl," said O'Hara, prodding her off the end of the pier. "And there goes a possible scouting job," he added. "Good work, Red."

"Don't call me Red!" Bronwen began trudging toward the log kitchen behind the cottage, furious with Pinkerton and with herself.

Darting ahead to block her way, O'Hara said, "Yes, sir, Red! Where are we going?"

"*We're* not going anywhere. Now stand aside." When he didn't move, she said, "Again, why are you here, O'Hara? You're supposed to be in Richmond, finding a way to remove Marsh from Chimborazo Hospital."

"I was ordered to come here first."

"By whom, and why?"

"By our supreme chieftain, Bevan the Welsh, who else. And if you recall, I'm from West Virginia, that soon-to-be bright new star in the Union firmament."

Rhys would of course call on O'Hara in the tobacco crisis. Why had this not been mentioned at the time she and Rhys had discussed it? Probably because he knew very well what her reaction would be to O'Hara's involvement. She felt anger rise at his subterfuge, and then reminded herself that subterfuge was precisely what they were all practicing.

"Besides," O'Hara went on, with his irritatingly cheerful smile, "Bevan thought you could use some help from a skilled scout like myself in passing through the Confederate lines. The Rebs are retreating to the far side of the Chickahominy River, which means they're standing smack between us and Richmond."

Bronwen wanted to retort that she didn't need his wretched help, but having foolishly lost her temper with Pinkerton, she held herself in check while she considered what O'Hara had said. She had already decided to take the girl to Chantal Dupont at Riverain, then ask her to learn whether Absinthe's brother was still at Berkeley Plantation. But given O'Hara's news, it would now be a more dangerous trek. She reluctantly conceded that he might be of some help. And if Rhys had sent him, it seemed she had little choice anyway, at least for the time being. She did not trust O'Hara, but could devise a way to rid herself of him later.

"All right," she said, "we'll take the girl with us and head straight south for the James."

He shook his head. "Heading south to avoid the Rebs is smart, taking the girl is not. Why can't she stay with your sister on the hospital ship?"

"Because Kathryn already has the boy to fret about,

and because Absinthe is a Negro. Natty overheard someone say the girl wasn't wanted on board."

O'Hara's eyes rolled toward the sky before he said,
"Can you be talked out of this?"

"No."

"That's it, then. We take the girl with us."

Bronwen nearly thanked him for not arguing further,
but gratitude would make him even more cocky. Instead
she walked on to the kitchen.

There she opened the door on an empty room.

The girl was gone. So was Natty. And, Bronwen saw
with a dawning realization that left her knees weak, so
was the honey jar, the sack of apples, and the loaf of
bread.

11

—⚬—

Richmond must not be given up; it shall not be given up.

—General Robert E. Lee, May 1862

East of Richmond, Virginia

"How smart is that kid Natty?" O'Hara asked her.

They were hiking alongside the tracks of the Union-held, eastern section of the Richmond and York River Railroad. The tracks ran roughly southwest of the snaking Pamunkey River.

"He's smart," answered Bronwen, continuing to glance around them, although she could not see much except pine woods, and the tangled underbrush to either side of the track could easily conceal a herd of moose. If Virginia *had* moose; her briefings had not included native fauna. Every few minutes she raised her field glasses, but the view revealed only more finely detailed flora.

So far they had not spotted too many Union troops, although McClellan's Army of the Potomac was westward bound, and White House Landing lay only twenty-three miles from Richmond.

Somewhere ahead of them, thought Bronwen uneasily as she continued to scan, stood the Confederate Army of

Northern Virginia. Its number of troops was unknown by
Union command, and the approximation of it varied anywhere from 100,000 to 200,000, the latter being Allan
Pinkerton's estimate. Pinkerton had arrived at this figure
by interviewing civilians at Yorktown and Williamsburg
who had been members of the Virginia state militia. While
some questioned the objectivity of these interviewees,
McClellan accepted Pinkerton's estimate as convincing
proof that his army was greatly outmanned. In fact, he
had stated, the Confederates had "perhaps double my
numbers."

McClellan had demanded that Lincoln send him more
troops, but the president was said to have found the two-
to-one odds cited by McClellan as "a curious mystery."
So did others in the Union command. And Rhys Bevan,
when he had sketched this state of affairs to Bronwen,
concluded that what McClellan really should have demanded was reliable intelligence information.

Before she and O'Hara had left White House Landing,
a Confederate deserter had been brought in, and he swore,
as O'Hara had earlier claimed, that General Johnston was
pulling his troops back across the Chickahominy River
and closer to the Confederate capital. Although General
McClellan was waiting for Lincoln's response to his demand for more men, Bronwen and O'Hara had been seeing some forward movement. It included what appeared
to be several corps of engineers setting out in the direction
of the Chickahominy.

All in all, it was small wonder the British were anxious
about their tobacco's future in Richmond.

"Natty is smart," she repeated to O'Hara. "I think the
girl Absinthe is, too, so if brains alone could save them,
I wouldn't be worried. But they're just youngsters. . . ."

Words failed her as she imagined the calamities that
could befall them while wandering through countryside
known for its treacherous terrain. It was now made even
more hazardous by tense Union soldiers in enemy terri-

tory, who might understandably shoot first and inquire later as to why two figures were tiptoeing around their camp.

"You know this is your fault, don't you, O'Hara? If you hadn't made that witless remark about handing Absinthe over to McClellan, they wouldn't have run."

"What kind of name is that . . . Absinthe?"

Bronwen ignored the question as he had ignored her accusation. For the past half hour she had been listening for the rumble of a train under O'Hara's running commentary, but now decided it was too late in the day for one.

There had been no choice but to set out for Richmond, and hope the youngsters were doing likewise and that they might be overtaken before meeting disaster. Natty would know the railroad ran into the city, and Bronwen reasoned that he would be apt to head for an urban setting that he had learned to exploit. If his repute as a pickpocket was deserved, at least he and the girl might not starve.

On the other hand, they could be headed south, bound for Berkeley Plantation if the girl believed she remembered the way there from her previous trip. In which case, since it was almost twilight, they would probably become hopelessly lost and stumble into a bog, or fall into a river, or . . . worse.

O'Hara was saying something to her, but then he usually was, so it startled her when he barked, "Red!" and grabbed her shoulder.

"What's the matter with you?" In pushing his hand away, she dropped her duffle bag.

"I hear something."

"Sounds like a train."

"Coming from behind or ahead of us?" he asked. "These woods make it hard to tell which."

"O'Hara, why would a train be coming from behind us? Where would one from White House Landing be headed at this hour? I doubt McClellan is intending a night attack by locomotive on Johnston's retreating troops. Some scout you are!"

O'Hara had moved onto the track and was hunkered down with one hand on the rail. When he straightened, he grinned at her, saying, "Hate to tell you this, Red, but you're not the only authority on railroads around here. I grew up with them. And that train's behind us."

Bronwen stepped onto a rail, listened, then shrugged. "Okay, you're right," she conceded, "but where is it going at this hour?"

"Could be it's hauling lumber and equipment for Young Napoleon's everlasting bridge-building plans. I swear that if McClellan has his way, there'll be some kind of span for every last soldier in the Union army. Just step right up and take your pick, my boys! Cross any river on your very own bridge!"

Bronwen turned aside to cover an involuntary smile. O'Hara's make-up included a number of characteristics. Respect was not one of them.

"Only trouble there," O'Hara continued, warming to his favorite subject, "is that Mac insists he can't advance on Richmond—no, sir!—not until every last one of those long, expensive, difficult, new bridges has been built. Funny thing is, his chief engineer says Mac doesn't need any more bridges. Unless, of course, he manages to hold off advancing until it rains again and washes out all the ones he's already got!"

"O'Hara, stop the treasonous talk about our commanding general."

"Commanding general? Who's that? Oh, you mean the one who proclaimed a 'brilliant victory' at Yorktown, after the Rebs just picked up and stole off in the middle of the night? Or the one who forgot to show up for the battle at Williamsburg?"

"That's enough," Bronwen said, reminded of her brother's capture.

"Why? You don't think Mac's actually going to take

part in a fight! Anybody who waits around for that to happen should start practicing 'Dixie' as our national anthem. In fact, I'm willing to put up some sizable stakes that say he won't personally attend a single, solitary battle down here."

She remembered with discomfort that O'Hara was a gambler by trade.

Since the train's rumble was growing louder, she moved a few yards from the track and drew her map from the duffle bag. It was one she had copied herself, concentrating on Virginia's land routes and waterways. In the slanting light it was difficult to judge distance, but she believed a short distance beyond was the beginning of a substantial curve to the south, since she had ridden this same rail line some weeks before. The speed of trains hauling freight averaged—on a good day with plenty of fuel—anywhere from twelve to eighteen miles an hour, and the one behind her would have to slow when approaching that curve.

She stuffed the map in her trouser pocket and, after grabbing her duffle bag, she took off at a jog.

"Hey!" O'Hara yelled. "What's the hurry?"

"Jumping a train," she threw over her shoulder.

"Right!" he said, easily catching up to jog beside her. "You're going to leap aboard a moving behemoth. Or maybe you think it's the Central Peninsula Local and it'll stop for you. Especially since you look so well-to-do in those dirty overalls that you couldn't possibly be mistaken for a hobo."

"I said *jump* it."

"Never! You haven't got the muscle, Red."

She didn't respond. The locomotive was gaining on them, and with any luck she would leave him standing beside the tracks gaping after her. She had learned to make do without a male's superior strength by vaulting sideways into baggage and freight and cattle cars, when she and Tristan Marshall had been dodging assassins all the way from Montgomery, Alabama, to Richmond, Virginia. That had meant a good many trains.

"Remember," Bronwen shouted to O'Hara over the rolling thunder behind them, "Marsh needs help at that hospital!"

Whatever he replied she could not hear over the locomotive's growing roar. Its oil-burning headlight had appeared behind them, glaring into the dusk like a Cyclops eye.

Bronwen began to jog faster as the train slowed on its approach to the curve. When the locomotive and its tender steamed past her, she flinched beside the spinning iron wheels, trying not to think about what would happen if she slipped and plunged beneath them. To her surprise the first car was for passengers. The next two were flatcars loaded with long lengths of timbers that left no room for her to land. The fourth and last was another flatcar, but it carried large pieces of equipment. Tossing her duffle bag ahead of her, she gathered herself for the leap.

She landed cleanly, and then rolled without conscious thought, her inner memory of how to do it still strong. The clacking of wheels steadily grew louder as the train began to pick up steam after rounding the curve, so she heard nothing before a hand clamped her shoulder.

A voice in her ear yelled, "Thought you'd leave me in the dust, didn't you?"

She clutched the nearest support to keep herself from swaying. "I could always hope. So where did you learn to jump trains, O'Hara? I thought your favored means of transportation were riverboats with gambling salons."

The train, having settled into a steady *clack-clack* rhythm, did not make as much noise, and he answered clearly, "Riverboats came later. The Baltimore and Ohio Railroad runs through the fair city of Wheeling, and before the siren call of riverboats lured me astray, I jumped many a freight car. And my Uncle Padraic was an engineer for the B and O, so I learned how to operate Paddy's newest locomotive, a thirty-ton Tyson ten-wheeler. Easy to derail, but a powerful workhorse."

Bronwen eyed him with suspicion. "O'Hara, did you actually run a train, or are you making it up?"

O'Hara smiled. "When have I ever lied to you? I have to admit, Red, that when it comes to sheer train-jumping style, you've got me beat. Wouldn't have thought you could do it."

Bronwen did not acknowledge this rare concession, but watched the glow of western sky above the trees and scanned along the track, hoping, but not expecting, to see two small figures trudging beside it.

"Why are we on this particular train?" O'Hara asked. "It *is* toting bridge-building equipment—see those pontoon frames behind you?"

"Might as well reach Richmond as fast as we can, unless you're especially fond of walking. Did you see that passenger car?"

"Yeah. Strange, at this hour. There's no place much to go, other than Richmond, and I can't imagine anybody from White House Landing is headed there."

"Maybe the car's empty," she guessed.

"No, saw some heads inside. Could be this train made a stop somewhere after White House. You're the map maker—does another rail line cross this one?"

She shook her head. "I wonder if we were seen."

"Now, Red, who would be looking for two Treasury agents along a railroad track in the middle of nowhere?"

"That's not what I meant and you know it."

Wedging herself between several of the pontoon frames, she sat back and pointedly ignored him for the next bumpy miles. Although the late May twilight was lingering, it was difficult to know with any certainty how fast they were traveling, but Bronwen assumed, because of the bridge-building equipment on board, that the train would stop somewhere short of the Chickahominy River.

That would put her within striking distance of Richmond . . .

She was suddenly jolted backward with a force that banged her against a pontoon frame, then was jerked forward, then backward and forward again. At the same time iron wheels screeched with ear-splitting shrillness.

The engineer must be using hook motions to slow because there were no driving-wheel brakes on these locomotives, only on their tenders. But why was he trying to stop?

O'Hara had climbed to his feet and was yelling something she couldn't make out over the howl of grating iron. The flatcar had begun to rock wildly, and Bronwen, gripping a wooden frame, saw him swing his arm as if signaling to her. Then he suddenly pivoted and leapt from the car.

She launched herself toward the spot where he had just been and landed short of it, needing to dig her nails into the violently pitching wooden floor as she scrabbled for purchase. A series of massive shudders shook the car, tearing her hands loose, followed by the deafening roar of iron slamming into iron. As she tensed for a last desperate lunge to clear the car, the floor buckled under her feet and sent her hurtling over the side.

She hit the spongy dirt beside the track and tumbled down a slight incline. Hearing behind her the spine-chilling screech of grinding, twisting metal, she scrambled to her feet and plunged toward the woods. Flaming chunks of wood and metal shot through the air like meteors, and fiery sparks rained down around her, but she kept on sprinting, praying she could outrun them.

Her heart was pounding so fast she could hardly breathe, and just when she felt one more step would kill her, she tripped over a tree root. She sprawled face-down on a bristly mat of pine needles, while behind her she could hear wood creaking and metal groaning. At last the terrible noise seemed to have stopped, but the silence was broken several more times by resounding crashes. Bronwen lay panting, trying to regain her breath, while around her hissing tendrils of steam rose as sparks were extinguished by rain-soaked earth. The first billows of smoke slowly began to disperse, drifting among the pine and oak trees like long streamers.

The scrunch of pine needles under uneven footfalls finally brought her head up. Peering through the dusky haze she saw O'Hara stumbling toward her.

"You okay?" he asked.

"I think so." Her shoulders ached when she pushed herself to a seated position. "Do you know what caused the wreck?"

"Rebs must have destroyed some track before they pulled back," O'Hara told her, in a voice that for once was not cheerful. "A couple hundred yards of it this side of the river have been torn up. Trainman probably couldn't spot it was gone until the last minute, and when he tried to stop . . . well, it's one hell of a mess back there."

Bronwen swallowed her curse, reminding herself that Union troops would undoubtedly tear up enemy track when given the opportunity. "Were there many passengers?"

He nodded, and Bronwen, having gotten to her feet, saw in the fading light that he was blanketed in ashes.

"What shape are they in, O'Hara?"

"Most are dead, and the rest aren't good."

"So why haven't you gone for help?"

"Because the two who could walk have already started back to White House. They're all engineers, supposed to check the condition of the tracks and the railroad bridge ahead, see if they need work, since troops advancing south of the river need supplies. But the bridge is gone. Rebs burned it."

Bronwen said nothing, determined to steer her thoughts to manageable things such as how long it would take to hike what she had planned to ride, and where there might be another bridge across the river. She realized O'Hara was watching her, and that he was waiting for her to offer assistance. It was a hard, grim decision to make.

"I'm moving on," she told him.

"*Moving on?* A couple of those men need help."

"Then by all means help them! O'Hara, I have an urgent assignment in Richmond."

He turned away, and minus his usual springy step, he plodded toward the tracks.

Bronwen forced herself to follow him. When they neared the still smoking wreckage, and she looked upon the lantern-lit remains of mangled men and machine, she had to turn aside to retch. Then she stumbled back into the darkening Virginia woods.

12

—m—

No man, *not even a doctor, ever gives any other definition of what a nurse should be than this—"devoted and obedient." This definition would do just as well for a porter. It might even do for a horse.*

—Florence Nightingale, 1860

White House Landing

Kathryn, walking down the length of the pier to the shore, glanced up at the blackening sky as night settled over the lantern-studded anchorage. For her to leave the Sanitary Commission ship, unescorted and after dark, flew in the face of guidelines that Frederick Olmsted had established for the women nurses, and she would have felt guilty about it except for her destination. She had been told by Dr. Gregg Travis to meet him, and since he was the army medical service's liaison with Sanitary, she decided it must be permissible. In any event, she had been unable to locate Olmsted, not that she had looked for him very thoroughly.

The ship transporting the sick troops, which had docked just as Bronwen and O'Hara were leaving for Richmond, had also brought Dr. Travis. He had given the on-duty doctors his orders for treating the men, and after quietly telling Kathryn where to meet him later, he had gone ashore. She, in the meantime, had rolled up her sleeves and begun dispensing blankets and beef broth to the chilled patients, while attempting to stay clear of the older army doctors.

"Give those to me, young woman!" one of the surgeons had demanded, snatching forceps and cotton bandaging from her as she knelt beside a man whose open sores were swarming with maggots. "We do not have time to revive you when you faint, so brew some tea or knit socks if you insist on being here."

His had not been an isolated remark.

Kathryn had backed away, trying not to show her distress, and keeping uppermost in her mind that she was here for the sick and wounded, not for the army medical staff. Although a few of the younger surgeons—those with whom she had worked on the *Aeneid*—had recently started to ask for her assistance, she knew that much of the time she was viewed as a nuisance and an intruder. Despite Mr. Olmsted's quiet support, she was too shy to protest. The worst of it was her sense of always being tested, not on her ability but on her submission. It was no wonder the army surgeons said that if they were forced to use women nurses, they would take only nuns, whose orders demanded total obedience.

By the time she had done all she was allowed to do aboard the transport ship, darkness had been gathering. Where was Natty? Bronwen, having unexpectedly returned to the pier before she left White House Landing, had stood for a minute at the foot of the gangplank. Her gestures had indicated that she wanted to talk, but there had been too much confusion, too much emergency care needed for Kathryn to leave the men. If her sister's appearance had involved Natty, he still should have returned before nightfall. Since he had not, Kathryn feared that he was gambling, or something worse.

"You must stop cheating the soldiers at cards," she had told him repeatedly.

"I ain't cheatin'! Kin I help it if they's rotten players?"

"And you must stop pilfering the supplies."

When he had started to object, she had interrupted him, saying, "Please don't lie, because I've been told that you're selling things like lemons and socks, and they're items you could only have found in the *Aeneid*'s supply cupboards. You mustn't steal, and you don't need to. I will provide for you."

Nothing she said changed his ways. She suspected he enjoyed setting up his marks as much as he did the money they brought him. She would undoubtedly hear complaints about tonight's mischief all too soon.

Gregg Travis was now coming toward her along the shoreline, and as usual his long strides were less hurried than she would expect from a man who seemed so rarely at ease. The lift in her own step when she saw him confused her, since she had known him for such a short time.

When he reached her, he said nothing, and Kathryn could not seem to find her own voice. He stood gazing down at her before he ran his fingers along the curve of her cheek.

"Come along," he said, and without a glance around to see if they were observed, he reached for her hand.

"We'll walk down the shore to that grove of river birch ahead," he told her. "I want you to see where the hospital tents will be raised. God knows we're going to need the few we have."

Kathryn nodded because by this time she knew that the army medical service was unprepared for anything other than the most minimal number of casualties. She also knew that Gregg and Frederick Olmsted were constantly wiring Washington with urgent requests and recommendations. Both men were frustrated by the lack of response.

Once they had cleared the wharves, most of the Union encampment seemed asleep, and only an occasional voice giving an order, or the low laughter of officers playing cards, broke the night's near-silence. After they reached the shelter of the trees, Gregg drew Kathryn closer to him, looking down at her again with his intense gaze.

"The days we spent in that makeshift hospital in Washington seem long ago, Kathryn. Do you ever think of them?"

"Yes, at least the last ones, I do."

"After you'd been convinced I wasn't a would-be murderer."

"And after you stopped treating me as if I were a not-too-smart schoolgirl."

"I never thought of you as dull. Contrary and stubborn at times, perhaps, but certainly never dull."

Kathryn started to bristle, but reminded herself how relentlessly direct he was. He had obviously learned manners, since he could use them skillfully when he chose, but he often seemed to deliberately discard them. Oddly enough, since she had known him, her shyness had somewhat lessened, even though he often misread her intentions and on occasion seemed to hold her entire sex suspect. It was not the first time she had been forced to wonder where his attitude had come from, and where it would leave her.

But now, as if he wanted to avoid disagreement as much as she did, he asked, "What have you heard of your brother?"

"Nothing more than what you already know. Bronwen is on her way to Richmond to see what can be done. Heaven knows she's resourceful, but I fear for both her and Seth, and I can't begin to think what . . ." She shook her head, not wanting to think. "And now Natty seems to have gone off somewhere. Have you seen him since you arrived?"

"Not the boy again! Kathryn, you are not his keeper."

"Well, yes, I am. He has no one else."

"So because he decided to appoint you his personal guardian angel, you feel obligated to fulfill the role? That's unreasonable!"

"It is not unreasonable. And——"

"Kathryn, I have waited too long to see you for us to argue."

He pulled her against him, and his hand under her chin lifted her face to his. "I've missed you," he said. "And as I recall, the first time in Washington I had you alone, it was Natty who interrupted us. Now, damn it, he'll not do it again."

His mouth on hers smothered her soft, startled laugh.

Distant shouts made Kathryn at last draw away from him. "Gregg, what if someone sees us?"

"It's too dark." But he let her go, keeping only her hand grasped firmly in his. "You're right," he said, "and I don't want you compromised. It won't happen again . . . not soon, anyway," he added with a rare smile. "I need you here."

"I really should go back to the ship," she said reluctantly as she heard the shouts again. "Mr. Olmsted has said——"

"I intend to talk to Olmsted about that," he interrupted, and released her hand, abruptly becoming the commanding Dr. Travis again. "If you're needed in the field, I want you available."

"But Mr. Olmsted . . . doesn't want us women ashore," Kathryn said haltingly, as usual taken aback at his ability to instantly transform himself, like the frog-prince in the fairy tale. "He hasn't allowed us far from the hospital ship."

"I'll take responsibility for you, and I'll tell Olmsted that. I certainly won't intentionally place you in danger! But you're a good nurse, good with the men, and as we both well know, there won't be anywhere near enough doctors when McClellan advances on Richmond. The next engagements are bound to be large ones. Most important, I've seen how level-headed you are in a crisis."

They had begun walking back along the shoreline, but Kathryn stopped to look up at him, surprised at his words.

She was further startled when he added, "But I won't talk to Olmsted unless you agree."

This comment was so unexpected from him that Kathryn needed a moment to take it in. She was starting to reply when she heard the shouting again. It was closer now and more distinct. Her growing uneasiness turned to real fear when one voice yelled clearly, "Need help . . . real bad train crash! Track to Richmond . . . at the river! It's one helluva wreck!"

13

—⁂—

The Chickahominy is a deep, sluggish river, bordered by marshes and tangled wood. There were small tracts of cleared land [along it] but most of the ground was wooded.

—Jefferson Davis, letter to his wife, Varina, 1862

Beside the Chickahominy

On a bluff above the river, Bronwen crouched in a stand of tall, plumed grasses, wearily watching both the charcoal horizon for a flicker of sunrise and the pickets at the bridge below.

When she had been ready to drop from fatigue, having hiked five or six miles along the Chickahominy's north side, searching for a place where she could cross to the south, she had spotted a rise in the land ahead. After she had cautiously climbed the bluff, the dark shape of a bridge below came into view. It was the first bridge she had found that the retreating Confederate troops had not destroyed, and this one stood directly on the path to Richmond.

Other than a map and the forged passport in her pocket, and a pouch of Federal coins strapped to her thigh, everything had been lost in the train wreck. Since she at least needed clothes, she had decided to head directly south to Riverain Plantation. It stood about halfway between Richmond and Berkeley Plantation, and she still had Natty and Absinthe on her conscience. Concern for Seth should not make her rush recklessly into Richmond. What more could befall him in the space of another day?

The clear moonlit night had meant she could stay more or less on course by watching the North Star and the river, but now with those pickets ahead, she wished it had been darker. No matter what else she did, she *had* to cross that bridge.

She looked east again for a hint of sun, since those pickets might pull out at dawn. Maybe she should inch closer, ready to sprint across the bridge if there was an opening when the guard changed, but she was so tired and hungry she questioned whether she owned the stamina. She questioned whether she could even think straight.

When she crept forward for a better view of the sky and the pickets, she noticed the grass becoming sparser, and she stopped moving. At the same moment she heard a footfall behind her.

She leaped forward, stumbled, and went sprawling into a slight depression. Before she could reach for her stiletto, a large hand grabbed her shoulder, and she was hauled to her feet like a sack of meal. Squirming in the strong grip, she saw two other Confederate soldiers positioned beside the one who had just seized her.

"Now just what d'y'all s'pose this is?" her strapping captor said to the others. "Maybe a rabbit fixin' to scoot down its hole?"

"Nah, it's too big for a rabbit, Tommy Lee," said one holding up a sputtering, dying lantern. "S'pect it's maybe a polecat."

Having retrieved her wits scattered by fright, Bronwen retorted, "I ain't no skunk!"

The sky overhead was shading from charcoal to gray, and in the dusky light the men looked as if they might be smiling, but it was hard to see. She just hoped it was equally hard for them to see, because those smiles would not last long if they found her map and the Federal coins. Her cap was fortunately still down over her forehead, so she should keep her face averted. And stop trying to wrench free, since the struggle was pulling the bib of her overalls too tightly across her chest, and the soldiers might notice they did not have here a *male* polecat.

"So, what *are* you?" asked Tommy Lee, giving her shoulder a shake, which at his size could have been much more jarring than it was. "And what are you doin' here?"

"Jest watchin' you," she answered, praying that the truth might set her free. "An' my pa's a farmer, so I guess I's a farm boy."

She tilted her head a little to give them a foolish grin, which might convince them that for their trouble they had caught themselves a simpleton. Now if only the light would stay dim: *Please Lord, hold back the sun.*

"And just what are you watchin' us *for?*" said Tommy Lee, who abruptly released her. She took a step back, racking her brain for a way out of this.

"I was thinkin' on mebbe joinin' the army," she mumbled. "You reckon I kin do that?"

Their smiles broadened and, scared as she was, she managed to recall she was in the intelligence-gathering business. Having noted their British Enfield rifles, she asked, "What are y'all Rebs doin' here . . . and where y'all from?"

One of them held up his rifle. "We're from Texas, boy, just out doin' some squirrel shootin'. Rabbits, too, if'n they come along," he added with grin.

Bronwen decided "squirrel shootin' " was probably another name for picking off Union stragglers and pickets. Texans were reputed to be matchless sharpshooters.

"So where *you* come from, boy?" Tommy Lee asked, his voice more good-natured than before. She noticed now his sergeant's stripe, and an appealing, crooked smile.

Bronwen jerked her thumb toward the Chickahominy.

"Come from across that there river. Got to get back home—lessen I kin join up."

"Think we can use him?" one of them asked the sergeant with a chuckle.

"With Yankees comin', guess we can use anything we'all can get. Boy, your pa by chance own any horses?"

Bronwen frantically tried to guess what her answer should be. And maybe . . . if these soldiers needed horses, and if horses just happened to be across the river, it might see her over that bridge.

"Yeah, he got lots o' horses," she said, nodding and casting a furtive glance at the lightening eastern sky. "Good ones, too. I s'pect I could get 'em for y'all."

"Well, now, that'd be just fine," said Tommy Lee, with the lopsided but incandescent smile. "Y'all go on ahead, boy, and round 'em up. We'll be along in a shake. You fetch us those horses, and then we'll talk about you joinin' up."

With hope routing her fatigue, Bronwen raced down the slope to the bridge. When she neared the first pickets, she loudly announced her errand, pointed to her former captors, and then waved at the Texans. She stood waiting in front of six tired-looking, armed Confederate soldiers, and prayed hard. Sergeant Tommy Lee had not looked stupid, even if he *was* gullible. Or maybe he was simply a decent, honest man. And if so, why didn't he wave her on through?

One of the pickets began to walk toward her, and her mouth went so dry it would be impossible to speak. She looked back at the three men on the bluff and swung her arms vigorously over her head.

Their returning waves brought weary nods from the guards, sending her over the bridge, where ahead of her the first rays of sun were striking the south bank of the Chickahominy.

14

—⁊⁊⁊—

New Orleans gone—and with it the Confederacy.
Are we not cut in two? That Mississippi ruins us
if lost.

—Mary Chesnut, 1862

Richmond

When Colonel Dorian de Warde emerged from the War
Department office and stepped onto the Broad Street sidewalk, he paused to glance around, experiencing a need to
reaffirm his sanity. He had just met again with the Confederate clerk Jones, an individual whose state of mind
teetered alarmingly on the unstable. Thus de Warde now
viewed his tobacco as more imperiled than ever.

It was possible, he told himself, that Jones was only
temporarily unstrung, and had become so only after reading the morning newspapers, a practice which de Warde
himself avoided whenever possible. The news was grim
indeed, although the Richmond *Enquirer,* lying open on
Jones's desk, merely confirmed in detail what had been
known for nearly a month: New Orleans, the South's largest city and vital Gulf port, had fallen to the Union navy.
It was so disastrous a defeat that one could almost hear
the death knell of the Confederacy begin to sound.

De Warde had once toyed with the idea of spiriting his

tobacco out of the warring country by way of New Orleans and one of the blockade-runners operating in the Gulf of Mexico. The Union victory had effectively cut off that potential solution. He also guessed that Admiral Farragut's U.S. Navy fleet would begin steaming up the Mississippi to meet another Union flotilla that was battling its way downriver. Between the two stood Memphis and Vicksburg, but if the Federals took those, they would control the Mississippi, splitting the Confederacy and severing its supply lines of Midwestern grain and Texas beef. The *Enquirer* had not seen fit to print mention of this looming catastrophe. Nor had de Warde alerted Jones to it, lest the clerk lose an already tenuous grip on his incendiary urges vis-à-vis the tobacco.

What had sent de Warde to Jones's office had been a positive development: the British and French consuls had succeeded in persuading the Confederate secretary of state, Judah Benjamin, to move their tobacco to separate warehouses, from atop which now flew their national flags. But while Benjamin had grasped the potential diplomatic benefits to be reaped by this concession, his reasoning had obviously not penetrated the closed mind of Mr. Jones.

"No, Colonel de Warde," the clerk had stated emphatically, "there is no need for you to inspect the warehouse. There is nothing to be gained by it."

"My good man," de Warde had responded affably, "I should simply like to see for myself that Britain's tobacco is secure."

"There is no need," restated the implacable Jones.

De Warde had stood before the clerk's desk, attempting an assessment of the man. Jones's name identified his origins as Welsh, and, as any Englishman well knew, the Welsh were prone to irrationality. In addition, here obviously was a small man who, by the fickle winds of fate, had been tossed into a position that afforded great power. The sum total of these factors was an unreasoning tyrant.

Therefore how to proceed? Where was the man's weakness?

"My dear Mr. Jones," de Warde had begun, "it occurs to me that one such as yourself, with such weighty burdens as you have been given to shoulder, should surely deserve some . . . shall we say, *compensation* from those who are in your debt."

Although it had taken a moment for Jones to think this through, de Warde learned soon enough that he had guessed wrongly.

The clerk had jumped to his feet and, with eyes blazing, shrilled, "Are you suggesting a *bribe?* How dare you . . . you dishonorable, conniving foreigner!"

"Not at all, sir," de Warde had denied, startled by Jones's uncivilized response, but recognizing the need to recover lost ground. "On the contrary, I was merely suggest—"

"I *know* what you were suggesting," Jones had interrupted. "Well, let me tell you this, *Mr.* de Warde. It does not matter what despicable, underhanded bargain you and the French frogs have made with the greedy Benjamin and his ilk, because the law states explicitly that *all* the tobacco is to be destroyed! *All of it!*"

De Warde, when faced with such distasteful demagoguery, made for the door, but Jones had raged on, "This is a holy cause we are embarked on! And I give you my word, that if one man can prevent it, the South shall never be betrayed for a crop of tobacco!"

Hence De Warde, now finding the Broad Street sidewalk reassuringly firm beneath his feet, withdrew a pristine white handkerchief from his frock coat pocket and thoroughly wiped his hands.

After replacing the handkerchief, he then checked his pocket watch, another pillar of normality, because he had earlier received a message from Major William Norris. A meeting had been requested for ten o'clock this morning. With his walking stick swinging at his side, de Warde began moving smartly along the sidewalk in the direction of the river and Libby Prison.

Standing in the hall outside the prison office, de Warde heard from within an unpleasant muffled thump, accompanied by a barely audible groan. Someone voicing what sounded like sharp criticism followed it. After de Warde's knock, and a short delay, the door swung open to admit him to the room.

He recognized all but one of its four occupants, these being provost marshal General John Winder, Richmond police chief Samuel McCubbin, and Major William Norris, whose youthful, clean-shaven face, since de Warde last saw him, had sprouted a full mustache and beard, aging him by at least a decade. The fourth figure there was a spare young man strapped onto a stool.

De Warde underwent a sudden, odd sense of recognition; odd because he was quite certain he had never before seen this young man. Although the sensation had been fleeting, he continued to study the prisoner's fine-boned face with its high cheekbones, dark blond hair with a strong glint of red, light brown eyes holding a cast of green, and a fair complexion that bore an unnatural tinge of prison gray. The skin around one eye had begun to show evidence of bruising.

"Good morning, Colonel de Warde," said Norris, stepping toward him and extending his hand. "Good of you to come."

The other two men voiced their greetings. But de Warde, for reasons he could not name other than dislike of the crude mayhem he had overheard, replied with cool reserve, "I am ordinarily prepared to accommodate Confederate intelligence, Major Norris."

As he said this he glanced sideways at the young man, and was rewarded by an expression of unguarded surprise, quickly replaced by one of wariness. It gave de Warde a perverse satisfaction to note that the youth now knew with whom he was dealing.

He saw Norris's frown of disapproval, but feigned ignorance of it when he asked, "How may I be of assistance, Major?"

The frown retreated as Norris answered, "I thought you might want to meet our young Union lieutenant here. We have only recently learned who he is."

"Indeed," said de Warde. "And did this information come before or after the blow I heard?"

Before Norris could respond, Police Chief McCubbin volunteered, "The prisoner tried to escape."

"Indeed," de Warde repeated, eyeing the leather straps that held the prisoner and making no effort to conceal his skepticism. "And may I inquire how useful it is?"

He did not mean solely the information, but assumed no one there would grasp that, so he did not expect the young man's mouth to twitch slightly. Something about the wry facial gesture made de Warde again sense that he had seen this man before, and yet knew that he had not.

General Winder backed up against the window and crossed his arms over his chest before saying, "Don't be taken in by this Yankee boy's innocent face, Colonel. He's guilty as sin."

De Warde refrained from again employing "Indeed." Instead he withdrew his pocket watch. "I have some pressing engagements this afternoon, gentlemen, so if you would be good enough to tell me the reason for my presence here?"

"I assumed that as a member of British intelligence you might want to question this man," Norris replied. "He's a Northern spy, captured at Williamsburg, where he was discovered skulking in the vicinity of a Confederate encampment hours after the engagement had ended. Once we learned his name, moreover, it became clear enough what he was doing."

"And what *is* his name?" asked de Warde, annoyed at

being made to play the dunce, and baffled as to why Norris was engaging in melodrama.

"I trust you will recognize it, Colonel de Warde. His surname is Llyr. *Llyr!*" Norris repeated with emphasis.

De Warde, who was seldom caught unawares and had now been caught twice this same day, stared dumbfounded at the young man. How irritating, not to have identified the obvious resemblance of the brother to the sister.

Meanwhile, young Llyr was gazing at the ceiling as if concentrating on a place somewhere other than his present one.

De Warde regained his voice, and crossed the room to stand in front of him. "And what is your given name, Lieutenant Llyr?" he asked pleasantly.

The prisoner's eyes, not as intensely green as his sister's, but similar all the same, lowered from the ceiling. "It's Seth," he answered.

"Ah, yes, the biblical third brother," De Warde murmured. *"And Eve called his name Seth, for God had given her another in place of Abel whom Cain slew."*

The young man looked directly at de Warde while declaring, "That's all I'm saying, except that I am not a spy. I'm just a Union soldier who happened to be in the wrong place at the wrong time."

When he said this, his voice was steady and his eyes held no guile.

With this, the Englishman discovered how Seth Llyr differed from his sister: she, with only a moment's notice, could mock, mislead, beseech, and beguile, but the brother could not. He was no actor. Consequently de Warde, who had made a study of such things, believed him.

Not that he would inform Norris and the others of his belief. It might be used to advantage at some future date and, in fact, even now came the first flicker of an idea. It was far-fetched, certainly audacious, but it just might work. The first step would be to find the man whom Count

Mercier had introduced as Lincoln's confidant, James Quiller.

He turned to Norris. "What do you propose to do with this young man?"

He received a dry smile. "Have you heard the old adage, Colonel de Warde, that says 'Use a thief to catch a thief'?"

"I have. And an apt one it is in the espionage trade. But if you intend to offer the lieutenant here as bait, I suggest you refrain from further damaging his face, and see to it that he remains in good health."

"Rest assured of that," said General Winder. "We do understand, Colonel, that it's no earthly use to put on trial and convict and hang a man who's already dead."

15

—⚮—

*The most dreaded, the most hated of all beings
was the "Yankee."*

—Sallie Brock Putnam, Richmond, 1862

Riverain

Bronwen sat drowsing in a rocking chair on the wide,
vine-veiled front porch of Riverain, a plantation house
that sat on a slope of land facing the James River. The
air smelled of hot iron, as if rain was again approaching,
and the setting sun dropped like a blazing ball through
haze as thick as morning fog. Beside a small table holding
a tray of glasses and a pitcher of lemonade sat Riverain's
mistress, Chantal Dupont.

"I've never appreciated a bath so much," Bronwen
said, rousing herself to run fingers through her damp hair
and smooth the jean cloth skirt Chantal had lent her.
"Given my state when I arrived on your doorstep, I'm
surprised you allowed me into your house."

"I'm just relieved you came here first because Elizabeth Van Lew's place may be watched," said Chantal, her
blue eyes the dark shade of her indigo skirt. She shook
her head in disgust, making the cloud of thick, curly
white-blond hair swirl around her face, adding, "Then

again, it may not be, but at least you will have been warned."

From what Bronwen had heard, most of Richmond's known Union loyalists were under some surveillance. A number had been imprisoned. While Riverain's distance made it less dangerous than the city itself, she knew Chantal took some risk by harboring a Yankee.

She glanced down the slope at a narrow road that ran between Riverain's fields and the river.

As if reading her thoughts, Chantal said, "It will still be some time before we have any word from Berkeley Plantation. But I'm afraid, as I told you earlier, there's not much hope of the two youngsters having reached it."

"I know that," Bronwen said, nodding affirmatively, "but Natty is quick-witted, and he has survived this long because of those wits. Chantal, on the way here I passed a number of abandoned farmhouses. Why did the farmers leave?"

"Because they and others in the outlying areas are fleeing the rumored advance of Union troops. They're flooding into Richmond, but I doubt it will be much safer there. Ironically, members of the government, or at least their families, are at the same time leaving the city to move farther south."

After consideration of Richmond as a turnstile, Bronwen nodded in affirmation again. "I stopped at one of the most isolated of those farmhouses, since by that time I was half-starved."

After poking around in its root cellar, she had found some stored food. She wolfed a hearty slab of smoked ham, pickled beets and red cabbage, and some walnuts, washing them down with cold well water.

She left after placing a coin on the kitchen table for the food, and had resisted sleep. "I was afraid the stalwart Texas sergeant Tommy Lee and his men might come looking for their horses," she told Chantal, with a small smile. "But I rather liked that Texan."

Several hours later she had chanced upon an unmarked crossroads, and hearing plaintive, braying noises, she had ducked into some tall grass. Inching forward, she had come upon two lone, struggling mules, harnessed to a wagon whose wheels were mired hub-deep in mud. Since the mud had begun to dry, the mules must have been there for a while. It could have been evidence that the retreating Confederates were being hard pushed by their commanding general to race toward Richmond.

"I scouted the area, and saw no troops or anyone else," she told Chantal, "so I unharnessed the mules, jumped on one of them, and headed south again. Even caught some sleep on the way here. I assume you can use another mule?"

Chantal smiled, nodded, and gestured toward her spacious pasture. Beyond it lay well-tended fields, in which a worker or two could be seen. Upon her husband's death nearly a decade before, she had freed Riverain's slaves, and most of them had stayed on with her as paid servants and farmhands.

When Bronwen had first told Chantal about Natty and Absinthe, the woman had sent her trusted servant Masika to Berkeley Plantation to inquire about the youngsters. That had been hours ago. They were still awaiting Masika's return.

"If you're determined to go into Richmond," Chantal said to her, "which, I must repeat, is a dangerous idea, you'll need clothes. You're welcome to some of mine. We're never close to the same size, and Elizabeth Van Lew's would never fit you—she's such a tiny woman to be so ferociously daring."

A clatter of wooden wheels made them both look toward the drive, where a horse and buggy was approaching. "That will be Masika," said Chantal.

After pulling the buggy up to the hitching post, a statuesque black woman climbed down, her hair covered by a red turban, and wearing a graceful, yellow cotton dress and large gold hoop earrings. While it was impossible to guess her age, she could not have been as young as the forty or forty-five that she looked.

Watching the woman, Bronwen was struck by how far the tentacles of slavery extended: Masika was the grandmother of Zeph Waters, the deputy chief constable of Seneca Falls, New York, where her Aunt Glynis lived. A hired slave-catcher had killed Zeph's mother—Masika's daughter—and her infant son had been left for dead in a western New York woods. Those who worked with the Underground Railroad had found him. As far as Bronwen knew, Masika had not seen her grandson for twenty-one years, not since her daughter had made that deadly flight from slavery.

As she came unhurriedly up the porch steps, her impassive face told Bronwen nothing, but she feared the worst. She had hoped that against the odds, the youngsters had somehow managed to reach Berkeley. It had probably been only wishful thinking.

Chantal rose wordlessly to hand Masika a glass of lemonade and wave the woman toward a chair. Masika took her time lowering herself into it while Bronwen, as always, found herself frustrated by the stately pace of Southerners. By now almost any Northerner would have asked the obvious and been answered three times over.

Masika, after several swallows of lemonade, at last said, "Powhatan Starke, he left some weeks past. Run to the city."

When Chantal merely nodded, Bronwen could not help leaping to her feet. "The *youngsters!* Has anyone seen them?"

Masika gave her a level look. "You just hold your horses, missy, and we'll get to where we goin' together."

Bronwen dropped to the edge of the rocker, her jaw clenched, while Chantal, with a hint of amusement, told her, "Powhatan Starke is the current owner of Berkeley." She turned to Masika, asking, "Who's guarding the house and fields?"

"His slaves," Masika answered flatly. She flicked a glance at Bronwen, an odd glimmer in her eyes that might have meant anything, but Bronwen was beyond guessing.

"Was a young black man there," Masika went on, "who says he's freed some time past now. Said he might know somethin' 'bout those two young 'uns this gal here's so jumpy over."

Bronwen did not move a muscle.

"He said," Masika went on, "that maybe I'd like to see the chile who showed up there just this mornin'. Said she's his li'l sister."

Bronwen's breath caught. "Absinthe?"

"It's a mighty poor name, but that's it."

Incredulous, Bronwen got to her feet again. "And the boy? Was a white boy with her?"

"The chile says he was, but he's gone now."

"Gone? Gone *where?*"

"Said he was bound for the city."

"Richmond?"

"S'pect it's the only city round here."

"Did Absinthe know why? Did Natty say before he left?"

"All's he said was that he's goin' to fetch someone for a poor sad soul."

"What does that mean?" Bronwen said to no one in particular. "But . . . wait! Did he say 'sad soul' or did he say 'sad *lady*'?"

"Could have been that," Masika answered, nodding.

"Oh, no! Damnation!"

"Bronwen?" Chantal rose from her chair. "What is it?"

"Natty calls my sister 'Lady.' " In response to Chantal's baffled expression, Bronwen explained, "I hope I'm wrong—Lord, how I hope I'm wrong—but I have a feeling that little wretch thinks he can get Seth out of prison. Or 'fetch him,' as he apparently said."

"But Richmond has hundreds of buildings. How would

the boy know where to even begin looking for your brother?"

At that Bronwen felt an upsurge of hope, before her memory dashed it as she recalled aloud, "Natty was there listening when Kathryn and I first learned of Seth's capture, and he could have overheard me guessing where Seth might be held. Aren't officers being confined in the Libby warehouse?"

"Yes."

"Chantal, I have to leave for Richmond!"

"You can't do that tonight. You need sleep. And it will be safer in the morning, when you can blend into the city more easily. I think it would be unwise for both of us if I were to bring you directly into Richmond, but I can take you most of the way by buggy."

"No, I won't put you at risk," Bronwen protested, "and I should start out tonight."

"Missy," said Masika, "y'all surely are pigheaded. Before you go throwin' yourself in a hot fry pan like a side of bacon, you might need to hear some more things I picked up at the big house."

"At Berkeley?"

Masika nodded, and moved her gaze to the crimson and violet western sky, then pointed at the rocking chair. "Sun's got 'nough sense to set a spell, and I s'pect you best do the same."

Gray morning fog was rising from the James River as Bronwen cautiously made her way along the road into Richmond. It was a good thing she had been too tired to argue with both Chantal and Masika last night because a monstrous thunderstorm had struck. It rivaled even those that frequented western New York. The rain had pelted down, drumming against the roof and windowpanes; the wind had howled and the thunder had boomed, as if foreshadowing the noise of a battlefield.

When its fury had finally been spent, she had managed

some much-needed sleep. She had also been warned by
Masika about the Confederate troops now massing on the
city's eastern outskirts.

Apparently even Jefferson Davis had been unaware
that General Johnston planned to retreat to the very gates
of Richmond. Masika had said a Berkeley slave told her
this after he had gone into town to sell produce and learn
the latest grapevine gossip from Union sympathizers. It
seemed the wily Elizabeth Van Lew had succeeded in
placing Mary Bowser, one of her freed black servants, in
the Confederate White House. Varina Davis had hired
Mrs. Bowser on a friend's recommendation just before the
president's wife had fled the city. As reported by Mrs.
Bowser, a shocked Jefferson Davis refused to accept a
courier's account of his troops' proximity to the capital,
and in disbelief had galloped through the city to see for
himself.

It appeared, Bronwen thought, that Lincoln was not the
only president to own a nervous commander. If General
Johnston intended to make a stand against the Union army
directly in front of his endangered capital, it would seem
to be a tactic born of desperation. Perhaps, as most Northerners predicted, the war *could* end here in Virginia.

In the meantime, Seth remained in danger. He might
be in even graver danger now if his identity were to be
discovered. Timothy Webster had been hanged here in
this city. A desperate Confederate government would not
hesitate to hang another Union man, not if it could accuse
him of spying and use him as a scapegoat to appease
angry, panicked citizens.

Natty had possibly compounded the nightmarish situation, and it would serve him right if *he* landed in prison.
It might teach him a lesson.

Bronwen shifted the carpetbag of clothes given to her
by Chantal, and made ready to wave down one of the
public coaches rumbling past. She felt safe for the moment, disguised by a green linen frock and a large-

brimmed, beribboned straw hat; merely another Richmond citizen watching Confederate troops digging trench after muddy trench to protect her against the hated Yankee invader.

The first thing she needed to do, once into the city, was to find Lincoln's friend James Quiller.

16

———❦———

If you can't send money, send tobacco.

—George Washington

Richmond

"I wish to have a note delivered to a gentleman who is staying here," Bronwen quietly told the Spotswood's aloof and bored-looking maître d'hôtel. She had averted her face so the large hat brim would shadow it, while wondering if her voice could even be heard over the noise in the lobby.

"He's an acquaintance of mine, and I believe he is expecting this," she added with a forced smile, handing the man a sealed envelope across the face of which she had written *James Quiller*. It contained a brief message and a Treasury coin. "Please have this taken to his room."

The man scanned the envelope and, apparently recognizing the name, abruptly came to attention. "It would be my pleasure. Will the lady wait for a reply?"

"Yes."

He nodded, bowed, and snapped his fingers. The envelope was instantly plucked from his other hand by a white-suited bellboy, who scampered with it up a red-carpeted staircase whose breadth could accommodate a team of horses.

"I should like to leave my baggage while I'm waiting," Bronwen told the maître d'hôtel.

"Very good, milady. I will see to it myself. May I please have your name?"

"Miss Larkin."

He scribbled this on a sheet of vellum before rounding the desk and taking the carpetbag from her. There was nothing in it to identify her, and Bronwen had been afraid that a young woman who looked as if she was traveling alone might provoke unwanted attention.

She cautiously glanced around before moving to a place where she could observe the hotel entrance while she waited. When coming into the lobby, she had noticed a group of oil paintings hanging on a wall adjacent to the glass and oak entry doors. She strolled, unobtrusively she hoped, to stand beneath them. Although she faced the wall, the spot allowed her a sideways view of the front lobby as well as the doors.

Nervousness was making her blood race, and if she had known beforehand how bustling a trade the impressive Spotswood enjoyed, she would have thought twice about coming here in broad daylight. And once here, only the determination to free Seth made her stay. A fourth of the Confederate reserve officers in Richmond must be passing through those doors on their way to the barroom. Possibly a fourth of the government, too; for all she knew, Major William Norris was among them. She had not expected so much indoor activity on a Saturday afternoon, but it might have been due to the gray, showery weather. The previous night's storm must have raised every river and stream to flood level.

She told herself, after recalling her last conversation with Rhys Bevan, that no one here could identify her. It was also useful to keep reminding herself that Richmond now held over 120,000 people. Not all of them could be waiting to pounce on her. That being the case, she should probably be more attentive, since there was unlikely to be a better place in the entire city to observe members of the Confederacy coming and going.

The five-story brick Spotswood, at the corner of Eighth Street, had been completed just before the war started. It quickly became the place in Richmond in which to see and be seen. Chantal Dupont had told her that after the Confederate capital was moved from Montgomery, Alabama, Jefferson Davis had stayed in this hotel until a home was furnished.

She now worried that Quiller might have left the hotel, or else was bewildered by the Miss Larkin pseudonym she had used as a signature on the note. But surely the Treasury coin she had included would suffice. Given what Lincoln had said in Washington, Quiller should be expecting her.

Determined to squash her anxiety, Bronwen gazed up at the paintings, probably done by some Richmond artist as renderings of well-known American works. It was a fairly common practice. She liked art—her own efforts at it having been confined of late to sketching maps—and recognized some of these renderings as representing Copley's Revolutionary War panoramas. And in a startling irony, she recognized a Trumbull portrait of George Washington reviewing his troops after the British defeat at Yorktown.

She glanced over her shoulder, half-fearing that Colonel de Warde would suddenly materialize to demand retribution. Instead she saw a stylishly dressed woman crossing the lobby, the hoopskirt of her gray velvet dress so wide at the hem that it made her look like a gliding equilateral triangle. She drew the eye because of her poise and fashionable attire, but there was something else about her that made Bronwen blink and look again. After swiveling her head slightly more, she sucked in her breath. The small lace hat the woman was wearing rested on upswept hair so black it almost looked . . . blue!

Bronwen whirled back to face the wall before she remembered that she should not be recognizable to Bluebell. The woman had not seen her after her hair had been cut and dyed a darker shade, and certainly not in the guise of a lady of leisure. She turned slightly again, warily, just in time to see Bluebell pause at the entry and wait until a bellboy pulled open both doors to allow her skirt to pass through. Quite a flamboyant display, Bronwen thought, for a woman who just days ago had been confined in Old Capitol Prison. But while Bluebell hardly had to worry about being extradited from Virginia, why was she in this hotel? Simply because nearly everyone else in Richmond seemed to be here?

Bronwen did not have time to speculate further, because the maître d'hôtel was at her side. "Will the lady please follow me?"

He led her back across the lobby to the staircase. To one side of it towered a robust-looking man whose morning suit spoke of an expensive tailor and whose thick silver hair had been barbered by an expert. Friendly brown eyes in a square, clean-shaven face brightened as she went toward him.

"How do you do," he said in a pleasant baritone, smiling as he stepped forward to extend a large hand. "What a pleasure to make your acquaintance . . . Miss Larkin."

Bronwen gave him her hand and returned the smile. Quiller's grip was solid, authoritative, and what she would expect from a successful businessman. His elegance was not expected. She smiled again, involuntarily, when recalling that Lincoln's drawling "Jimmy" had made this man sound like a backwoodsman.

"I have taken the liberty of ordering a light meal in one of the small dining rooms," he said. "At this hour it shouldn't be crowded."

Her consent was evidently not required, since he had taken firm hold of her arm and was already sweeping her toward an archway across from the large, busy barroom. The archway opened directly onto a smaller room graced by two crystal chandeliers, where four amply spaced, unoccupied tables stood covered by gleaming white linen. Red velvet drapery framed the road beyond the one window. When Bronwen took in the leaded crystal vases on each table, overflowing with scarlet lilies and set between ornate silver candlesticks, she found herself remembering the thin, raggedly clothed children she had seen on Richmond's streets. Natty was now probably one of them, doing only the devil knew what. She thrust the image from her mind as a waiter pulled out a chair.

"I'm simply delighted you are here," Quiller said to her, nodding to the waiter, who promptly vanished. "I have heard commendable things about you from . . . from our mutual acquaintance."

The waiter had swiftly reappeared, and now stood uncorking a Bordeaux claret. Quiller sniffed, tasted, and nodded his approval. While the wine was being poured, he unfolded one of the snowy napkins with a snap of his wrist and whipped it across his lap, while launching into the profits to be made by investing in French vineyards. Bronwen wondered if she was expected to comment, and, when surveying the table setting's array of silverware and crystal, also wondered if Quiller intended to devote the next several days to wining and dining here. If this was to be a "light meal," she could not think what would constitute a full-course dinner.

He put down his glass suddenly and said to her, "It has just occurred to me, since I trust you did not travel to Richmond alone, if perhaps a . . . a colleague might care to join us? Please forgive me for not thinking of it sooner."

"Not at all. Especially since I've come alone."

A frown clouded his amiable face. "But surely, my dear, it must have been a perilous journey. There are troops, both North and South, literally swarming over the countryside."

"I saw a few," she agreed.

"I cannot imagine that your employer allowed you to make the trip without any of your fellows."

Bronwen must have looked dismayed, because as she glanced around, he said, "We are the only ones here, as I arranged, but if you are uncomfortable, we needn't talk of it. However, I must insist upon knowing if you have adequate accommodations. Decent rooms have become difficult to find in Richmond because the population has swelled in recent weeks."

"I haven't decided where I'll stay," she answered, which was the truth, but his comment unsettled her.

It had not really occurred to her to worry about a room, because in the past she had gone to Elizabeth Van Lew's—which might now be risky if the woman had come under surveillance. But surely she could find a boardinghouse or, if worst came to worst, go to the tavern where Marsh had last stayed. Still, the tavern owner might not welcome her, since Marsh had been shot in his attic.

Quiller was looking genuinely shocked. "You have *nowhere* to stay?"

Bronwen began to tell him there was no need for concern when he stated, "Our mutual acquaintance would quite rightly find it unforgivable if I did not correct this situation. You shall stay here."

"Here?" Bronwen echoed incredulously.

"I can assure you the Spotswood is a clean hotel, and the management will find something suitable."

"I can't stay in this hotel."

"Of course you can."

"Mr. Quiller, you are kind to be concerned, but in the first place it would be too expensive, and in—"

"Nonsense, my dear, the cost is trifling. You have in the past done me a great favor, and it would be my pleasure to take care of this. I must insist!"

"No, please!" Bronwen protested, feeling as if she were trying to stop a charging rhinoceros with a butterfly net. She lowered her voice to give him the most persuasive argument. "Mr. Quiller, with all due respect, it would not be prudent for me to stay at this hotel. There are too many people here, people I should avoid. In the lobby and barroom alone—"

"That is no obstacle," he interrupted with a wave of his hand. "If you wish to avoid them, there are back stairways at either end of the building. No one need even know you are here."

He motioned to one of the waiters, who came to hover at his elbow, and said, "Ask the maître d'hôtel to step in, if you please."

Bronwen sat dumbstruck, trying to think her way out of this sticky problem. Quiller was clearly unaccustomed to being thwarted, and given his financial success it was unlikely that many even attempted it. And now that she thought about it, if she were cautious, having a room in this hotel might be an advantage. She would have access to Quiller, and what was more, Rhys Bevan would never forgive her for passing up a ready-made opportunity to overhear rumors that in this place must circulate like mill water. Naturally she would quickly need to make discreet inquiry about whether the hotel also lodged a Mrs. Bleuette. Though it was possible the woman had merely been lunching with someone.

Since Quiller was apparently not prepared to give an inch, it might seem boorish to argue further. She could also find lodging elsewhere, and two ports in a storm were always better than one.

"Mr. Quiller," said the arriving maître d'hôtel, "how may I assist you, sir?"

Quiller rose, and after a few quiet words, he received an obsequious nod. He said to Bronwen, "Do you have luggage?"

"It is with the maître d'hôtel."

"Indeed it is, Miss Larkin," said the man, adding to Quiller, "I shall have it taken to her room immediately, sir."

Quiller had reached into his coat pocket and withdrawn a wallet. The transfer of a sizable gratuity was handled with such finesse that Bronwen nearly missed it. The next thing she knew Quiller was reseating himself, asking the maître d'hôtel to deliver her room key at his next opportunity.

The entire transaction had taken less than three minutes.

It was followed by the arrival of bouillon, for which Quiller apologized. "There are, lamentably, no fresh oysters to be had at the end of May. And before long, there will be no beef of quality here, either. A tragic prospect! If you have investments in cattle, my dear, I suggest you divest yourself of them without delay."

Bronwen smiled at his supposition.

"I imagine you have heard of New Orleans's fall?" he went on. "A prelude to control of the Mississippi. I trust we have witnessed the beginning of the end."

As she nodded, she fingered the stem of her wine glass, trying to decide—if she were ever able to fit a word in edgewise—how best to broach the subject of Union prisoners of war. She knew unpleasant matters were never to be discussed while dining, but she would be wasting precious time if she kept silent. That her brother was confined in a warehouse less than a mile from this prosperous hotel was causing her growing distress. While she wavered between waiting for dessert and simply blurting it out, a waiter whisked away her wine glass and soup bowl as another waiter deposited before her a plate of croquettes encircled by green peas and fragrant morel mushrooms. Followed immediately by the *pop* of a champagne cork.

She needed to find her voice. The champagne was already being poured when she said to the waiter, "I would prefer water, if you please."

The waiter looked aghast. Quiller looked thunder-struck, then sincerely contrite. "Please forgive my lack of manners, Miss Llyr! Of course I should have asked your preference."

His "Miss Llyr" could not have boomed as loudly as she imagined. She restrained the impulse to glance around, deciding the waiters were not likely to be agents of Confederate intelligence. Gritting her teeth, she was about to quietly remind Quiller not to use her name, when a familiar voice directly behind her made the hair on the back of her neck rise.

"My dear Mr. Quiller!" the voice had said. "What an agreeable surprise."

Bronwen knew before she turned that she would look up into the sharp, black eyes of Colonel Dorian de Warde.

While Quiller got to his feet, extending his hand to the Englishman, a score of urges raced through Bronwen's mind, the most compelling by far being flight. But since she had nowhere to flee to, she remained frozen to the chair, watching de Warde's every move, except for one of her hands inching of its own volition toward the stiletto in her high, laced shoe. The rest of her body felt like a block of ice.

"Allow me, Colonel de Warde," said the affable and oblivious Quiller, "to introduce you to my dining com-panion, Miss Larkin."

De Warde's expression did not alter one single iota. He bent slightly at the waist, saying, "I am delighted to make your acquaintance, Miss Larkin. You are a fortunate man indeed, Mr. Quiller, to enjoy such beauteous com-pany."

In rapid succession, Bronwen underwent astonishment at his complicity, awe at his straight-faced duplicity, and profound alarm. The Spotswood Hotel was not the place to run head-on into de Warde, the one person who could positively identify her as a Treasury agent. Nor would she have found herself face-to-face with him had it not been for an ill-advised appearance with Quiller. But Lincoln's friend could not possibly have known that by "introducing" her to the British agent, he was placing her in peril. He wouldn't know de Warde even *was* an agent. In truth, by a mere flick of de Warde's finger, those officers in the barroom could seize her for espionage.

So what was the man playing at? The questions and possible explanations that surrounded his coming into this dining room at this particular moment were too numerous to count. Of one thing only was Bronwen certain: in return for not publicly exposing her as a Federal intelligence agent, de Warde wanted something.

And now, to her even greater alarm, Quiller was graciously asking de Warde to join them. Bronwen assured herself this was only a required social exercise, and she could expect de Warde to decline. Quiller would expect the same. While she waited for the Englishman to make an excuse for leaving, her eyes darted over the room. Her present predicament was at least partially her own fault. Because of Lincoln's relationship with Quiller, she could not have gracefully declined the man's invitation to dine, but when coming in here with him, she had failed to remember one of Pinkerton's most frequently growled directives: *Always have an alternate exit!* As a result, short of plunging through the velvet-draped window, she was trapped.

De Warde was now saying, "I don't wish to intrude," which did not sound to her like a sufficiently firm refusal.

Quiller was required to respond, "Not at all, Colonel. We would be pleased to have your company."

"Then if you insist, my dear sir, and do not object to sharing the lovely Miss Larkin, I should be delighted to join you." De Warde even contrived to look defeated.

Bronwen reached for a champagne glass.

The next moment, coming from somewhere far beyond the window, a long deep-pitched rumble sounded. She glanced at Quiller and de Warde, who had both obviously heard it too, and were still listening.

"Thunder," announced Quiller decisively, and he took his seat, followed by the Englishman's seating himself. Bronwen hid her dismay, knowing she could never mention Seth now; de Warde had ready access to Major Norris.

While waiters began scurrying to lay a setting for de Warde, she took two very small sips of champagne, attempting to look nonchalant about this nasty turn of events. Fortunately, his ploy had finally aroused her anger, which until now had retreated in the face of terror. To execute her assignment she had to see him sometime, anyway, though she would have chosen a different time and place than one with Confederate military not twenty yards away. But so be it. She might now learn what he wanted.

Several more far-away rumbles sounded, but were heard by all as the approach of another storm.

By the time she had endured in near silence the two men's speculation about coal and lumber commodities and, somewhat more interesting, a transcontinental railroad that would connect the country's markets from coast to coast, the coffee had arrived. It was evening, or so said the dusky light beyond the window. Seth was no closer to being released. Making Bronwen still more uneasy were the distant reverberations, which had now persisted for so long that they did not strike her as being typical of a thunderstorm.

When she excused herself and went to the ladies' lounge located beyond the dining room, she observed that, strangely enough, almost no one remained in the lobby. Everyone seemed to be in the barroom, where near-quiet had descended after what she noticed had been the departure of most Confederate officers.

"It is distressing," de Warde had been saying upon her return. While he and Quiller were rising to their feet, he finished his thought. "There seems no end to this dilemma." He explained to Bronwen, "We were discussing the European investments in Virginia tobacco."

Having reseated herself in the chair Quiller held for her, Bronwen had been about to raise the evening's hundredth glass of water to her lips, but her hand stopped in mid-air: *tobacco?*

"Yes," agreed Quiller, "the tobacco presents a vexing problem. As you know, Colonel, I've recently returned from France."

How would de Warde know that? wondered Bronwen. In fact, how *did* these two men know each other?

The question must have been obvious because de Warde turned to her, saying, "Mr. Quiller had just arrived here in Richmond when the French minister introduced us. One can only surmise the meeting will prove beneficial to us all," he added cryptically.

"My understanding," said Quiller, "is that the British and French tobacco has been transferred from its original location into separate warehouses. Surely that is a positive sign the Confederacy intends to protect it in all eventualities."

"I do not think that a foregone conclusion," disagreed de Warde. "No, I do not think so."

"The French have been reassured by Secretary Benjamin's attitude," Quiller said. "However, they naturally remain anxious."

"With good reason. So does my queen, and as you may have learned, she is newly widowed. A tragic thing, poor Albert's death. It has left her quite inconsolable, hence it is my duty to spare her from financial worries."

Rubbish, thought Bronwen. Queen Victoria probably knew or cared nothing at all about the fortune residing in a threatened city in North America. De Warde's overriding concern, as always, would be for his own interests. And she suddenly wondered how much of an investment he personally had at stake.

He unexpectedly asked, "What would you suggest be done, Miss Larkin?"

Aha, thought Bronwen, was this the reason for de Warde's forcing himself upon Quiller's hospitality? She replied carefully, "If that tobacco belongs to Europe, I imagine it could be to everyone's mutual advantage to have it removed from Richmond without delay."

"Secretary Benjamin might prevail in his efforts to do just that," de Warde replied, "but there is no point in pursuing it if the tobacco cannot travel beyond Virginia."

"Then perhaps it needs to be taken out of the Confederacy entirely," said Bronwen, feeling her way along with caution, "and sent across the Atlantic before the storm here becomes more violent."

"Unfortunately, my dear," Quiller inserted kindly, "the Union's Atlantic blockade prevents the French from doing that. If I am not mistaken, Colonel de Warde, a shipment of your cotton was recently lost when a blockade-runner was captured."

Bronwen, noting his singular reference to the French— and certain that Warde did too—smiled in feigned embarrassment at her lapse into stupidity. "Mr. Quiller, thank you for your reminder. I overlooked the fact that the tobacco must travel *east* to reach Europe."

In saying this, she almost bit her tongue; she, who drew her own maps.

Quiller, the businessman who published maps, smiled benevolently, and may or may not have been taken in. De Warde, on the other hand, was eyeing her speculatively.

"Perhaps," said Quiller, "it would be best to continue this discussion at—"

Interrupting whatever he had been about to say came an explosion of shouting from the direction of the lobby. More shouting erupted from the barroom, and in a matter of moments the noise had increased to an uproar.

De Warde and Quiller both rose quickly and started toward the archway. Guardedly Bronwen followed them, but stopped when she saw that just beyond her, men were pouring from the barroom. The lobby was rapidly filling with people coming in from the street, so many of them that the entry doors were jammed.

An unreasoning fear coursed through her, one rooted in the unknown, and she strained to quiet it while trying to discover what was causing the furor. Quiller and de Warde had stepped into the whirlpool of bodies, so she lost track of them, but now she began to pick up the ominous words "battle" and "Yankees."

Quiller suddenly reappeared beside her. Taking her arm, he placed something in her hand, at the same time bending down to say, "Here is the key to your room. I think it wise for you to go there immediately."

"What's happened?"

"A large engagement, not too distant from the city. I gather it's been going on for several hours or more, creating the noise we earlier dismissed as a storm. The agitation here started when word came that General Johnston had been wounded. Apparently severely wounded."

Bronwen tried to disengage herself from Quiller's grasp and move toward the lobby to learn more, but he began tugging her in the opposite direction. The crowd now swirled not far from where they stood.

"I must insist that you go up to your room," Quiller repeated, his brown eyes radiating concern. "It's on the top floor at the east side of the building."

"Yes, very well," Bronwen agreed reluctantly, her need for information having been replaced by a more basic instinct, that of self-preservation. This crowd would not have reason to treat any Yankee with detachment when one of them had just removed their commanding general.

She glanced toward the red-carpeted staircase to see it mobbed with people racing up and down it.

"No, not those stairs," Quiller told her. "Go straight down the hallway next to the room where we were dining. At the end of it is a stairway that will take you to the fifth-floor corridor. Your room should be at the far end. I'd take you myself, but someone might see us, and it could place you in a compromising position."

He pressed her hand, and as Bronwen hurried toward the hallway, she marveled at the tenacious grip of propriety. Here they were with pitched combat taking place a few miles from Richmond, with the commanding general of the Confederate army wounded—and Quiller was concerned for her reputation!

Midway down the corridor, she heard quick footsteps coming up close behind her. She bent over, her hand swooping under her skirt and into her shoe before the voice reached her.

"One moment, if you please, Miss . . . *Larkin!*"

Spinning toward de Warde, she saw that he was alone, and his lethal walking stick was held loosely at his side. She watched with wary suspicion as he neared, the stiletto balanced in her fingers; it had not been that long since she saw him coolly dispatch a man who had not even threatened him, although she conceded that the man, a murderer several times over, deserved to die. But now she heard voices floating toward them and her fear lessened. De Warde would be loath to use violence in a public place.

"My dear young lady," he said, "you hardly need the weapon, or the ferocious expression."

"I'll decide that, de Warde."

She stiffened when he reached into his pocket, but he withdrew only a folded piece of notepaper. When he handed it to her, glancing down the hall as he did so, she took it gingerly.

Without another word, he pivoted on his heels and walked quickly back the way he had come.

She waited until he was a safe distance away before she continued toward the stairs, shaking open the notepaper as she went. There were several sentences on it, but three words jumped out at her: *tobacco* and *your brother.*

17

—ᗜᗜ—

*Men in their generations are like leaves of the
trees. The wind blows and one year's leaves are
scattered on the ground; but the trees burst into
bud and put on fresh ones when the spring comes
round.*

—Homer

Seneca Falls, New York

Glynis Tryon hurried up the shallow steps from her library to Fall Street, wondering how she could have lost track of the hour; unless by some unconscious impulse she had made herself late intentionally, thus leaving her no time to think about what lay ahead. The incoming train, if on schedule, would steam into the railroad depot within the next thirty minutes. And it would steam out again shortly thereafter.

Since the war began, the library had become busier than ever, and her hours there had grown longer. Despite this she had spent some of the morning with her niece; one year ago Emma had wed attorney Adam MacAlistair and was now expecting a child. For several days she had been experiencing the mild cramps of incipient labor, but today Dr. Cardoza-Levy had said the birth was likely a week away. Which meant that Glynis had lost the last good reason for not facing the fact that Cullen Stuart would be leaving Seneca Falls.

As she hastened up the edge of the wide dirt road in the shade of soaring elms, she listened for a locomotive's whistle, afraid she would hear it, while knowing that if she did, it would be the first time in memory a train had arrived early. She had told Cullen yesterday that she could not bear to take leave of him at the rail station. He had agreed it would be too hard on them both. Instead, he would wait for her, he had said, at his office in the firehouse.

Now noticing a few startled glances from those in wagons and buggies along the road, Glynis realized that her frantic pace was unbecoming the town librarian, so she reluctantly slowed it. Below the slope to her left, the Seneca River sparkled under a high, brilliant sun and she was obliged to shade her eyes with a hand. In her haste she had forgotten her large-brimmed hat, but by any measure it should not be such a glorious June day. A dismal rainy one would have been more fitting. Then, recalling how she always had the same thought on sunlit days that held funerals, she pushed it from her mind.

When she rounded the corner and turned down the slope to the firehouse, she saw standing in front of it Cullen's three deputies. They were too young to be given the task of policing an entire town, but the county sheriff had said he could not spare any of his own men. The war was draining the region of capable law officers, while at the same time violence was increasing because of the number of army-issued firearms brought home by returning soldiers. It was not often the soldiers themselves who committed the crimes, but the misfits into whose hands the firearms fell.

All of which, Glynis thought, made it even more senseless for Cullen to leave. It was simply unthinkable to her. He had been considering it, she knew, for over a year, ever since the first New York regiment had left at Lincoln's initial call for troops. And now he would be bound for Virginia, where a Seneca County regiment stood somewhere east of the Confederate capital.

Glynis was aware that her distress was not, in truth, because the town constable was leaving but because the town constable was Cullen.

"Afternoon, Miss Tryon," said Liam Cleary. "Constable's been waiting for you. 'Fraid you wouldn't get here in time 'cause the train's coming soon."

Glynis sighed at Liam's customary lack of subtlety, while the effervescent Danny Ross at least had the sensibility to straighten his face. Chief Deputy Zeph Waters shot Liam a look of long-suffering exasperation that nearly made Glynis smile. She clasped Zeph's hand gratefully, and his responding pressure told her he understood how wrenching this was.

"We'll wait out here," he told her in a low voice.

"Yeah, make sure nobody interrupts you," said Liam in a loud and clear one, thus earning another scowl from Zeph.

When Glynis went through the doorway of Cullen's office, the first thing she saw was his battered old leather valise. Her eyes at once filled, even though she had pledged herself to no weeping.

He was seated behind his desk, chair tipped back with his boots up on the desktop as if he had all day to just park himself there. His shaggy sand-brown hair was shot through with paler strands, but his mustache was untouched by the color of time, and women still sent him coy, inviting smiles. When he got to his feet, he stood for a minute in silence while they looked long at each other, then he rounded the desk to grasp her shoulders.

"Glad you made it," he said, drawing her to him. "I was beginning to think you wouldn't. Or couldn't."

"Cullen, I still cannot understand why you're going through with this . . . this . . . ."

Words failed her, and her eyes overflowed as she pressed her forehead into the hollow of his throat.

"Don't make this harder than it is, Glynis. I've told you I have to go."

"But you *don't* have to! There are already too many men gone."

Even as she said it, she heard the shrill whistle of a train, and his arms around her tightened. Tears were coursing down her face when he kissed her, and somewhere in the back of her mind she thought he might not be going if, all those years ago, she had consented to marry him. He had asked only once, both his pride and hers having shaped much in the years that followed.

He gazed down at her and ran his fingers over her wet face. "I'm sure you know this," he said quietly, "but I'll say it anyway. I have always loved you, Glynis. Always will."

"I do know, and I love you, too," she whispered, looking at him through a veil of tears. "Please be safe, Cullen."

He released her slowly, then stepped back and picked up his valise. He was in the doorway when he turned to say, "If Jacques Sundown shows up—and I'm damn certain he will—you make sure he understands I'll be back!"

Then he went through the door and was gone.

It was long after she heard the train rumbling away before she felt collected enough to leave Cullen's office. She could not remember ever feeling so stricken, so . . . bereaved, as if some vital part of her had been irretrievably lost.

Cullen's last words about Jacques Sundown had been heartbreaking. She had never been able to choose between these two men she loved, and neither of them had forced a choice. She had come to believe, or perhaps simply wanted to believe, that the three of them would weave in and out of one another's lives for as long as they lived. But the war that had begun to take so much from so many had now taken Cullen, and Glynis thought she could never in her life be whole again if he did not come back.

Tears again welled, and she pressed the heel of her hands against her eyes. Finally she stood and walked around the desk, running her fingers a last time over its scarred surface.

Closing his office door behind her, she went reluctantly into the warm, hay-scented afternoon of early summer, a season when western New York became Eden regained. She stared down at the road to keep anyone from approaching her. She could not possibly return to the library; she just wanted to reach her boardinghouse without intrusion. When she heard her name called, she quickened her pace to discourage whoever it was.

"Miss Tryon, wait!" came the voice again, and now she recognized it as belonging to Zeph.

Turning, she watched him lope toward her, the sun lending his skin the sheen of polished ebony wood. She hoped Frederick Douglass's call for the acceptance of Negro troops in the Union army would go unanswered, because if it did not, she knew without question that Zeph would be among the first to go.

"You're the only one I would have stopped for, Zeph."

He nodded understanding, and said, "I wouldn't have bothered you if it weren't important. Dr. Cardoza-Levy wants you at the MacAlistair house, soon as you can get there, she said."

"She's at Emma's? Oh Lord, Zeph, did she say why?" He shook his head.

"How long ago was that?" she asked, having resumed walking, her gait as rapid as she could manage without tangling herself in the long skirt.

"I went looking for you at the library first, so it's been . . . maybe fifteen, twenty minutes."

"I pray something hasn't gone terribly wrong. And I've just remembered that since Emma's baby wasn't due yet, her husband went to Waterloo this morning on some legal matter."

"I've sent Danny Ross to fetch him."

"Zeph, thank you!" Glynis tried to think what might have happened, but it was too frightening to imagine. It could be any one of a hundred things, and so many women were lost in childbirth.

The walk to Cayuga Street and the large Italianate house Adam had purchased, a few doors up the road from Glynis's boardinghouse, seemed to take forever. At last it was just ahead, and she gathered up her skirt to quicken her pace still more.

After rushing up the front steps and through the open front door into the entrance hall, she stopped abruptly. Dr. Neva Cardoza-Levy was coming down the stairs, but Glynis could not read her expression.

"Neva, what *is* it? Is Emma . . . has she . . . ?"

"Emma is fine," Neva said, and Glynis's racing heart began to slow. "From your swollen eyes, I gather Cullen has gone, but otherwise I must say, Glynis, that you look too striking to be anyone's great-aunt."

"Yes, Cullen left . . . what did you say?"

"Emma sent a neighbor for me, and the baby arrived not more than ten minutes after I did."

Glynis grasped the stair railing for support. "But how could . . . Neva, you said it wasn't due for another week."

"I was wrong," she shrugged. "And it was one of the easiest deliveries I've ever attended. Infant slid out like a greased piglet down a chute."

Glynis, weak with relief, leaned on the railing and had to smile at Neva's turn of phrase.

"Emma wants to see you," Neva told her, "so go on up and meet the newest Tryon woman. She is being named, according to Emma, for a dauntless grandmother of yours who not only faced a band of Seneca braves with just a flintlock musket, but also lived to tell it."

"That was Miranda Tryon."

"It certainly goes a long way to explain Bronwen!"

"Yes," Glynis agreed. "I've often thought that about Bronwen."

Neva nodded. "In any case, Emma says her new daughter's name is to be Miranda. Miranda Glynis MacAlistair."

Halfway up the stairs Glynis paused, hearing above her a newborn's high, vulnerable cry. And in spite of her happiness for Emma, again the intense grief of parting from Cullen nearly overwhelmed her.

She stood there, wrenched by conflicting emotions and wondering how she could ever meet Emma's certain joy, when, like a gift of grace, memory gave to her the ancient wisdom of the biblical sage: *To everything there is a season; a time to weep and a time to laugh, a time to mourn and a time to dance . . .*

A time of war and a time of peace.

18

~m~

*Men too old or infirm to fight went on horseback
or afoot to meet the returning ambulances, and
in some cases served as escort to their own dying
sons. . . . Following the [Seven Pines] battles, the
streets were one vast hospital.*

—Constance Cary Harrison, Richmond, June 1862

Libby Prison

When Seth got to his feet and took a few steps forward,
the links of chain around his ankle rattled like a sack of
empty tin cans. He reached for the mug of soup brought
by Major Edmund Randall and nodded his thanks. The
soup smelled like rancid pork and sawdust.

"Sorry, lad, this is all they've given us today," Randall
told him. "And I suppose we're lucky to get it, what with
the whole city in an uproar."

Two days ago a cannonade of heavy artillery and the
sustained roar of musketry told of an intense battle, which
the prisoners estimated was only five or six miles east of
the city. At daybreak on the following day it had begun
again, but not with the same concentration. Just after midday, it had ceased altogether. Not so the confusion and
panic of people on the streets outside the prison.

"Any news yet?" Seth asked.

"Nothing in detail," Randall replied, "but we may have
something soon. Guards have allowed the peddlers back

in here, and the men are trying to gather information from them. We should hear something anytime now."

Seth nodded, gulped the thin soup in several swallows, and after Randall started back toward the stairs, he sank to the floor again. At least he had been returned to the relative comfort of the warehouse room after two days and nights spent in a cell the size of a cloak closet next to Winder's office. It was strange how a small thing like being able to stretch out his legs seemed a luxury.

They had questioned him for hours, and he had not told them more than his name and his regiment, other than denying over and over that he was a spy. It had not been a brutal interrogation until Police Chief McCubbin had begun to strike him, more in exasperation than anything else. A Major Norris had stopped McCubbin, and later, after the puzzling Colonel de Warde had come and gone, he had been left alone. Yesterday noon he was released from the cell, but when he had moved toward the stairs to the second floor, two guards grabbed him.

"Can't go up there," they had said.

Ordinarily prisoners were permitted fairly free access to all three stories of the warehouse. Some even cooked meals in the first-floor fireplace. Most of the officers could buy food and other items sold by the street peddlers who were allowed into Libby twice a day. Oddly enough their Federal money had not been confiscated. This was said to be on Winder's orders.

"Why can't I go to the second floor?" Seth had asked the guards.

"Got to keep a close eye on you, that's why."

"I'm not going much of anywhere."

"That's the truth, 'cause we got to chain y'all, Yankee boy. Can't have you hurtin' yourself by tryin' to run off. General Winder, he says we don't want that good-lookin' face all black 'n' blue for the trial."

When Seth did not respond, the guard seemed disappointed, and added, "If y'all look out that window there, you can see a stack of wood they's been collectin'. That wood's gonna build your gallows, Yankee boy. An' your coffin, too."

The length of his chain was looped and attached to a padlocked metal collar clamped around his ankle, and the chain attached to an iron ring sunk into the floor. It was longer than he expected, since it reached to a window opening above Canal Street. Seth had tested the chain's strength last night; it was stronger than it looked.

Worse than the accusations of spying or the uncertainty of what would happen next was his belief that a fellow officer must be an informer. It could not have been co-incidence that he was hauled into Winder's office shortly after young Carson had died.

He had gone over the scene in his mind a hundred times, trying to remember what exactly he and Carson had said, and who had been close enough to overhear it. He thought the most likely one was Thompson. A rough, loud bully, Thompson was unlike most men here. When Seth had been brought back to the room yesterday, he started to ask Randall and Lieutenant Rafe Andrews what they knew about Thompson, but had not finished his question. It was wrong to spread suspicion about the man, about any man, without solid evidence. Then too, much as Seth resisted the idea, it was possible that Randall or Andrews might themselves be informers. It might be anybody.

It gave him a hollow, forsaken feeling, the same as if he had been exiled, that he dared not trust a single man here.

Randall was now coming back across the floor with Rafe Andrews.

"We finally got some word, for what it's worth," the grave-faced Andrews told Seth. "Seems nobody knows for sure what the outcome was, or if the Rebels retreated, but it must have been one hell of a battle. Streets out there are swamped with ambulances and litters bringing in wounded, and they're still coming. By the looks of it, there must be thousands of casualties—a lot worse than Bull Run was for us. Maybe even as bad as Shiloh. Never saw anything like it."

Thompson joined them to blare, "But the biggest and best damn news is that ol' Joe Johnston caught himself a shell or two. S'posed to be in sorry shape, or maybe he's dead. Nobody knows for sure. But we can hope."

"General Johnston?" Seth asked, trying not to seem too eager for information, even though the others must know his fate lay with whoever held Richmond.

"Commander Joe himself," said Thompson with a grin.

"Anybody say who's replacing him?" asked Andrews.

Thompson shrugged and shook his head. "So, how's our boy?" he said to Seth. "Heard yet when they're draggin' you to the kangaroo court?"

"Thompson," snapped Randall, looking behind him, "are you out of your head? You'll put everyone here in jeopardy."

"And we're not now? Hell, Randall, you can't b'lieve Llyr's in for a fair trial," Thompson said loudly. "Listen to 'em out there on the streets—sounds like a madhouse. Rebs got to blame somebody besides their own for the mess they've got themselves into."

Seth suspected that Thompson, informer or not, was probably right.

"Peddlers are coming in," Andrews said, looking across the room to the Cary Street door. "You need anything, Llyr?"

Seth forced a smile and gestured at the padlock. "Just a key, if you can find one."

"Hey, there's that kid who's been here a couple times before," Thompson said. "The one with the cigars. Wonder where in hell the little bugger stole 'em. You want a smoke, Llyr? Take your mind off your troubles?"

When Seth shook his head, Thompson went off, following Andrews and Randall.

Seth watched them join the others clustered around a

thin, dirty-faced boy who was peddling cigars. The last time the boy had been here, he made his way across the entire length of the room, hawking his wares like a seasoned pitchman. He had stopped in front of Seth, where he stood eyeing the chain.

"You wanta buy a cigar?" he had finally asked.

"No, thanks. Looks like you had a good day, and don't have any left even if I did want one."

"I got this here," the boy had said, pulling a cigar stub out of his trouser pocket. "An' I'll letcha have it cheap."

"You better look out," Thompson had said to the boy as he came up behind him. "They got this man in chains 'cause he's a dangerous Yankee. And I'll take that cigar."

He had reached out to snatch it, but not quickly enough. In a split second the boy had yanked it back, spun like a top, and darted away.

Seth now leaned his head back against the wall and flexed his legs. He had to keep his strength up, and at least the sprained ankle wasn't bothering him much, even though the chain was attached to it.

He must have dozed off, but wakened suddenly with the uneasy sense he was being watched. The boy was standing a few feet away.

"Hello, again," Seth said.

"You wanta cigar?"

"No, thanks. But if you're selling water I'd sure take some."

"Don't sell no water."

Seth smiled. "I was afraid you'd say that. Sell all your cigars today?"

"Why you got a chain on you?"

"I'm a prisoner."

The boy's alert hazel eyes narrowed. "So's the rest o' these guys priz-ners, an' they ain't got no chains."

Seth glanced around. He didn't want the boy to get in trouble by talking to him, but there was nobody close enough to notice. "I guess the prison guards think I'm a bad risk," he said.

"What's thet mean?"

"Means they think I might run away if I got the chance."

"Would ya?"

"You bet. It's no fun in here."

He saw Randall and Thompson coming back across the floor. "You better go," he told the boy, moving his head in Thompson's direction.

"Thet big guy don't skeer me none."

"He should. You watch out for him."

The boy's eyes narrowed again, before he nodded and moved away, skillfully avoiding Thompson, who had changed course and was headed for the Cary Street windows.

Seth watched after the boy for a minute before closing his eyes again. Good to talk to someone who wasn't a potential informer.

A few minutes later he heard a faint sound beside him. Likely a rat, he thought, and without looking he slapped his hand on the floorboards. By the time he bothered to check, there was no rat there. Instead, on the floor beside him, was a tin cup of water and a cigar.

He glimpsed the boy running out the Canal Street door, and got to his feet. Stretching the chain to its limit, he stood beside the window and looked out.

The boy was darting along the narrow, crowded road, nimbly dodging ambulance wagons and litters. Catching Seth's eye as well was a tall woman in a metal-colored gown, carrying a fringed parasol. She was standing near the prison door and looked bizarrely out of place in the grim setting. For some reason she appeared to be staring after the boy. A moment later she started out in the same direction he had taken. She was walking rapidly, but still managed to push back into place several loosened strands of her upswept, glossy black hair.

19

—m—

Men in every condition of horror, shattered and shrieking, were being brought in by stretchers. . . . To think or speak of the things we see would be fatal. No one must come here who cannot put away all feeling.

—Katharine Prescott Wormeley, June 1862

Field Hospital

Kathryn slumped against the foundation of the farm-house porch, with the certainty that she didn't have the strength to lift the cup of coffee she held to her mouth. On the damp, trampled ground surrounding the porch sprawled wounded soldiers, who, after many hours, were still waiting for medical attention. The stretchermen had told them they were not in immediate need. Those in un-relenting pain questioned this diagnosis, but most bore it stoically. Kathryn questioned it, too, not that it mattered. There were not enough doctors or stewards.

Wounded were still straggling in through a misty driz-zle. Kathryn tried to make them comfortable while they waited for the doctors, but it was like dipping out the ocean with a teaspoon. They just kept coming. Nothing she did in the face of such vast suffering seemed even half enough. Right now she expected some returning stewards, hoping they would bring the additional blankets and whiskey she had requested when the most recent trainload of wounded had left for the transport ships at White House Landing.

She vaguely recalled Bronwen saying, at the York River anchorage after Williamsburg, that it looked like a scene from Hades. Perhaps, but this *was* Hades.

A while ago Micah Rosen, one of the doctors performing surgery inside the farmhouse, had said he guessed it might be Sunday afternoon, or maybe it was Monday. No one disagreed, since most of them had no idea what day it was. They seemed to have been here forever.

Kathryn was certain it had been Saturday afternoon when the first rumbles of heavy artillery had reached White House Landing. Several hours later a young private attached to the quartermaster corps had dashed down the *Aeneid*'s pier from the railroad depot, bringing a handwritten message for Kathryn: *Come immediately. Brown farmhouse. GT.*

There had been time only to stuff a change of clothes and a few other items into a carpetbag, snatch her shawl, and follow the private to where army wagons were being loaded with medical supplies. Shortly after Kathryn arrived, mules and their drivers pulled the wagons into standing freight cars. The private pointed to one of the smaller cars, and Kathryn had started toward it when she spotted a small, overlooked box labeled CANDLES. She had grabbed the box and tucked it under her arm before the private hoisted her into the car.

"Thank you," she said to him, while he spread her shawl over a wooden bench against the wall of the car. "May I ask your name, Private?"

"Hall, Miss Llyr. Private Randy Hall, at your service, ma'am."

He gave her an uneasy smile, nervously fingering his cap and appearing to be very young. She started to ask him how long he had been with the army, but then thought better of it. He would be embarrassed if he thought she had noticed his nervousness. For the same reason, she also refrained from saying, "We're all frightened, Private."

She had been the only woman among the drivers and a few red-sashed stewards. After they threw her some surprised looks, and she heard some disgruntled muttering, Private Hall lowered himself to the wooden floor near her feet, either appointing himself her protector or the other way round. The others then for the most part ignored her.

The train had run west on the Union-held portion of the Richmond and York River track, passing any number of troop encampments before stopping beside a dilapidated wooden shed. The wagons were taken off the railroad cars, and Private Hall helped Kathryn into one of them. What followed was a rough, jolting ride in the rain over a marshy road for what seemed to be two or three miles. The other wagons followed like a clattering tail.

"Not much farther, if I remember," Hall said to the grizzle-haired driver.

"Nope. Can't go much farther, son, less you want to take a swim in the Chickahominy—flooded its banks and a right mess it is!"

Kathryn had begun to hear shouting and the high whinnies of horses as the wagon labored up a shallow rise, and at its crown she leaned forward on the seat beside the driver to peer through the rainy dusk. She drew in her breath and clutched the wagon seat.

The rain-soaked fields below held a churning maelstrom of men and horses, beast and human nearly indistinguishable, swirling around carts and caissons and battery wagons.

She could hardly take in its enormity, but in the midst of the roiling mass of bodies, she made out a brown farmhouse and barns, and the white blur of tents being pitched. Those were the only stationary objects she could see in the eddying sea of men and horses. At the same time, sporadic artillery fire was coming from the south.

She gripped the sides of the wagon as it lurched forward, the driver saying, "Miss, you sure you want to go down there?"

Private Hall looked at her anxiously. "It's a lot worse than when I left. Maybe Dr. Travis didn't know how bad it would get . . . and you shouldn't be here."

Kathryn clenched her teeth and did not answer. The wagon jounced in the direction of the farmhouse, now passing ragged lines of countless numbers of soldiers headed the same way. While all of them had visible injuries, at least, Kathryn thought, they could manage to walk. How many others could not?

Then she saw the stretchermen, scores of them, coming in with the others. Agonized screams began to soar over the tumultuous clamor, while the stench of vomit and blood drew the black turkey vultures that were wheeling overhead.

When the wagon neared the farmhouse, its wheels began to sink into the soggy ground. While the mules strained to plod forward, Kathryn saw below her on a stretcher a soldier whose open head wound bled so profusely that his features had become a distorted red mask. He was coughing clots of blood as he thrashed on the stretcher, gasping for air, and Kathryn signaled the driver to let her down. She seized her carpetbag and climbed over the side of the wagon.

"Private Hall," she shouted to him over the clamor, "please fetch those candles. And hand down a box of bandaging—bring as many boxes of it as you can carry."

Snatching a handful of the cotton bandaging from the box he had lowered to her, she asked the stretchermen with the bleeding soldier to stop, thinking she might at least try to stanch the terrible flow, but the men ignored her and hurried on. She stumbled after them, struggling to keep her footing while holding her skirt above the mud.

"Miss Llyr," panted Private Hall, as he came along beside her, his arms heaped with boxes, "where do you want these?"

Kathryn pointed at the brown farmhouse. "On the porch."

They wove through the wounded going toward the farmhouse and barns and the tents just beyond, forced to shoulder aside the milling horses. Kathryn made the mistake of looking past the buildings to the swampy fields and woods where men, hundreds of them, were being transported by wagons and stretchers. *There were so many.*

She kept walking, her eyes on the mud-mired ground, but drawing near to the farmhouse she stopped to lean against the trunk of a tree, fighting the terror that she could do nothing but fail these men.

She had to concentrate only on what needed to be done.

Some small distance from her, a soldier on a litter, deposited and left on the ground despite a gaping wound in his chest, had been asking weakly for water. Kathryn glanced around her, spied a barrel of rainwater, and made herself move forward on leaden feet. By the time she got back with a filled tin cup, the soldier was dead.

He had only asked for water. Something she could have easily given him. It was unforgivable to be absorbed by her own wretched self-doubt in the midst of all this suffering.

She had not prayed, not with any real conviction, for a long while, but the need to do it now was so powerful she did not even think to bow her head. She simply looked up at the sodden, weeping clouds, and then found she hardly knew what to pray for. *Help me,* she whispered. *Please help me to help these men.*

"Out of the way, dammit!" came a shout from behind her. "Let this wagon through!"

Kathryn quickly moved aside as an ambulance wagon jolted past, the shrieks of the wounded it carried more terrible than anything she had ever known, but she refused to look. She would not think of anything other than what lay directly before her. She would not lift her eyes above the farmyard to see what lay helpless in the muddy, torn fields beyond.

There were so many.

She made herself resume walking, intent only on putting one foot in front of the other, until finally the farmhouse rose just ahead. The noise was not quite as clamorous here, and over it came a mercifully familiar voice, one she recognized as Micah Rosen's, a civilian surgeon who had been a medical school classmate of Gregg Travis. He was shouting at four or five nearby soldiers wielding shovels.

"No, not here!" he yelled.

The men kept digging, and as Kathryn moved toward Dr. Rosen, he yelled again, "Don't dig them *here!*"

The soldiers must have heard him, but they continued to heave clumps of mud, digging what were likely latrine sinks. At the same time she saw other soldiers struggling to erect a large tent for food distribution just a short distance from the shovel brigade. Since she knew from experience at White House Landing that soldiers would not take orders from a civilian, she started toward Dr. Rosen to tell him he needed an officer.

A voice from the porch suddenly cut through the sticky air like a hot blade through lard. "Soldiers! Dig those sinks down that slope, and keep them away from the tents and buildings. That's an order! Now move out!"

Gregg Travis scanned those below where he stood, his search stopping at Kathryn, and he gave her a brief nod before he turned and went back into the farmhouse. His arms below the rolled-up sleeves had been glistening with blood, the apron he wore soaked with it.

As the soldiers with the shovels trudged away, Dr. Rosen came toward her. "Miss Llyr! I thought Gregg was insane when he sent for you. But you can help, if you're willing."

"Just tell me what to do."

He looked at her with an expression of contained rage.

"To start, you can get rid of the army medical bureau. What was the army thinking, sending thousands of men into battle without preparing for casualties?"

Kathryn just nodded, trying not to think. "What should I do?" she asked again, aware that more wounded were pouring in every minute.

The anger in his eyes retreated. "Gregg said for you to help the stewards determine which wounded arriving on stretchers need the most immediate help. We have to establish some kind of order here, so the men who can wait should go by train to White House, or on to the next field hospital site. There's one being set up near the railroad."

"There was nothing being done there when I came through," she told him. "And the track's several miles away, so how can the men get there?"

"By ambulance wagon—but there aren't near enough. If you have trouble with the stewards, Gregg said to come to him, and to keep in mind you have as much skill as they do. Good luck."

He leaped to the porch and disappeared inside.

Kathryn jumped as someone touched her shoulder. Private Randy Hall had come up beside her, and he looked every bit as scared as she felt.

"Miss Llyr, my orders are to report to Captain Travis. He knows you're here, doesn't he?"

"Yes, I believe so."

"Is he doing, ah . . . surgery in there? In the farmhouse?"

"Yes, which means he can't be interrupted."

The young soldier looked pathetically relieved when he nodded.

Kathryn had started to walk toward a clump of trees at the right of the farmhouse, where the stretchers were being taken. "When there's opportunity I'll talk to Dr. Travis, but in the meantime, Private Hall, you can assist me, if you will."

Again came a nod, a more enthusiastic one this time.

The next hours passed as in the blur of nightmare. She discovered there were also surgeons operating in the barns, and that she and those in the farmhouse were not alone in their frustration. Everyone was doing the best they could, trying to manage the unmanageable. Night fell, and the wounded kept staggering in; men cold, thirsty, hungry, and most of them in pain. The artillery fire had long since stopped, but still they came. Since the stewards ignored her, Kathryn worked around them, unwilling to go to Gregg Travis with complaints. She dispensed blankets, cleaned and bound wounds, and made sure the men had water and food.

She did not know how she would have coped without Private Hall.

"We need much more drinking water," she told him. "The river's so close by. Is there a way to get a good supply to here from there? Perhaps by using some of those barrels over by that tent? And a wagon to cart them, if you can beg or borrow one?"

"Yeah, I can try," he said readily, and took off at a run. He was back with the barrels in a shorter time than she would have thought possible.

"Where did you get the wagon?" she asked him.

"You might not want to know," he answered.

She thought of Natty. Where *was* he?

As it grew darker, she worked up the courage to ask a steward, "Please, could we have some lanterns here?"

He turned away as if she had said nothing.

Private Hall went foraging and came back with three. This time Kathryn did not ask.

The big soup kettles under the tent were too distant to be reached by the soldiers who had dropped in their tracks by the farmhouse.

"If there were only a way to bring one of those kettles nearer," Kathryn said to Randy Hall. "Something with wheels to set it and move it on."

Private Hall went off, and with the help of two

wounded soldiers, returned with one of the soup kettles balanced on a caisson coupled to a two-wheeled limber. The kettle teetered precariously, but they braced it with tree limbs.

"Somebody might come looking for the limber," Hall told her. "We more or less . . . uh, we borrowed it from artillery."

The wounded were grateful for any kindness, and she tried not to think about their immediate future. It would be a miracle if some of the worst injured, loaded into the jolting wagons, made it alive to the train stop, or to White House Landing and the transport ships north. The ones who survived surgery were being taken there, too.

The lantern light inside the farmhouse began to dim as the oil burned down. A few lanterns went out entirely. When Kathryn heard Gregg Travis cursing, she remembered the box. She had to step over and between the men to reach the porch, and after a search in the near blackness, she found it. Knocking on the sill of a window that opened into the kitchen, she called, "Dr. Travis! There are candles here."

She waited, and when there was no response, she balanced the box on the sill and started to leave. A wet hand shot out of the gloom and grabbed her wrist.

"Thank God" was all Gregg said before releasing her. He was only a black shape on the other side of the window.

"I sent soup in to you a while ago," she told him. "Do you need more?"

"We need twenty more surgeons! There are only the three of us. Miller is too old for this pace, and he's ready to drop any minute."

Then he disappeared. A minute later she saw candlelight flickering.

Hearing a man call for water, she went quickly down the porch steps, nearly colliding with a bearded sergeant, one who had ignored her earlier.

"Need more soup?" he said gruffly.

"Yes, we do." She was distracted by a stream of curses from inside the farmhouse, but when she turned back to point the sergeant toward the makeshift soup cart, he was already wheeling it toward the tent.

Private Hall was coming with more barrels of water. He reined in the mule and jumped from the wagon, jerking his thumb over one shoulder. "What's he doing with our kettle?"

"Getting more soup. Why?"

"Thought we might be in trouble."

"Not yet."

More than anything else, it had been the anguished cries of the wounded that she most wanted to flee. They were something that all the training in the world could not erase from memory. There was so little she could do. There were so many in need.

At daybreak this morning, she had found herself slumped against one of the trees, covered with a blanket, and with no idea when she had crumpled there. And to the south the artillery firing had begun again, though not as fiercely as the day before.

She had slowly recognized that there was somewhat more space around her, and somewhat less confusion. Dr. Rosen had been nearby, leaning against the soup cart, and she went to ask him about it.

"Another field hospital, one closer to the railroad track, has been set up," he had said, rubbing his red eyes. "Some of the wounded have been directed to go there. The only reason it came about was because Gregg read the riot act to some general who showed up a couple hours ago. Our Dr. Travis was fearsome! Good thing you slept through it. The general sure couldn't."

"It wasn't General McClellan, I assume."

Rosen had shaken his head and, bending toward her, said quietly, "Wouldn't have mattered to Gregg if it *had* been McClellan, but it seems Young Napoleon's been indisposed. He made a quick ride from his headquarters to survey the damages—it was *after* yesterday's battle—but now we hear he's taken to his sick bed again."

"So who's in command?"

"That's a good question. It's one Gregg asked the big brass who was here. I don't know the answer, but Gregg surely caught his attention, and we've got another field hospital. A couple more surgeons are supposed to be on their way here, too."

As far as Kathryn knew, those other surgeons had not arrived. The elderly Dr. Miller had collapsed a half hour ago, brought out of the farmhouse on a litter just as a thin stream of wounded began arriving from the battlefield.

Now mid-afternoon, the gruff sergeant who had continued to replenish her soup supply was approaching her with a stack of blankets.

"Thank you, Sergeant. I'm very grateful."

"It's okay, miss. Figure you know what to do with 'em better than anybody."

This gave her such heart that she asked him, "Does anyone know what's happening?" She gestured south toward the river.

"Nope. But there's a whole lot of casualties, we know that. One of the brass sent out a scout a few hours back, so we might hear . . . if he comes back."

Kathryn nodded, and began to thank him again, when she heard Gregg's voice erupt from the farmhouse. He seemed to be yelling something to the stretchermen.

A few minutes later, when, heading away from the house, they grumbled past her, she heard one mutter, "He only wants the wounded who've got a chance. How the hell are we s'posed to know that?"

Kathryn stood there, paralyzed by the thought of men making decisions only God should have to make.

Gregg appeared in the farmhouse doorway. "Miss Llyr, did you *hear* me?" he said sharply, standing above her on the porch.

She stared up at him, shook her head, and started to move to another soldier asking for water.

"I *said* come into the house," he told her brusquely. "With only two of us doing surgery, we need help in here."

His gaze went to the bleak sky. "Damnable rain!"

Scowling as if the weather were a personal affront, he said, "If it doesn't stop soon, I'm moving outside anyway. Chloroform fumes are making me light-headed." He shouted at several young, reasonably able-bodied soldiers, "Raise the best tents available! Right here and right now!"

"Ain't got no more tents, sir," was the laconic reply.

Gregg came down the steps and with an expression that made Kathryn flinch, he went over to the soldiers. Whatever he said, it was spoken in such a low voice it could not be overheard, but a minute later the young men took off at a quick pace for the officers' tents. Gregg stood and watched them until several of the tents began to collapse, and then he strode back to the porch.

By this time Kathryn had fetched the water, and she followed him into the farmhouse. She fearfully imagined, given the screams and the odors that had come through its open windows and doors, that inside she would find something that resembled a charnel house. The reality proved to be much worse.

She moved to the end of a long, blood-dripping wooden table where Gregg directed her to stand.

"There's only a few towels left until the stewards get back, and the chloroform's over there," he indicated, the scalpel in his hand pointing to a smaller table nearby. "I'm not sparing with it, but it's not always necessary if a man is in shock."

He went to the open back door and said tersely, "Next."

Please help me, Kathryn whispered.

She straightened her spine and picked up a towel and the bottle of chloroform.

20

We tramped down Main Street through the hot
sun over the burning pavements, from one scene
of horror to another. . . . The impression of that
day was ineffaceable. It left me permanently convinced that nothing is worth war.

—Constance Cary Harrison, Richmond, June 1862

Richmond

The window of Bronwen's fifth-floor hotel room overlooked the roof of a four-story office building adjacent to
the Spotswood, so before descending the back stairs, she
peered out a hall window to the street below. The moon,
rising in a rare cloudless sky, shone down on a city become one vast field hospital.

For days the Confederate casualties from the Seven
Pines Battle had been streaming into Richmond. Wounded
had overflowed the available hospital space, as well as
churches and schoolhouses and private homes, and soldiers were now sleeping in doorways, on front porches,
and along the roads. In the turmoil, Richmond's police
were virtually powerless to enforce martial law or to
check passports, and when she had left the hotel it had
been without sensing constant danger. One of those times
she had even crept unmolested down Canal Street for a
furtive look at the Libby warehouse. The choice of its site
for a prison had been a shrewd one, since it was relatively

removed from other structures, making it easier to guard.

She had crouched a safe distance away, gazing up at the dark windows and wondering where her brother was behind them, until the painful frustration of being unable to help him drove her back to the city streets.

By now she was frantic for word of Seth. And she desperately needed information before responding to de Warde's cryptic message: *Do you wish to consider a mutually beneficial proposal regarding a solution to the captivity of my tobacco and your brother? Reply requested at your earliest convenience. Room 315.*

That de Warde knew of Seth's imprisonment made her skin crawl with fear. Had Confederate intelligence informed him of her brother's identity, or had the Englishman informed them? Or had it been someone else entirely? It did not reassure her that she had seen Bluebell exiting the Spotswood since de Warde knew the woman through the Confederate intelligence network, but his allegiance to Major Norris seemed open to question if he were offering to bargain. Or maybe not, because de Warde always played both ends against the middle. It was still possible that while the Englishman knew Seth's identity, Norris and his network had not yet discovered it. She needed more facts, and quickly.

She also needed to evade the well-meaning but hovering Quiller. He had been almost fatherly in his insistence that for her protection he should escort her everywhere, despite her protests to the contrary. She feared having hurt his feelings on at least one occasion by too firmly refusing his offer to take her to an afternoon tea. A *tea!* In the midst of casualty-laden, Union-threatened Richmond, there were still tea parties being held. She had not told Quiller about de Warde's message, deciding she could not risk Seth's freedom being compromised by a possible dispute between British and French economic interests. Even if Quiller was Lincoln's friend, he was first of all a businessman.

Thus far, he had learned nothing new about Seth. "I am wary of appearing too forward," he had told her the first morning there, while adjusting his wire-rimmed spectacles to peer at her over the Richmond *Enquirer*. "General Winder is receiving harsh criticism for the rising prices here, and he may not welcome a Northern businessman whom he might view as meddling. But I will watch diligently for an opportunity."

It had now been several nights since de Warde had given her that message. Last evening she had tried to sneak to Elizabeth Van Lew's mansion on Church Hill. If anyone outside the Confederate's inner circle could get information about Seth, it was Van Lew. But as Bronwen had feared, the muddy roads had been clogged with troops and with ambulance wagons turned away from the fully occupied Chimborazo Hospital. When the rain had begun to fall in torrents, all civilians were halted and forbidden to leave the city.

When she had returned to the hotel, she tried to reach Quiller to learn if he had any news, but he had not been in his room. Now adding more fuel to her anxiety over Seth, sometime this evening another note had been slipped under her door: *Time is swiftly running out. Suggest you reply* without delay *or consider proposal to cooperate withdrawn. Room 315.*

This threat was likely a ploy, and de Warde's intention in sending it simply to unnerve her and force her compliance with his timetable. If so, he had been partially successful. She had to fight her impulse to find out immediately what he had in mind because she needed time for one more stab at information about Seth. Since she could apparently not count on Quiller's assistance tonight, she had given a note to a hotel bellboy to deliver to Room 315: *Expect reply within twenty-four hours.*

Now, with that rising moon, she obviously needed to take advantage of it. Pulling a dark-blue, hooded cloak out of Chantal Dupont's carpetbag, she drew it on, and then cautiously opened the door into the hall to check whether the coast was clear. Dashing to the back stairs, she waited impatiently until the stairwell was empty. When she reached the first floor, she made a short detour to the waiter's station just inside the small dining room, where she snatched several candles before slipping out one of the hotel's back doors.

The gutters along the streets smelled like open latrines, and rats scurried underfoot as she weaved stealthily in and out of back alleys, her stiletto held ready. She avoided the taverns where crowds gathered, but suddenly, coming from somewhere around a dark corner, she heard the loud, belligerent voices of confrontation.

People began spilling into the alley, driven, it appeared, by some of McCubbin's police force. Bronwen ducked into the next doorway, immediately stumbling over a uniformed figure huddled on the stoop.

"S'cuse me, miss," the soldier mumbled. "Didn't think anybody lived here."

He began struggling to his feet, but Bronwen, casting an anxious glance over her shoulder, whispered, "Never y'all mind, soldier. I'll just set here for a spell 'til things quiet down."

She seated herself closely beside him, watching the disturbance rapidly dissipate when police wielding nightsticks began scattering the crowd. With alarm, Bronwen saw two of them approach, and they paused before the doorway.

She nodded up at them, smiling, with her stomach lurching. "Evenin', sirs. Me and my soldier were enjoyin' the pleasant night 'til all the rumpus started."

"You live here?" one of the policemen asked the soldier, raising a lantern to scan the doorway.

Bronwen was about to lie, when to her astonishment the soldier answered promptly, "Yes, sir, I do."

Her face averted from the light, Bronwen quickly added, "We all just stepped out for a breath of air."

"Wouldn't stay on the street too long," said one of the policemen. "Lot of vermin out tonight, some of 'em human."

Bronwen held her breath until the police moved on, then, watching them from the tail of her eye, she asked the soldier, "Are you wounded?"

"Yes'm. Caught some shot in my arm. Been waitin' two days to see an army doctor. And I thank you kindly, for not lettin' on to the police, 'cause I surely do not care to spend a night in one of those tents the city got set up. The smell's enough to knock over a mule."

Bronwen turned aside and reached under her skirt for the money pouch on her thigh, fingering the gold coins until she found a quarter eagle.

"Much obliged for your company, sir," she said, pressing the coin into his hand as she rose.

"Oh, no, miss, I can't take this."

"Yes, you can. Money talks, so tomorrow you find yourself a Richmond doctor and let that coin speak up."

Before he could protest further, she hurried away. It had become increasingly hard for her to view the ordinary Confederate soldier as The Enemy. Most of them were unfailingly decent even when in extreme distress.

She continued to zigzag through the streets. As she had guessed, there was enough disorder and sheer misery to cover her passage through the eastern section of the city. When she reached the foot of Church Hill, she lit one of the candles to guide her through a wet, wooded ravine. She had made this trek before under less hazardous conditions, and finally she saw above her the outline of a huge, vase-shaped elm that stood at the rear of the Van Lew grounds. After she climbed the slope, she crouched behind the tree, scrutinizing Grace Street and, on its far side, the moonlit St. John's Church and cemetery. When she felt confident that Van Lew's was not under surveillance, at least not tonight, she darted to the stucco mansion's back steps.

As usual, the door opened instantly. Bronwen had wondered before if there could be a mounted spyglass trained on the rear yard.

"I've been expecting you, my dear," Elizabeth told her, as if they had last met yesterday, and drew her quickly into the large candlelit kitchen, closing the door firmly behind them.

"I couldn't get here before now."

"I have some news," Elizabeth said, nudging one of her scores of cats off the kitchen table. "I'm about to send it to Fort Monroe by way of the farmers along the James. Sit down and I'll fetch us some tea."

Bronwen shrugged out of the cloak, trying to conceal her impatience. She knew from experience that Elizabeth Van Lew could seldom be hurried. But perhaps it was her deliberate pace that made her a good spy, together with her pretense of mental instability, convincing her neighbors that she was a harmless, if deranged, middle-aged spinster. Her genuine eccentricities only magnified the impression.

Elizabeth placed the teapot on a trivet, announcing, "One of my servants is now working up the road at Chimborazo Hospital."

Bronwen blinked in surprise as the woman poured tea into two cups. "I'm afraid there is no sugar, my dear. The inflated prices, you know."

"Whom do you have at Chimborazo?"

"Oh, it's Jim's son, Hosea—you must remember him."

Bronwen nodded.

"Hosea's helping with the ambulance wagons, among other things, and is picking up all manner of useful items. For instance, that young man you brought here?"

"Marsh? How is he?"

"Recovering, but very slowly. I think he's safe for the moment, because of all the confusion there at the hospital—you know of the battle, I assume?"

"Not much. What have you learned?"

"According to Hosea, it has been calculated that there are between five and six thousand Confederate casualties."

"Good Lord, that *many*? More than the population of a town? Although, from the number of wounded I've seen in the city, I guess it's possible. And the Union casualties?"

"I've had no means of gathering those figures yet. But I do know that since General Johnston was wounded, the Confederates have named a new commander."

"Who is he?"

"Jefferson Davis's former military adviser, General Lee. A Virginian and a traitor," Elizabeth said, with repugnance; "turned against his own country."

But not against his own homeland, Bronwen thought, while she fingered her teacup. She found she was now almost afraid to ask about Seth.

"Elizabeth, my brother was captured at Williamsburg. I believe he is here in Richmond and, since he's an officer, is probably being held in Libby Prison. Have you by chance heard anything about him?"

Elizabeth's thin brows had lifted, and she pushed a blond corkscrew curl off her forehead. "Oh, my dear, I fear that I have. When I heard the name Llyr, I had hoped he was not a relative of yours."

Bronwen nearly jumped off the chair but managed to restrain herself and instead leaned across the table. "*What* did you hear? And how?"

"From a peddler. Chaucer said—"

"*Chaucer?*"

"It's an assumed name. The poor man was a professor of literature at the college until his loyalist sentiments were suspected. It's a terrible injustice that he has been reduced to—"

"Elizabeth, please! I apologize for interrupting, but please go on about Seth."

"Oh, yes. Chaucer is one of the peddlers who's allowed into Libby, and he said a young Union officer named Llyr was in solitary confinement for several days."

Bronwen moaned and sank back in the chair. "Did this peddler know why?"

Elizabeth shook her head. "I'm afraid there's a bit more. Chaucer said the young man is now in chains."

"Chains!" Bronwen leapt off the chair, heart in her mouth. "Is that common practice?"

"No. General Winder does not ordinarily chain prisoners, or not to my knowledge."

"Then why would Seth be singled out? Unless there is some reason to think he might try to escape. Elizabeth, is that all you know from this peddler?"

"Yes . . . well, no, there is one other small oddity, but it's likely not important."

"What is it?"

"Chaucer mentioned that a youngster has been peddling cigars in Libby, and several times the boy was seen talking to the young chained officer."

"Natty!" Bronwen exploded. "It must be Natty!"

Elizabeth frowned. "James Fenimore Cooper's character, but since I did not know him *personally,* I don't believe I'm acquainted with anyone by that name."

"Be grateful! This character is a Washington street urchin. My sister Kathryn befriended him, but God only knows why!"

"Perhaps she's kindhearted?" Elizabeth's pale blue eyes held an artful innocence.

"The boy is a dodger, Elizabeth. A pickpocket."

"What else would he be, my dear? And he must be very good at it, if he's managed to acquire cigars in Richmond these days."

Bronwen did not want to discuss Natty's dubious talents. The little wretch! His attention to Seth might add to her brother's danger, although no one here in Richmond could connect Natty to . . . Bluebell! Bluebell could certainly recognize Natty!

Bronwen must have groaned again, because Elizabeth hastily poured more tea.

"Where can I find this Chaucer?" Bronwen asked.

"I doubt you should look for him, my dear. If General Winder or Police Chief McCubbin were to make an association between you and your brother, it could go hard for him. No, I should not think it's a good idea for you to be anywhere near Libby warehouse. We must think of something else."

Everytime Bronwen feared Elizabeth Van Lew was veering toward the lunacy that her neighbors believed of her, she came out with a piece of perfect sense.

"You're probably right," she said. "If Confederate intelligence were to learn Seth's identity—"

She broke off, sure she had just heard something at the kitchen door, and motioned Elizabeth to silence.

The woman listened, then shook her head. "I imagine it's one of the cats scratching to come in."

It did not sound to Bronwen like any cat fumbling with the latch. She slipped the stiletto from her boot and advanced with it toward the door, while Elizabeth abruptly arose and disappeared into the dining room. Bronwen was sidling up beside the window when the woman reappeared seconds later, holding a musket. The cobwebs trailing from it indicated the musket's last use had been in Revolutionary times.

Into the silence came a sudden sharp rap on the door.

Bronwen edged sideways to the window and squinted out into the darkness, unable to see anything. Elizabeth meanwhile was moving resolutely toward the door, armed with her ancient weapon. Even as Bronwen put up a hand to quiet her, the woman called out, "Who is there? Speak now or I shall not be responsible for the consequences."

Bronwen tensed, ready to break and run for the secret attic chamber used for years to hide escaping slaves.

"Madam," came a subdued voice from outside, "I am here to award one of your cats a medal for bravery—just as soon as I can detach its claws from my ankle."

"Damnation!" swore Bronwen, lunging forward to yank open the door.

"How y'all doin', Red?"

"O'Hara, I should cut your throat."

"Do you know this man?" Elizabeth asked, waving the musket barrel at O'Hara.

"Yes, and you might want to shoot him," Bronwen responded, as O'Hara stepped into the kitchen, carrying a large, gray-haired, and benignly purring tabby.

"Dear lady," he said to Elizabeth with a slight bow, "allow me to return this magnificent animal to your tender care." He handed over the cat, at the same time dexterously relieving Elizabeth of the musket. "And please let me introduce myself. Kerry O'Hara, United States Treasury agent and feline aficionado, at your service, madam."

To Bronwen's disgust, Elizabeth eyed O'Hara with approval. "Please be seated, Mr. O'Hara," she said, and turning to Bronwen, commented mildly, "You certainly do have a great many young men following you about."

"And speaking of Marsh," Bronwen said to O'Hara, "are you here to remove him from Chimborazo?"

"Can't get near the place," O'Hara answered. "It's swarming with wounded and other military types. And no, that's not why I'm here. But I have just braved the wilds of Virginia, crossed flooded rivers and quicksand bogs while risking capture by the enemy, and frankly, Red, I think you could show a little more enthusiasm about my arrival."

Bronwen dropped into the nearest chair. "How did you know I was here?"

"It's where you were the last time I came looking."

"You were here before?" Elizabeth asked him, bringing another cup to the table.

"Yes, but I did not have the pleasure of meeting you then, Miss Van Lew, because I was engaged in rescuing the young damsel here, who was at the time being pursued through your bushes."

Bronwen, disregarding Elizabeth's raised brows, said, "That was some rescue. You nearly had me killed! And *why* are you here?"

"I thought you'd never ask. To assist you, naturally."

"Assist me with what?"

O'Hara took a swallow of tea and beamed at Elizabeth. "Delicious," he said, "and not too sweet."

"I'd like some answers!" Bronwen demanded. "Did Rhys Bevan order you to come?"

"Of course, and I'm always glad to be of help."

"Help with what?"

O'Hara rolled his eyes and glanced at Elizabeth, as if he were weary of so obviously evading questions.

"If you have business to discuss, I shall retire," stated the woman with admirable perception. "Please lodge here if you like, my dear," she said to Bronwen.

"Thank you, but no. I've already led one too many polecats to your door."

O'Hara, typically, grinned.

"But Elizabeth, I still think I need to find this Chaucer."

"Chaucer?" O'Hara, choking on his tea, sputtered, " *'And he knew the taverns well in every town.'* "

"When is the peddler usually at the prison?" Bronwen persisted.

"Before noon," Elizabeth answered. "But as I said before, I think it would be dangerous for you to be seen near Libby. If you insist, however, let me know how I can help. And in the meantime, good evening."

O'Hara was on his feet in a flash. "Your faithful musket, madam—where may I put it for you?"

Elizabeth gestured toward the dining room, and his engaging smile followed her through the doorway.

When he returned, he dropped into the chair next to Bronwen and reached for the teapot. "I don't suppose," he said, "that the lady of the house keeps anything stronger than this tea?"

Absently Bronwen shook her head. It occurred to her that if only she could trust O'Hara, he might be of use. "Is it possible," she asked him, "for you to be serious for any length of time? Because my brother is in real danger."

"Bevan told me. Said he'd been captured."

"Seth's in Libby Prison, a former warehouse down on Canal Street. I take it you've been back to Washington since the train wreck?" She asked reluctantly, not eager to remind either of them of that night.

"Went straight to Washington from White House Landing. Went through there again on the way here, too— your sister had just made it back."

"Back from where?"

"Some field hospital, north of the Chickahominy, where she'd been since the Seven Pines fiasco."

"*Fiasco?* O'Hara, have you no respect for anything?"

"You're a fine one to talk about respect, Red!"

"There were thousands of Confederate casualties at that battle," she protested. "It's not something to scoff at."

"Since when have you been worried about Rebs? Maybe you should worry more about Union casualties— close to five thousand, they're saying, or about a thousand less than the Rebs. Which means one hell of a lot of men dead, wounded, captured, et cetera. And for what?"

Bronwen stared at him, taken aback by his bitter tone. "For *what?*"

"For nothing! Rebs retreated to where they had been originally, couple miles east of here, and the Yanks went nowhere either. Both armies in the same damn places they started, eleven thousand men later."

"My God!"

"God, as far as I know, was not in command. But then, neither was our self-anointed savior McClellan. No, true to form, Young Napoleon was snug in his bed during the whole messy to-do."

Bronwen could find no response, and for once O'Hara did not take advantage of it.

Instead; he asked, "Okay, what's the story with your brother?"

She was so fearful for Seth, and O'Hara looked so uncharacteristically somber, that while she still did not completely trust him, she decided to risk telling him. Rhys Bevan had already given him part of it anyway.

"And so," she finished with the little she knew, "the fact that they now have him in chains looks bad."

"I agree. And you probably won't have to wait long before finding out *how* bad."

"I've seen the Libby warehouse and I'd say escape from it would be difficult. But he needs to be taken out of there somehow, and quickly!"

"If they have him in chains, they're not likely to invite you in there with a saw and a getaway horse, Red."

She shouldn't mention Lincoln's friend James Quiller. Her work for the president had to remain clandestine, and she was positive the only other person who knew about it, Rhys Bevan, would not have told O'Hara. Not that it mattered, because O'Hara had been sent to Richmond, or so he had claimed, to help free the tobacco.

"I've had dangled before me a proposition," she told him. "I don't know what it includes yet, but British intelligence agent Colonel Dorian de Warde—"

"De Warde?" O'Hara interrupted.

"Do you know him?"

"Not personally, I don't. Bevan told me this Brit is the one who needs to get his tobacco out of Richmond. Turns out I already knew de Warde's name. Remember in Norfolk, when the Rebs pulled out?"

"I'm not likely to forget it." But O'Hara presumably should know nothing about the *Monitor* plot that had been foiled there, since Gustavus Fox, the navy's assistant secretary, had exacted a pledge of silence from her regarding the navy's part in it.

O'Hara went on, "You couldn't know this, Red, since you weren't in the thick of things, but that day a blockade-runner was spotted hightailing it out of the Chesapeake Bay. After a U.S. Navy ship was ordered to capture it, and did, this blockade-runner was caught red-handed with a full hold of cotton headed for Britain. And guess who's name appeared on the cargo manifest?"

"De Warde's?"

"The same. Of course there's no crime in simply buying cotton. But before the captain of the blockade-runner could be questioned about the shipment, where it originated and who was paying his salary, he allegedly tried to escape. And was shot. Dead."

"That sounds like something de Warde would do to silence a source," Bronwen remarked. "But as it happens, I know de Warde was not on a ship that day."

"How do you know?"

"Because he was in Norfolk," she hedged. "Although that doesn't mean he couldn't have had a hand in it."

"I doubt that," said O'Hara, eyeing her narrowly.

"Why?"

"I was at Fort Monroe when the blockade-runner was towed into port with its dead captain. The one who had ordered him shot was a U.S. naval officer."

"Who was it?"

"Don't remember the name."

"And the captain of the blockade-runner?"

"Never knew his name."

"O'Hara, can you find out? Both names?"

"Probably. Why?"

"I need to know everything I can about de Warde's Confederate connections."

A clock began chiming in another room, and O'Hara got to his feet, apparently to find it. When he came back into the kitchen, he said, "Where are you staying in Richmond?"

"Why do you need to know?"

"Because I'm staying with you."

"The devil you are!"

"Red, we loiter here any longer and we risk getting caught—there's a curfew in effect, as if you didn't know."

Bronwen knew, but had not kept track of the time and didn't want to admit it. She stood up and started toward the door. "You can't stay with me, O'Hara. Find other lodgings."

He suddenly strode across the floor, swinging an arm around her shoulders in a vise-like grip. It was so unexpected that Bronwen was taken utterly by surprise. She tried to jerk away, but had forgotten how strong he was, and his arm only tightened.

His face came within inches from hers when he said, "Climb down off that high horse, my girl. You need help, and lodgings are at a premium in this city. Besides which, Bevan sent me here with orders to help get that tobacco transported, and I intend to do it. Especially since West Virginia may be in the scheme of things."

"Fine, so—"

He clapped a hand over her mouth and held it there.

"I'm not finished, Red! Suppose you just remove from that hard head of yours any idea that you are so damn desirable that I would risk my job by ravishing you. You aren't, and I wouldn't. Hell, I'd sooner take on that mangy cat over there!"

His puckish smile, as he released her, bared even, white teeth, and his breath held the scent of chocolate.

Bronwen snatched the cloak and wordlessly yanked open the door. No matter how unpleasant the reality, she needed O'Hara.

21

Spies were there who for gold were ready at any moment to deliver the city into the hands of our enemies.

—Sallie Brock Putnam, Richmond, 1862

Military Tribunal, Richmond

"This tribunal is convened to determine the guilt or innocence of Second Lieutenant Seth Llyr, United States Army, on the charge of espionage. Let the record show that the presiding military commission is composed of three ranking officers in the service of the Confederate States of America. Let the record also show that defense counsel Lieutenant T. J. Oates, Confederate Army of Northern Virginia, represents the accused. Counselor, how does the accused plead?"

"He pleads not guilty, sir."

"The prosecution may proceed. Captain Rogers?"

"May it please the commission, the accused Lieutenant Llyr was placed under arrest by Richmond provost marshal General John Winder. Prior to that time, the accused had been detained as a prisoner of war. General Winder received notification that Lieutenant Llyr is a member of an espionage unit operating under the auspices of the Federal Treasury Department; therefore he is not entitled to the customary protection afforded prisoners of war. Sub-sequent investigation has disclosed overwhelming evidence to support the espionage charge."

"The commission will decide whether the evidence is overwhelming, Captain Rogers. Continue."

"Yes, sir."

Seth looked at defense counsel seated beside him, but First Lieutenant T. J. Oates, probably four or five years older than himself, determinedly stared straight ahead. Prior to today, Seth had seen the man only once.

On that occasion, after Seth had been brought into a room used as a holding cell in Libby, Oates had immediately announced, "I'm not going to ask if you are guilty."

"Okay, but I'm not," Seth had replied.

"I was ordered to take this assignment," Oates had gone on without pause, "despite my objections to defending an enemy spy. My only recommendation to you, Llyr, is to plead guilty and throw yourself on the mercy of the commission. The evidence against you is substantial."

"Then it's either circumstantial or fabricated evidence. I'm not a spy."

"You know something about the law?" Oates said, eyeing Seth even more skeptically.

"I was taking preliminary law courses in college when I enlisted."

"Meaning civilian law," Oates said. "This is a military tribunal you're facing, and it's altogether a different arena."

" 'Arena' seems to be the right word. You're telling me I'm to be tossed to the lions in spite of what the facts may be."

"No, I'm telling you they have the facts."

"There *aren't* any facts to prove I was spying, because I wasn't."

"I expect that's what all spies say. But this city anticipates being attacked momentarily by your army, Llyr, and people believe they see enemy spies everywhere they turn. You couldn't have picked a single worse time to get captured."

By then Seth had guessed what really lay behind the accusation: it was Bronwen the Confederates had targeted. Once he had seen this, he also saw that his hands were tied. He had no way of knowing whether his sister had been seized and was now in custody, but if she was, the Confederates were likely using him as a tool to convict her. Which meant he could not say anything in his own defense without possibly endangering her life as well as his own.

He had asked Oates, "Can I be forced to testify?"

"If you don't, it will be seen as an admission of guilt. Not that I think it matters," Oates had answered bluntly.

"Haven't you people down here read the Constitution?"

"If you're referring to the Fifth Amendment protection against self-incrimination, Llyr, I just told you this won't be a civilian court but a military tribunal operating within the common laws of war. Even if it weren't, Richmond is under martial law, which means written law has no authority here. Finally, what you are relying on is the *United States* Constitution."

On that note, Oates had picked up his unopened valise and had left.

Now prosecutor Rogers was placing into evidence a statement made in a prior deposition by one Private Billy Harkness, who had fought at Williamsburg. The grounds for this private having been deposed were that he was serving in the field and could not appear here in person.

At first Seth did not even recognize the name, not until the prosecutor read: "We was going along to the camp, when that there Yankee spy attacked me. Grabbed my gun and swung it at me, and just about busted my knees, he did. And for no good reason."

Seth glanced at Oates and received a shrug that said

that Billy couldn't be cross-examined if he were not here.

The prosecutor now asked permission to introduce another deposition; this one made by Major General Daniel H. Hill. "General Hill," Rogers said dramatically, "is engaged in defending his country against its invaders, and thus could not be present today."

"Proceed, Captain Rogers."

General Hill's statement, which more or less corroborated Billy Harkness's, included what prosecutor Rogers termed "irrefutable evidence against the accused. General Hill states here in his deposition that 'The prisoner Llyr must have been acting as a courier. Subsequent to his capture, we found on his person an order to Union general Hancock from his superior, General Sumner. The order directed Hancock *once again* to withdraw from his position west of Cub Creek dam, which indicated to me that it had not been the first order so directing Hancock. In retrospect, it was Hancock's failure to withdraw his troops that led to their slaughter of the Fifth North Carolina regiment, one of the most awful things I ever saw,' concluded General Hill."

Seth sat rigid in the silence that followed what even he could acknowledge had been, from General Hill's point of view, an accurate statement.

One of the commission's officers now asked, "How does General Hill's testimony affirm the guilt of the accused, Captain Rogers?"

"Sir, it is plainly evident from General Sumner's order to Hancock that Union command was not in possession of crucial information regarding Confederate positions or troop strength. Had it been, General Hancock, with his superior position, would almost certainly not have been ordered to withdraw. Once Union command recognized their deficiency, it became a situation that called for immediate remedy. And Lieutenant Llyr, in his capacity as an espionage agent, was dispatched to gather the information needed."

Seth nearly groaned, but clenched his jaw to restrain himself. Oates shot him a dark look.

"At this time I should like to remind the commission," said prosecutor Rogers, "that the Union's lack of intelligence information, and their urgent need to acquire it, came about because they had recently lost four Pinkerton agents operating here in Richmond. Three of those agents are now imprisoned, and the fourth, Timothy Webster, was hanged little over a month ago—or, tellingly, *five days before the Williamsburg engagement!* Webster had been found guilty of the very crime of which Lieutenant Llyr now stands accused."

At this, Oates stirred himself enough to raise an objection. Although it was sustained, Seth knew the damage done by linking him to Webster was irreparable.

The prosecutor began reading yet another deposed statement, this one from a Sergeant Bellows: "When I first saw Llyr he was sitting and talking to a young boy. The boy was dying, and me and my men didn't know then he was a drummer with the Fifth North Carolina. When we found out, and I asks Llyr why he stood on there after the fighting was over, he tells me the boy didn't want to be left alone. And I believed him."

The prosecutor now turned to Seth saying, "I must add, Lieutenant Llyr, that it takes a man of particularly low character to interrogate a dying boy."

Seth ignored Oates's glare and looked Rogers straight in the eye, anger keeping his spine rigid and his shoulders squared.

Prosecutor Rogers turned back to the commission members. "I now call General John Winder to testify."

After establishing Winder's credentials, among them his graduation from West Point and commission as brigadier general, Rogers asked him, "Have you questioned the accused, General?"

"I have. He refused to give anything other than his

name, his New York regiment, and the denial that he was a spy."

"In your experience, General Winder, is that the typical behavior of an innocent man?"

"No, it's not, and I—"

To Seth's surprise, Oates interrupted with an objection. When it was overruled, Winder went on to state that he had never known any prisoner to refuse the opportunity of explaining himself, even if the explanation was untrue.

Oates shifted to give Seth an I-told-you-so look, but rose to his feet.

"Do you care to cross-examine the witness, Lieutenant Oates?"

"Yes, sir, I do. General Winder, how many prisoners charged with espionage had you questioned before Lieutenant Llyr?"

"Well . . . none."

"So your testimony that the accused displayed behavior not in keeping with innocence has no basis, correct?"

"I'd say it's obvious on the face of it."

"That was not my question. Is it possible that by his silence the accused was simply refusing to incriminate himself?"

"Lieutenant Oates," a member of the commission said, "Your attention to duty here is commendable, but the accused will have the right to inform this body if that is the case."

"I recognize that, sir, but if he refuses to speak, it should not in the eyes of the law be necessarily construed as guilt."

"Where did y'all attend law school, Lieutenant Oates?"

"Yale, sir."

"That will be all, Lieutenant."

Seth gave Oates another sideways glance and caught a barely perceptible smile.

After the commission members conferred briefly among themselves, the major who appeared to be in charge said to Seth, "We have some few questions, Lieutenant Llyr. You have pled not guilty to the charge of which you are accused. You surely are aware that it is a charge of the most serious nature. In light of that, and of the testimony presented here today, do you wish to change your plea?"

"No, I do not."

"Very well. Let the record show that the accused was given the opportunity to change his plea and refused to do so."

The major turned to the officer on his left and asked him something inaudible, receiving a brisk "Yes, sir," before he turned again to face Seth. "Lieutenant Llyr, in addition to the evidence presented here today, it has been brought to the attention of this commission that you have a family member in the employ of the United States Treasury. Is this not true?"

Seth felt the air rush from his lungs as if they had been punctured. He had still been hoping against hope that they did not know about Bronwen. Everything else here had consisted of circumstantial evidence, no matter how damning it might appear, and up until now there might have been a whisper of a chance for him to convince these men of that. Now he could do nothing because whatever he said might be twisted, as his own actions at Williamsburg had been twisted, and used to incriminate his sister.

"The accused is ordered to answer the question!"

"I cannot say," Seth answered. He sensed rather than saw Lieutenant Oates move in his chair.

"And isn't it true that your sister is part of an intelligence unit, which operates for the express purpose of gathering information to be used against the Confederacy?"

"I cannot say."

"And have you not been, and are you not presently, a member of the same organization to which your sister belongs?"

The question, Seth thought with an inner grimace, was constructed like the old trick one: *Have you stopped beating your wife?* Damned if he had and damned if he hadn't. "I cannot say."

The major straightened and leaned forward across the table. "Do you have anything at all to add in your own defense, Lieutenant Llyr?"

"Yes. I am innocent of the charge."

"Let the record show," stated the major, sitting back in the chair, his face flushed with what had to be anger, "that the accused has refused to provide answers to the questions put to him by this commission. And that he has also refused the opportunity to rebut the charges with any evidence of his innocence."

The commission members rose and left the room.

"You are a damn fool, Llyr," said Oates. "On top of everything else, you managed to add insult to injury by not appealing to them as fellow officers."

"They're not United States officers. Besides, it wouldn't have done one shred of good, Oates, and you know it. Why did you even bother with that last objection?"

"I don't like Winder."

"I've met worse. He could've been tougher on me in Libby than he has been. Somehow I don't think this farce was his idea."

"It is not a farce! You look guilty as sin."

"*Look* guilty? What's this, Oates—are you having some doubts?"

"Not anymore. I might have had a few reservations if it were only a case of your refusal to answer. I might even have respected a man who wouldn't betray his country or take part in what he saw as a kangaroo court. But how the hell, Llyr, could you take advantage of a dying boy?"

"How the hell could you people send onto a battlefield a boy so young he didn't even know why he was there? He was just a little kid, Oates—younger than my own brother—whose greatest fear was that his father might think he'd been a coward *because* he was dying! So don't talk to me about taking advantage."

Oates had turned to look directly at him and was beginning to frown. Then he shook his head. "No, your sister was the finishing stroke. For God's sake, Llyr, she's a Union *spy?*" As if to himself he muttered, "They could have at least warned me."

Seth stared at him dumbfounded. Oates wasn't told? Did that mean Bronwen had not been captured? Maybe. Or at least not yet, because if she was somewhere out there and knew he was in here, she would move heaven and earth to try to free him, and might well get herself caught in the trying. She was daring, and she was loyal. Always had been.

Coming to mind was a winter day, years ago, when a young neighborhood girl had broken through ice on the Erie Canal. Bronwen—at the time not much older than the hapless girl—had been the only one of a frantic group rushing to the towpath who had kept her head and acted quickly. Dragging the long, fallen limb of a river birch, she had told Seth and others to hold it fast. Only her agility and light weight, and her sheer grit, had allowed her to crawl along the limb, dipping frequently into the icy water, to grab and clutch the drowning girl's hands. After both had been hauled back to safety, Bronwen had ignored everyone's admiration. She had refused a thankful father's offer of his gold watch. Her sole comment had been, "Lizabeth's my friend. She was 'bout to die, so I went and stopped her."

The military commission members were now returning to stand behind their long table. Seth calculated their deliberations had taken less than five minutes.

Oates dragged him to his feet, as the major began speaking.

"This commission finds the accused, Second Lieutenant Seth Llyr, guilty of the charge of espionage. The sentence is death by hanging. Execution is to take place at sunrise on June 27.

"This commission is now adjourned."

22

The laws are silent in times of war.

—Cicero

Richmond

The climbing sun slanted through the hotel room window where Bronwen stood staring out, seeing only an image of her brother held in chains. When she had joined Treasury's special unit, it had not occurred to her that her own family would become vulnerable because of it, or that this Southern war of secession would grow such long and treacherous tentacles.

The scrape of a key in the lock, although she had been expecting it, made her whirl anxiously toward the door. It had opened a crack, and O'Hara was edging inside, needing to flatten himself to sidle around the heavy bureau that the night before Bronwen had insisted be shifted to stand in front of it.

"You mean to tell me you move this behemoth every night?" O'Hara had asked her, his shoulder shoving the bureau sideways with relative ease.

Bronwen had shrugged to avoid answering.

"You know, Red, I'd never have suspected you of tidiness, but this room looks as if you've never used it."

She had given him another shrug.

O'Hara appeared to be none the worse for having spent the night on the floor, sprawled across a thick, costly Spotswood carpet, but Bronwen noticed that his expression was less annoyingly cheerful than usual. Eyeing him more closely, she saw that he actually looked grim. "O'Hara, what's happened?"

"Picked up a morning newspaper in the lobby, and you'd better brace yourself, Red, 'cause it is *not* good news," he told her, tossing the paper on the bed. "In fact, I'd say it's about as bad as it gets!"

Bronwen seized the paper, collapsing to the edge of the goose-down mattress when she saw the boldface headline.

YANKEE SPY SENTENCED TO DEATH

> Richmond provost marshal General John Winder has disclosed that Union officer Seth Llyr, a prisoner of war housed in Libby Prison, appeared yesterday before a military tribunal. Llyr was found guilty of espionage and sentenced to hang on June 27.

Bronwen's hands grasped the paper in a death grip. "No! They can't *do* this!"

"They can do anything they choose," said O'Hara. "Read on."

> Llyr was captured following last month's engagement at Williamsburg. "He was caught prowling near a Confederate encampment," Winder said, "hours after the battle had taken place. Obviously he had been scouting the area for information on troop movements and numbers."
>
> When asked why there had been no prior

announcement of the charges pending against Llyr, military prosecutor Captain C. Rogers stated, "It was feared that this information might unduly alarm Richmond citizens. The decision was made to withhold it from the public until the scope of the crime committed had been determined. We now have every reason to believe that Lieutenant Llyr acted alone in this instance, but he is likely part of an extensive espionage organization." General Winder went on to explain that spies like Llyr pose a serious threat to the security of . . .

Bronwen hurled the newspaper at the wall. "This is ridiculous! Absolute hogwash! They can't have had grounds to even charge Seth with spying, much less to convict him."

"You sure about that?"

"Of course I am. Other than that absurd comment of Winder's about Seth 'prowling' after the battle—when he was probably just wandering around dazed, or lost in some infernal woods—what did they have? Nothing! *Nothing!* And don't ask me again if I'm sure, O'Hara. I know my brother. Seth was not spying!"

She slid off the bed and went again to the window, looking down on rain puddles dwindling in the sun on the flat roof of the next building. "They somehow trapped him," she said in a lowered voice, "because Seth could never lie, even when it was stupid to tell the truth."

"So it's not something that runs in the family?"

"This is not a joke! In case you've forgotten, they hanged Timothy Webster!" Bronwen heard her voice crack, and added, "Just go away and leave me alone!"

"Can't do that. You're not thinking clearly enough yet to be left alone, and besides, I've got orders. Now you have a halfway decent brain, Red, so use it! If you're convinced the Confederates had no proof your brother is a spy—"

"They couldn't! Obviously proof doesn't matter to a Confederate military tribunal."

"But what they *did* have was guilt by association. They must have learned you're his sister, and you *are* a spy! Since they haven't been nimble enough to catch you red-handed with the goods, they settled on the next best thing."

"There can't be any true *evidence* involving Seth, or me either, for that matter."

"C'mon, Red, grow up! This is a war zone, my girl, and truth can be twisted here faster than you can sneeze. That newspaper says the Rebel military conducted your brother's trial. Believe me, they wouldn't have bothered unless they planned to convict him."

"I can read, O'Hara, and I can see what they did." She had to admit that his insistent needling was clearing her mind. "But how could Seth even come to their attention?"

"Who knows? Maybe an informer inside the prison. Norris and his gang aren't just sitting around waiting for Lady Luck to drop goodies in their laps."

"It's what I was most afraid of—that Norris would learn of Seth."

"I think you could have counted on that. Especially since they probably want to smoke you out."

Bronwen had resisted putting into words what had been Rhys Bevan's concern. And O'Hara's comment immediately brought to mind de Warde and his tobacco. She turned back to the window.

O'Hara hammered on relentlessly, "That's it, Red! They want to exchange your brother for you. Why else would the Rebels risk having their own captured men falsely accused of spying? They must think this is worth the price, because the uproar over Timothy Webster's execution brought some strong threats from the Feds about retaliation. Hell, if this goes on, hanging soldiers as spies could get to be daily entertainment. A regular Roman circus."

Bronwen spun to face him. "Stop making light of this! I may be terrified, O'Hara, but I am not dim-witted."

"Glad to hear it. And it's too late now to make some noble but moronic sacrifice, so I trust you're not considering it."

"I'm not."

"That's good, because you know too much about Federal intelligence—such as it is—and I'd have to shoot you."

Bronwen walked past him and threw herself on the bed.

"In which case," he went on, "you'd bleed all over this expensive rug. And who would pay for it?"

Her mind racing, she murmured, "De Warde."

"The Brit's that generous?"

"He's been pressing me to talk about the tobacco, so to play for time, I agreed to contact him within twenty-four hours. That was early last night. Now suddenly this newspaper horror tale about Seth appears."

"And the plot thickens."

Yes, it was just too convenient, she thought. Someone must have handed Seth to Winder. Winder then naturally informed Norris. Norris passed it on to de Warde of British intelligence—maybe to demonstrate Confederate efficiency in uncovering a dangerous spy. But it might have been the other way around, and de Warde had been the informer. And while he could not know that Lincoln was prepared to appease Britain by looking the other way while its tobacco shipped north, de Warde *did* know she had access to the president. It was after the oblique reference to the tobacco at dinner with Quiller that de Warde immediately proposed to bargain—with what? If he had either learned about Seth or discovered Seth's identity himself . . . did he now want her collaboration in saving his tobacco in exchange for somehow saving her brother? A devil's bargain to be sure, but not one she would turn down if it could free Seth.

"O'Hara, I need a gun—"

"Suicide's not your style, Red. And there'd still be the problem of the rug."

"—small enough to be concealed in a lady's purse, but large enough to be effective."

The rented buggy jounced and rattled as Bronwen uneasily guided the old livery horse along a narrow, winding road, just one of many in the park-like setting of Hollywood Cemetery. Situated west of the city and overlooking the James River, Hollywood was a maze of carriage lanes and footpaths, the very reason she had chosen it, but now she worried she might have taken a wrong turn.

To avoid the heat of midday, burials took place in the evening or early morning, so this afternoon was quiet and cedar-scented, and very few people were strolling the hills and soft green glades that were shaded by holly trees. The cemetery had been the only place Bronwen could imagine in Richmond that would be secluded but still afford some safety. The note she had given a Spotswood bellboy to deliver had named the time and the summit point of the cemetery.

She reasoned it would be a spot open enough for her to see de Warde coming, and anyone else as well.

The buggy climbed a shallow rise lined with cedar and pine, but just ahead the trees began to thin. When she saw the summit, open except for a few spreading oaks, she reined in the horse beside a low brick wall. After climbing down from the buggy, she tossed the reins over a shaft of marble statuary, and then smoothed the skirt of Chantal Dupont's pale yellow frock before plucking from the buggy seat a large-brimmed hat.

Having decided that she could not credibly negotiate with the urbane de Warde when looking like a chimney sweep, she had sent O'Hara to the shops. Her mistake had been telling him only that the hat must be large enough to conceal her face from a distance. He had returned with an extravagant, cream-colored straw the size of a serving platter, trimmed with an opulent green silk bow that trailed long, green ribbons. There could not be many in impoverished Richmond who could have afforded it, adding yet another twisted thread to a situation enmeshed in painful irony. Here she was, the guilty one, gussied up like Marie Antoinette on her way to a ball, while Seth, the blameless one, sat in chains awaiting a hangman.

"I've changed my mind," O'Hara had said while circling her before she left the hotel, his turquoise eyes glowing with uncommon but unmistakable warmth. "I think I'll ravish you after all."

"O'Hara, just hand me the gun and spyglass."

Now checking that the small, newly designed double derringer made no telltale bulge, she looped the drawstrings of her purse over her arm and lifted the spyglass. Seeing no one, she edged along the wall, stopping again to scan the hill. She had deliberately arrived here early, but began to worry again that she was in the wrong place.

Just as the likelihood of de Warde also arriving early occurred to her, with the consequence that he might now be watching her, she saw a flash of light from one of the oaks. The glint of sun on a glass? She cautiously edged forward again.

The Englishman stepped from behind the oak. "Good day, Miss Larkin. How enchanting you look."

De Warde's gray morning suit looked as if it had just left a presser's hand, and his white linen was spotless. Held at his side as he walked toward her was the walking stick, its silver ferrule flashing when it caught the filtered sunlight. He never failed to remind Bronwen of a bird of prey, a sleek and cunning falcon or a hawk. A shudder ran down her spine, and only the fact that he could hold the key to her brother's fate made her resolutely stand her ground.

"Shall we stroll while we talk?" he asked her, making

Bronwen want to scan the glossy-leaved holly for signs of protruding gun barrels.

She must have telegraphed her distrust, because de Warde said, "My dear girl, you should put aside your suspicions, else we cannot have a fruitful discussion. You must believe that you are safer than you have ever been in Richmond. On this I pledge my word of honor."

"You forget, Colonel de Warde, that I've heard your word pledged before, so you'll understand if I hold onto a fair amount of skepticism."

His black eyes narrowed. "You have misjudged me. I give my word very seldom, for the simple reason that I cannot always afford to keep it. However, in this case I can assure you that for the moment you are not in danger, the most compelling reason for it being that my Southern acquaintances have no knowledge of this meeting. But if they did, and were determined to dispatch either one of us, they would more than likely strike me first as the bigger target. And they would be fools indeed to shoot the goose that may lay a golden egg."

Bronwen almost smiled at the supreme self-confidence that allowed a falcon to call itself a goose.

"A smile," said de Warde approvingly, "would be much more becoming to you, and would remind me of your charming aunt. I trust Miss Tryon is well?"

"We're not here to discuss the health of my aunt," Bronwen said, her eyes darting around them warily.

"There is a vine-covered arbor over there," de Warde said, gesturing with the ebony stick, "where you may feel more at ease."

Bronwen had spotted it earlier, but since he now suggested it, she said, "No, I like the looks of that gazebo on the slope."

"A prudent choice," de Warde said.

As they started toward the latticework pavilion, he offered his arm, smiling ruefully when she refused it. It galled her that she could not voice her suspicion of him as possibly the one who had brought Seth's identity to Winder's attention. But there was nothing to be gained by accusing him now and much to be lost by showing her hand too early.

"It is a shame indeed," he said, "that the world has become so barbarous that one as young as you must be sent to war on American soil."

He was reminding her who, by virtue of seniority, was in charge here, she thought with irritation, but refrained from pointing out that his own country had decades before now sent younger than she to war on this soil. And that she and de Warde were here precisely because Britain was weighing the merits of doing so again.

"Never mistake it, my dear girl," he added with a melodramatic flourish, "you are a warrior as surely as those who toil in the trenches."

When they reached the gazebo, Bronwen risked de Warde's mockery by raising her spyglass. He merely gave her a benign smile. Once inside the three-sided latticework frame, it would be nearly impossible to target her. The fourth side opened onto a grassed slope with the rapids of the James tumbling below it, the sublime beauty of the cemetery contrasting starkly with the melancholy use to which it was now being put ever more frequently.

De Warde seated himself on a bench, while Bronwen remained on her feet. She might need to make a fast escape, and standing kept her in control.

"My dear girl, if you are still concerned about your safety," De Warde offered, "why don't you remove the weapon from your purse and thus be better prepared. Remember that it would take the same amount of time for me to ready my stick."

"At last," she said, "we have a straightforward statement. Since I'm willing to put my cards on the table, what is your proposal?"

If she had startled him by her abruptness, he covered

it by agreeing. "Very well, I have a troublesome matter before me. As do you."

"You can't ship your tobacco to Britain."

"And you cannot let your brother hang for espionage he did not commit."

This stopped her momentarily, but she didn't ask how he knew of Seth's innocence. It would appear weak and allow him to take the upper hand. "You're right. I'm not going to let him hang."

"What do you have to offer?" asked de Warde, surprising her for once with his directness.

"In return for what?"

"For your brother's liberation and his safe passage out of Richmond."

"Is that your offer?"

"It may be. I am eagerly awaiting yours."

"Your tobacco's removal from Richmond." She kept her ace concealed.

"It must first be released from the warehouse."

"I think you can find a Confederate official who's willing to make that possible," Bronwen said, "if only to keep the British lion well-fed and friendly. I believe Secretary of State Judah Benjamin approved the recent change of warehouse requested by your embassy."

De Warde smiled. "You have done your research well. And you are correct. Mr. Benjamin is a pragmatic man. He knows that nothing is of greater importance to me than the happiness of my queen."

Bronwen ignored the puffery, saying, "Since the Confederates have no legitimate charge against my brother, other than the fact that he *is* my brother—"

"Which is quite enough. Forgive me for interrupting, Miss Llyr, but legitimacy has nothing whatsoever to do with this."

So he was conceding the charges against Seth had been fabricated. "I'm aware of that," she replied.

His eyes widened slightly with surprise before he said,

"Good. Then we'll not waste time with recriminations that will benefit us not at all. However, I should add that I have recently seen your brother Seth. He lacks your guile, my dear, but is similarly loyal."

He paused, obviously waiting for a question, and she had to struggle to resist asking if Seth was all right. More and more it sounded as if de Warde could have been responsible for her brother's peril in order to set up this opportunity. He must also know that she suspected him of it.

"I regret to observe, Miss Llyr, that you seem to have lost a certain attractive impetuosity. A year ago you would have leapt at the chance to learn—"

She interrupted, "How can you affect Seth's release?"

"You must trust me to find the way."

"I need more concrete assurance than *that!* Or your tobacco can just sit there and rot while you and the Confederate government play hide-and-seek over British intervention—or rather, interference—in this war. Better still, that tobacco can burn to cinders, torched by a vengeful Confederacy just before the Federals capture Richmond."

She saw the instant she struck a nerve. There had been a subtle shift in the black eyes. "You cannot get that tobacco out of Virginia without help, de Warde."

"I'm afraid that is overstating your case. The blockade-runners are—"

"Excuse me, but you have already tried running the blockade. Your cotton didn't get through, did it? So you've tested the waters."

He smiled in response, but not fast enough for her to miss the fact that he had been caught unawares.

"Of course you are in error," he said. "Where would you have received such misinformation?"

For him to ask meant something had gone badly awry with that cotton shipment. Bronwen reminded herself that O'Hara needed to find out more about that naval incident.

"Shall we return to the tobacco," she evaded, "since McClellan is prepared to advance on Richmond at any time now?"

"Perhaps, but the South has a new general who has yet to show his mettle. General Lee may be made of sterner stuff than your McClellan."

"Lee would need to be a wizard to improve the plight of your tobacco," she said quickly, fearing he might turn this into a waiting game. "And as you said in your message, time is running out."

"Your brother is to be executed on the twenty-seventh, I believe?"

Bronwen fought down a surge of panic, making herself say crisply, "I am prepared to address your tobacco situation if I am satisfied with the terms."

"First, Miss Llyr, shall we review the details to make certain we understand one another? The Confederate government, even if it allows the tobacco out of the Richmond warehouse, will never allow it out of Virginia, and the Federal government will not allow it past their blockade. That is the dilemma for which I am seeking relief. I assumed you understood that from your comment during the conversation with Mr. Quiller."

She scanned their surroundings. While she did not want to stay here any longer than necessary, she needed to learn, if possible, something about Quiller. She had left several messages for him and was troubled by his lack of response.

"Speaking of Mr. Quiller, I've not had a chance to talk with him recently," she said, also believing she should at least try to include Lincoln's friend in this maneuver. "He had indicated interest in the French tobacco, and perhaps they, the French, might also be interested in . . . an arrangement."

"*Indeed not!*" de Warde responded. "The French would insist, as they always do, upon complicating matters far beyond reason. No, we shall not deal with the

French. And please believe me, my dear, your M. Quiller is of no earthly use to you."

This startled her, as did de Warde's vehemence, which was out of character. It most likely stemmed from some tangled political dispute, rather than suggesting that in the past day or two some economic disaster had befallen Quiller. But this was no time to question it.

"All right, de Warde; let's imagine I could guarantee that your tobacco will leave Confederate Virginia and, without Federal interference, be allowed to head north and into Canada. You do remember that route, don't you? If not, does the port of Oswego on Lake Ontario jog your memory?"

He gave her a dry smile of concession. "Ah, yes, Miss Llyr, you have caused me some inconvenience in the past, which is why I am delighted that we are to be allies."

"Don't be too delighted yet. And the word 'allies' doesn't appeal to me."

"Mutual benefactors, perhaps? Am I to assume that you have, shall we say, *permission* to make this offer in good faith?"

"If I make it, you can assume it."

"Excellent. Then let us also imagine that I can guarantee your brother will travel north with that tobacco."

"He needs to be gotten out of Libby first! How can you arrange that? And don't tell me again that I simply should trust you!"

"I have some connections. A padlock key, lost by a careless guard, could allow your brother to slip his chains. He could then be put on the wagons . . . there *will* be wagons to transport the tobacco?"

"The details, de Warde," she said, managing a faint smile, "are my business."

She caught a hint of exasperation when he said, "I must at least insist on knowing where the tobacco will be taken before heading north—with your brother, of course."

"It will initially go to West Virginia."

"Ah, yes, I am acquainted with that controversial region. How remarkable, Miss Llyr. I am impressed beyond measure."

"Keep in mind, de Warde, that the permission granted can be withdrawn anywhere along the tobacco's Northern route."

"It is hardly necessary to remind me of that. Trust is essential between partners. Now, do we have a bargain?"

Bronwen answered only, "I will alert those necessary to make this transfer work smoothly."

"Your need to act quickly," de Warde said, "is even more compelling than mine, so let us begin the process at once. You may reach me at the hotel when you are ready to proceed." He rose from the bench and extended his hand.

She did not respond.

"Come, come," said de Warde, smiling as if he refused to take offense. "Instead of ensuring your brother's life, you behave as if you are making a pact with the devil."

"My thoughts exactly."

"But, dear girl, what choice do you have?"

He stepped from the gazebo and began walking across the slope, but he suddenly turned to say, "Do be cautious, Miss Larkin. I believe I detect a wily snake here amongst Eden's greenery."

He bowed and continued on, but Bronwen noted that his walking stick was now held at a different angle, its silver ferrule cap between his fingers, ready to snatch off if he needed to fire.

She drew the derringer from her purse, and with the spyglass searched the surrounding area before edging warily out of the gazebo. Heading back to the buggy, she raised the derringer only once, and that was when she caught a slight movement among the lower branches of a holly tree.

Her gun hand dropped to her side when her spyglass found among the glossy leaves a glitter of turquoise.

Had de Warde been warning her generally, or warning her explicitly of O'Hara? Or had the Englishman merely been sowing discord and suspicion from sheer force of habit?

Whichever, there was no turning back now, not with Seth's execution date looming so near. Unfortunately de Warde had been right on the mark about one thing: What choice did she have?

23

*As I think both parties are wrong in this fratri-
cidal war, there is nothing comforting even in the
hope God may prosper the right, for I see no right
in the matter.*

—Mary Custis Lee, 1861

Richmond

Bronwen, after returning the horse and buggy to the livery, was taking a circuitous route back to the Spotswood
when she paused, ostensibly to peer at the coils of plaited
rope displayed in the window of a dry-goods store. For
several minutes she had sensed a shadow behind her, but
now could glimpse no one reflected in the window glass.
So either her imagination was too active or the one tailing
her was too good. If the latter, it could mean that her
shadow was O'Hara.

She had not made up her mind to confront him about
following her to the meeting with de Warde, but guessed
this tactic would not yield much information. Better to
wait and see if he voluntarily admitted it.

As she gazed into the shop window, darting furtive
sideways glances at the many soldiers and few shoppers
on the street, she also decided that the room at the Spotswood was becoming a luxury she could ill afford. Especially given de Warde's earlier comment, "this Quiller is

of no earthly use to you," which implied the business-man's failure to answer her messages meant something more than simply a lack of time. With Seth in such danger she had no time to investigate Quiller's absence, but the reason for the hotel room had been access to him and, more important, as a message drop. It would likely be tempting fate to keep the room longer than necessary to complete plans for the tobacco's transfer and to notify de Warde.

She took several steps past the window, hesitated, and then, as if impulsively changing her mind, turned back and boldly entered the dry-goods store. Some short time later, she emerged through its back door into an alleyway, carrying a new and bulging duffel bag. Richmond shop-keepers, it seemed, still eagerly welcomed Federal money. By backtracking through side streets, she reached a rear-alley entrance of the four-story office building adjacent to the Spotswood. Once inside, she strolled along the ground floor hallway until she reached the stairway, and then be-gan a familiar climb.

When O'Hara finally returned to the hotel room, Bronwen had been waiting there for several hours, growing more edgy by the minute. His expression, as it had been that morning, was far more somber than usual.

"I've got some news," he told her, while sinking into a plump, velvet-upholstered chair.

"About my brother?"

He shook his head. "Not him. How was the meeting with the Brit?"

Unnerved by the long wait, and despite her earlier res-olution, she retorted, "You ought to know!"

To her surprise, he responded sheepishly, "You caught me, I take it?"

"I could hardly miss you, O'Hara. I thought you were better at surveillance than that!"

"I usually am. And I agree it was rotten cover. That

holly's got sharp-pointed leaves—every time I moved I got stabbed. Anyway, you and de Warde walked too far away for me to overhear."

"Why the devil were you there?" she asked, feeling somewhat less suspicious because of his ready confession, but wondering if he might have made it for just that reason. "Couldn't trust me to take care of myself?"

"Just wanted to make sure de Warde had no evil motive, such as snatching you for Norris. I don't trust him."

"Who does? But I didn't think—to use his words— that he would shoot the goose who could lay a golden egg."

"Did you? Lay an egg?" he asked, at last smiling.

"I held out the prospect. And we need to start work on it right now."

"I said my news doesn't concern your brother, but—"

"Then can't it wait? There's a mountain of details to climb."

He started to reply, but shrugged and answered, "It can wait."

Earlier, Bronwen had decided it would be safer not to disclose to O'Hara her brother's part in the bargain with de Warde, but she could not openly defy Rhys Bevan's directive to include O'Hara in the tobacco transport. More important, the strategy she was developing could not work without him.

She filled him in as to what she had proposed to de Warde, and added, "He doesn't know the particulars, or that I plan to use a train."

O'Hara was frowning. "Red, I don't think this has a chance. I'd even bet on it! For starters, how many tobacco hogsheads are there to transport?"

Bronwen shrugged. "Millions of dollars' worth."

"Do you know how much a packed hogshead weighs?"

"No. Do you?"

"Anywhere from several hundred to a thousand pounds."

"A *thousand* . . . no, that can't be right!" she protested. "Tobacco is dried by the time it's packed."

"A hogshead is heavy no matter what it holds, and it's too much weight for a man to lift. Can't be done. You've given yourself an impossible assignment here, Red, and from what Rhys Bevan told me, a hell of a lot is riding on it. Like keeping the Redcoats out of our war!"

"O'Hara, you do not have to remind me how crucial this is!" And he didn't even know it was Lincoln who had called for this mission, who trusted her to accomplish it, and who, in the meantime, was holding at bay the acquisitive British Empire.

"I'd say you better leave town fast," O'Hara told her. "In fact, leave the country, leave the world, because you've promised de Warde something you can't deliver!"

"I *have* to deliver!" She managed to catch herself just in time, nearly blurting that her brother's life was also at stake here. But given the way O'Hara was eyeing her, she was afraid he might have guessed it.

In an effort to calm herself, she took a deep breath, then another, before saying, "I passed by that warehouse today, the one holding the British tobacco. Here's what I think *could* work, if you'll listen to me instead of throwing up obstacles."

He regarded her skeptically. "Okay, go ahead. But do you have to keep pacing back and forth?"

She went to stand against the windowsill, talking fast to keep him from interrupting, and with relief saw that he had begun to smile. The smile had broadened by the time she finished.

"Red, you're crazy! Plumb crazy, but your scheme just might work! I said *might*. And what after the tobacco leaves Richmond?"

"Once it's in Union-occupied Virginia it will zigzag north by train to the Baltimore and Ohio line, and then west to your stamping ground of West Virginia. Until Rhys Bevan gets clearance to send it on by rail through

Pennsylvania and New York State, I assume you'll be able to store it in Wheeling?"

"Nothing to it!" he said, with considerably more enthusiasm than he had shown earlier. "The Wheeling surveyor of customs is Thomas Hornbrook, a rabid Union loyalist and guess what else? He's supervisor of the Baltimore and Ohio Railroad there."

Bronwen, still trying to think through a complicated chain of events, asked him, "Wouldn't this Hornbrook have access to boxcars from other eastern rail companies? From, say, the Virginia Central? In large railroad yards there are usually cars from other lines sitting idle on sidings until they're needed for a long haul back."

O'Hara for a moment looked puzzled, but then he chuckled. "I see where you're headed, Red. Damn smart! And you can count on it, because Hornbrook will undoubtedly agree. Hell, he even let the army store kegs of *gunpowder* in the basement of the Custom House. Didn't make Hornbrook any too popular in town. Not that he cared."

"But is the Wheeling Custom House large enough to store those hogsheads? However many there are?"

"Let me take care of that! If the Custom House can't hold them, we can always commandeer the John Street theater-cum-prison. The city's Southern sympathizers call it Lincoln's Bastille—"

"Wait," she interrupted, another link in the chain taking shape. "Does that mean it houses Confederate prisoners? With Confederate *uniforms?*"

"It houses everything!"

As she nodded, he said cheerfully, "What a scheme this is! A something-for-everybody caper! The Confederacy's Judah Benjamin curries favor with Britain by releasing the tobacco from Richmond. Lincoln makes the Brits happy by looking the other way while it travels north. West Virginia scores points with Lincoln so he'll grant it statehood, and you . . . do you get your brother?"

With her mind on what lay ahead, Bronwen answered without thinking, "So de Warde claims."

When she saw O'Hara nod in obvious understanding, she cringed at the thought of Seth's life depending on de Warde, who she knew was untrustworthy, and on O'Hara, who she still feared might be.

He was chuckling again as he said, "The secessionists in Wheeling will hate this idea, so Hornbrook will love it! I'll leave for there tonight."

"Before you go west," she told him, "you need to make a side trip to Washington. Rhys Bevan has to be alerted that de Warde's accepted the offer, and that railroad schedules will need to be arranged accordingly. You also should tell Rhys—and please get this straight, O'Hara, because it's important—that our mutual friend's chum may have gone astray again."

O'Hara gave her a blank look, which somewhat eased Bronwen's concern, but he nodded again. "Okay, and I shouldn't have any trouble leaving Richmond. General Lee has his troops digging earthworks—trenches and redoubts—to hold off the Yankee hordes from the east. Those Reb soldiers are up to their ears in mud, so they won't hear me tiptoeing by. They've taken to calling Lee the 'King of Spades.'"

"How much do you know about him?"

"Enough to think it could be a big mistake to underestimate him. I saw him riding up Church Hill this afternoon, and if appearances count, he looks every inch a commanding general. Handsome man. Has a face with character, the kind that arouses respect from even a cynic like me—as contrasted with our Union counterpart."

"O'Hara, General McClellan is—"

"An ass. Next to Lee, McClellan looks like an ass running against a Thoroughbred."

Bronwen eyed him with annoyance, which admittedly was a more comfortable emotion than suspicion. But she did not have time to concern herself further with O'Hara's loyalty. She wanted him on his way, starting the wheels of the tobacco plan turning.

"Travel to Washington and then to Wheeling as fast as you can," she said, "and . . . oh, hellfire! I've just remembered there's still the problem of Marsh in Chimborazo."

"If you're so damn worried about him, Red, go get him yourself."

"You should have done it before now!"

"How? Maybe lift him out in one of McClellan's surveillance balloons? Besides," O'Hara said, abruptly sobering, "Marshall's not the only one in trouble."

"My brother is—"

"When I came in," he interrupted, "I said there was news."

Bronwen felt a sudden coldness, mostly because of O'Hara's expression. "What kind of news?"

"It's not good. After I returned the horse to the livery—the one I used to follow you to the cemetery—I went down Canal Street to Libby warehouse. Wanted to see if I could find this Chaucer character Elizabeth Van Lew mentioned, and maybe learn something about the prison's layout."

"And?"

"And I found Chaucer, all right. He told me something peculiar had happened a few hours before. Seems an enclosed carriage pulled up to the warehouse entrance, and then it just sat there. When the peddlers came out, somebody inside the carriage called to one of them. This Chaucer thought he heard a voice asking if this peddler wanted some cheap cigars to sell."

Bronwen, already disturbed by a premonition of what was coming, said, "This peddler wasn't . . . tell me it wasn't Natty."

"Afraid so. The kid had no sooner reached the carriage when someone inside it—and Chaucer said he couldn't see who—flung open the door and dragged him into it. The carriage took off hell-for-leather, the kid screeching like a banshee."

Bronwen had dropped to the edge of the bed. "There's only one person in Richmond who could recognize that boy."

"I figured as much."

"But *why?* Why on earth would Bluebell snatch Natty?"

O'Hara shrugged. "I expect she'll let you know."

"Why me?"

"Because she must want something. Why else?"

"You mean such as . . . ransom? That's insane! Bluebell would actually kidnap Natty for ransom money?"

"Why are you even asking—I thought you said she was *insane!* And frankly, Red, I think it'll be one hell of a lucky day if money is *all* she wants!"

Joshua Jared had gripped the side of the carriage as it went lurching around the street corner, swaying so precariously it had thrown the bound boy up against him. He heard a muffled snarl of anger, but the gag tied over the youngster's mouth had at least eliminated the worst of his screaming, a sound like that of a hog being slaughtered. The boy had not seemed so much frightened as enraged. Jared thought it a curious response from one so young after having been plucked without warning from the road.

It remained unclear to Jared just why this tactic had been necessary.

"Because he's a guttersnipe," Simone Bleuette had told him, gazing up at him with eyes like shards of opaque glass. "It will be no use trying to persuade him with words he cannot understand. He needs to be taken by surprise and taken forcefully."

"A child?" Jared had protested.

"He's not really a child, Joshua. He's a dwarf masquerading as a child."

He had not found the will to oppose her. For this he viewed himself with revulsion; a fly caught in a web spun by what he could only speculate must be his grotesque obsession with the woman. She at once repelled and fascinated him. In a matter of seconds, she could transform herself from a lady to a harlot, from a fissure of ice to a tongue of flame, until Jared feared for his sanity by wanting her more than he wanted release. He had always believed himself a rational man, but he no longer knew what he believed. Except that he could not escape.

Now, after arriving at a small farmhouse outside of Richmond, she at last spoke to the blindfolded boy. "If you don't stop struggling, brat, I will carve you up and mail you in pieces to your lady nurse."

Jared stared at her with aversion. The boy either did not believe her or was too furious to care, because he continued to thrash wildly as she attempted to drag him toward the root cellar.

"Joshua," she demanded, "come help me with him!"

"No, this was your idea."

"Very well. He may be as useful dead as he is alive, and he'll surely be less trouble."

"Simone!"

She shoved the boy from her and walked purposefully toward the front of the house, calling over her shoulder, "I'm serious, Joshua, and I am bringing back a butcher's knife. Quiet him or I'll use it."

The boy was stumbling around in circles when Jared caught his shoulder. "Lad, stand still and I'll take off the blindfold."

Within seconds the boy complied. When the blindfold was untied he blinked hazel eyes against the light, looked around warily, and then glowered at Jared.

"I'll take off the gag, too, if you won't start screaming again." Jared received a nod and removed the gag.

"Mister," the boy said instantly, "you gotta get me

outta here! Thet there"—he jerked his head toward the house—"is gonna ice me!"

"She intends you no harm."

"The 'ell she don't! You heered what she said."

"She did that just to frighten you."

"It worked."

Jared nearly smiled. The boy was thin but wiry, attractive in a feral sort of way despite his unkempt hair and clothes, and his eyes held intelligence.

"Now listen up, mister," the boy said. "You looks like an okay kinda gent, so what's you hangin' round her fer? She's a witch!"

"Perhaps," Jared said, thinking this as apt a description as any that he himself had attempted.

"No 'per-haps' 'bout it! Bet you dint know she burned up a house in thet there Washing-town thet had peoples in it."

Jared stiffened, then shook his head. "Boy, you don't have to make up stories—"

"It ain't no story! I wuz *there!* An' what's she want with me anyhow?"

"It's not you she wants."

"But it's me she's *got!* So you go an' tell her she made a mis-take."

"It's more complicated than that."

"Mister, is you as daft as you sounds? 'Cause you gotta b'lieve me, she's a bad one. Jest lookit her eyes an' you kin tell. Like a dead fish's they is."

"Lad, you'll be out of here safely in no time."

"Outta here on a slab is what I'll be."

"No, I can give you my word on that."

The alert hazel eyes narrowed as the boy studied him.

"Mister, what's goin' on? An' are you gonna let thet there witch keep me tied up?"

"I told you, it's just for a short time. Until she does . . . what she needs to do."

"Like what?"

"Like collecting a ransom."

"What's thet?"

"It's money she wants delivered for your release."

"Mister, you *is* daft! An' she's crazy as a loon, 'cause nobody'd pay money fer me."

Jared turned as Simone came from the house with a knife in her hand. "Now, don't make an uproar," he said to the boy, "and you won't be harmed."

The distrustful eyes regarded him. "I shur hopes you don't never sleep, mister!"

As the woman approached them, she eyed the boy with distaste. "I see you've charmed the little snake into silence, Joshua. What a soothing man you are, my darling. Close him up in that cellar!"

"That's not necessary. He can stay in the house."

"Not with us, he can't." She reached up and ran her fingernails down the side of his neck. "Joshua, where do you suppose he's spent most of his wretched life? That is, until he hoodwinked Miss Gullible Nightingale Llyr."

Jared saw the boy frown, the tension in his face painful to see. "If you want him in that cellar, Simone, put him there yourself."

Her ivory complexion blanched to harsh white. "I can't . . . no, I can't do that."

"Why not?"

She hesitated before saying, "It's too dark."

For the first time since he had met her outside Old Capitol Prison, Jared felt a cleansing surge of anger. It allowed him to retort maliciously, "It's not the *dark* you're afraid of down there!"

The boy was watching them intently.

When Simone shuddered, lowering her head against Jared's shoulder like a frightened child, he bit off what he had been about to add. Instead he took a tight grip on the boy's arm and marched him toward a hinged trapdoor leading down to the sunken root cellar.

Just before they reached the top step, the boy jerked

backward, his heels digging into the soft mud.

Jared held his arm firmly. "I'll bring you something to eat, and untie the rope around your wrists. Don't worry, she won't go down there."

The boy's sudden expression of fear, one completely absent until now, surprised Jared.

"Mister," the boy whispered, "what all's down there? It must be gawd-awful if'n *she's* even skeered! What *is* it?"

Jared shook his head, and told him.

24

I am tired of the sickening sight of the battlefield, with its mangled corpses & poor suffering wounded! Victory has no charms for me when purchased at such cost.

—General George B. McClellan, June 1862

White House Landing

"The boy has been *kidnapped?*" said Gregg Travis, incredulously echoing what Kathryn had just told him. "Where did you hear that?"

"From Kerry O'Hara. He stopped here on his way from Richmond to Washington," she answered, aware that her voice was trembling and that her eyes were welling with uncontrollable tears.

"Kathryn, where is he, this O'Hara? And who is he?"

"A Treasury agent, and he just left on a transport ship. It seems Bronwen and he are working on a plan to free Seth."

"You've had word of your brother?"

She nodded. "Seth has . . . he's been . . ." She could not say the words.

"Come along outside," Gregg said, hurriedly taking her arm to lead her from the four-walled officer's tent he was using as an office.

They were at some distance from White House Land-

ing's wharves, on a broad, sparsely treed plain that ran in
a shallow slope to the bank of the Pamunkey River. The
base camp of the Army of the Potomac now held row
upon row of hospital tents, pitched after the Battle of
Seven Pines—or Fair Oaks, as the Union command was
calling it. No matter what its name, Kathryn thought, it
had been followed by days at the field hospital on the
Chickahominy that would forever be fixed in her mind as
a long, nearly unrelieved, heartrending tragedy.

"We'll go over there by those wagons," Gregg directed, guiding her toward a somewhat isolated area of
artillery equipment. "Kathryn, I've never seen you so dis-
traught. You went through that whole nightmare at the
field hospital without once breaking down."

When they reached the shade of one of the few trees,
he stopped beside several long-bodied battery wagons and
their limbers. "For the moment we seem to be alone here.
Now, what's happened to your brother?"

Kathryn took a deep breath, resolutely forcing back the
useless tears. "He appeared before a Confederate military
commission in Richmond. It convicted him, and . . . and
sentenced him to execution."

"Good God, no! Has the Confederacy nothing better to
do than execute Union soldiers?"

"The commission claimed Seth was spying. That
couldn't be true, but he was convicted anyway. Gregg,
they're going to hang him!"

His hand gripped her shoulder, its firm grasp holding
her steady. "Where is your sister?"

"She's in Richmond. I'm terrified they'll capture her,
too."

"I'd say, from what little I saw of her, that she won't
make it easy for them to catch her."

"And now Natty's been taken."

"Did this O'Hara have any idea who seized him?"

"Yes, it was . . ." Kathryn grasped the edge of a wagon,
gritting her teeth in an effort to keep her eyes dry. She

felt Gregg's arm encircle her, which brought her sense of helplessness even closer to the surface. "It was that woman."

"What wom—you can't mean that Bleuette creature!"

She nodded. "Kerry O'Hara said it couldn't have been anyone else."

"But the woman's in Old Capitol in Washington."

"No, she somehow managed to escape. She's in Richmond and she has Natty. Gregg, she intends to kill him! O'Hara said that just before he left Bronwen, she had received a message from the woman."

"Kathryn, I'm not following you, but this is hard to take in. How the devil did the woman know where to find your sister?"

"Bronwen has a room in a hotel there. She's been using it to receive messages, and the woman apparently left one at the main desk, addressed to Bronwen's current alias. O'Hara said he couldn't figure out how the Bleuette woman learned the alias, or how she even knew my sister was staying there. He thinks Bronwen has some suspicions about how, but she wouldn't tell him."

Gregg released her and leaned against one of the wagons. "If I didn't know you, Kathryn—or rather, if I didn't know your sister—I would say this all sounds too bizarre to be even remotely plausible. Does she ever stop to consider the consequences to others because of her regrettable activities?"

Kathryn wiped her eyes and looked up at him. "*Regrettable* activities?"

"A young woman—or, for that matter, any woman—should not be involved in hazardous espionage work. Look what she's brought upon your brother! And now the boy!"

"Gregg, you can't be suggesting that Bronwen is in some way to blame—"

"Of course she's to blame! Why do you think your brother's been sentenced as a spy? Why did the Bleuette woman kidnap the boy and then send a message to your sister? She is rash and willful, and she's selfish, thinking only of herself."

Kathryn took a step back. "Bronwen acts at the direction of her superior at Treasury. And she's serving her country like any soldier in this war."

"A soldier learns obedience and the necessity of discipline, not only for his own sake, but for that of others who may depend on him. Your sister doesn't know the meaning of those two words."

He was not saying anything that had not already been said about Bronwen by most of her own family, including, at times, Kathryn herself. But she had come to see that intelligence work called for those who were daring, who could think quickly and act decisively, and whose lives in the field often depended upon their own resources alone. There were not many who could qualify, and undoubtedly most of them were men. But should Bronwen be condemned for owning the very same traits that in a man would be valued? That in a man would not be named "rash and willful" but bold and determined? Not "selfish" but self-reliant?

Rhys Bevan evidently understood this. But since Gregg Travis probably would not, or could not, it seemed pointless to pursue it.

"I don't think," Kathryn said, drawing away from him, "that I care to discuss my sister any further."

"As long as she wields such influence on your life, we have to discuss her, Kathryn. Did she ask your brother's permission, or the boy's either, before placing them in jeopardy?"

"Gregg, I need to go to Richmond."

"You . . . *what?*"

"With Seth and Natty in so much danger—"

"Kathryn, you're overwrought."

"Yes, I am. The message from the Bleuette woman

stated that Bronwen *alone* is to deliver the ransom money, or Natty will be killed."

Gregg caught her shoulders, holding her in place, and said, "Listen to me, Kathryn, and think! First, while your sister supposedly knows how to take care of herself, you can't have forgotten that the Bleuette woman nearly killed you in that fire! Second, you can't personally affect the outcome of your brother's situation. Third—and most important—you cannot simply walk away from your obligations here."

"Have you heard me at all?" Kathryn asked him, anger beginning to displace the helpless fear she could not control. "Natty will be killed, and Bronwen will be too, given the wording of that message. And Seth is to be *executed.* You can't be saying I should just ignore it."

"War requires sacrifice from everyone," he answered, his arm sweeping to indicate the hospital tents below. "The sick and wounded men here have brothers and sisters too, Kathryn, and right now your brother and sister must be secondary to your duties."

"My brother and sister are secondary to *nothing!*"

His expression hardened, and his words were clipped when he said, "This is exactly why I've had grave reservations about women serving as nurses."

"I thought your position might have changed," Kathryn said, more tentatively now, because she was suddenly afraid of where this could lead.

"I had conceded I might be wrong," he agreed. "I was ready to believe in you, especially after your work at the field hospital, where you were as courageous as any man I have worked with. But now your emotional response to the plight of a few individuals at the expense of the many here is typical of a woman."

"I *am* a woman, Gregg."

"I had hoped you were not just any woman," he said, his expression softening somewhat, before it again became inflexible. "Your present way of thinking cannot be tolcratcd, Kathryn. Since you seem unable to come to terms with this, you force me into a posture I prefer not to take—"

"Please try to understand."

"—but as you give me no choice, I must forbid you to leave."

"Forbid me?"

"And because I have found you at times to be nearly as willful as your sister, I am also forced to say that if you choose to deliberately disregard my order, and you leave here anyway, then . . . then do *not* come back!"

"Gregg, you can't mean that."

"I mean it! You won't be the first woman I've seen walk away when emotion clashed with obligation. You will be the last, however."

She had been desperate to make him see through her eyes, but with his last words, she realized he could not. Something had made him this way, but it had been no fault of hers.

For a moment she thought he might unbend when he said, "If you wish to reconsider, Kathryn, I am willing to forget this conversation. Otherwise . . . I have already deferred my responsibilities too long."

His rigid stance and expression told her that he would not relent. Kathryn tried to think of some compromise, some way to appease him, because she would never be able to forgive herself, or him, if she did as he demanded.

He stared down at her, his eyes unyielding, and then he turned away and started down the slope. Only once did his pace slow, and she hoped he might have changed his mind. She took a step toward him, but he shook his head as if an argument with himself had ended, and continued striding on toward the tents.

25

*And it came to pass, when they were in the field,
that Cain rose up against Abel and slew him. . . .
And the Lord said unto Cain, where is Abel thy
brother? And he said, I know not: Am I my
brother's keeper?*

—Book of Genesis

Road to Richmond

Kathryn could sense through the reins an eager readiness
in the bay gelding that drew her lightweight wagon. She
was not the splendid rider that Bronwen had always been,
though she was as good with horses as most women who
had grown up with them. But her long skirt and petticoat
made it impossible to ride astride without creating a spectacle, and since an encampment of men had not owned a
woman's sidesaddle, she had gratefully accepted the
wagon and the bay when offered by a soldier in the quartermaster corps.

"Can't have you taking just any nag, Miss Llyr," he
had said to her. "This one's getting on some in years, but
he'll do you fine."

Getting on or not, he was a strong horse, and Kathryn
now wondered if a plodding mule might have been a better choice. But concentrating her attention on the horse
and the road kept her from imagining what could lie ahead
for Seth and Natty, or from replaying in her mind the

scene with Gregg Travis. How had he become so unyielding? She supposed the reason did not matter now, and she
should stop guessing about it, which was easier said than
done. Despite the bitter antagonism he had displayed today, she still cared for him, and had often seen that he
could be a less rigid man. She must stop thinking of him,
or she would begin weeping again.

The warm June day carried only the buzz of insects
and the call of birds, and the dull thud of the horse's
hooves. When she had first started from White House
Landing, other wagons had occasionally passed her, but
now it seemed eerily quiet on the rutted dirt road. Alongside it stood pine and sweet gum and oak overgrown with
creeping vines and thorny shrubs that formed a long tunnel of green. Since she had been assured that this road
ran straight into Richmond, there was small threat of her
becoming lost.

When she left the Union encampment, she had been
so upset that she didn't take time to change her clothes
and was still wearing her nurse's snood and apron. Perhaps it was just as well, if she should encounter Southern
troops. But even Bronwen had never suggested that Confederate soldiers would deliberately harm a woman.

Kathryn began to trust the horse not to bolt. Since she
could not recall when she had last slept more than a few
hours at a stretch, she let herself be lulled into drowsiness
by the quiet warmth of the afternoon. She neither
glimpsed nor heard any warning when suddenly riders
burst from the trees like highwaymen.

As she jerked upright on the seat, Kathryn counted four
men in Confederate uniform, and although she could see
no sabers, all were armed with revolvers. One was shouting at her, and in startled fright she instinctively slapped
the reins on the horse's rump. The bay, already made
skittish by the riders' explosive appearance, responded by
jumping forward. He was at a gallop before Kathryn fully

grasped the absurdity of trying to escape in a wagon, but now she could not stop him.

Over the wagon's clatter and the bay's pounding hooves she could hear the men yelling. The isolation she had found soothing minutes before was now terrifying, and the thick growth to either side of the road became a green blur as her horse raced past it. The lightweight wagon careened wildly, tossing Kathryn about as if she were a leaf in a whirlwind. She had all she could do to keep her seat and hang onto the reins.

In moments riders were thundering on both sides of her, shouting at her to pull up, and Kathryn caught sideways glances of their grimly purposeful expressions. A vision of her sister astride a pony, racing the neighbor boys along the Erie Canal towpath, flashed through her mind. If it were Bronwen now being threatened, she would not halt until her horse dropped in its tracks.

The wagon lurched from side to side while Kathryn made wasted efforts to haul on the reins. Two horses were now running alongside the bay, their riders grabbing for its harness. It seemed only seconds before the wagon shuddered to a stop. Kathryn sat in dumb silence, her heart thumping like a kettledrum, and watched the men unharness the lathered bay.

"He worked up a sweat, ma'am," one of them said to her, "so's he needs to be walked. Good horse like this, have to take care of him."

He startled Kathryn with this ordinary remark, since she had been waiting for the man with braid on his sleeves to tell her she was under arrest. She had nothing to identify her, having allowed her anxiety about Seth and Natty, and the argument with Gregg Travis, to sweep away common sense.

"Ma'am, you'd best come on down from there," said the officer.

He held up a gloved hand. After a moment's hesitation, during which Kathryn decided that even token resistance would be pointless, she took his hand and allowed him to help her climb down.

When she stood by the wagon, he said, "Captain Sorrel, ma'am," and touched the brim of his forage cap. Gesturing at her headdress, he asked, "Does that have some significance?"

"I'm a nurse," Kathryn answered, trying to keep fear from cracking her voice. She was bathed in perspiration, yet the men were not even breathing hard.

"We guessed you might be," the captain replied. "Heard there were some women nurses with the Union army."

"I'm not employed by the army," Kathryn murmured, thinking this might make her seem less an enemy. But it also might convey an unsavory meaning to him, since female nurses were in some people's minds more disreputable even than actresses, so she added, "I'm with the U.S. Sanitary Commission. It's a volunteer organization."

She could not tell from his face, or from those of the others standing with him, if this explained anything. They might even believe, she thought with growing fear, that she was one of the prostitutes who had begun to follow the army.

The captain took her upper arm in a firm grip. Frightening her still more, he propelled her to the roadside, saying, "You need to come with us."

He gestured toward what appeared to be impenetrable underbrush, while the other men watched her with expressions ranging from faint smiles to cold sobriety. It had already occurred to Kathryn that there might be more men camped in the woods.

Her mouth too dry to speak, she tried to wrench away from her captor, but his grip on her arm was too strong. "Come along!"

"No!" she finally forced out, terror now so overpowering it made her legs weak. Her voice was shaking, but she repeated as loudly as she could, "No! If what I

have heard about Confederate officers is true, then you
are a gentleman—so please let me go!"

This brought from the captain a frown, which Kathryn
found more reassuring than a grin, but he did not release
her. He seemed about to say something, but turned as a
figure appeared in what proved to be a break in the underbrush.

The tall, muscular man coming toward them through
the trees looked much like a tree himself, Kathryn
thought, with an irrational surge of hope. Everything
about him was big: his broad high forehead, his shoulders
under the cadet gray tunic coat, his long gauntlets, his
full, brown beard and mustache; even his felt hat was
oversized. She did not need to see his sleeves or the but-
tons on his coat to know he was in command here, but
his insignia said he was a general.

"Sorrel, what's the—" The general stopped, having evidently seen Kathryn, and he looked at her with level eyes
of cool blue-gray. Then he turned to the captain. "I
thought I heard a woman's voice. Why is she being detained?"

"We believed, sir, that she might be a nurse and could
help those men."

"Well, let go of her."

The captain released Kathryn's arm immediately, his
startled expression saying he had not realized he was still
gripping it. From somewhere in the distance came the
muffled reports of rifles. The big man turned to listen,
then moved his head in the direction of the sounds. All
but this man and Captain Sorrel were gone in seconds,
and Sorrel stood to one side, holding the bay.

"Are you from a nearby farm?" the general asked Kathryn.

"No, I'm not from here." She guessed that was obvious
from the moment she opened her mouth, and she repeated
what she had told the captain. "The Sanitary Commission
ships are moored at . . . that is . . ." She stammered to an

abrupt stop, remembering the vulnerable, wounded men behind her at the field hospital.

"I know where the Federals are," said the general, "and I expect they know where we are. But why are you on this road?"

"Excuse me, sir," Kathryn said, her teeth beginning to chatter from nervousness, but she needed to take this man's measure before admitting to anything. "May I know to whom I am speaking?"

"General James Longstreet. And you are?"

These men could have access to Richmond newspapers, in which case they might have read about Seth *Llyr*. "My name," she answered, "is Kathryn Tryon."

"Come along then, Miss Tryon. We have some casualties back there and no medical personnel at this immediate time. Do you have objection to aiding Southern soldiers? Because if you do, I'll have you placed under guard."

"I have no objection," she said. "I'm a nurse, not a combatant, and I'll do whatever I can to help."

The general gave her an appraising glance, and nodded to the other man. "From the looks of it, Captain Sorrel, this young woman was needlessly frightened and is owed an apology."

"Yes, sir." Sorrel turned to her, saying, "I didn't know you were frightened, Miss Tryon, since we intended you no harm. If you were, my sincere apologies."

Unless he were blind he must have known she had been terrified, but Kathryn said only, "My carpetbag is in the wagon, Captain Sorrel, if you would be kind enough to retrieve it?" She would spare him the embarrassment of adding that if the bag wasn't there, it had been lost during her flight from his men.

He went back to the wagon and General Longstreet motioned her down the rough trail through the trees. The woods abruptly opened onto a field of tents and what was now to her familiar military gear, but the general veered toward several small rude cabins.

"The casualties are in one of those," he told her. "If you need something, Captain Sorrel will see to it."

Kathryn found three Confederate soldiers inside a one-room cabin. Two of them were on canvas cots and the other was seated on the dirt floor, his arm cradled in his lap. One of those on the cots had a yellowish, dehydrated look that she guessed might be caused by liver problems and diarrhea. It was a fairly safe guess. Diarrhea was the single most common ailment of soldiers, although Gregg Travis believed the worst cases of it were often symptomatic of some underlying disease.

The other man on a cot was ominously pale and lay still, so she went to him first. His eyes were open and did not flicker when she passed her hand close in front of them, making her think he was in shock. Which meant that while she could do nothing for him, he probably was not in pain.

The soldier holding his arm was eyeing her with suspicion, so she moved past him to the man on the other cot. "How long have you been sick?" she asked.

"Beggin' your pardon, ma'am, but who're you?"

"Miss . . . Tryon. I'm a nurse."

"You sound like a Yankee."

"I'm a Yankee nurse."

"Yanks are usin' ladies for nurses? They always so hard on their women?"

She gave him a smile. "The Yankee doctors are hard, but most soldiers seem to like the idea of women nurses. Have you been unusually thirsty? Had stomach cramps?" she asked, disregarding his curious but not unfriendly gaze.

"Now, that's a fact, ma'am," he answered. "Got a bellyache an' the Tennessee quickstep."

"Any blood with the quickstep?" she asked matter-of-factly, as if she normally asked everyone she met this question. One moment's hesitation—a mere blink of the eye or an averted glance—could make a man clam up and refuse to discuss this with a woman. "No blood," came his response.

"Good." With luck it might not be dysentery. "What do you usually eat, soldier?"

His eyes held sudden mischief under the raised eyebrows. "Oh, I eat steak, oysters, apple pie—though I've got me a strong taste for lemonade."

Kathryn smiled. "And when you can't get steak, oysters, and apple pie? Then I'll wager fried beans and salt pork are high on your list, am I right?"

"Ma'am, I've had nothin' but them for three weeks."

"Which may be why you're having trouble. And it's no wonder you crave lemonade. I know it's hard to do in the field, but try to eat potatoes instead of the beans, and fruit if you can find it, and stew the meat instead of frying it."

She knew he probably wouldn't or couldn't do this, and opened her carpetbag to extract a pouch of tea leaves. "I can't say exactly what's making you sick," she told him, "but it could be all the fried food you're eating. If you possibly can, boil the water you drink. And you need lots of water. Tea should give you some comfort, too."

She looked around for water and saw none, but Captain Sorrel had obviously anticipated the need, because a soldier was coming through the open doorway with a bucket.

"Thank you," Kathryn said to him. "Where was this water drawn?"

"From the creek out there," the soldier answered, gesturing to a slow-running stream Kathryn could see some yards beyond.

"Does that stream pass anywhere near the latrine sinks?"

She saw his distaste at a woman raising such a subject, so she added quickly, "The reason I asked is because the Sanitary Commission doctors believe that men are sickened when the sinks are dug upstream from the water supply. Or are located close to the camp kitchens."

She could tell that he believed her daft, and decided that anything she said would be suspect. "Soldier, I saw a fire when I came, so would you please boil some water for this man. And bring me a fresh bucketful *upstream* from the sinks?"

The soldier gaped at her, then shrugged and went off.

Unexpectedly, the man seated on the floor commented, "That there makes some kind of sense, ma'am. Mostly 'cause when we first make camp nobody gets sick right off."

She spun to look at him, surprised to find an ally. "Yes," she said, "and some doctors think the camps should be moved every few days."

To her further surprise, she received a nod from him.

Seizing the moment, she asked, "Is it your arm that was wounded?" while going to kneel beside him.

"You could say so." He raised his forearm, wrapped with a filthy rag.

"I need to take that wrapping off," she told him, and he held his arm out to her readily enough. She unwound the rag cautiously, anticipating at the very least a festering infection and possibly gangrene, although unquestionably she would have smelled it by now.

"I s'pect the sawbones are gonna want to cut it off," he said.

Although his voice was fairly steady, she heard the fear in it. "How long ago did this happen?" she asked.

" 'Bout five, maybe six days now. Caught a bullet. Not even a Yank bullet—one of my own company was horsin' round with his fool rifle," he added, the irony producing a grim smile.

"Did it pass through your arm?"

"Straight through."

She rocked back on her heels. "You're a lucky man."

"Don't feel lucky."

"Well, you are. Look here at the wound. It's already closed, healing over with good, healthy-looking tissue, and with no sign at all of infection. After this amount of time has passed, it's probably safe to say you won't lose the arm."

"That so?" came the laconic reply.

"I know you're gladder than you sound, soldier. I have some clean cotton here in my bag, so let me wrap it back up again for protection. While I'm doing that, tell me what you know about the young man on that other cot."

"Got his gut blown open," he replied quietly. "Two days ago. He won't make it—can't figure how he lasted this long. But he keeps askin' for somebody named Mandy, so maybe he's tryin' to hang on 'til she gets here."

"Mandy?" Kathryn repeated in an overly loud voice to see if it would bring a response.

The young man stirred slightly, and murmured something. As soon as she was done bandaging the other's forearm, she went to crouch beside the younger man's cot, but she questioned whether he saw her. The pupils of his eyes were huge, his face drained of color like the soft gray ashes of a damped fire. She raised the dirty cotton blanket covering his mid-section and silently agreed with the other soldier; clearly this man should not be alive. He was just barely so, hanging by a slender thread of sheer will. She lowered the blanket, knowing she could give him nothing other than comfort. But she could pray that God would have pity and take him.

"You asked for Mandy?" she said to him, kneeling beside him.

"Mandy? Is . . . that y'all?"

Kathryn had learned that even men barely conscious could sometimes have moments of lucidity just before they died, but the phenomenon never lost its wonder for her. Perhaps Mandy was the name of this man's sweetheart or his wife.

"I knew . . . knew you'd come . . . Mandy." His hand as he spoke jerked spasmodically as if he were trying to raise it. Kathryn took hold of the hand and held it. His pulse was so feeble she could barely find it.

"Yes, I've come," she told him.

A faint smile began to curve his lips, then vanished as he cried softly, "Now don't tell the young-uns. . . . Don't go tellin' 'em I'm sick. You promise me?"

"No, I won't tell them. Not just yet."

"I been wishin' you'd sing, Mandy. You always did . . . when I couldn't sleep."

"What would you like to hear?" It came to Kathryn that she had not sung once since leaving home, although for years she had, every Sunday morning in Rochester's Presbyterian church choir. She wondered if the same hymns were sung here in the South.

"Sing the one 'bout the stranger goin' over Jordan, Mandy . . .'cause I'd like to go there."

"Stranger going over Jordan?" Kathryn repeated, silently begging her memory to oblige as she felt the man's pulse stop altogether, then start again in a thready, broken cadence. "Do you mean 'The Wayfaring Stranger'?"

His lips quivered, but whatever words he had were drowned in a choking gasp. His eyelids flickered as his breathing stopped again. A rattling sigh escaped and Kathryn, still holding his hand, hummed the first notes, her memory giving back to her the mournful revival hymn as if she had last sung it yesterday.

"Is that the one?" she asked him.

No answer, but a flutter of his hand, light as a butterfly wing. She bent over him to hear the rasping sound of air as his lungs collapsed.

"Sing his song for him, miss," said the soldier on the other cot.

Kathryn settled back on her knees and sang softly, *"I am a poor way-faring stranger / While journe'ing thru this land of woe / Yet, there's no sick-ness, toil nor danger / In that bright land to which I go."*

She sang it again, hesitating when she felt his pulse stop, and then went on with her eyes filling, *"I'm going there to see my Father / I'm going there no more to roam / I'm only going over Jordan / I'm only going over home."*

His hand was limp as she repeated the last phrase. *"I'm only going over home."*

She put her hand to the side of his throat, and finding no pulse there either, she closed his eyes, whispering, "Go with God, soldier."

As she lifted a corner of her apron to wipe her eyes and cheeks, she was reminded of a sound that had come from the doorway some minutes earlier. Twisting on her knees, she saw General Longstreet standing there, leaned back against the doorjamb with his arms folded across his chest and an unlit cigar in one hand. He must have been there for a while.

Kathryn got to her feet and shook out her skirt when the general stepped back outside and began to light the cigar.

Following him, she said, "The man's gone. I'm so sorry I couldn't have done more."

"Appears you did all you could. Haven't heard that hymn for some time. Long time."

Kathryn felt a dull throb of anger. Of late it seemed always there just below the surface, ready to rise whenever she had time to think of these deaths as such a terrible waste.

"General Longstreet," the anger asked, "why can't you men stop this?"

He made an abrupt motion with his head, as if to dismiss her, but then looked down at her with those blue-gray eyes, answering, "If I understand the question, you shouldn't have to ask it."

"I think I do," Kathryn said, gesturing toward the inside of the cabin. "I've seen too much of this not to ask it."

"You read the Bible, Miss Tryon? Book of Genesis?"

"I have, yes."

"Read it again."

He looked levelly at her, as if to see whether she understood what he meant.

She did understand. "Cain and his brother," she said.

"We're all Cain's brothers. It's as good an answer as any I've found."

Kathryn said nothing, looking off toward the lush green Virginia woods and fields, soon to be battlefields if the Bible parable was true. And the history of man said it was.

Smoke from the cigar rose in a pale blue column before he said, "I'm obliged to you for my men. I'll see you have an escort back to the Union lines."

"I have to go into Richmond."

He shook his head.

Kathryn said the one thing she thought might reach this man, even if it had not moved Gregg Travis. "General Longstreet, please understand. My brother is a prisoner of war in Richmond."

A frown crossed his impassive face, and although it was gone in an instant, he asked, "Where was your brother captured?"

"I heard it was near Williamsburg. I just want to see him, and make sure he's all right. Then I'll return to . . . to the Sanitary Commission ships where I was working," she finished, having stumbled over the recollection of being told not to come back to the field hospital.

"Can't take you into the city," Longstreet said. "Could get you as far as Chimborazo Hospital—I expect nurses are always needed."

"I would be very grateful, sir. And thank you."

"I'll have Captain Sorrel see to it."

A short time later a mule was harnessed to the wagon.

Captain Sorrel explained, without apology, that the bay gelding was too valuable to relinquish, but he had been ordered to provide her with an escort. As the wagon clattered out of the camp, Kathryn turned to look back. General Longstreet was still standing against the doorway of the cabin, and he raised one gauntleted hand to touch the brim of his hat.

26

—⚏—

O, what a tangled web we weave,
  When first we practice to deceive.

—Sir Walter Scott

Richmond

ᴮronwen paced up and down the length of the Spotswood carpet, making frequent and useless detours to the
window. Through a haze of mist the sun was beginning
to lower over the city, but there had been no new word
from de Warde. It was perilous for her to remain in the
hotel, and she had returned only this once after receiving
the ransom note. Bluebell had apparently left it, addressed
to *Miss Larkin,* with the maître d'hôtel. How the woman
had learned of her alias and her room here was just one
more source of anxiety.

  Written in a bold hand, the note had read:

> *I have in my possession your sister's gutter-*
> *snipe. On Thursday next at 7 o'clock in the*
> *evening, bring a pouch containing ten thou-*
> *sand dollars (Federal) to Hollywood Ceme-*
> *tery. Go to the burial plot of President James*
> *Monroe and deposit the money at the base of*

the wrought iron cage surrounding the vault.
You must *come alone! Failure to follow these*
instructions to the letter will result in the
boy's acutely unpleasant death. Again, you
must be alone, or have no doubt the boy will
die.

There had been no signature, but the identity of Bluebell, a.k.a. Simone Cartier Bleuette, had been transparent
through the vicious threat.

At first Bronwen thought this demand must be a sa-
distic jest. Even a deranged Bluebell could not think that
ten thousand dollars would be available to a Treasury
agent. The whole thing seemed only a ploy to draw Bronwen to the cemetery. She did not question for a minute
that the woman intended to kill Natty, and she could only
pray that the deed had not already been done. But did
Bluebell truly believe that this simpleminded lure would
make a Treasury agent run headlong into certain capture
or death? Either she had succumbed to a need for revenge
or was desperate for attention from Norris and Confederate intelligence.

Bronwen had included the ransom demand in her most
recent communication to de Warde, reasoning that he
wanted his tobacco more than he wanted her dead, and
that it was in his own best interests to make sure she
stayed alive. But he might not have received her message
or, worse, was stirring up some new deviltry of which she
was unaware. But how much more could there be? Natty
was in Bluebell's brutal clutches, Marsh was trapped in
the Confederate Chimborazo Hospital, and Seth was in
chains awaiting execution. James Quiller's whereabouts
remained unknown, but his absence for so long a time
was more than troubling.

Was there a single Northern male of her acquaintance
still at large in Richmond and not in need of immediate
rescue?

In a moment of weakness she almost missed O'Hara, who always at least landed on his feet; unless of course the reason for this was not his talent but his treachery. Was that why she had not heard from de Warde? Because O'Hara had not gone to Washington to confirm the tobacco transfer, and de Warde knew it?

Her glance darted to the door barricaded behind the bureau, thinking she had heard something in the hallway outside. It was just as probable that she was driving herself mad with wild imaginings when reality was more than enough to accomplish the same thing. Still, she crept toward the door, and then she spotted it—the corner of a white envelope barely visible under the bureau's squat bulk.

She ripped it open to find a sheet of vellum containing a message written in a neat cursive hand.

> *Your message acknowledged. My acquaintances in northern climes confirm your offer is legitimate. Proceed. However, be advised: a viper lurks in yon confining nest. And lacking an attentive gardener, a deadly flora grows wild, and must be pruned this night,* without delay, *beyond Eden's northwest border. Repeat: without delay. All due haste required.*

It was also unsigned.

Blast de Warde and his absurd riddles! Did he believe she would read this message aloud in the presence of others? Leave it lying around the hotel, or possibly post it in the Spotswood lobby? More likely, it was simply the Englishman making sure there would be nothing whatsoever to incriminate himself. But one item had leapt out, giving her immediate relief—namely that O'Hara *had* reached Washington's "northern climes," and de Warde's contacts there had verified her tobacco proposal.

She edged around the bureau to listen for sounds in

the hallway. Hearing none, she checked the lock and went to the window to quickly reread the message, and then stood tearing it into scraps. "A deadly flora" was of course Bluebell. The "grows wild" allusion could mean that kidnapping Natty was her own idea, done without the approval, or the collusion, of Confederate intelligence. But how would de Warde have learned that? Unless someone like Norris had voiced disapproval, which might mean that he thought Bluebell had become a liability. If Bronwen had not known the history between Norris and Simone Cartier Bleuette, she would have wondered, as Rhys Bevan had, how Norris even came to know the woman.

De Warde's "a viper lurks in yon confining nest" unnerved her. Bronwen stood with her forehead pressed against the window, resisting the idea that his warning meant one of Seth's fellow Union officers in Libby Prison was a traitor. Which also meant that this traitor must at all costs be kept from hearing of an escape attempt. But even Seth himself knew nothing about it, and forewarned was forearmed.

Nearly as alarming was de Warde's emphasis on urgency in dealing with Bluebell tonight, so Bronwen yanked on the shirt and overalls purchased at the dry-goods store, and slipped the derringer into a pocket. She wadded up her dress around the spyglass. While stuffing the bundle into Chantal Dupont's carpetbag, she heard a faint scratching at the lock of the door.

She rushed to the window to jerk it open, flinging out the scraps of de Warde's note and tossing the carpetbag after them.

A sharp noise resounded as if someone had slapped the door with the flat of a hand.

"Open it!" an unfamiliar voice shouted.

It had to be a Richmond policeman, because no one else these days would be arrogant enough to assume a door would be opened simply because it was demanded. The worst part of it was that she had been betrayed. She could not bear to think who was the most obvious betrayer.

"Open the door! Don't make us break it down!"

She hadn't anticipated the "us," but now she could hear several voices and caught the word "axe." There would be no room to bargain with men prepared to chop up the Spotswood's expensive walnut.

Hauling up her overalls, she heard a blade strike the door and scrambled onto the windowsill. She had just time enough to gather herself before a crash of splintering wood sent her leaping from the fifth-floor window.

Practice had taught her exactly where to land on the roof of the adjacent building.

After seizing the carpetbag, she raced to the far edge of the roof and found the coiled rope she had earlier tethered to a metal girder. Ordinarily she entered the office building by way of a staircase that ran from the roof to the top floor. The storage room she used for sleeping was located there, but the building would no doubt be searched and the entrance closed off as soon as they found her gone from the Spotswood. A quick glance at the cobblestone alley below showed it holding only the usual overflowing trash barrels. Threading an arm through the carpetbag handles, she climbed down the rope to the stones, and skirted the barrels to emerge onto a side street.

For a brief moment she wished she could have seen the men breaking into her Spotswood room. Anyone stupid enough to believe she would actually reside in a hotel with Confederates around every corner deserved the large chamber pot poised on the top edge of the bureau.

She urged the rented horse up a road that climbed northwest beyond the "Eden" of Hollywood cemetery, again aware she had been forced to place her trust in untrustworthy de Warde. No other choice had appeared, and she reminded herself that the Englishman needed her alive for the tobacco transfer.

Her roan mare, the last decent animal available at a livery where most had been taken for the war effort, was costing the U.S. Treasury plenty. Again she had seen no other choice. De Warde's message had stressed haste, which meant astride, not afoot.

After pulling up the mare at the top of the rise, she looked down on a farmhouse located under several spreading trees. On the near side of it were the last cemetery headstones, and beyond it was an expanse of field gone to scrub growth. As Bronwen scanned the surrounding countryside, still more urgency was added in the form of an open carriage that rumbled along the dirt road leading to the house.

She glanced around her, saw the beginning of a waist-high hedgerow that ran down the slope to within yards of the farmhouse, and prodded the mare toward it. Dismounting, she threw the reins over one of the bushes. After rooting in the carpetbag and withdrawing the spyglass, she strapped the bag behind the saddle.

Creeping forward a short distance, she raised the glass. The sun sat above the horizon, bright enough for her to see a stocky, uniformed man descending from the carriage. He walked toward two figures coming down the house's front steps, and Bronwen was unpleasantly aware that the man fit Rhys Bevan's description of the agent rumored to be Major William Norris's immediate subordinate. Of the two figures waiting, she did not recognize the nondescript man, but the black-haired woman was Bluebell.

If Bronwen had deciphered de Warde's message correctly, Confederate intelligence had not been involved in Natty's capture, so why was Norris's man here? She pulled the derringer from her pocket, knowing she had only two possible shots against three adversaries, and hugging the hedgerow, she started stealthily down the slope.

Joshua Jared glanced toward the root cellar as Simone Bleuette pointed it out to the Confederate officer. She had introduced him as Major William Norris's assistant, Captain Raymond Kohler. A quick look from Kohler told Jared he was not to acknowledge their previous meeting, when they had planned Simone's escape from Washington's Old Capitol, or to mention that Norris had ordered Jared to keep a close watch on her. Jared had not been given a reason for this order, but at first he assumed Norris had some basis for distrusting her. Why, since her loyalty to the South was beyond question? Jared now thought perhaps it was not her loyalty that Norris distrusted.

"I have the urchin and will soon have the Treasury agent, too," Simone was saying tensely to Kohler, for whom she seemed to harbor dislike. She appeared more nervous than usual when insisting, "It was not necessary for you to come out here."

"After we received your communiqué," Kohler replied, brushing dust from the stripes on his sleeve, "Norris thought it was necessary. For various reasons, Simone, we believe your actions to have been unwise."

"You are mistaken!"

"No! We want that agent, but her seizure has to appear legitimate. We have moved against her cautiously for good reason—another cause célèbre like Timothy Webster's execution must be avoided. It is difficult enough to convince a jury or tribunal that a beautiful young woman should be hanged! We also want information about other Treasury agents, and for interrogation purposes we need that woman *alive*. You have, as Norris and I are aware, an unfortunate tendency to kill without considering the consequences."

Simone's brows lifted as she replied archly, "Naturally I will comply with Norris's wishes, although the plan is *not* unwise. The boy is only an urchin and no one other than the Treasury bitch and her sister would miss him."

Jared observed Kohler giving Simone a long look of appraisal. "We have found the means to bring that young woman into our grasp," he said finally. "In fact, orders have come down to arrest her, something which should be taking place even as we speak. But kidnapping a child, no matter who he is, could have unpleasant implications should the newspapers learn of it."

"The newspapers! You *can't* think that agent will actually inform the Richmond press."

"She is inventive, and she may well have loyalist Union connections here in Richmond," responded Kohler, "so we can't discount the possibility that the press will be alerted about the boy. Moreover, as you have been told, Major Norris does not and will not condone the killing of civilians. And the British agent Colonel de Warde has repeatedly warned against it."

"De Warde!" she scoffed. "He is without scruples himself, so he is a fine one to talk."

"The Confederacy *needs* Britain's goodwill!" Kohler told her sharply.

Jared, listening closely, thought it safe to assume that Kohler had arrived here, unannounced, because something more critical than the boy's welfare was worrying Norris.

"But enough of this!" declared Kohler abruptly. "I want to see the boy."

"See him? Why?" Simone asked, inclining her head so she could gaze up at Kohler under a fringe of long black lashes.

Jared cringed at the obvious tactic. Simone understood she was on shaky ground with Norris's man and had changed her persona to that of an artless ingenue. He wondered why he had not noticed before how unappealing this role was for a woman patently beyond the age of innocence.

Kohler, in any case, appeared unmoved by it and sent Jared an odd, almost accusatory look before he said, "Frankly, Simone, Major Norris is not reassured by your conduct of late. We need agents who are sound, and I, for one, am not convinced that you qualify. And then too, there is your regrettable history."

Jared stiffened, at once hoping that Kohler would go

on to describe this history and not wanting to hear it if he did.

But with this Simone had reverted to her former self and was now bristling. "Norris and I agreed long ago that the past was dead," she snapped.

"And we want to assure ourselves that it remains so," Kohler said smoothly. "Now get the boy."

Simone, clearly frustrated by the man's inflexible attitude, gave Jared her child-like look of appeal. He glanced at Kohler, who was observing this, and the captain repeated, *"Get the boy!"*

"Very well. Joshua, do bring him here," she said, her silver eyes sending him a plea. "I am unsteady on those steps."

"No, Simone," Kohler contradicted, *"you* get him! Mr. Jared and I have some matters to discuss."

Simone hesitated, received a relentless stare from Kohler, and then started with reluctant steps toward the cellar.

Jared knew she had not seen the boy since they had brought him here. It had been he who had taken food to her captive, and had several times been on the verge of flinging the trapdoor open and looking the other way. Only the certainty of Simone's fury and subsequent rejection of him had stayed his hand. Jared had also begun to fear that the boy could lose his mind in the bleak cell, where the only light came from the cracks between damp foundation stones and from one grimy, barred window just above the ground. The last time Jared had entered the cellar space, he thought the boy was concealing something behind his back, but upon investigation he found only some empty canning jars.

"I don't care if you eat what's here," he had told the boy. "You don't have to hide the evidence."

He had been eyed warily and received only a shrug. It seemed odd the youngster had not pushed past him and tried to escape. Jared would have thought the lad owned more spirit than to resign so readily. Or perhaps he was too clever to risk provoking Simone's murderous wrath.

Kohler was now watching her slow progress toward the cellar steps with narrowed eyes. Not turning, he said to Jared, "You've been ensnared by her. Don't bother to deny it and don't feel damned for it either. I was myself trapped by her."

Jared did not respond to this confession.

"Simone has, or she had, an uncanny ability to gauge the needs of men," Kohler went on, undeterred by Jared's silence, "and she uses that knowledge ruthlessly. It could be a priceless asset for a woman in espionage work, provided she was balanced enough to use it selectively. Simone loathes men, Jared—all men. I hadn't realized the loathing now includes *anyone* who thwarts her—even women and children. Norris fears it has made her vindictive and thus unsound, in which case she is worthless to him. But is the boy still alive?"

"He's alive."

"How can you be sure?"

"I'm the only one who goes into that cellar."

"Is she afraid of him?"

"Not of him," Jared answered, seeing Simone standing transfixed in front of the trapdoor.

Kohler gave him a searching look before demanding, "Simone, open the door, and do it now!"

She reached out a hand for the door handle, but quickly withdrew it.

"I can't wait any longer," Kohler said loudly, and began walking toward the carriage. "Your refusal to carry out an express order, Simone, means your work for Norris is finished! You will leave Richmond immediately."

"No! No, wait!"

Jared did not know if Kohler was bluffing but he doubted it, and apparently so did Simone because she grasped the handle and yanked. The door squealed noisily on three rusty hinges as it swung upward. Simone gave it a shove, making it fall against the ground with a clatter to reveal the sunken cellar stairs. After one tentative step downward, she peered into the near darkness.

There was nothing to hear but silence. Simone glanced at Kohler, who shook his head as he took another several strides toward the carriage. She sent him a gesture of appeal, and then went down two more steps of the cellar stairs. The silence stretched on.

Suddenly it was broken by the sound of shattering glass. And Simone's unearthly shriek rent the air. She jerked backward, falling over the upper steps, and clawing at herself as if possessed. Her shrieks scaled upward as she struggled to rise while tearing at her clothes in frenzy.

Jared stood frozen in shock, and what followed happened so fast he could scarcely track it.

The boy came bursting up the steps into the light. The next instant a slim figure erupted from behind a hedgerow, yelling "Natty! Over here!"

Kohler grabbed a revolver from the carriage seat, and was turning to level it at the figure when something flashed through the air. The revolver went flying and the Confederate agent bellowed in pain, clutching at his right arm where a stiletto blade was embedded. Meanwhile the boy had leapt over the screaming Simone and was dashing toward the revolver. He snatched it up as Kohler stumbled toward him. Natty took a step back and, gripping the gun tightly, cocked the hammer and aimed the weapon directly at Kohler. The agent skidded to a stop as Simone's shrieks grew more hysterical.

Jared took a step toward the boy. Directly to his right, the figure shouted, "Stop right there, mister!"

He swung to look at what first appeared to be a young man in overalls pointing a double derringer.

"Keep that revolver on him, Natty! Fire if he even twitches!" yelled the figure, moving closer to Jared with quick, lithe steps, and he now saw the fine-boned features of a young woman. Her face was grim with determination, and Jared did not question that she would fire. She edged past him, the derringer held ready. She said something to the boy she called Natty, but it was lost to Jared in the crescendo of Simone's shrieks as she clawed viciously at herself, writhing on the ground as if in agony.

"Woman, stop that screaming!" shouted Kohler.

He needn't have bothered. Her reddened eyes held madness, and saliva ran from her slack mouth as the screams continued mindlessly. Jared now saw that the roiled earth around her seemed to be alive and crawling.

It was spiders, hundreds and hundreds of them, and on the steps lay shards of broken glass, which must have been the canning jars that had held them. Jared remembered then what he had told the boy.

The young woman, now holding both revolver and derringer, motioned at him with one of them, while the boy circled Simone and ran back down the cellar steps.

"Move!" she shouted at Jared, jerking her head toward Kohler, who looked unsteady as he stood with the blade still protruding from his arm, blood dripping in a stream from the torn, gray sleeve. It was nothing compared to the blood there would be if he tried to remove the knife.

With the revolver pointed at him, Jared moved slowly toward Kohler. Simone's shrill screams had at last weakened, and her prone form had become a shuddering, sobbing mass that the boy cleared with a leap.

He carried several lengths of rope that Jared recognized as having been the boy's own bonds. Natty straddled Simone, whipping the rope around her wrists as if he did it every day of his life.

"Down on the ground!" the young woman told Kohler, her voice holding a terse authority. His pallor was becoming pronounced, and he swayed before dropping to his knees.

As if reading Jared's mind, the young woman said to him, "I will shoot you without a qualm, mister, so don't consider moving a muscle. Natty, tie up our uniformed friend here next," she said to the boy, indicating Kohler.

"I say we jest shoot 'em all," the boy answered.

"I'll give it some thought, but meantime tie him up."

The boy told Kohler to put his hands behind him. When the stiletto handle got in the way, the boy simply wound the rope tightly around his body. He used another length to tie his feet, while the agent winced in either pain or humiliation.

"Move away," the young woman directed the boy, and with her eyes focused on Jared, she said to Kohler, "I assume you're with Confederate intelligence, Captain. What's your name?"

"Kohler," he answered in a low tone.

"Is kidnapping a child Norris's idea of an espionage operation?"

"Who the hell *are* you?" Kohler asked, but Jared thought the agent already knew, as did he.

Believing Kohler had distracted her, Jared made his move with an abrupt lunge at the boy. The revolver barked once. He staggered before toppling onto his side, a bullet lodged in his thigh.

"And now you know I'm a good shot," the woman said, "because if you think I missed killing you by accident, you're wrong. But I might let you bleed to death."

"What do you want?" Kohler asked, his face having grown still whiter.

Instead of answering, she told the boy to tie Jared's hands behind him.

When he had finished, she directed him to fetch cotton sheets or towels from the house, and when he returned with them, she had him tear them into strips. After handing the revolver to the boy, she wound several strips as a tourniquet around Kohler's arm above the blade. Jared wondered where she had learned to do it.

"I'm reclaiming my knife, Captain," she said, bracing her feet before withdrawing the stiletto from his forearm in a single smooth motion. Blood spurted from the wound and then slowed to a dribble.

With more cotton strips she stanched the sluggish flow of blood from Jared's leg, all the while glancing at Simone Bleuette, who sprawled over the top cellar step, the agitated sobbing finally quieted. It disgusted Jared that even now he felt some pity for her, since she had brought this calamity raining down on them both. How would Norris react? That was, if any of them lived to tell him. On second thought, it might be better to die here than to face Norris.

"There's another farm about a half mile up the road," the young woman told them. "Dredge up some of that fabled Rebel grit, and one of you should be able to make it that far."

"What do you want?" Kohler asked again.

"I doubt you have the authority to offer me anything," she stated, and Jared saw a puzzling, almost wistful expression cross her face. Then, so suddenly she must have intended to catch Kohler unawares, she added, "Do you know the whereabouts of James Quiller?"

Jared caught the flicker of Kohler's eyes. It was a barely perceptible reaction, but if he saw it, the woman saw it too. When Kohler did not reply, she bent down and untied his feet, then stood back to glance around her.

"Natty, a roan mare is up that rise there. Go fetch her and we'll tie her to the back of the carriage."

"You're taking my carriage?" Kohler sounded surprised and irritated.

"You bet I am, Captain. It was your vicious operative over on those steps who brought the boy and me here in the first place, so your carriage can bloody well take us out! And you can thank your lucky stars it's all I'm taking."

"How did you know where to find the boy?" asked Jared. He imagined that Kohler had the same question but pride kept him from asking it. Jared now noticed the other agent was watching every move the young woman made, and his expression had altered from angry to faintly admiring.

She nearly smiled, her green eyes glinting in the faded twilight, and answered, "I'm a gypsy fortune-teller, mister. And I don't believe I caught your name."

"Joshua Jared."

"Also Confederate intelligence, I presume?"

The boy reappeared leading a roan horse. His tone of voice was belligerent when he said to the woman, "I don't see why we can't jest shoot thet hoity-toit witch. She was gonna kill me! And you, too, 'cause I heered her say so."

"We are not cold-blooded murderers, Natty, my man."

After a glance toward Simone, she turned to Kohler. "Captain, you might mention to Major Norris that I'm disappointed in Confederate intelligence. I can understand if you skip the details of your own performance here tonight, but you tell Norris I thought he had more sense than to employ a security risk like her."

After a pause Kohler replied, "I'll pass the message along."

She nodded. "You can also tell Norris—and make no mistake about this, Captain—that if the woman over there ever crosses my path again, I will shoot to kill. Before I even ask which direction she's headed!"

Kohler responded in a dry voice, "I expect you'll have to stand in line."

27

—⚹—

[General Jeb Stuart's Chickahominy Raid] excites as much admiration in the Union army as it does in Richmond. We regard it as a feather of the very tallest sort in the rebel cap.

—*The New York Times,* June 1862

Richmond

"Why cain't we pinch the buggy, too?" Natty complained to Bronwen, as they left the livery on the muscular brown Morgan horse that had earlier drawn Captain Kohler's carriage.

"Because the buggy's too easily identified. This horse is another matter. He's sturdy, good-tempered like most Morgans, and has no markings that stand out when seen from any distance. And I'm not exactly 'pinching' him."

"Shur looks like it to me."

"Captain Kohler lost the battle, which means his horse is the spoils of war, which means what I'm doing is a more or less permissible type of—"

"Stealin'."

"I am naturally delighted you have grasped the basics, Natty, but let's just leave it there."

She had decided Elizabeth Van Lew's was the only place she could take the boy safely and keep an eye on him, so they were now climbing Church Hill. She had wrapped the shivering Natty in a carriage blanket, one *he* had misappropriated from the livery with a practiced sleight of hand that even she had not caught. No question that he was a superb thief, she thought, and something moved at the back of her mind.

"Tell me how you knew that woman was insanely terrified of spiders?"

"Thet gent told me, day I got there. Cellars got lots o' spiders."

"It was a very smart thing you did, collecting them in those jars."

"It weren't smart not to shoot thet witch," he said accusingly, "on 'count of now she's prob-ly gonna go after Lady."

Bronwen felt the hair on the back of her neck rise. "What on earth makes you say that?"

" 'Cause Lady ain't tough as you."

"Lady Kathryn is a nurse, which means she's much tougher than she looks or you think. And there's no need to worry about her. As you know, she's where you left her with the Union army. As you also know, that is nowhere near Richmond. Besides, I imagine Bluebell's days with Confederate intelligence are finished. The one we *do* have to worry about is my brother Seth."

After what appeared to be a doubtful nod, he asked, "Where we goin'?"

"You'll see soon enough. But if we run into soldiers or police, remember that you're my little brother who's deathly sick, and I'm taking you to Chimborazo Hospital—"

"The 'ell you is!"

"—because it's only a quarter mile from where we're really bound, and don't swear at me!"

Riding in front of Bronwen, Natty squirmed around to give her a skeptical look. "You think yer gonna git yers and Lady's brother outta thet there war-house place?"

"Yes! But I may need your help with the war-house,

my man. You and I were a pretty good team back there at the farm, so what do you say?"

"How much do I git paid?"

"Paid?"

"I don't work fer nothin', an' I don't come cheap."

"And here I've been laboring under the impression that you wanted to help Seth because he is Lady's brother."

"Don't mean I hafta do it fer free!"

A few minutes later he grumbled again, "You shoulda shot thet witch!"

"Natty, you can't kill people just because you have the upper hand and they're hateful," she said, realizing with some dismay that she sounded exactly like her mother.

"Why not, if'n you got the gun?"

"Because it's immoral, dishonorable, and just plain wrong! It's also illegal."

"Then how come sol-jurs kin do it?"

This leaving Bronwen groping for words, they warily made their way up the hill. Only once, just before they turned onto Grace Street, did she have cause to worry. Ahead in the moonlight she saw a group of mounted Confederate military approaching, presumably heading down to the city and perhaps even to the stucco executive mansion called the Gray House by those who refused to call it the White House of the Confederacy.

"Don't make a sound," she whispered to Natty, her arms encircling him.

"How kin I? Yer squeezin' my gut!"

Bronwen pulled the Morgan to the side of the road as the horses drew closer. She recognized one of the lead riders, a cinnamon-bearded officer wearing a cape, gold-braided jacket, and ostrich-plumed hat. Quickly she averted her face, recalling vividly the accidental encounter with Jeb Stuart in northern Virginia when she and O'Hara had been scouting Confederate troops. Stuart's familiarity with her fellow Treasury agent was what had triggered her continuing distrust of O'Hara.

Stuart and the men now passing all looked fatigued, with one notable exception—a handsome, silver-haired officer riding beside Stuart and mounted on an almost equally handsome pale gray horse. As they rode by with only a glance toward the Morgan, the others obviously deferred to this man. His bearing and self-possessed expression reminded Bronwen of something O'Hara had recently said: *He looks every inch a commanding general.*

It would seem that she and Natty might be within a stone's throw of the Confederate army's new commander, General Lee.

She waited, watching the men until they disappeared under the trees along the road before urging the Morgan forward. Glancing down at Natty, she wondered at his uncommon stillness, and guessed he might have been as anxious as she. Then she realized that he was asleep.

As usual, the Van Lew back door swung open at their approach. It surprised Bronwen that the street had been nearly deserted, and standing on the stone stoop, she asked Elizabeth about it.

The slight-framed woman shook her head, fair curlicues bobbing around a face markedly troubled. "There's an ill wind blowing, my dear. Come in, and I'll acquaint you with recent events."

"I've put a Morgan horse in your carriage house," Bronwen said to her. "And this lad here, eyeing your orange cat, is Natty."

"How do you do, young man. I have fried chicken and biscuits over there on the table. And are you familiar with lemon cake?"

"I s'pect I kin be," Natty answered, edging toward the food.

"Then help yourself."

Motioning toward the table, Elizabeth handed Bronwen a stack of newspapers, all of them some days old. The Richmond *Examiner* and *Enquirer* both carried headlines that made Bronwen drop stunned into the nearest chair, and upon reading more her shock increased.

General Jeb Stuart and twelve hundred Confederate cavalry had succeeded, with little or no opposition, in riding completely around McClellan's army. Stuart and his men had then returned triumphant to Richmond with recaptured slaves, scores of Yankee prisoners, and several hundred confiscated mules. The Southern newspapers crowed with glee. Even a dog-eared copy of the June 21 *New York Times,* probably come into Van Lew's possession via her James River network, nearsightedly trumpeted what Bronwen saw immediately as a strong threat to the Federal objective of taking Richmond.

Elizabeth, evidently mistaking Bronwen's horrified silence for awe, said, "My dear, the newspapers have as usual blown that popinjay Stuart's escapade all out of proportion. He and his men were simply having a joyride at our expense, thumbing their noses at the Union."

"I'm afraid you're wrong, Elizabeth. No one who works in intelligence could dismiss that as a joyride."

"You are making too much of it," the woman protested. "It's a terrible thing that Union soldiers were taken prisoner, but it's not reason for despair."

Bronwen left the chair to pace around the table where Elizabeth sat, clearly puzzled by her reaction, and Natty went on stuffing chicken and lemon cake into his mouth. The orange cat crouched at his elbow, fastidiously nibbling fallen crumbs.

The news articles reported that Stuart and his cavalry, while circling Union positions on the Chickahominy River, had met with only a few minor challenges by Union pickets and an ill-fated foray by some disorganized Union cavalry. When Stuart's men struck a supply depot on the York River Railroad, situated less than five miles from the Federal supply base at White House Landing, they had encountered only token resistance. The Richmond papers implied that Stuart had refrained from raiding White House itself only because he believed Union command might finally have been alerted to his presence. Bronwen thought otherwise.

She would wager that Stuart's assignment had not been to engage the enemy but to collect information—a scouting expedition, which, she gathered from the newspapers, must have succeeded far beyond his or his commander's wildest expectations. Humiliation of a foe ten times greater in number was simply an amusing side benefit.

Surely McClellan would understand this. But would Pinkerton, whose conceit was so large that it made him underrate everyone except himself? And again Bronwen was reminded of O'Hara's assessment of General Lee: *It could be a big mistake to underestimate him.*

If, due to Stuart's expedition, Lee now held information about Federal positions and approximate troop numbers, what would he do with that information?

In the meantime, there was her brother. She could not even try to reach Washington for new instructions, not with Seth's execution date in three days! Besides, in the unlikely event that no one in Union command recognized Stuart's alleged romp for what it really was, Rhys Bevan certainly would. He had unquestionably already alerted Secretary of War Stanton.

Bronwen again sank into a chair, noticing that the platter of chicken was now mostly heaped with bones, the lemon cake was almost gone, and Natty was slumped forward, his head resting on the tabletop.

Elizabeth was regarding the boy with a smile, and Bronwen was about to suggest putting him in an upstairs bedroom, under armed guard, when a series of rhythmic raps on the back door made her jump from the chair.

"It's only Hosea, come from Chimborazo," Elizabeth declared with a seer's certainty, and went to open the door to admit her servant.

"I smell chicken," announced Hosea upon entering, "but I don't see none."

Elizabeth looked at the table, shook her head, and went to pull another platter of chicken from the warming oven.

"Do you have news?" she asked Hosea, placing plates in front of him and Bronwen, and shooing the cat from the table.

Hosea nodded as he forked a drumstick from the platter, at the same time casting a baleful eye at Bronwen, who had involved him or his father in a number of unpleasant episodes in the past year. The last one had been driving Marsh and her to Timothy Webster's hanging.

"Is it about Marsh?" Bronwen asked, with no hope that Hosea's news might be good.

"Not 'zactly," he said, reviving her momentarily, until he added, "but y'all got kinfolk down here?"

"Kinfolk?" Bronwen repeated loudly in surprise, making Natty's head jerk up from the table.

Hosea nodded again. "Tonight when I went to check on Marse Marsh, there's a young lady with him. After he tells the lady who I am, she asks if I've seen you. Says she's your sister."

"Kathryn's at *Chimborazo?*" said Bronwen incredulously, while grabbing Natty, who had darted toward the door. She managed to hook her fingers into the back of his breeches and drag him to a halt. "And where do you think you're going, young man?"

"To see Lady! Leggo o' me, you . . . you horse-thief!"

She pushed him into a chair and held him there with her hands pressed against his shoulders. "Hosea, did Kathryn say how she had arrived there?"

"She did, but you best hear it from her. Said she wanted to see y'all tomorrow night."

"Not tonight?"

"No, missy. Too many ambulance wagons there now, 'cause the hospital's takin' more sick soldiers from the city. But your sister says tomorrow evenin' for certain, 'cause she's got important news to tell."

"What news?"

Hosea shook his head. "Didn't say."

"I imagine Kathryn's found Marsh there at Chimbo-razo, and since I need him for Seth's rescue, we'll have to spirit him out of that hospital. Tomorrow will be cutting it close to the bone, but I'm so badly in need of sleep I can't think straight. And that's a dangerous state to be in right now."

She needed to be fully alert the next day while arranging the fine points of the clandestine tobacco transport, which included hiring Chaucer and his fellow peddlers for labor detail. As she headed upstairs, pushing Natty ahead of her, she experienced a belated prick of apprehension.

If locating Marsh was Kathryn's news, why hadn't she simply relayed it through Hosea?

28

—m—

While [Confederate] hospitals were still partly unorganized, soldiers were brought in from camp or field, and placed in divisions of them, irrespective of rank or state.

—Phoebe Yates Pember

Chimborazo Hospital

As soon as dusk promised to gather the following evening, Bronwen and Hosea, together with Natty, who adamantly refused to stay behind, made the hike from the Van Lew grounds to Chimborazo. The hospital's wooden structures sprawled across a flat bluff overlooking the James River. Hosea, guiding them through a wide gully at the western edge of the huge Confederate installation, said it would have been faster to take the road, but Bronwen chose the gully route. If longer and tougher, it would be safer. The guards Hosea told her were posted at Chimborazo's main entrance could not be expecting infiltration from the direction of their own capital, and Seth weighed too heavily on Bronwen's mind for her to ignore caution. She was acutely aware of being her brother's means of escaping the hangman.

During the afternoon, the wind had brought snatches of protracted artillery fire from the southeast, possibly somewhere along the Williamsburg road, but whether it indicated the onset of a serious engagement neither she nor Elizabeth were able to learn. Bronwen decided that with Confederate troops entrenched just ahead, the use of their lanterns would be too risky, so what by broad daylight would have been a brief trek to Chimborazo took almost an hour by sunset. Even that was frequently darkened due to shifting clouds that sprinkled rain.

"I had no idea it was this large," she whispered to Hosea, when, after climbing out of the gully, they reached level ground and darted behind the first of numerous squat, wood-framed buildings.

As they approached a whitewashed structure resembling a one-story house, Bronwen clapped her hand over Natty's mouth when he demanded loudly, "Where's Lady?"

"Wait here," Hosea told Bronwen, and went forward to disappear through a doorway.

Minutes later he emerged with Kathryn, and Bronwen noted her sister's expression of relief when she saw Natty. She must have learned of his kidnapping from the ever-chatty O'Hara.

Kathryn whispered, "Come this way." They quickly followed her to another frame house, whose raw wood exterior and lack of a door indicated it was still under construction.

"I'll keep watch," Hosea volunteered, stationing himself in front.

The room they entered smelled of fresh paint. Kathryn, after setting her candleholder on a plank positioned between two sawhorses, lit the candle's wick. As Bronwen watched the small flame sputter and then waver upward, an idea half-shaped until now took distinct form.

"Thank heavens you and Natty are safe," her sister said, "but what about Seth? It's just two days—"

"He's still in Libby," Bronwen interrupted with a stab of frustration. She refrained from saying she did not need reminding of his execution date, asking instead, "How did you come to be here?"

When Kathryn quickly related the sequence of events, she gave scant attention to an argument with Dr. Travis, although Bronwen could hear in her voice the distress it was still causing.

"After I arrived here with General Longstreet's escort, I was shown to that house back there." Kathryn gestured in the direction of the whitewashed structure. "I learned it was the nurses' quarters, and the only thing that seemed to interest anyone was that I had previous experience."

"No one questioned your northern accent?" Bronwen asked in disbelief.

"No one has challenged me, at least not yet. It's probably because those in charge here are still learning the ropes themselves, and there are too many sick and wounded soldiers for them to be turning away a trained nurse."

"This must be a pretty disorganized place if nobody's expressed doubt."

"Of what?" Kathryn asked. "I *am* a nurse."

Natty, who had dropped to sit cross-legged on the floor near Kathryn's feet, piped up, "But these here sol-jers are Rebs!"

"They should have care regardless," Kathryn told him softly, a sentiment not unexpected by Bronwen, but Natty reacted with a look of confusion.

"What about Seth?" Kathryn anxiously repeated. "I know you too well, Bronwen, to believe you're leaving his fate to others. I'm terrified for both of you."

Bronwen decided against further terrifying her with the vast uncertainties. "I'm working on it," she answered, "and I urgently need Marsh, so where can I find him?"

Kathryn, looking even more anxious, said, "That's one reason I needed to see you. The gunshot wound Marsh received—"

"Was a surface wound," Bronwen broke in. "The bullet

grazed his head, and knocked him down. When I first saw him he was unconscious, but he came to not long after."

"He must have injured himself when he fell, Bronwen, because I've seen his records, and the diagnosis made by a surgeon here was that Marsh suffered a severe concussion. He's very unsteady on his feet and is having vision problems. We can pray it's only a temporary condition, but right now he can't see well enough to move about without assistance."

"Oh, my Lord!" Bronwen groaned, trying to absorb the devastating blow that Marsh was lost as a collaborator. Why, everywhere she turned, did fate seem to be conspiring against her?

The four scruffy peddlers she had attempted to hire that morning, including Chaucer himself, had been markedly less than eager to shift tobacco hogsheads. After she had offered them the equivalent of a king's ransom in Federal money, they still had refused to guarantee even their exalted presence, much less their willingness to work. When she had checked late this afternoon, only two of the three Virginia Central boxcars O'Hara had pledged stood on a spur of track running beside the British tobacco warehouse. There had been no peddlers in sight. There had also been no locomotive. And no O'Hara.

How was she going to load and move that tobacco? De Warde would never fulfill his part of the bargain with regard to Seth's escape unless it could be proved she was making good on the transfer of those wretched hogsheads.

But none of this was Marsh's fault, and she asked her sister, "Will he eventually be all right?"

"I pray so," Kathryn said, "but there's something else I must tell—"

She was interrupted by Natty, who had suddenly jumped to his feet, crossed his arms over his chest, and announced, "I kin do it!"

"Do *what?*" said Bronwen.

"Help git yer brother out, o' course—what else we bin jawin' 'bout?"

"If I accept your offer, my man," said Bronwen, so desperate she was only half in jest, "don't disgrace yourself by asking if you'll be paid! Take that matter up with President Lincoln."

Kathryn appeared shocked, while Natty sent Bronwen a disgusted look that said such a thing had never crossed his mind. "All I wants," he declared with fervor, "is to get outta this here Rich-man city."

Bronwen conceded this might contain a kernel of truth, but she could also picture Natty in the White House demanding that Lincoln pay up.

"Kathryn, would you be safe here for a few more days?"

"There's no reason to think I wouldn't. You must work on freeing Seth, Bronwen, without worrying about me, or about Marsh either. I can't imagine anyone here wanting to harm us."

Natty, abruptly seeming to recall something, whirled toward Bronwen. She could guess the source of his troubled expression.

"Kathryn, be aware that Bluebell is in Richmond," she warned, and gave her sister a brief account of the farm escapade. "All in all, I don't think we need to worry about her anymore. At least I certainly hope not."

Natty gave his head a violent shake. "Thet hoity-toit's a witch, an' who kin say what a witch'll do?"

Kathryn also looked doubtful, but she said, obviously to reassure the boy, "That woman couldn't possibly know I'm here. No one knows it."

He looked about to disagree again, so Bronwen said with finality, "Look, the sooner I get on with this, the sooner we can *all* leave Richmond!"

"But before you leave, Bronwen, there's something else, someone you *must* see," Kathryn told her, the strained, insistent edge to her voice persuading Bronwen to consent despite her impatience.

"All right, but it must be quick!"

"I wouldn't delay you if it weren't important. We need to go to another building," Kathryn added. "Natty, you wait here with Hosea."

She took Bronwen's hand and hurriedly drew her outside. The wind had picked up, sweeping clouds over a rising moon to make grotesque shadows weave across their path. Bronwen again voiced her impatience, but Kathryn remained intent on her mysterious mission. She stopped at another structure, which aside from being unpainted looked no different to Bronwen from any of the others. Her sister pointed to a door, and after inching it open enough to enter, she put a finger to her lips.

They stepped into a vacant hallway that smelled of new wood. A lantern swinging from a hook was the only source of light, and after Kathryn took it down, she signaled for Bronwen to follow her along the hall. They passed the open door of what in the dim lantern's glow looked to be a large room holding rows of empty cots.

Kathryn gestured at it, whispering, "That's just been made ready, and they plan to move wounded into it tomorrow. Which is why we had to do this tonight before anyone else was here."

"Anyone else? So far I haven't seen another soul."

"There's a room at the end of the hall."

When they reached its door, Kathryn indicated a piece of paper tacked to the wood frame that read in bold black lettering: *Authorized Persons ONLY.*

"Kathryn, what's this about?"

"That sign was put up after I mistakenly stumbled in there, looking for the new supply closet." Kathryn pushed open the door a few inches and poked her head around it to peer inside, then beckoned for Bronwen to follow her into the small room.

Bronwen could see by the light of Kathryn's raised

lantern only one bed, where a figure lay partially covered by a sheet. Kathryn pointed at the wall beside the bed where a white object was hanging; it resembled a padded coat with long laces that dangled from flap openings.

"That's a straitjacket," Kathryn whispered.

Bronwen took a quick step backward as a man's voice came from the bed. "Is that you, Miss Llyr?"

"Yes, sir, it is, and I've brought someone with me," Kathryn answered. Lifting the lantern, she approached the bed and motioned for her sister to follow.

Bronwen reluctantly moved to stand behind a bedside table that held a water pitcher and cup, and a tray of dishes that contained remnants of what, from the looks of the congealed brown gravy, had been an ample supper. There was a spoon on the tray but, tellingly, no knife or fork. Well within the man's reach were half a dozen books. Since the one title Bronwen could make out was *Moby Dick,* the man must expect to be here for some time.

Under the table sat an empty chamber pot. Impossible to ignore was a length of chain running from a ring bolted into the floorboard to a point somewhere under the lower edge of the sheet. It provided Bronwen with a wrenching reminder of Seth. But if this man were insane, why was her sister standing unguarded beside him? Now that Bronwen could see him better, she noted that he looked healthy for a bedridden patient. He had pleasantly regular features and a ruddy complexion, as if he had spent much of his previous life outside. He was also, as evidenced from the toes protruding slightly from the end of the bed, quite a tall man.

"This is my sister, Bronwen," Kathryn told him. "You said you had heard of her."

"I've heard much. My apologies for not standing to be properly introduced, Miss Llyr," he said, peering at Bronwen and then gesturing at the chain, "but my hosts have made it awkward to do so. I hasten to add that aside from the restraint, I am quite comfortable. But I am also at a disadvantage because I cannot see you clearly. Would you please come a bit closer? Your sister can likely assure you that I'm not mad, at least not dangerously so."

He smiled, and when Bronwen stepped forward, she could see bright, brown eyes absent the slightest hint of insanity. She had never met this man, but something tugged at her memory.

"I'm the one at a disadvantage, sir," she said, sending Kathryn an accusatory glance. "My sister didn't tell me who you are."

The eyes crinkled at the edges. "I asked her not to, until I could see you myself," he answered. "Given my confinement, I've become somewhat distrustful. You may understand better when I tell you that I am a friend of a friend."

Bronwen's memory tossed her a fragment. Startled, she bent to look more closely at the man, her intuition suggesting who he might be, while logic argued that he could not be.

He responded to her astonished gaze with a chuckle. "Our friend told me you are a clever lass."

Fear shot through her, and Bronwen gripped the table to steady herself before asking, "Sir, how recently have you suffered from eye trouble?"

"Excellent, young lady! Yes, I am indeed James Quiller."

The implications were staggering, and when Bronwen returned to where Natty and Hosea waited, it was with such fury joined by mind-numbing terror that she recognized the signs of panic.

She kept her head long enough to tell Hosea to remain there at Chimborazo and to keep an eye on Kathryn and Marsh until either she returned or Union troops arrived. Meanwhile, they should all watch closely over the "insane patient." At the moment, the only other thing she could do for James Quiller was to alert Elizabeth Van Lew and her loyalist network to his situation, because freeing Seth must come before all else.

And for that she needed Natty. As she and the boy made their way toward the gully, she prayed the hike to the Van Lew mansion would clear her head.

The plan to rescue her brother was dangerously compromised, as it now seemed evident that de Warde intended to double-cross her. De Warde, who by his own admission several days ago had formerly met Quiller in Washington, had then deliberately failed to mention what he knew to be the substitution of a counterfeit Quiller in Richmond.

James Quiller had just told her that his capture occurred while he awaited a carriage at the Richmond rail station. One had drawn up beside him, its door already open, and in a matter of seconds several men had whisked him into an enclosed phaeton. From the station he had been transported directly to Chimborazo. He claimed he was not being mistreated and, with good-natured gallows humor, said the captivity allowed him to catch up on his reading.

He could have done the same thing in more comfort at the Spotswood.

Bronwen remembered how insistent his impostor had been that she lodge there. Insistent, too, that he escort her everywhere, which had bothered her enough at the time to take evasive action. It must have been instinct that warned her something was amiss, since she could not recall having been actively suspicious of him. He was after all Lincoln's *friend.* When his reading glasses had struck her as odd, she told herself it was only because Lincoln had made such a point of Quiller's recovered eyesight. When he had asked too many questions, including ones about her "colleagues," she assured herself he was just being solicitous. But her instincts had protected her. She had not only evaded him, she had given him no answers.

The switch had almost certainly been made by Norris

and Confederate intelligence. De Warde's silence about it undoubtedly involved some self-serving double-dealing, but whatever it was, it put her brother's life in still more jeopardy.

She now realized that if Quiller's impostor was a member of Confederate intelligence, he had likely supplied her alias and whereabouts to Bluebell. Which answered the nagging question of how the woman had found her. Perhaps Simone Bleuette had met with him at the Spotswood the day Bronwen had seen her there. It also explained the Richmond police breaking down her door. She remembered that at the time Quiller had fleetingly occurred to her as the single most obvious one to inform them of her whereabouts, but she had refused to even consider him as a betrayer.

She had sincerely liked the bogus Quiller, and it galled her to think this might have made her more trusting of him. O'Hara would find it hilarious.

O'Hara . . . who had said he could persuade the West Virginian Hornbrook to provide a locomotive and an engineer. Both were to have arrived in Richmond yesterday at the earliest, today at the latest, and both had done neither. With only two boxcars delivered, O'Hara must have failed her. Despite her past mistrust of him, it was now unbearable to speculate that he too had betrayed her.

"Natty!" she whispered as they climbed out of the gully's western rim. "Keep that lantern down, or somebody could spot us!"

"Cain't see nothin' ahead o' me. Almost jest stepped on one o' them polecat skunks. That'd shur make *everybody* spot us!"

"Hush!"

She had to keep her wits about her and devise a new plan. The original one had called for Seth's escape to take place late tomorrow, after the tobacco had been loaded into the boxcars and the train ready to leave Richmond. Now she was faced with the prospect that Confederate intelligence could be, or already had been, alerted.

De Warde's tobacco could just go to the devil . . . but no, she could not dismiss the British threat causing Lincoln's deep concern. He had trusted her enough to send her to Richmond. But what could she do? She had to free Seth from Libby *tonight*.

When she and Natty reached level ground, she found still another cause for alarm. The wind had increased, and when it veered toward the west, she could hear a deep and continuous rumble of wagons. Pitched over it were the keyed-up sounds of men and horses that usually signaled significant troop movement. There was no way of knowing if this activity was connected to the afternoon's artillery fire. Was Lee's army preparing for siege behind the earthworks, meaning that McClellan had at last begun an advance on Richmond?

She hesitated only an instant before the fresh urgency of freeing her brother overwhelmed everything else. After a quick word to the boy, they dashed for the mansion under clouds racing like phantom frigates across the face of a watery moon.

29

—m—

One becomes a critic when one cannot be an artist, just as a man becomes a stool pigeon when he cannot be a soldier.

—Flaubert

Richmond

𝔄 short time later, when they descended Church Hill to the road that ran along the wind-roughened canal, Bronwen was leading the brown Morgan horse. She sensed Natty giving her sideways glances, probably because she had been muttering under her breath ever since leaving the Van Lew mansion. It helped her to focus on the obvious pitfalls ahead, and kept her from paralyzing anxiety over the unforeseen ones. There were too many things that could go wrong.

She had stopped at Van Lew's to retrieve the horse and the carpetbag. The bag now held, among other things, the Colt revolver, recent issues of the Richmond *Enquirer,* and, carefully wrapped in strips of sheeting, two flasks of kerosene and a bottle of brandy. The gear of a desperado.

She had asked Elizabeth if there were any messages from O'Hara. Since none had come, there remained no hope that he would make it in time, if at all.

The only development Bronwen could count in her fa-

vor was the Confederate troop movement. It meant fewer
soldiers to launch a manhunt. Citizens, too, were less
likely to leave their homes, and in fact, the traffic on the
streets was already sparse.

Also in her favor might be the element of surprise, but
she could find precious little else to boost her confidence.

Ahead on Canal Street the hulking Libby warehouse
came into view, its darkness relieved only by the window
openings in which feeble light flickered from what Natty
said were candle stubs sold by the peddlers.

Bronwen pulled him into the moon shadow of an abandoned waterfront shack and looped the Morgan's reins
over a post. She was reluctant to use the boy in this new
and more perilous plan, but whom else did she have? Not
Marsh in Chimborazo, or O'Hara, presumably in West
Virginia. Natty was also uniquely qualified.

"Do you understand what you're to do," she asked him,
"and the exact order you're to do it in?"

"I ain't no dummy."

"That's not what I asked. Everything depends on your
doing precisely as we've planned."

"I *know* thet!"

It did not reassure her that the boy looked drawn and
a little less full of himself than he usually did. He would
need every ounce of his irritating boldness plus a dash of
recklessness to ignore what otherwise might be crippling
fear. Not in her wildest dreams had she ever imagined
relying on a young pickpocket, but she did not doubt his
devotion to Kathryn, and hence to their brother. And at
the moment he looked a far sight more trustworthy than
Colonel Dorian de Warde.

"I think," she whispered, giving his hair a quick tousle,
"that you are a plucky lad, and if this works, I believe I'll
pay you myself."

He gave her a surprised if dubious look, and then with
a jerk of his head in the direction of the warehouse, he
grumbled, "So lemme git goin'!"

She nodded, and watched as he began creeping stealthily toward a side door of Libby. He had learned as a peddler that it was the one nearest to the guards' quarters.

Seth slumped back against the wall in frustration, pocketing the penknife that he had surreptitiously been using to work at the padlock holding the metal shackle around his ankle. He knew the effort was futile, but he could not sit idly waiting for execution, even though he tried to make it appear that way to the guards.

As darkness fell, the pounding noises outside the window had finally ceased. That morning, the first hammer blows from workmen raising the scaffold for his gallows had rung like death knells, and all day he had struggled against despair. Hope of escape had dimmed as every hour brought the next sunrise closer. Each time he shut his eyes it was to see the image of his body swinging from a hangman's noose.

Thinking he had heard some faint odd noise at the window opening above him, he glanced up. All he could see was what resembled a mop bobbing above the ledge.

It must be one of the street urchins who regularly begged outside the prison, but why would one be here at this hour? There was no one handing out money now, not even the guards. So far the number of prisoners was few enough, and the warehouse isolated enough, that two of the guards would be sleeping while the other two played cards and drank beer, leaving the remaining pair to patrol the outside walls. Reason told them a Yankee officer could not go far if he did manage to break out.

Seth looked around at what he could see in the dim glow of candle stubs. A few men were squinting at newspapers brought in earlier by the peddlers. Some yards beyond him, Major Edmund Randall, Lieutenant Rafe Andrews, and the burly Thompson were playing poker by a sputtering flame. Yesterday Seth had asked Rafe what he knew about Thompson.

"I don't know anything," Rafe had answered. "Don't even know his first name. Closed-mouthed about himself, even if he's loud enough about everything else."

Randall had said much the same thing, but added, "The others here are suspicious that Thompson betrayed you. Which means if given the chance he would inform on any of us, so I doubt you'll receive any answers."

Seth now heard again the faint persistent noise at the window. Not wanting to draw attention to himself, he slowly climbed to his feet and made as if to stretch while he leaned toward the opening. The first thing he saw was the rising scaffold, but was startled by the mop appearing, disappearing, and reappearing as if its owner were jumping up and down. He glimpsed the face of the young peddler, who had not been there for the past several days.

When the boy's eyes next met Seth's, he lobbed a tiny, wadded scrap of paper through the opening. Seth, after his initial surprise, stretched again so he could move the length of his chain and block a view of the window from the room. After a furtive glance round him, he did a knee-bend and retrieved the paper. With his back to the others, he made a show of scratching his chest, smoothing the scrap in the process.

The light was so weak he could barely make out the black-penciled words: *On the ledge. Use east door. Be ready! B.*

With a dizzying rush of hope, Seth looked again at the window. The boy had disappeared, but on the ledge lay a small metal object. Just as Seth recognized it as a key, and felt another wild surge of hope, he heard a voice behind him. He balled the scrap and pretended to cough, raising his hand to pop the paper into his mouth. Then he made himself turn slowly to face Thompson.

"Others want to know if a hand of poker sounds good?" Thompson told him, his lips twisting in a grin that did not touch his eyes. "Said I'd ask, since you and me are such good chums."

Seth coughed again and covered his mouth while tonguing the ball into his cheek. "Just needed to stretch my legs," he mumbled, bending sideways to obstruct Thompson's view of the ledge. He did not dare look up, so he couldn't know if it had worked. But now the other man's gaze went beyond him, and Thompson took a step toward the window.

Seth swayed sideways to lurch hard against him. "Sorry," he muttered as Thompson staggered backward. "Chain makes me clumsy."

"Yeah, sure," Thompson said, having seized Seth's upper arm in a brutish grip. Again the man's gaze went to the window. How could he miss seeing the key that in Seth's mind was now the size of a cannonball?

"Wind's sure pickin' up out there," Thompson observed, while Seth's heart pounded against his rib cage. "Not a fit night for man nor beast." Thompson, with the odd grin again, released Seth's arm. "You don't wanna look out that window, Llyr, 'cause you won't like what you'll see! Sure you don't wanna play a last hand or two of poker?"

Seth shook his head.

Thompson turned, and over his shoulder said, "Suit yerself, chum."

Seth remained on his feet until the man had rejoined the poker game before he backed up the few more steps his chain would allow. Scanning the room, he waited again until he felt that none of the few men still awake were looking in his direction. After rubbing his neck, he stretched his arm to scratch his shoulder blade, and his fingers touched the ledge and moved to the metal key. He extended his index finger and was inching the key closer to the inside of the ledge when a sudden explosive crash made him jump. The key dropped to the floor with a soft chink, amid a succession of loud banging noises.

An outside door had blown open and was continuing to slam against the wall. It was at the east end of the

warehouse. Seth sank to the floorboards, quickly palming
the key as one of the guards ran to close the door. Then
the guard turned and unaccountably began to walk toward
where Seth was chained. He could feel sweat breaking out
on his forehead as the guard stopped a few feet away.

"Y'all need the privy?"

Seth shook his head as the man stood looking down at
him.

"Last call tonight. And those breeches, boy, are the last
ones y'all're goin' to get."

When Seth said nothing, the guard walked back across
the room.

The men settled down for the night as the candle stubs
guttered and went out. When it grew dark in the corner
where Seth was sitting, he leaned back against the wall
and pulled his legs under him, sliding the key down his
calf. By touch alone he inserted the key in the padlock.
It seemed to slip in, but then it jammed. It would not turn
and he could not even pull it back out. Agonizing seconds
passed while he jiggled and tugged at the key, until with
a whispered click it turned.

He let out his breath and with his eyes shifting over
the room, he gripped the padlock. Holding the looped
length of chain across his lap so it wouldn't rattle, he pried
open the lock and the metal shackle. After he drew out
the key, he slipped it into his pocket, then immediately
rearranged the padlock to look as if it were still in place.

He heard something above him, and looked up at the
window to see the moonlit blur of a small clenched fist.
Then it vanished.

Be ready! Bronwen had written.

Seth gathered himself into a tense crouch, peering into
the darkness to await whatever his sister dared.

It came with a thump.

Below an opposite window, a blazing torch had struck
the floor, its flames instantly spurting upward.

The prisoners nearest the window scrambled to their feet with yells of "Fire! It's *fire!*"

A second burning torch soared through another window.

Men were jumping to their feet as flame leaped from still another blazing missile, and then another. While they spewed smoke in rolling black clouds, Seth was sprinting for the east side of the warehouse when disheveled guards burst from their quarters with guns drawn.

"Water! Get water!" prisoners were shouting, even as the confused guards hollered and waved their weapons at those threatening to charge past them.

When a revolver spit twice, Seth stopped in his tracks. The two outside guards had rushed in with raised guns, and the noise was reaching a deafening pitch. Through the thickening smoke Seth tried to locate the guards' door, but could barely see a dozen feet beyond him. He was being pushed and jostled from every side as brawnier prisoners shoved their way ahead, some with pails from the privies, and he had lost all sense of direction. Where was the east door?

Suddenly deliverance in the form of Edmund Randall appeared a yard or two ahead. The major was frantically gesturing to him, the uproar too great to hear what he was shouting, but Seth could see Randall's lips shaping what looked like "This way!"

He plowed after Randall, pushing through clutches of other men desperately trying to find the doors. The smoke was thinner here, and Seth at last spotted a doorway where a handful of prisoners labored to drag a fire hose farther into the room. The canal must be straight ahead.

Starting for the doorway, Seth was jerked to a halt by a hand clamping his shoulder, and he felt the prick of a knifepoint at his neck. He could not see who had seized him. At the glint of the blade drawing back, ready to slash toward his throat, he wrenched himself free. At the same instant he was shoved forward, catching himself just

before smashing into a wall. Flattening himself against it
to feel his way, he inched along, not knowing where he
was, or who might be directly behind him with the knife.
His outstretched fingers broke into empty space, groping
in mid-air, and he prayed he had found an open door.

As he stumbled into the doorway, someone jumped
from behind to stand squarely in his path. Seth jerked his
head up to look into the narrowed eyes of Thompson. One
of his hands gripped the handle of a knife.

The big man grabbed Seth's shoulder and yanked him
forward. "Get the hell out of here!" he yelled. "Go on!
Move!"

In confusion Seth staggered on. He could hear Thompson shouting behind him as he flung himself into the fresh
night air. When he glanced back, he saw Rafe Andrews
positioned beside Thompson, the two of them blocking
access to the doorway from the room.

"Get going, dammit!" Thompson bellowed at him.

Rafe was also hollering, but he suddenly pivoted toward a man coming up behind him. Thompson turned,
too, and lunged forward to grab Major Edmund Randall
by the throat, shouting, "You goddamn stool pigeon! Traitor!"

"*Go!*" Rafe shouted to Seth. "We'll see to Randall.
And good luck!"

Seth turned to run, nearly smashing into a figure with
a kerchief tied like a highwayman's over the lower part
of the face.

He was raising his arm to deliver a blow, when one of
the eyes above the kerchief winked at the same time he
heard a familiar voice whisper "Seth!"

"Bronwen?"

She looked past her brother's shoulder and through a
thickening haze of smoke saw seven or eight bodies press-

ing to get through the doorway. They were packed together like tobacco in a . . .

"Seth, quick! Do you know those men?"

"Most of them."

"Tell them to follow us! Hurry, we don't have much
time!"

Seth did not question it, and turned immediately to yell
"Rafe! Thompson! C'mon! You others follow!"

Bronwen grabbed Natty, who was behind her holding
the Morgan, as a handful of choking men stumbled outside. Behind them smoke began rolling in huge, stifling
black billows. No more men could make it through that
door now. When she heard muffled gunshots from inside
the building, she boosted Natty onto the horse, climbed
up behind him, and shouted to Seth, "Hurry!"

"Where . . . where to?" gasped one of the seven men
around her brother.

Bronwen leaned down and said to Seth, "Tell them to
follow the Morgan—northwest to the railroad! Go west
along the tracks, and look for a warehouse with Virginia
Central boxcars! Now c'mon!"

Seth shouted the directions to the others, but when
Bronwen reached down for his hand to help him up behind her, he drew back. She knew him, knew he was
reluctant to ride while the others were on foot, so she did
the only thing she could think of. Pointing to the scaf-
folding, she screamed, "That's *your* gallows!"

After another moment of hesitation, Seth climbed up
behind her and she wheeled the Morgan toward the road.
Members of the fire brigade would be there before long.
They would find more smoke than fire, but it should keep
them occupied, long enough for the escaped officers to
reach the boxcars before the prison break was discovered.

When she turned to make sure the men were heading
in the right direction, Seth said in her ear, "How did you
manage the torches?"

"First two were Richmond newspapers soaked in

brandy," she yelled back, "like flaming plum pudding. For the next ones I used rags and kerosene. Didn't want to burn the place down with Union soldiers inside, and I figured all you'd really need was a good, thick smoke screen."

She felt his cheek press her hair and his arms around her waist tighten as they turned a corner and passed along a quiet street. When she heard fire bells clang, she again glanced back. The Union officers were dropping behind, so she grit her teeth against the urge to prod the Morgan faster.

Seth jerked his head at Natty, perched in front of her and clutching the horse's mane, and asked, "Who's your friend?"

"Best little pickpocket east of the Mississippi."

"Best *anywheres!*" the boy shot back.

"Pinching padlock keys is a new specialty," Bronwen added.

She breathed more easily when she saw the railroad tracks ahead. It wouldn't matter now if the Union officers lost sight of her. Her first concern had to be for Seth, and she intended to hide him in one of the empty boxcars. The others, too, if they acted fast enough.

As they moved along the moonlit tracks, she spotted a peculiar glow some distance ahead. Her breath caught in her throat when she realized it could be the British tobacco warehouse, located on a short spur that branched off just beyond a curve of the main track.

"Seth, we'd better dismount," she told him. "I don't like the looks of that light up there. Let me take a quick scout around, and you stay here with Natty."

"Not a chance," Seth answered. "If you go, we all go!"

There wasn't time to argue, and Bronwen was aware that he would not knowingly let her walk into danger alone, so she pulled up the horse near some scrubby trees.

They had to hurry, but it could be anything ahead, from Richmond police to more Confederate troops. Or Norris and his intelligence agents alerted by de Warde, even though Seth's escape had been planned for tomorrow.

After they slid off the Morgan and she took the carpetbag from Natty, she glimpsed movement back down the tracks. "Here come the others," she said to Seth. "Please stay here with them until I see what—"

She broke off at a sudden but unmistakable rumble.

"Gawd-a'mighty, it's a train!" yelped Natty, diving for the trees.

Bronwen looked to where the seven men were also moving from the railbed. But the sound, she was sure, had come from the west!

Her heart pounding, she began to run beside the tracks, aware of Seth and Natty beside her and the other men closing in behind them. They were all listening for sounds of horses, signaling a search party, while watching the track ahead for a locomotive's headlight. The rumble had somewhat increased in volume, and Bronwen now thought she could hear steam hissing. But where *was* it?

As they rounded a clump of trees, the dark shapes of two warehouses loomed ahead. Bronwen stopped when she saw that the light, as she had feared, did come from one of them. She snatched her spyglass out of the carpetbag and jammed it against her eye, then nearly dropped it in stunned disbelief.

After waving her arm for the others to follow, she dashed toward the first warehouse.

Lanterns lit a scene she could not have prayed into being. At least eight men, some of whom she recognized as the peddlers she had tried to hire, were rolling hogsheads down a wooden ramp that ran from the open doors of the warehouse directly into the second boxcar. A locomotive and tender stood coupled to the first car.

"Greetings, lassie!" shouted the rotund peddler who called himself Chaucer, while he wiped sweat from his face. "I brought some fellow knaves to attend thee."

As Bronwen and the escaped men stood there gaping,

another man ducked nimbly under the ramp to lope toward them.

"How y'all doin,' Red? Nice of you to drop by."

"O'Hara, I . . . I thought—"

"I know what you thought. But I got held up trying to find an engineer, is all. You have no faith, Red."

"Did you bring the supplies?" she asked, glancing at the Union officers and hoping O'Hara had done what she had suggested.

"You're not satisfied with a train and an engineer?"

"Where's the engineer?"

He clapped a striped cap on his head, saying, "At your service, ma'am!"

As Bronwen stood rooted there, unsure whether to laugh or cry with relief, O'Hara said to the officers, "Red, here, insisted those cars should tote supplies to look authentic in case we got stopped. So don't get too exercised if you find among the other stuff some Reb uniforms. Help yourselves."

Even as he was pointing to the first boxcar, the men had already sprung forward and were scrambling inside it.

"Have you been here long?" Bronwen asked him.

"Just sittin' around and waitin' on you, 'til that scruffy lot arrived," O'Hara said, gesturing to the peddlers. "Stoked the engine when I heard those fire bells—figured it was you, up to no good. What'd you do, burn down Jefferson Davis's house?"

"No, smoked up Libby Prison."

O'Hara grinned. "Guessed that good-lookin' fellow I saw might be your brother."

"You'd better get moving *now*."

"Right after we load some more of the tobacco," he answered adding, "It's my job, Red."

He turned away from her and shouted at the Union officers emerging from the boxcars, "We can leave this Reb town a whole lot faster if you start rollin'!"

•   •   •

Fearing they were running out of time, Bronwen looked nervously into the second car, where the number of tobacco casks had quickly increased. She started to ask O'Hara if he knew the hour, when he held up a hand, saying, "You hear something?"

After a moment, she said, "It's horses! The escape must have been discovered. Damnation, O'Hara, you should have left!"

He raised his voice to shout, "Take cover! Horses comin'."

"Excuse me," inquired Chaucer from the ramp, "but does that apply to me and mine, or solely to thee and thine?"

O'Hara rolled his eyes, answering, "You and yours keep working! Go on, Red," he said, pushing her toward the boxcar.

"How many hogsheads have they loaded so far?"

"More than half. Now get in that car!"

She had again forgotten how strong he was until he grabbed her waist and swung her up to the car. One of the Union officers, a bear of a man, caught and pulled her inside.

"You sure think of everything," the man said to her. "Even got tobacco for us. Major John Thompson, Second Michigan, and I do thank you, miss."

Seth, helping to stand a hogshead, said in surprise, "*Major* Thompson?"

The man nodded. "Owe you an apology, Lieutenant, for some rough treatment. I suspected Randall from the start on account of he disappeared right after young Carson died. Figured he'd gone to Winder. Thought if I made your life miserable enough, he might confide his dirty dealings."

"You saw that key in the window tonight, didn't you?"

Grinning, Thompson said, "Sure did. Got myself ready for some action, and once the fun started, watched Randall like a hawk. Trust me, his traitor days are over!"

At the sound of horses and riders approaching, the men crept behind the standing hogsheads. Bronwen crouched beside the door, furious with O'Hara and with herself for not demanding that he leave immediately after she and the others arrived. For what good it would have done!

"Evenin', sirs," she heard O'Hara say, and she could also hear the grin in his voice. "What brings you out tonight? Not too often I see the *Richmond police*."

His last words were loud enough to be heard in Wheeling, Bronwen thought, and felt Natty press against her.

A new voice said, "Prison break—down at Libby. Bunch of Yankees escaped. You see any men pass here?"

"How long ago?" came the relaxed-sounding reply.

"Within the last half hour or so."

Bronwen couldn't catch O'Hara's answer, but she did hear another voice say, "This warehouse is flyin' a British flag. So just what're y'all doin' here?"

Bronwen felt her pulse race, and cautiously peered around the door. O'Hara, standing in front of four men on horseback, was pulling a paper from his trouser pocket.

"Have orders here," he said, "from Secretary of State Judah Benjamin. Says to move this here tobacco and get it to Fredericksburg by mornin'."

"Don't sound right to me. Lemme see that order!"

Bronwen watched as the police officer snatched the paper from O'Hara, and then whirled to gesture to the Union officers behind her. Without a word spoken, they moved into the boxcar entrance, their Confederate uniforms dusty gray in the lantern light.

The police officer glanced up. "Y'all got soldiers on detail? Why didn't you say so?" He waved the order, saying, "I'll deliver this to Winder. In the meantime, keep your eyes peeled for those escapees!"

"I surely will do that," drawled O'Hara. "But bein' as how they're Yanks, it seems to me like they'd go north. 'Course if they do, they're headin' into a lot of trouble."

"Why's that?"

"Jackson's comin'! Saw his troops marchin' south on my run here. Those Yanks are likely to walk straight into a Stonewall!"

Bronwen heard gusts of laughter, but she didn't breathe fully again until the horses were turned and headed north. When she climbed down from the car, O'Hara was instructing the peddlers to remove the ramp.

"If you heard," he said, "you know we have to get the hell out of here. I forged that Benjamin order myself."

"Was that true what you told them—about Jackson coming south?"

"Would I lie to a policeman? Sure, it was true. Things could be about to explode here, and I'd just as soon not be tangled in it. Not with this damn tobacco!"

"How much has been loaded?"

"More than half, and then some. Maybe three-quarters."

She followed him as he went to the locomotive. "O'Hara, can you make it to Wheeling, taking my brother and the other men?"

"Sure! But not unless we move out fast before Winder and . . . don't you mean can *we* make it?"

"I'm not coming."

"Red, you *are* coming if I have to hogtie you and—"

"O'Hara, I can't."

She was aware of a few men coming up behind her, and knew she could not explain much.

"What do you mean you *can't!*" O'Hara demanded.

"My sister, Marsh, and James Quiller are all at Chimborazo, and I promised I'd come back for them. And it worries me that Bluebell's still on the loose. For that matter, Washington needs to be alerted about Jackson's movements."

"We can wire Rhys Bevan from Wheeling!" he argued.

"O'Hara, I have *my* job, too, and the . . . She broke off,

not free to mention Lincoln. "What time is it?" she asked him.

O'Hara pulled out a pocket watch. "Half past ten. Now listen, Red—"

"Get that engine steaming before Winder arrives with troops, O'Hara! That's an order. And I outrank you!"

Bronwen turned and walked toward the peddlers. It was payroll time.

She stood beside the tracks as the train gathered steam and rumbled away. O'Hara had actually looked as if he knew what he was doing, his elbow resting on the window of the cab as if he ran a train every day.

Natty stood beside her, holding the Morgan, and kept glancing up at her with a scowl. Bronwen swiped at her eyes and said, "Time to go, my man."

"You dint even say so-long to yer brother," he responded accusingly.

"At the last minute, I couldn't find him. But he's left Richmond and that's what matters. Now let's go!"

As she took the Morgan's reins from him, she heard footsteps behind her, and spun around to see a man in Confederate uniform emerging from the warehouse.

"No!" she shouted in helpless anger. "No! Why aren't you on that train?"

"You couldn't think I'd leave you here alone."

30

—∽—

The tobacco alleged *to be bought* [was in] *separate warehouses . . . saving the property claimed by foreigners whose governments refused to recognize us.*

—John B. Jones, 1862

Richmond

As they made their way toward Van Lew's kitchen door, trees tossed in a wind that was sweeping clouds before it to clear the sky.

"I'm goin' to see Lady," Natty abruptly announced.

"Who's Lady?" Seth asked, stopping a few yards from the back steps to glance around them.

"Our sister," Bronwen answered with a sigh. "Natty, there's no time to take you to Chimborazo. I need to see my brother behind the Union lines."

"You don't hafta take me! I kin git there by myself. It ain't far an' I knows the way."

"All right," she relented, knowing he would go no matter what she said, "but first let Miss Van Lew give you something to eat."

"Wait," Seth said. "We can't let the boy just go off by himself."

"He's not a boy," said Bronwen. "He's a tough, resourceful little rascal, and a good thing for us that he is!"

From the corner of her eye she saw Natty's mouth twitch, as though he might actually smile. He must have seen her glance, because he merely tossed his head as if her remark went without saying.

She fingered the coins in her trouser pocket. There were only two of the U.S. Treasury ones left, but its seal would afford protection for both Natty and Kathryn, and Marsh and Quiller, too, if Union troops occupied Chimborazo before she herself could return there. Or if the worst happened and she could never return.

She withdrew one of the gold coins and held it out to Natty.

"Take good care of this, my man. And let my sister know you have it."

He gawked wide-eyed at the coin, and she knew it would be safe with him. Who would suspect a youngster of carrying something so valuable?

Bronwen glanced around uneasily as the wind whistled through the trees. "There's no more time because I have an appointment to keep," she said, taking some smaller coins from her pocket and thrusting them toward the boy. "So take these before I change my mind."

He reached out and snatched them, shoving them all into his trouser pocket. Then, after a moment's thought, he hauled the gold one back out and thrust it deep into another pocket.

"Natty, tell Kathryn that I'll come back to Chimborazo after our brother is out of harm's way. Among other things, I need to return Mr. Quiller to Washington, or I'll lose the trust of a friend in the White House."

When Natty nodded at her, it was not his usual, impatient jerk of the head.

"Also tell her not to fret," Bronwen said, reaching out to ruffle the boy's hair, and adding, "Seth and I will be safe and sound."

Natty cocked his head to stare at her with a peculiar

expression. "Is thet the truth? I never seen you do *nothin'* thet's safe!"

Fortunately, Elizabeth was by this time stationed in the doorway.

Bronwen handed the revolver to Seth. "You may need this more than I do," she told him, "because I think Elizabeth's musket came here on the *Mayflower*. I'll be back soon."

When her brother started to protest, she cut him off, saying, "Don't worry, Seth, it's only some loose ends I have to tie up for the president." It was not quite the whole truth, but not a bold-faced lie, either.

As she rode away, she hoped her promise to return soon was one she could keep. Before she reined the Morgan around the next corner, she glanced back at the darkened mansion; a spring door behind a bureau gave entrance to the secret attic chamber located just above the columned portico. The chamber was little more than three feet high, and she imagined if her moderately tall brother needed to use it, he would think himself imprisoned again. But with any luck, it would not be for long.

When she and the Morgan reached the foot of Church Hill, the number of torches and lanterns around Libby showed that the contained fires had not created any observable damage. She turned the Morgan in the opposite direction to take a circuitous route.

Reining in some distance from her destination, she tethered the horse in a stand of grass. After checking the double derringer in her jacket pocket, and making herself take several deep breaths, she went once again to the warehouse door over which was flown the British flag.

The Englishman was already inside, standing near the door. As Bronwen had earlier directed, the first rows of hogsheads had not been removed, and the empty space behind them was not immediately visible.

"Good evening, Miss Llyr. I have myself only just arrived. I trust you have remained well since our last meeting?"

Bronwen, regarding him by the light of lanterns hanging overhead, could not know if he had learned of Seth's escape, but she trusted it was unlikely. De Warde would not loiter around prisons.

"I've been somewhat occupied," she answered briefly, watching for reaction in his sharp black eyes.

"Indeed," said de Warde, his expression giving nothing away. "Then, my dear, you might be disheartened to learn that you shall have to engage in some unexpected activity."

"Meaning?"

"We agreed on this rendezvous to complete our plans for tomorrow night," de Warde said, producing a rueful smile. "I now find that I must regretfully withdraw my contribution."

"Is that so?"

She thought he was caught unawares by her noncommittal response, but if so, his look of surprise had been fleeting. "Allow me to be more precise, Miss Llyr. Your brother, if he escapes the prison, cannot be afforded safe passage with my tobacco."

So he did not know about the prison break, but as she had foreseen, he was reneging anyway. She should tread softly until she discovered what game was being played. Under no circumstances should he learn that Seth had escaped. "I don't understand."

Since this might be underplaying her hand, making him suspicious of her lack of outrage, she added, "We made a bargain, de Warde! And you want this tobacco out of Richmond."

When he agreed, "Oh, I most certainly do!" his tone was less guarded. "I do indeed—eventually."

"Eventually?"

"I've learned the tobacco is not quite as imperiled as I formerly believed. Hence, attempting to remove it from here could involve more risk than allowing it to remain. This is not the time for premature alarm."

"Premature . . . de Warde, I don't *understand*!"

"It pains me greatly to disappoint you, my dear, because you have acted in good faith."

Bronwen concealed her skepticism regarding his pain, while she tried to guess why he considered his tobacco no longer endangered. *What* had changed his mind?

"I am truly apologetic," de Warde added, "but there it is."

"There *what* is? Admittedly, I am not overly fond of you, de Warde, but I did believe you to be a man of honor."

His faint frown said this flattering lie had struck home, even if it was only a glancing blow. It was from de Warde himself that she had learned everyone had some weakness. Even, so it seemed, a jaded intelligence agent.

"This has little to do with honor," he objected, "and much to do with practicality. It is hardly restricted information that the Confederate army has acquired a new commander. General Lee is a man of determination and initiative. I have persuasive reason to think your General McClellan has delayed too long, and his advance on this city will likely come too late."

"What makes you able to predict that?"

"If you mean what are my sources, naturally I cannot tell you. However, I am confident of my assessment, because I understand that a bold strategy is already being implemented. Under these conditions, it makes small sense to move the tobacco at this time."

It was an astonishing statement. De Warde must be among the very few to suppose that Richmond would not fall before McClellan's superior forces, yet on this supposition he was willing to wager a fortune? No, he would never pass up a Federal offer to safeguard his tobacco unless something solid had convinced him that it was unnecessary.

She then recalled the Confederate troop movement she had heard earlier.

Before she had time to consider this, he said, "I have kept our appointment here tonight, because of my regard for your noble efforts. This morning I made certain inquiries at the prison, and it still might be possible to attempt a rescue of your brother. I must repeat: it *might* be possible."

Bronwen worked hard to restrain her disgust at his insincerity, but what lay behind his remarks concerning General Lee?

As if reading her mind, he said, "I cannot divulge my sources, Miss Llyr, but as to your broth—"

He broke off at a sudden movement to his right, looking startled when a hooded figure slipped from behind the first row of hogsheads.

As Bronwen's hand closed around her derringer, she found a Colt revolver pointed directly at her.

"Take your hand from your pocket, or I will kill you instantly," came a familiar voice. It was accompanied by an ominous click.

The voice sounded only slightly less deranged than when Bronwen had last heard it. She quickly withdrew her hand and threw a glance at de Warde. His initial surprise had been real enough, but he had recovered his bland expression, and would now be calculating which way to jump.

Simone Bleuette tossed back the hood as another figure appeared behind her. The kindly man who had called himself Quiller, now studiously avoiding even a glance Bronwen's way.

Bronwen's furtive look toward the door told her the distance was too great to cover against the Colt. She was forced to wait, as was de Warde, to see what Bluebell and the man intended. But she could distract the woman to buy time.

"De Warde," she said brightly, "you might have told

me this would be a party. Have you invited still more revelers?"

Bluebell snapped, "Quiet, you wretched whore! Who else is coming here, de Warde?"

"My dear Mrs. Bleuette, surely you are aware by now that I deplore violence—"

"Answer my question!"

"Simone, please," protested the counterfeit Quiller. "There is no reason for such harshness and certainly none at all for the weapon. You insisted that I come here with you to gain information for Norris, but this is no way to obtain Britain's goodwill."

While Bronwen believed the impersonation of Quiller had been a brainchild of Norris and Confederate intelligence, she also trusted her instinct that this man was essentially decent. Hope flickered faintly.

"I would have thought," she nettled Bluebell, "you had made such a spectacle of yourself that Norris—"

She saw the woman's hand move, and twisted aside as the gun roared.

"Simone!" shouted the man, reacting as Bronwen had prayed he would. "Are you insane? Give that gun to me this instant!"

Bluebell pivoted toward him silently, and almost as an afterthought she fired the Colt again. This time her target had not seen it coming. His hand clawing at his chest, he sank to the warehouse floor with a look of stunned disbelief. The woman ignored him and swung the Colt back to cover Bronwen and de Warde.

While Bluebell's attention had momentarily been diverted, Bronwen had inched a hairsbreadth closer to the nearest tobacco cask. She darted another glance at de Warde, whose face was pale and perspiring. His walking stick remained at his side.

If he had not seen it before, he now knew the woman was mad. Bronwen had not enjoyed the benefit of doubt. Other than praying for a rain of spiders, what else was there? To move her hand toward her pocket meant Blue-bell would fire again, and if that Colt had been fully loaded, four bullets remained. More than enough.

The woman's eerie silence was now more frightening than if she had been shrieking.

All at once the wounded man on the floor groaned and looked as if he might try to raise himself. The gun moved and barked again. Bronwen leapt toward the hogshead, but fell short of it, while De Warde was pulling the silver cap from the end of the stick. Both cap and stick flew from his hands when Bluebell fired. The Englishman gasped, and gripped his profusely bleeding arm with the other hand.

He reeled backward to stumble against Bronwen, just as a sound like wind gusting outside the door made Blue-bell spin toward it. Bronwen, yanking out her derringer, dropped to hunker behind de Warde, but the little gun was unreliable at this distance. She would have only two chances and Bluebell would know it. De Warde could could be used as a shield, but there was no doubt in Bron-wen's mind that to reach her the woman would kill him without hesitation.

And indeed the woman had turned back toward de Warde, her strange silver eyes gleaming with mindless malice. The longer Bronwen hesitated, the less likely she was to survive a Colt fired twice at point-blank range.

The door suddenly swung open. When Bluebell whirled and took several steps toward it, Bronwen grabbed de Warde around the waist and dragged him be-hind the tobacco cask. He was still bleeding, but she could not further risk her life for his. God only knew who had opened that door.

It was much too quiet. Bronwen gripped the derringer and crawled past de Warde to find out why. But when she peered cautiously around the cask, Bluebell was advanc-ing on her. The Colt had a longer range than the derringer, and all Bronwen could do was freeze in place, hoping the woman would hoard her last bullets until she came close enough to—

Gunshots twice split the silence.

Bronwen leapt forward with the derringer, but held her fire because the woman was staggering, arms flailing, her head spurting gouts of blood. After a few more lurching steps she crumpled in a heap. In confusion, Bronwen's gaze went beyond the woman to a figure with a cane, shuffling lamely across the floor.

She sank to a crouch with the derringer held ready as she watched the man limp forward, the gun dangling from his hand still emitting wisps of smoke. He glanced down at it and abruptly tossed it away. After he took a few steps closer, Bronwen identified him. It was the Confederate agent Joshua Jared, whom she had winged at the farm after finding Natty. He hardly looked like the same man, having seemingly aged decades.

Bronwen took several steps backward as he went to his knees beside the woman whose features were obscured by blood-soaked ropes of black hair. Jared lifted her limp body to cradle it in his arms, and when he looked down at her, his own features were contorted beyond recognition.

Bronwen heard a soft groan behind her, and remembered de Warde. She first crept to pick up the revolver Jared had flung, and as she came back with it, he handed her the woman's Colt.

"Miss Llyr," came de Warde's voice, "it would seem that in terms of firearms you possess an embarrassment of riches. Thus, do you think you might safely assist me?"

"You don't deserve it," she muttered softly, as she bent over him, searching for a handkerchief in his waistcoat pocket. "But while it gives me no great pleasure to say it, I think you will live."

"That is glad tidings indeed. I must add that you are a far better and braver knight of the realm than I."

"That goes without saying," Bronwen replied, as she

wrapped de Warde's arm with the handkerchief, the blood now only a slow dripping.

Thinking she might catch him off guard, she asked, "Why did you say that about McClellan?"

"My dear girl, you should never come to the aid of an adversary from whom you want information. It leaves you with nothing to convincingly threaten."

She glanced over at Jared, who had barely moved. She could only guess at his reason for killing Simone Bleuette. It could have been that he was finally, belatedly, convinced of her madness. Her rampage tonight would have been too much for Confederate intelligence to tolerate, particularly if, in the bargain, she had killed a British agent. But Norris had known the woman's history, known she was a killer. It had occurred to Bronwen before now that Norris might have used that knowledge as a means of control, perhaps even of coercion. Or maybe de Warde had forced Norris to abandon her. By disposing of Bronwen, Simone might have hoped to regain his good graces.

Or Jared could have been ordered by Norris to assassinate her.

"There remains," de Warde said to her wearily, "the matter of your brother. I suppose as reward for saving my life, you will request—"

"I do *not* need you, de Warde! Look behind you! A good portion of your tobacco is safely in Federal hands and on its way to West Virginia. And when the rest of it here is burned by the Confederacy, you can't blame the North!"

His head swiveled, and she wished his following reaction could have been preserved in amber.

When he turned back to give her an unmistakable, if reluctant, nod of respect, she said only, "You'd better see a doctor soon about that arm. I'm afraid I don't have time to take you to one myself."

Jared unexpectedly said, "I'll take him. Simone and

Carl"—he pointed to the dead impersonator—"will have to be removed as well."

Bronwen got to her feet, placing the derringer and Jared's revolver in her pockets, but keeping in hand the woman's Colt with its two remaining bullets. Both men knew from experience that she was a good shot.

"De Warde, give one good reason for not telling me of Quiller's impostor."

"I do not inform on my friends."

"Except when it suits your purpose."

He smiled. "I did not know initially that the dead man over there was with Confederate intelligence. No, do not scoff, my dear, it is true. I believed he must be a French agent, since I first saw him with Count Mercier. I feared he was scheming to deprive my queen of her rightful tobacco. One must never trust the French."

"You British aren't looking any too trustworthy either," Bronwen countered. She turned to Jared. "I assume the impostor was to track me?"

When he nodded, she pressed, "To what purpose?"

Jared looked away, and de Warde chuckled. "A quick guess, my dear, is that Confederate intelligence had learned what fast friends you and I are. It would not want to risk my certain displeasure by harming you, especially since I have repeatedly counseled against killing unnecessarily—"

He suddenly broke off, but then said, "Mr. Jared, would you please step outside to see if the way is clear? I must insist that nothing whatsoever detain Miss Llyr."

The ploy was hardly worthy of him, and Jared must know he was being dismissed.

"I won't be working for Norris again," said Jared. "But I'll wait outside."

With a last grief-stricken glance at the woman's body, he limped to the door.

After Jared went out, de Warde said, "I shall continue, Miss Llyr. You deserve to know that Norris needed to keep track of you—although he obviously failed to do so—because he intends to implicate you in your brother's case. I don't wish to appear morbid, my dear, but you have earned my advice. Thus if your brother is hanged, I strongly advise that you not attend his execution. I have every reason to believe that if you do, you will be seized and arrested."

Bronwen simply nodded, and turned to leave.

"Would you be so kind, Miss Llyr," de Warde added, "to tell Jared that I have changed my mind and would like his assistance? I'm certain he said that he could be found at the front door."

She turned back to him, determined to make one last attempt to learn what had prompted his earlier decision. "Enjoy the remainder of your tobacco here while you can, Colonel. And when you have the time, remember to send a thank-you note to President Lincoln for saving much of your investment."

He gave her an enigmatic smile, but nothing more. On second thought, earlier he *had* given her something, if she could somehow decipher it.

She walked away, breaking her stride only slightly when she passed by the ebony walking stick.

"One must never trust the British," she said softly over her shoulder, before she crept cautiously from the warehouse, by way of its rear door.

31

Every man's sword shall be against his brother.

—Book of Ezekiel

North of Richmond

The sky to the east had begun to flush when Bronwen reined in the Morgan at the fringe of a thicket. When she raised her spyglass to search the misted landscape, all she could make out ahead was a shallow valley. She turned and signaled her brother to pull an old chestnut mare alongside.

"It's still too murky to see much," she told him, "and I'm uneasy about that rumbling noise we're hearing in the distance. It sounds like troops, so we need to keep clear of the roads."

"Okay," Seth agreed, "but you figured by going north we could avoid the Rebels heading east."

"That's because de Warde had said—or at least I thought he strongly implied—that General Lee was mounting an offensive, and it was already under way. Now I'm not so sure," she admitted.

"I think we should keep moving, Bronwen. Your first plan seemed like a good one, so let's stay with it."

Her uneasiness was growing, but she could not think of a better alternative. "We'll go north another mile," she said, "and take a look when the sun's higher."

But after only a half mile she again pulled up the Morgan. The low-pitched rumble had been steadily increasing in volume, and more alarming now were the individual sounds that had become distinct. She turned to signal Seth. He had already reined in the mare.

In her mind's eye Bronwen searched the maps she had studied. She and Seth had been riding up the fairly steep rise of a bluff that must overlook the Chickahominy River when a jungle of vine-covered trees had forced them closer to a road. It ran parallel to their course and was called the Mechanicsville Turnpike.

"We're still south of the river," her brother said, "and we can't have ridden more than four miles since we started out. Could Union troops be this close to Richmond?"

"I doubt it. Let's tether the horses in those trees over there and take a look."

They fought their way on foot through another tangle of shrubs and vines until it yielded to tall wild grasses. Even after they warily climbed the remainder of the bluff, Bronwen was not prepared for what she saw below. She and Seth threw themselves facedown and inched backward in the grass.

"My God," Seth breathed in her ear, "it's Rebels! Thousands of them! What the hell are they doing down *there?*"

Bronwen took a quick glance around her before crawling forward in the grass to look down again. Their eyes had not deceived them. Thousands of Confederate troops were massing below on the wooded riverbank and thousands more were advancing along the turnpike.

Why were they *here?* Here, when they should be protecting Richmond against McClellan?

As Seth crept up beside her, she shut her eyes against

the terrifying scene below, trying to find an explanation. When one came to her, it seemed so audacious, and so foolhardy of Confederate command, that she nearly discarded it. Until she reconsidered the Richmond newspaper accounts of General Jeb Stuart's cavalry ride around the Union army. It had almost certainly been an intelligence-gathering mission ordered by General Lee.

Lee, whom the cynical O'Hara had warned against underestimating. Whom the shrewd de Warde had characterized as a man of determination and initiative. Whose commanding presence she had seen herself that night on Church Hill.

"Bronwen?" Seth nudged her.

"I think after those troops cross the river," she told him, "that Lee plans to send them northeast toward White House Landing—Jeb Stuart scouted it just days ago. That's McClellan's main supply base, Seth. Tens of thousands of Union troops here in enemy territory can't be supported without a base of supplies!"

Anticipating her next thought, Seth asked, "Where is McClellan now?"

"Elizabeth Van Lew's sources said his current headquarters are somewhere near Savage's Station, and that's on the railroad this side of the Chickahominy. If we can just reach the Union lines—"

Seth was already sprinting toward the horses. Bronwen took one last scan with the spyglass, then raced after her brother.

Minutes later they descended to flat farmland. As Bronwen urged the Morgan eastward along the flooded Chickahominy, she was aware of ghostly silence on every side. There were no troops here. None, anywhere she looked.

A vast sea of white tents and brightly waving flags had led them inside the Union lines, and pickets directed them to the large farmhouse that was General McClellan's headquarters.

Seth had immediately asked if there were New York regiments camped in the vicinity. Told there were, he had left, hoping to find his own company among them.

Bronwen, now standing before a two-story frame structure, had watched her brother ride away. For now, today, he was safe. There was no use in dwelling on an unknown tomorrow.

The sun was high, and the young, sweating guards at the steps of the house looked miserable in their flannel uniforms. Before she approached them, she stopped to swipe at her face with a dirt-smudged hand, and brush weeds and dust from her overalls. She might look shabby, and an unlikely intelligence courier, but she did have an impressive calling card.

When she handed the gold Treasury coin to one of them, she wondered if she could be losing her sense of drama when she said, simply, "I need to see General Mc-Clellan."

The guard turned to climb the steps, and while she waited, Bronwen looked over her shoulder toward the Chickahominy River. Its surface looked tranquil enough, but it would not be for long. Not when massing to either side of its rain-swollen course were two great armies, which like slumbering giants had suddenly awakened and were now on the march.

HISTORICAL NOTES

—⁕—

Chimborazo Hospital

The huge Confederate institution Chimborazo Hospital,
said to be in its time the largest military hospital in the
world, was located a short distance from Elizabeth Van
Lew's Church Hill mansion. Chimborazo opened early
in the spring of 1862, and an estimated 76,000 men
were treated there during the Civil War. Its grounds
overlooking the James River are now open to the
public.

Hollywood Cemetery

Originally called Mount Vernon, Hollywood Cemetery
was designed by architect John Notman, who is said
to have named it Holly-wood for the profusion of holly
trees growing on the site. It opened in 1849, and
became the final resting place of President James
Monroe. Some of the best-known figures of the
American Civil War are buried there, including
Jefferson Davis, George Pickett, and Jeb Stuart.
Hollywood's beautiful tranquil site above the James
River can be visited today.

Hornbrook, Thomas

The surveyor of Customs in Wheeling, Thomas
Hornbrook appears to have been a man of high energy
and strongly held loyalist views. The Baltimore and

Ohio Railroad was under his supervision during the war. A letter of resignation, written by Hornbrook to President Andrew Johnson in 1866, is illuminating, and I quote in part: "Sir: . . . continuing in said office under your administration I shall belie the principles for which I have labored . . . besides seemingly approve the twaddle of your vetoes, the horrors of New Orleans, and the political treachery of your minions."

Jones, John B.

Before the Civil War began, John B. Jones (1810–1866) had achieved some reputation as an author of westerns. He became a clerk in the Confederate War Department, and appears to have been obsessively determined to deny delivery of previously purchased tobacco to "foreigners whose governments refused to recognize us." Before his death in 1866, Jones published *A Rebel War Clerk's Diary,* which provides a view of the intrigue that took place behind the scenes in the wartime Confederate capital. Through his diary, Jones's character is clearly revealed, and some of his own words appear as dialogue in the text of *Brothers of Cain*, such as "If one man can prevent it, the South shall never be betrayed for a crop of tobacco. This is a holy cause."

Libby Prison

With the exception of Andersonville, Libby is possibly the best known of Confederate military prisons. Formerly owned by Libby and Son, ship chandlers and grocers, during the war the warehouse held captured Federal officers. The most famous escape from Libby took place in February of 1864, when 109 officers crawled through a tunnel they had dug from its cellar to a warehouse shed. Almost half these officers were recaptured. In 1889, the warehouse was taken down and rebuilt in Chicago as a museum.

Norris, William

Originally from Reisterstown, located a short distance from Baltimore, William Norris received his law degree from Yale. By the age of forty he was a successful Baltimore businessman, but he picked up stakes and moved south to serve the Confederacy. He became chief of the Confederate States Army Signal Corps in Richmond. In his postwar correspondence with Jefferson Davis, Norris claimed to have also headed the Confederate War Department's Secret Service Bureau, but this bureau's official records were apparently destroyed, and its history remains shadowy. In addition, Norris is believed to have formed the famed "Secret Line"—an intelligence-gathering operation that, beginning early in the war, sent information from Washington to Richmond, and eventually stretched north to Quebec, Canada.

Spotswood Hotel

Completed in 1859 at the corner of Main and Eighth Streets, the Spotswood Hotel played a major role in Richmond. Confederate president Jefferson Davis was a resident for a time, as was General Robert E. Lee. After the war, Union generals Sherman, Sheridan, and Grant stayed there. The flat-roofed building adjacent to the Spotswood held offices, such as those of Alfriend and Son, agents for fire, marine, and life insurance.

The Tobacco

Clerk **John B. Jones**, in his diary entry of May 21, 1862, writes: "Count Mercier has been here on a mysterious errand. . . . I think it was concerning tobacco. There are [sic] $60,000,000 worth in Richmond."

Van Lew, Elizabeth

Elizabeth Van Lew (1818–1900), a courageous woman from an old, respected family, had a long career of providing the Union with what Ulysses S. Grant called "the most valuable intelligence I received from Richmond during the War." When Grant became president in 1869, he rewarded Van Lew by appointing her postmistress of Richmond. (She was unmarried and reputed to house scores of cats.) Van Lew was described as being fearless to the point of recklessness, and her lengthy, nineteenth-century career in espionage cannot be viewed, as so many things historical cannot, in the same light as we view things in the present day. Other women spies, both North and South, behaved with outspoken daring and also had long careers, such as Belle Boyd, Rose O'Neal Greenhow, and Pauline Cushman, to name but a few. The actress Cushman, it is reported, went so far as to proclaim her Union loyalty from the stage of a Southern theater, something even our valiant Bronwen would have been unlikely to dare. I think it probable that nineteenth-century military men seldom saw women as serious threats to security—if they saw them at all.

West Virginia

Once called the "Child of the Storm," West Virginia was born of the Civil War. On December 31, the last day of 1862, President Lincoln signed its admission bill. In June of the following year, it entered the Union as the thirty-fifth state.

West Virginia Independence Hall

West Virginia Independence Hall, an intriguing, three-story, hand-cut sandstone building where much of West Virginia's early history was made, is a National

Historic Landmark in Wheeling and is open to the public. Its basement is where **Thomas Hornbrook** allowed the army to store guns and gunpowder.

Note: With the exception of Elizabeth Van Lew, who is a major character in *Brothers of Cain,* the items that appeared in the Historical Notes of *Sisters of Cain* have not been repeated here lest this section threaten to grow longer than the novel itself. For the same reason, I made the choice to exclude other historical items that may have been of interest to some—in which event my apologies to readers—but this remains a work of fiction.